BEGGING FOR IT

BERKLEY TITLES BY LILAH PACE

Asking for It
Begging for It

BEGGING FOR IT

Lilah Pace

BERKLEY BOOKS, NEW YORK

BERKLEY
An imprint of Penguin Random House LLC
375 Hudson Street, New York, New York 10014

This book is an original publication of Penguin Random House LLC.

For more information, visit penguin.com.

Library of Congress Cataloging-in-Publication Data

Pace, Lilah.
Begging for it / Lilah Pace. — Berkley trade paperback edition.
pages ; cm
ISBN 978-0-425-27949-6 (softcover)
1. Man-woman relationships—Fiction. 2. Bondage (Sexual behavior)—Fiction. 3. Sexual dominance and submission—Fiction. I. Title.
PS3616.A3255B44 2015
813'.6—dc23
2015015244

PUBLISHING HISTORY
Berkley trade paperback edition / September 2015

PRINTED IN THE UNITED STATES OF AMERICA

10 9 8 7 6 5 4 3 2 1

Cover photo by Scala / Art Resource, New York.

Penguin
Random
House

PROLOGUE

I'm ashamed of what I want.

I want it anyway.

Although I've tried to break the habit, it never works. Sometimes I indulge in fantasies that would bring most women over the edge. A hot guy with his face buried between my legs, his muscular arms wrapped around my open thighs; that sexy professor from my undergrad poli sci class, bending me over the desk in his office; even Robert Downey, Jr., and Chris Evans inviting me into an Avengers three-way and proving they have superpowers of their own.

None of it gets me off. Every time, my fantasies ultimately bring me back to my most secret shame. The hands that caress me hold me down; the moan of satisfaction I imagine turn into screams for help, screams no one hears. As the fantasy becomes more savage, more brutal, I glory in it more and more.

And in the end, I only come when I imagine being raped.

I loathe this about myself. Rape is a vicious criminal act, one that makes the victim feel like a hollowed-out, broken *thing*; I should know. Countless self-help books, sex toys, and therapy sessions have taught me more about why I have these fantasies.

They've also taught me that lots of people get off on this—female and male. But my desires still betray me, own me.

For a long time I kept my needs secret. My boyfriends had no idea what I was imagining behind my closed eyes while they were inside me. Once I tried to tell my ex-boyfriend Geordie about it—lightly, playing it as no more than a kinky whim—but that was a kink we didn't share. He couldn't go along, not even for me, and I wound up feeling humiliated and even more ashamed than before.

But I'm glad I told Geordie. Because in a drunken haze at a party months later, he blurted out my secret. Most of the people who overheard him snickered or leered, knowing only that I wanted to try something crazy in bed.

One man heard the truth even Geordie hadn't understood. One man realized exactly what I wanted, and how I wanted it.

Jonah Marks understood because he wanted it too.

We began a sexual relationship built on our shared secret. At first we tried to remain unknown to each other, coming together only as strangers, to intensify the fantasy. Jonah understood what I needed and how to give it to me. He let me become a victim; I let him become a monster. And yet we always stayed within the limits we'd set. He understood how to walk the line that let me feel scared and safe at once.

Over time, though, we were no longer strangers. We knew only one thing about each other—but it was the most intimate thing anyone could know. We had looked into each other's souls.

Finally we saw too much. Saw the truth. Jonah pulled back. Now he's lost to me—for now, and maybe forever.

But not if I can help it.

ONE

Normally I don't worry much about walking across campus to my car. My schedule as a graduate teaching assistant allows me to leave before dark most of the time, and the University of Texas at Austin is one of the biggest colleges in the nation, meaning people are usually around.

However, this is the Saturday night after Thanksgiving. Most students are still at home with their families. Professors too. Me, I left New Orleans sooner than I'd planned. The enormous pile of research papers I had to grade could've been split into a couple of days' work, but I was close enough to finishing this evening to keep on to the end.

That's why I'm walking across a nearly deserted campus, not far from downtown, at 11 o'clock at night.

A white truck drives along the nearest road. Its headlights sweep past me, and I blink against the glare. For a moment I think the truck might be about to stop, and I wonder if it's stopping for me. But then it drives on, and I breathe out a sigh of relief.

The world spends so much time telling women how not to be raped—more time than it spends telling men not to rape. So I remind myself that I know what to do. I keep my head up. I look around me so that I'm alert and aware of my surroundings. No earbuds to deafen me to the sound of approaching footsteps, no phone in hand to distract me with texts or games. What I'm wearing shouldn't attract undue attention: denim skirt, wine-colored cardigan. And I've got on flats I could run in, if I had to.

And I also know to meet the eyes of any man I see, so he'll realize I've registered his presence. That I could identify him later.

Which is why, when I hear the dull thud of boots on the ground near me, I turn my head—and stop in my tracks.

The man walking so close is tall, six-foot-two or -three. Muscular too, as his low-slung jeans and tight-fitting shirt reveal. Yet he's not some bodybuilder type; his waist is almost impossibly narrow beneath such broad shoulders, his neck long. His proportions suggest both brutality and fragility. One glance would tell anyone this man is stretched to the breaking point, and make you wonder what he'd do if he broke. In the bluish glare of the streetlight, his features are almost too beautiful to be rugged, but not quite. Straight nose, high cheekbones like slashes, his thin-lipped mouth set in a firm line. One of his broad hands could circle my throat. The description for the police would begin *Caucasian, fair skin, dark hair cropped short, clean-shaven.* His eyes are the shade of steel.

And they are locked on me.

I felt so sure of myself a few moments ago. So strong and prepared. Now I see myself as an attacker would. A woman in her midtwenties, all alone, weighed down by a messenger bag stuffed with seven pounds of papers. The bag's strap cuts diagonally across my torso, pressing my sweater tightly against my breasts. Nobody else is within sight or hearing. My car must be at least a hundred feet away.

If he wanted to come at me, nobody could stop him. Not even me.

"You're out late," he says, his deep voice tight. Tense.

"Well, you know." The kind of meaningless nonstatement we all make to strangers. I shrug the messenger bag behind me. I could run easier that way. But the strap only twists my cardigan, sliding the hem up enough to bare a few inches of my skin to the cool night air. Our endless Texas summer has finally ended; the chill has come.

But I'm not shivering with the cold.

It's anticipation.

"Girls shouldn't walk around outside late at night," he says, stepping closer. The streetlight elongates his shadow; the dark line of it slices across the ground between us. "It's dangerous."

"Walking isn't dangerous," I retort. "People are."

His voice deepens further, almost a growl. "Yes. So why are you out here?"

"I'm going to my car."

"You could've gone home anytime you liked." He's speaking to me stranger to stranger, like a naughty little girl he has the right to chastise. "But you stayed late, on purpose. So you could walk out here all alone."

My breath catches in my throat. The mood between us shifts by the instant.

And then it turns sharp as a knife as he finishes, "Some people would say you were begging for it."

The possibilities multiply within my mind, a pornographic kaleidoscope. He could force me into his car, or mine. Hold me down in the backseat, rip off my panties, and fuck me senseless. Or maybe he'll play it cooler, offer to give me a ride on a cold night, swear to act like a gentleman. But instead of dropping me off as he'd promised, he forces his way into my house, ties me up, and does whatever he wants with me, for hours. He could even drag me down right here.

Any other woman would go for her phone. Or scream. Or run.

Instead I stand there, drinking him in. The other edge of fear is desire, and it's desire that has me now. Not only desire—lust. I don't care how cold the night is; I don't care how dangerous it would be. I just want *him*, so badly I'll do anything.

And he wants me just as much. I can tell by the way his jaw clenches, by how he keeps trying not to look at me but still can't resist.

We have become hunter and prey.

Come on, Jonah, I think as I look at the man I have feared and fought and maybe begun to love. *Let go. Take me.*

He takes one step forward—and then we both freeze as the white truck circles around again and stops nearby. Someone leans out the open driver's side window; through the glare of the headlights I recognize a friend of a friend, this guy named Mack. "Hey, Vivienne!" he calls. "You need a ride to your car?"

"I'm good!" I answer. I would've turned the ride down no matter what. Mack's always struck me as the stereotypical frat bro, hardly my type. Then again, when he saw me walking around alone and vulnerable late at night, he tried to help out. Maybe I misjudged the guy.

Doesn't change the fact that right now I could scream at him for interrupting Jonah and me.

Mack simply waves before he puts his car back in drive and heads out, leaving me alone with Jonah again. But it's too late.

The spell has been broken, the game ended. I look into Jonah's eyes and what I see there is not desire. Not only desire, anyway. What I see most strongly is pain.

Very quietly he says, "We're not doing this. I'm sorry."

Damn it. "You started it . . ."

"Because you make me lose control." Jonah half-turns from me, giving the lie to his own words. This man has *iron* self-control. I wish he didn't. "Vivienne, you know why we have to stop."

"You're the one with the—" But what do I say? *Hang-up* is too trivial; *problem* too judgmental. The truth would be closer to *wound*, or *scar*. Yet the last thing he wants is my pity.

More resolutely, he continues, "I can't play for a while. Maybe not ever. I don't know."

Not ever? He can't think like that. We'll never find an answer if he's not even looking for it. "Jonah—"

"I just can't do it to you. Not knowing what I know." His shoulders slump, like he's been carrying a tremendous weight for far too long. "It changes things."

"You're not protecting me with this, you know. Maybe you think you are, but all you've done is make me ashamed." Jonah Marks was the first person who ever got me past that shame, who gave me the freedom to own my desires. Having that ripped away from me aches with an almost physical pain.

"Vivienne—"

"You decided I'm too fragile to touch. Which is what broke me." My voice cracks. "Ironic, huh?"

I walk past him, hurrying to my Honda Civic. I toss the heavy messenger bag in ahead of me, get in, slam the door. Jonah stands in the distance—watching me to make sure I get in the car safely. He punishes me and protects me; that's the paradox of the man.

That same paradox is now tearing both of us apart, from each other and within ourselves.

As I put the car in reverse and pull out, I catch one last glimpse of Jonah in the rearview mirror. He's staring after me with an expression so bruised that, despite my anger, my heart hurts for him.

But whatever he's feeling isn't enough to make him come after me, and I drive off into the darkness alone.

TWO

My therapist deserves a raise.

Doreen leans back in her easy chair. "Are you surprised your meeting with Jonah didn't end the way you wanted?"

"It *began* the way I wanted, and then we got interrupted." Jonah wanted it as badly as I did, if not more. I know that in my bones. "But I should've realized he wouldn't follow through regardless."

"Why so?"

"Because I thought he'd put aside all his misgivings so we could fix our problems with sex," I say. "When our problem *is* the sex."

"Is it?"

"Jonah thinks so."

I curl my sock-clad feet under me on the sofa. Doreen makes her patients leave shoes at the door, probably to make us feel less formal, more comfortable. It works too. None of the other psychologists I've talked to over the years were able to put me at ease, but Doreen's practice is different. Her office is a sunny, cozy room in the corner of her house. Instead of the usual diplomas and certifications on the walls, she decorates with thriving houseplants and African art.

We broke off our sessions for a few weeks, just before Jonah and I hit the shoals. Doreen prodded me a little too hard about my fixation on my rape fantasy. I didn't want to hear it; honestly, I still don't. But when I came back to her, she understood. Doreen's wise enough to know when to let something go for a while, and when to remain quiet so that I'm forced to find the truth that fills the silence.

Which is what she's doing now.

"Jonah and I have both struggled with our fantasies. Neither of us has ever come to peace with what we want, or why we want it. But when we were together, living it out—I didn't feel so guilty and ashamed anymore. Jonah was so careful to make me feel safe. We set our boundaries, and he never, ever violated them. He never would. So when I was with him, I could let go. Completely."

Doreen nods. "You established trust and intimacy."

"We thought we were being so smart," I murmur, almost to myself. "Like we could wall off that part of our lives and preserve the fantasy. But we didn't understand what we were getting into."

That first night together had been brutal, terrifying, and perfect. Jonah had wrecked me—ripped my clothes from my body, forced me to my knees, thrown me down onto the hotel room desk, and fucked me mercilessly. I came harder than I'd ever come in my life, crying out even as he pounded into me. The sound had made him laugh in triumph. In that moment, Jonah owned me, and he knew it.

But afterward, as I trembled and struggled to catch my breath, Jonah had held me tenderly. He'd brought me water, made sure I was okay, and gave me one of the gentlest kisses I've ever known.

That kiss was my first hint that I'd found more than my ultimate sexual partner. In Jonah I had discovered something far more rare.

"So you expanded that relationship," Doreen says, bringing me back to the now. "It seemed to be working for a while."

"When he came home to New Orleans with me, it changed everything." I sit up straighter, energized by the memory of righteous anger. "It wasn't just that he was there for me when we were so scared about Dad—I mean, it was that too. But Jonah stood up to my family. He saw through the lies. For once, just once, finally someone was *on my side* and it made all the difference in the world."

"Your family betrayed you."

Doreen is simply telling the truth. Yet even after all these years I find it hard to put it that bluntly. Instead I shrug, folding my arms atop my knees. "They took Anthony's side."

She shakes her head. "They took their own. The side of convenience and luxury and denial. They chose to believe what was easy instead of what was hard and true, and they didn't give a damn about what it did to you."

Even Doreen has rarely put it that harshly before. I find it bracing. "Jonah saw the truth without having to be told. He believed in me implicitly. I've been waiting for that my whole life. So why did that truth have to be the exact thing that drove him away?"

"Because Jonah was uncomfortable living out rape fantasies with someone who had actually been raped," Doreen replies firmly.

I duck my head so I don't have to meet her eyes. "We set our boundaries. He made it okay for me. So why isn't that enough for him?"

"Boundaries protect both the person who sets them *and* the person who obeys them. When Jonah learned the truth about you, he needed to redraw the lines."

"The lines he's drawn now keep us apart." My frustration boils over, and I wrap my arms around myself as if that could keep the agitation inside. "It's like we always said—I want to be a survivor. Not a victim. But that's what I am to Jonah now. Just a victim."

"I doubt it's that simple. His feelings about this are bound to be complex. After all, he's a survivor too."

Jonah was never raped. Never molested. What happened to him was stranger, and maybe even sicker.

We've traveled parallel paths, he and I. We were betrayed by those who should have protected us. We've fought for our sanity and won. We've dealt with the dark desires spun from our worst secrets and found ultimate pleasure in them, together.

Yet what we shared is also what has torn us apart.

Doreen says, "How are the other people in your life reacting to the split? As I recall, you'd just introduced Jonah to your friends."

Despite everything, I laugh. "I don't think any of them have noticed."

Not because they don't care—because all our lives turned upside down at once, in different ways.

Times like this make you believe in astrology. Mercury in retrograde.

Later that day, I walk into the Mullins Recovery Center, an outpatient facility on the far south side of town. Although I'm casually dressed in skinny jeans and a drapey black sweater, I feel conspicuous anyway. You don't enter Mullins unless you're an addict or somebody who cares about an addict very much. This isn't a place I ever expected to be. But I guess that's true for everyone who comes here. Nobody plans to become an alcoholic, or to love one.

Certainly nobody plans to be her ex-boyfriend's main support system more than six months after the breakup. Yet here I am.

Geordie emerges from one of the long corridors, the rubber soles of his Chucks squeaking against the linoleum. As these kinds of facilities go, Mullins is top notch. Still, there's that slightly depressing, antiseptic quality to the furnishings, even to the scent of the air. It seems to me that Geordie looks . . . faded.

That's exhaustion, I remind myself. *He's doing hard work, and his body is fighting to recover from abuse. Of course he's not going to be his usual self.*

Then again, I might not even know Geordie's real self. In some ways, I am only now meeting him, the person he could be without alcohol.

"Bless," he says, his Scottish accent stronger than usual as he comes up and busses me on the cheek. "You not only came, you came early."

"Hey, you said you needed a ride."

"Still, thank you." Geordie zips his fleece jacket as if he already feels the outdoor chill. "I'm not sure my ego could've taken the bruising if I'd had to call a taxi to pick me up from the drunk tank."

The phrase *drunk tank* earns him a glare from the worker behind the reception desk, but it takes more than this to repress Geordie Hilton. He grins as the two of us head out, as if daring the day to knock him down.

When we get into my Civic, he immediately syncs his phone with the sound system, an old habit from when we were dating. I never minded, because Geordie has great taste in music and introduced me to artists I wouldn't have discovered otherwise. At the moment I also appreciate the moment it buys us—the opening for us to talk. "How are you doing?" I say.

Geordie pauses, phone in his hand. PJ Harvey's bass beat begins to thump through the speakers. He glances over at me, his usual cheeky smile slightly . . . bent. "Don't suppose you'll let me get off with 'fine, thanks.'"

"Not this time."

He leans back in the passenger seat. Even the pale light of this overcast afternoon reveals the dark circles under his eyes, the new hollows in his cheeks. Geordie has gone from being wiry to being too thin. Only his floppy brown hair remains as rakish as ever; everything else about him is cast in shadow.

Finally Geordie says, "One day at a time. That's what they keep telling us here. Over and over, until you think you'll slap the next person who lets those words come out of his mouth. But they repeat it for a reason, don't they? You really can't look any further ahead. You try to get on top of things today, and leave tomorrow until it comes. So that's what I'm doing."

We're silent for a long, awkward pause. Finally I manage to say, "The withdrawal—was it terrible?"

"They say I got off lucky. I didn't go through DTs, which is the part of withdrawal that actually kills some people." He sighs. "Me, all I had to deal with was vomiting, nausea, a bad case of the shakes, and a three-day-long anxiety attack. Imagine that party, if you will. But as of now, drumroll, flourish of trumpets, I have been sober for two whole weeks. Please, hold your applause to the end."

"You're trying to make it sound like it's not a big deal." I smile, partly to cover my horror at the thought of Geordie as sick and weak as that. Mostly, though, I'm smiling out of pride. "But you're beating this. You really are."

He shrugs. "Two weeks. No more than that."

"No less than that either." Surely the first few weeks are the hardest. Then again, I don't understand how addiction works; it's not one of my demons. I don't want to take Geordie's struggle for granted. "When I talked to you about this, I honestly didn't believe you'd accept that you had a problem. Instead you took action, immediately. That takes a lot of courage, Geordie."

He laughs ruefully. "You're not the first person who ever brought up my drinking. Just the first one I could hear."

I wonder who spoke to him about it in the past. How many friends or lovers might have fallen by the wayside because Geordie wasn't ready to face the truth? "Then I'm glad you heard me."

"All right then, enough of my dismal story. How are things with Arturo and Shay? I can't believe I haven't seen wee Nicolas yet."

"We'll change that," I promise as I put the car into gear and pull out. "It's crazy over there of course, but the baby's so adorable. You just want to pick him up and smell his head."

"Smell his head?" Geordie shakes his head in disbelief. He'll see. "Did you go home for Thanksgiving?"

"Yeah."

He grimaces. "Oh, God, I'm sorry. How many extra hours in therapy did that require?"

"It wasn't bad this time, actually." I can't tell Geordie *why* things were better, because while he knows my family stresses me out, he's never known the full story behind it. The fact of my rape is one I've shared with only a handful of people. So he couldn't know what Jonah's defense meant to me. "Dad's recovering well; I wound up only staying a couple of days because Mom said they were finally getting 'back in their routine.' Anthony and Chloe went on some kind of trip, so it was just my parents, Libby, and me." Finally I could've spent time with my family without Anthony, and *this* is the year my mom doesn't demand I stay as long as humanly possible. Figures.

"Your sister and her husband went on holiday at Thanksgiving?" Geordie asks. "Left their daughter behind?"

"I know. It's weird." Especially given how hard a guilt trip Chloe gave me about coming home for Thanksgiving this year. Then again, she laid down that ultimatum before she finally heard Anthony admit part of what he'd done to me. No doubt neither of them wanted another confrontation so soon. It feels good knowing that, this time, they blinked first. "We had a low-fat, low-sodium meal because of Dad's heart condition, *ugh*. But I sneaked Libby out for pecan pie the next day. So that pretty much counts as my best Thanksgiving in the past decade or so."

"Beats the hell out of mine. I mean, my family, we're Scots, so it's not like we ever made a big deal of it even after we'd been living over here for a while. Sometimes Mum would buy a turkey at the grocer's. End of story. But this year, I was at Mullins for the 'celebration,' and no, you cannot mock me for those air quotes, for they are well earned. If you ever want to taste the actual flavor of depression, I'm here to tell you, it's reconstituted mashed potatoes at an alcohol-rehab facility."

By now I'm giggling. "Was it that bad?"

"Says she who's never eaten reconstituted mashed potatoes. Tastes like fake butter and failed dreams. And oh! They served some monstrosity called a *turducken*."

"What are you talking about? Turducken is *delicious*."

Geordie gives me a look. "Then why have I never heard of it before? What kind of animal is that even supposed to be?"

"They call it that because it's a chicken stuffed inside a duck stuffed inside a turkey."

"That's supposed to be a holiday meal? Sounds more like a botched experiment by Doctor Moreau."

It feels so good to laugh like this again. Geordie and I were always more friends than lovers, which is why we're able to have this second act to our relationship. He needs a friend right now—and, in a smaller way, so do I.

As if he'd read my mind, Geordie said, "Did Jonah come home with you for Thanksgiving? You said he'd been down to New Orleans with you before."

He speaks precisely, politely. It's not that Geordie is jealous of Jonah, exactly; our breakup was mutual. But accepting the next guy is probably always awkward.

Or it would be, if Jonah were still in my life.

"He didn't." I despise the sudden brittleness in my voice. It makes me sound like my mother. "We're—taking a break."

Geordie gives me a sidelong look. "Is this a Ross-and-Rachel break? Or the more permanent variety?"

The only way to stop sounding like my mother is to do something she never does—tell the absolute truth. "I wish I knew."

We fall silent, and the music on the stereo takes over. Geordie pats my arm once. It's an awkward gesture, but I appreciate it anyway. These days, it helps to remember that I'm not alone.

Between my counseling session, picking up Geordie, and dealing with students' last-minute, panicked e-mails about their impending final projects, I keep my mind occupied throughout the day. It's when I go home at night that my imagination begins to wander in dangerous directions.

I live in the odd little zone between South Congress and First Street, which ought to be one of the most desirable spots in the city. But most of the houses here were built long before the restaurants and clubs came, before average homes had foyers, cathedral ceilings or master suites. We have small yards and wire fences. We have driveways instead of garages. My neighbors are a mix of older couples hanging on, would-be gentrifiers who always have a project in progress, and college students who hang obscure flags or beer signs in their windows.

My place is a notch above its surroundings, located close to my landlord's grander house, which is one of the older ones in this area. I've wondered if it was intended as a guest house, or even servants' quarters. No matter why this was built, I'm glad it's mine. I love my tiny house of white brick, with tons of bookshelves (all of which I've filled) and a freestanding fireplace that doesn't get much use. Bedroom, living room, the smallest kitchenette in the world and an even smaller bathroom—that's it. When I'm in here, I feel like I'm in a snug little nest safely above the rest of the world.

Though, once, I let Jonah break in.

As I sit on my love seat, my e-reader dangles in my hand, almost forgotten. I can't see the words on the screen, not while I'm remembering that night.

We always set the rules of the games in advance. Different

encounters, different force, different ways. Once he pretended to be a not-so-good Samaritan, offering to help me change a flat but raising the price of his assistance second by second—from putting my hand on his cock all the way to spreading my legs for him in the backseat of his car while he fucked me senseless. Another time—he pretended to be a stranger at a charity event who tricked me into going backstage, then took me while he kept one hand firmly gripped around my throat. Each encounter was different. Each fulfilled a different kind of fantasy.

The night he broke in here, he mocked me. Humiliated me with my own sex toy. I fought him, cursed him out, and it didn't make any difference. Jonah forced me to suck him off; he came in my mouth for the first time. By then I'd already had two orgasms myself and was . . . limp, almost weak in the aftermath. But I still relished drinking him down. He could've fucked me all night if he wanted. I wouldn't have taken us out of the game. I would have been his victim, his slave. Just thinking about him taking control makes my pulse race. I feel it in my gut, in my throat, and between my legs.

Jonah, I think, flopping back onto the white cushions of my love seat. *Why can't you get past this?*

But that's not a fair question. We don't always get to choose our own limits. If he can't live out our fantasies after knowing what I've been through, then . . . that's it.

The end.

I never let myself think that before. Despite the silence between me and Jonah, I've believed so strongly that we would find our way back to each other—that what we shared together would be more powerful than what was done to us. My belief alone isn't enough, though. Jonah has to believe that too, and maybe he doesn't.

That night on campus in my mind—the hope and desperation that must have been radiating from me, the hunger in his gaze as he checked out my short skirt, then the haunted look as he pulled away, unwilling to go any further.

Is that the last time we'll ever be together? Is our ending so stunted and sad?

We deserved better than that. Both of us.

Tears well in my eyes. I haven't let myself break down about this even once because I was so determined to believe Jonah's withdrawal was a detour instead of a dead end. Now, though, I let it out, curling into a ball for a good long cry.

As I sob into the crook of my arm, I tell myself, *let it go*. But it's too much to let go of. The weight of the fantasy, the guilt, my anger toward Anthony, and most of all Jonah and everything we might have been—so much more than partners in a fantasy—it's more than I can lay aside in a night.

I do my best, though. I cry until I'm out of tears, and I lift my head from the damp cushion only to crawl into bed. By then my head aches from sobbing and exhaustion drags me down within seconds, into a sleep too deep for dreams.

The next morning, I awaken with still-swollen eyes and a dull dread at the thought of muddling through this day.

Which is why it's so shocking to check my phone and find a message from Jonah.

He's sent back to me the first words I sent to him: Let's talk.

THREE

As I drive downtown that evening, I'm so nervous I can hardly pay attention to my surroundings. Maybe I should've called a cab. I pull up a mellow playlist, hoping the soothing tones of Norah Jones will calm me down.

But who am I kidding? Calm is not on the menu for tonight. I've missed Jonah so much, body and soul. It feels like I've waited years for this moment, not merely a few weeks.

We can work through this, I remind myself. *Jonah finally sees that too. If he hadn't, would he have reached out to you like this? You two have another chance. Don't blow it by freaking out.*

Just as I think this, my phone rings, and I patch it through the car system. Maybe it's Jonah; I feel a stab of fear that he's going to call the date off, say he can't handle it after all.

When I hear who it is, however, I smile. "Vivienne, darling!"

"Hiya, Kip."

Kip Rucker is our fine arts department secretary. He's seventy percent ruthless efficiency, twenty percent sass, and ten percent omniscience. Even his new, red-hot romance with a bartender named Ryan hasn't shaken his ability to turn around, transfer, or otherwise control pretty much anything at the University of Texas at Austin. It's as if he has both Hermione Granger's Time-Turner and Sauron's all-seeing eye.

Luckily, Kip likes me.

"You are going to worship the ground I walk upon," he continues. "Assuming you don't already, which you should."

"Of course I do. So why am I going to worship you even more?" I continue as I steer toward downtown Austin.

"Tanisha, my friend in the registrar's office—"

Virtually everyone at the university is Kip's friend . . . or, at least, owes him a favor.

"—she's putting together the schedules, and thanks to my advice, a certain someone only has two class days per week next semester, and not a single reason to be on campus before one P.M.," he finishes with satisfaction. "The adulation may now commence."

"That's fantastic!" I laugh out loud. "Oh, God, is this the part where you say I have to give you my firstborn child?"

"What on earth would I do with *that*? All I ask in return is your undying gratitude, of course. And a favor should I ever require one."

"You've got it."

"Any plans this evening?"

"Nothing in particular."

I wish I could bite back the words as soon as I've said them. Lying to Kip never works. "*Ohhhh*," he says, maddeningly knowing. "The combination of dishonesty and hesitation intrigues. Either you've found someone to make Jonah Marks jealous, or the elusive Mr. Marks has come to his senses of his own volition."

"We're not having this conversation yet."

"Aha! He *has* come to his senses." I can just imagine Kip's face—half-expectant, half-ravenous, like a cat about to pounce. "Tell me all."

"There's not much to tell at this point, I swear. Don't you have a hot boyfriend of your own to spend time with?"

"Come to think of it, I do. But don't think this gets you out of explaining the entire thing the very next time I see you."

"Good night, Kip." I disconnect the call, and I realize I'm grateful for that brief interruption. Hearing from Kip was exactly what I needed to stop worrying. Now I can allow myself to look forward to this evening with Jonah. To talking with him again.

I can allow myself to hope.

We meet in the same hotel bar where we first got together to negotiate our arrangement. This is where we set our limits, where all the boundary lines are drawn.

Maybe we can demolish a few boundaries tonight.

Some hotel bars seem to be designed for conventions—long tables perfect for a dozen boisterous strangers wearing name tags, cutesy plastic drink menus in bright orange or green on every flat space. But this place? It's meant for seduction. The lobby bar area is broken up into white-walled, nearly separate rooms lined with low couches the color of cream. Earth-toned pillows and carpet, plus the enormous blazing fire, give the space a sort of *Arabian Nights* feel.

Sunday night would be quieter here regardless of the week. Since this is the end of the Thanksgiving holiday, tonight I have the bar to myself—until Jonah walks in.

His dark V-neck sweater hugs the striking dimensions of his body—the wide shoulders, the long, slim waist. His wheat-colored trousers suggest his muscled thighs rather than revealing them, but suggestion can do a lot. His gray eyes sweep over me, reminiscent of the cool appraisal he's given me so many times, always driving me wild.

Tonight, though, his gaze is shadowed. Raw.

Although this conversation is definitely just that—talk only, no games, no sex—I dressed to remind Jonah just what he's missing. Tight black jeans, a nude camisole to create the illusion of bare skin beneath my slightly sheer red top, sky-high heels: The kind of thing that would normally turn him on. But when I sense the sadness within him, I feel foolish for believing a sexy outfit could fix anything.

Our problem isn't a lack of attraction. Merely being in the same room together sets us each on fire.

Our problem is that this fire could burn us both down.

Jonah leans close enough to me that I think he might kiss my cheek, but he doesn't. He sits just next to me, our knees almost brushing. I am so near I can smell the scent of his skin. When I breathe that scent again, it hits me how badly I've missed that. Him. Us.

"I'm sorry," he says. Jonah's not big on hellos or good-byes. "The other night—coming onto you like that—it wasn't fair."

"It would have been, if you hadn't stopped." I want him to know that it's all right to touch me. More than all right. *Begging for it,* he said to me, and right now, I'd fucking beg if I thought it would help. It wouldn't.

"Don't." He can no longer look me in the face. Instead his gaze falls on the bottle of wine I ordered for us—pinot noir, the deep red of it brought out by the firelight just beyond. Two glasses wait.

"I went ahead and ordered," I say, slightly flustered by his silence. "I hope that's okay." We both know he doesn't give a damn what we drink.

Jonah continues, "I should've said hello like a normal person. Walked you to your car. But the sight of you in that skirt—out there all alone—"

His fantasies all begin with a woman alone and vulnerable. That's how my fantasies begin too.

When our eyes meet, I see the Jonah I know and want. The one he tries to hide from everyone else in the world but me. He whispers, "I couldn't stop thinking about you all night."

Heat flushes through me as I imagine Jonah back in his apartment, fist tight around his erection as he stands in the shower, jerking himself off to the memory of me that night. Maybe he envisioned one of the scenarios that tantalized me, like dragging me into my car, taking me on my own backseat. I think of his lips slightly parted as he breathes harder and faster—the water from the shower beading on his pale skin—the dark head of his cock sliding back and forth within his grip. When he did that, he was remembering me.

My power over him comes from my powerlessness in his arms. The paradox intoxicates us both.

I lean forward and pour us each a glass of wine. It's not that I want to get him drunk, convince him to do something he doesn't want to do. He's respected my boundaries, and I want to respect his. But this is a difficult subject to discuss, even after months of living out our shared fantasies. The wine can only help.

We need a little lubrication, I think, a joke I can never share. My panties are already so wet just from the sight of him that I can feel the crotch of my jeans getting damp.

"Is that why you wanted us to meet?" I say. "Because you can't stop thinking about me?"

Jonah breathes out, not quite a sigh. "Of course."

Hope blazes brighter within me. "You're ready to play our games again?"

His expression darkens. "That's not what I said."

Why? I want to plead. But we both know why.

In our last intimate conversation, Jonah finally told me the primal origin of his fantasies. He was born into so much privilege and wealth that he might as well have been a prince in a fairy tale: His mother, Lorena Marks, was an heiress, perhaps the richest and loveliest girl in Chicago's upper crust, and his father, Alexander Marks, was a self-made man, the founder of Oceanic Airlines. Both Jonah and his little sister Rebecca were raised in Redgrave House, a mansion so baroque and beautiful that it's a landmark known around the nation. They were dressed in velvet, tended by nurses, untouched by care.

But fairy tales always take a turn for the dark. Jonah's father died, and his mother—perhaps weakened by grief—remarried. To the outside world, Jonah's stepfather would have seemed to fit the role of king equally well. Carter Maddox Hale is a luxury hotel mogul who appears on the covers of magazines like *Forbes*. He brought with him two more children from his first marriage, a girl called Elise and a boy named Maddox. According to Jonah, the children all loved each other from their very first day together, and never called each other *stepbrother* or *stepsister*. The bond was as deep as blood.

Within Redgrave House, however, Carter Hale revealed his true self. The fairy tale shifted into reverse as the prince turned into a beast.

Carter raped his wife regularly, and brutally. That would be enough to make him a monster. But his needs were even more depraved. When Jonah was five years old . . . Carter began forcing him to watch.

Jonah might be made to stand against the wall; he might be commanded to climb in the bed and lie right next to them. Elise had to watch too, sometimes. He and Elise worked hard to make sure that Carter never turned on the younger two; I don't even know if Rebecca and Maddox ever learned the truth. But Jonah feels that he kept them safe, that they're not as twisted up inside as he will always be.

Because that was Jonah's first impression of sex—violent, forcible, and merciless. Over and over, as a child, he would ask his mother what was wrong. Over and over, she refused to accept the truth of what was happening. Denial was easier for her. So she told Jonah that what was happening was normal between men and women.

He learned better, thank God. But the damage to his psyche was done. For him, the sights and sounds of force will always be arousing. He can't change that any more than I can.

Rape was my first experience of sex too.

"Knowing that you've been hurt," he says, "realizing what Anthony did to you—it changes things for me."

I was *so fucking happy* when Jonah stood up to Anthony. He'd seen the truth hidden beneath our actions, the same truth my family refused to see even when I told them in plain words. Nobody had ever defended me; nobody had ever made Anthony back down.

If I'd known it would signal the end of my relationship with Jonah, I would've broken down and wept instead. I wouldn't even have cared that Anthony was watching.

Jonah continues, "It used to turn me on so hard, thinking about you tied up, at my mercy. And now all I want to do is get between you and anyone or anything that could do you harm."

Tears prick at my eyes. I've waited so long for someone to feel this way about me.

And yet I also waited just as long for someone to make love to me the way I really wanted—to accept me as I am, kinks and all. Will I always have to choose between the two?

"You know how much I need this," I whisper.

But he shakes his head. "There can't be anything that either of us wants in bed as much as we need each other."

I can't argue with that. I don't want to. Jonah's voice has become ragged; his hand grasps my forearm like he will never let go.

"You're the only one who's ever understood, Jonah. The only

one who ever could understand completely." The words tremble. I'm on the brink. "But you've pulled away."

"I'm sorry. I should have tried harder, thought it through. At the time, I hated myself so much for hurting you that I couldn't see anything else. Couldn't feel anyone's pain but my own."

You weren't hurting me, Jonah. You gave me what I wanted when no one else would. Why can't you see that?

He continues, "There has to be another way for us to be together."

"Like normal people?" It's a joke. We both smile crookedly. Whatever Jonah and I are together, it ain't *normal.* "Does that mean we won't ever—play our games again?"

The euphemism fades his smile. "We can have a relationship without that."

"Yeah, we can—we could—but I don't want to. You didn't just give me the fantasy I wanted; you gave me something I *needed.*" Then I tilt my head, inviting him to be less serious for a moment. "And it was absolutely the best sex of my life. Are you going to tell me it wasn't that good for you too?"

"You know it was. No other woman would ever—completely give herself to—Jesus. You're perfection." Jonah cuts himself off. "But the game isn't necessary for me to enjoy having sex with you. Remember Scotland?"

He swept me off to the Highlands for one amazing week earlier this fall. While he did whatever it is earthquake scientists do off the Scottish coast, I drew constantly—pages and pages a day of heather-covered hills and otters darting beneath dark water. I plan to turn those drawings into a series of etchings soon. We ate our dinners together in the tiny seashore inn where we stayed, and at night Jonah took me to bed, treated me like the most fragile treasure in the world, caressing me, going down on me longer and better than any other man ever has—

—and it wasn't enough.

Which isn't his fault. I know good oral when I get it, and damn, does Jonah give it. Most other women would have been screaming his name within seconds. But my brain was wired for perversity long before Jonah ever came along.

"I enjoyed making love with you in Scotland," I say honestly. Simply being that close to him, having him treat me so tenderly—that had its own kind of magic. "But by now you have to have guessed that it didn't work for me on its own."

"You mean you were faking it." He sounds so stung. So cheated.

"No, I wasn't! I've never had to do that with you, Jonah. Not even once." I take his hand in mine. "I should've been honest with you from the beginning. But it was so hard to admit to you that I don't—that I can't ever get off without imagining being raped."

Just said the *R*-word in public. But nobody's sitting particularly close, and the low music muffles anything we would say so that nobody else can hear.

I continue, "It's hard to admit that to myself, sometimes. I hate it. I've spent so many years in therapy trying to change it, but it never changes. So even when you weren't playing the game, I still was."

Jonah leans back on the sofa. He looks disappointed—no, worse. Wounded. Like he's not hurting because of me; he's hurting for me.

"Never," he says. "You've never gotten off any other way."

"Before Anthony—" But I stop. For me, sexually, there is almost no such time as before Anthony. I was fourteen. An age when girls might begin to wonder, or explore. Me, I went straight from daydreams to nightmares. "I touched myself like any other kid would, or I did, beforehand."

"Afterward?"

"I didn't get myself off again for four years."

Jonah's broad hand closes over mine, as if he could reach into that awful time and pull me out. "It wasn't like that for me," he says, quietly. "So I didn't realize what it was like for you."

Of course it wasn't like that for him. Guys are lucky, with their dicks. No matter how fucked-up they are, the mechanism usually works. It's like they have an expressway to orgasm, while even the happiest women sometimes have to wind their way through a maze. "That's how it is for me," I say. "I want to work on it, but—that's my truth, that's where I am. If you can't be with me until I'm over it . . . Jonah, that's going to be a long time."

He doesn't answer right away; he's deep in thought, weighing what I've said. I want him to take this seriously, but I also want an answer. More than anything, I want him to drag me back to his apartment and ravage me until the pleasure in my body drowns the pain in my head.

I take a sip of wine. Killing time. The suspense stretches me thin.

Finally, Jonah says, "You know why this is hard for me. It's not like I drew some arbitrary line."

"I know." What must it have been like for him, watching his mother broken down night after night, year after year? "But I don't understand why what Anthony did to me has to define what we do together."

"When you put it that way, it sounds cruel. I don't mean for it to be." The silence between us lasts even longer this time. Jonah's gaze turns inward, toward other people and other times. "What my stepfather did to my mother wasn't only meant to hurt her. Elise and I weren't merely props for his sick games; it took me a long time to realize he enjoyed victimizing us just as much. I think he wanted Elise to feel helpless. To expect nothing but pain from any man. He's the kind of man who would want his daughter to believe that. And Carter wanted me to be that kind of man too."

"You aren't. You have to know that, Jonah. You've always taken such good care of me."

His gray eyes search mine. "I want to believe you," he says. "Sometimes I do. Other times I wonder whether all the evil I saw in Carter is in me too, but—silent. Ticking like a time bomb. Waiting to detonate."

I understand what Jonah means. No, I don't believe he's grown up to be anything like that bastard Carter Hale. But I know what it's like to feel like a parent's script is forever waiting for you to speak the lines. My father's denial, my mother's sharp, shallow judgments: I hear echoes of those in my own thoughts from time to time. The fact that I don't believe the words will never fully stop me from hearing them.

Jonah continues, "Knowing what you've been through—that you've been hurt—that brings us too close to what I lived through before. I can't forget what's been done to you, and I can't pretend it doesn't affect me."

"It's like—like you stopped seeing me as *me*. Now you can only see me as a victim."

"That's not true."

"Okay, then you can only *treat* me as a victim. And you were the one who helped me feel less like a victim than I ever had since the day Anthony raped me. With you, it was like I *owned* this. I'd felt so sick and ashamed, but with you—when we acted out our scenes together—I could let the shame go. You set me free."

"Vivienne," he says, leaning closer. Jonah folds my hand against his chest. He wants to kiss me, but he doesn't. Neither of us moves. We are bound together and yet parted. Two halves that can't be glued into a whole. Maybe that's how it is when you find someone whose wounds are the same as your own.

But I'm not willing to give up on Jonah. Not the sex, not the emotions between us, not any of it. If I'm going to fight for this man, I'm going to fight for everything.

"Jonah, you and I—we're walking through the same dark place, together," I whisper. "Don't leave me there alone."

"I don't want to leave you. I don't even think I could, unless it's the only way to keep you safe. Make you whole."

I want to cry. I want to scream. Jonah holds so much power over me—but this is the one power nobody else can ever have.

"You don't get to make me whole," I say. "You have to take me as I am, or we're lost."

Jonah wants to protest, but even as he opens his mouth, I sling my handbag over one shoulder and stand. The firelight plays across his face, tricks of light and shadow obscuring what he feels in this moment.

But I know myself, and that's enough.

So I say, "Listen to me. Tomorrow night, I'll be at home. At ten P.M., I'm going to unlock my front door. At eleven, I'll lock it again. If you're still on the other side of the door—then I'm locking you out. For good."

"What?" He looks stunned. No, hurt.

"I know it's not fair," I confess. "I don't like giving you an ultimatum. But what I've had with you is the one honest sexual relationship of my entire life, and if giving up that honesty is the price of getting you back, it's too high. I won't live a lie again."

"You're giving me *one day*?"

My voice trembles as I say, "How much time would be enough? A month? A year? This isn't about waiting until we're both comfortable and 'healthy' or whatever the hell else our goals should be. It's about accepting that we're both *twisted as fuck* and the only way we'll ever work this out is together. If you can't deal with that now, then you're probably not going to be able to deal with it ever. And if that's the case, then the best thing for both of us is to move on as soon as we can."

Jonah finally gets it, I can tell. Slowly he nods. But his expression has become completely unreadable—those steely eyes closed to me again—and I have no idea which way he'll jump.

"Tomorrow night," I repeat. "Ten to eleven P.M. I'll be waiting."

Instead of waiting for a reply, I turn and walk out, refusing to glance back even once.

As I fumble for my car keys in my purse, blinking back tears, I ask myself if I'm really ready to draw that line in the sand. A traitorous voice inside me whispers, *It's not too late to return to the bar and take everything back.*

But I *am* ready. I have to be. Because the barrier between me and Jonah isn't one that will slowly disappear with time.

Jonah has to tear it down.

FOUR

The next morning, I keep myself busy at the university. Exams are upon us, which means I have to lead two exam-review sessions, read a few late papers, and sort through e-mails about a statistically improbable number of dead grandmothers. Normally I'd get through this by reminding myself that I've got the afternoon off—

—but free hours today are hours of almost unbearable suspense. Every second is one more tick on the clock counting down to the moment Jonah comes for me, or I learn I've lost him forever. My mind refuses to focus. The disconnect between my inner tension and the outside world makes everything slightly surreal.

Luckily, I can invite myself to a place where focus is impossible anyway—to a house with a newborn baby.

"Thank God," Shay breathes as I enter the town house with a couple bags of groceries. She's propped up in this puffy red recliner she and Arturo bought at Goodwill. In her arms, Nicolas nurses hungrily, his tiny pink hands opening and closing against her breast. "Tell me you brought chocolate."

"Not just any chocolate." I swung by World Market on the way over; they carry various snacks from all over the world, including

Shay's native Australia. As I triumphantly pull out a red-and-brown packet, Shay lights up.

"Tim Tams! *Thank you*. I swear, I'm going to eat the lot in one go." She sighs in anticipatory delight. "Nursing a baby—it's like you can't get enough calories in you, no matter how hard you try."

"Sounds like fun. The calorie part, I mean."

She laughs. "Not the rest, huh? Oh, God, I must look like hell."

Shay's hair, usually tinted some outlandish shade of maroon or purple, now shows an inch of plain brown roots. Her thick-framed glasses are slightly askew on her face, and she's wearing the same pajamas I saw her in two days ago. Having a new baby might be one of the greatest joys human beings can experience, but from what I can see, it's also completely fucking exhausting.

I peel open the Tim Tams and set the packet next to her. Shay stuffs one in her mouth with her free hand, then gives me a big-cheeked smile.

"Hey, baby," I whisper as I brush one fingertip along Nicolas's arm. He keeps feeding hungrily, his heavy-lidded eyes shut against this unfamiliar world. "I'm here to help your mom and dad out today. So where do I start?"

"Ask Arturo." Shay sighs as she reaches for another Tim Tam. "I have no idea what's happening in the rest of the house. I don't think I've left this recliner since four A.M. except to pee."

My real family lives one state over, in the physical sense. In the emotional sense, they might as well be on the moon. That distance might be harder to bear if I hadn't found an adopted family to love and be loved by. Carmen Ortiz began as my randomly assigned freshman year roommate. Within a couple months, she'd become my best friend. When her younger brother Arturo joined us at UT Austin, we both took him under our wing, and for the past few years, I've been the unofficial third sibling. They even brought me back to their home in San Antonio to spend a couple of Thanksgivings with them and their parents. The way they love each other—openly, unabashedly—it shows me what a healthy family looks like. My parents and Chloe don't have a clue.

Not to say that Arturo and Carmen don't argue. They do, and it can be fierce. Carmen's attitude about his early marriage to Shay and the pregnancy—let's say it took her a while to adjust. But Ortizes even fight fair. Even at their angriest, they're always talking to each other from a place of love.

Where do you learn how to do that? And how? The habits of a functional family seem alien to me—literally, like something from an entirely different planet. Different from the one I grew up on, anyway.

I find both brother and sister on the second story of the town house, in the nursery, disassembling Nicolas's crib. "Uh, guys?" I say. "Doesn't the baby need that?"

Arturo never looks up from his place on the floor, where he's hurriedly unscrewing board from board. "Product recall. Who makes a baby crib that kills babies? This is what we get for shopping at the Salvation Army"

"Don't blame yourself," Carmen says. She's in her San Antonio Stars jersey, carefully detaching the stars-and-moon mobile from what remains of the crib. "The charity should've checked to see if there were past recalls on any of these products before they sold them again. Or the parents who donated it in the first place! I bet they threw it out at the original recall and donated it for the tax benefits, and they didn't even care if some other kid got hurt. They're *scum*."

Maybe the donors had no idea that their baby crib was a white wooden death trap, but the mood in the room keeps me from defending these unknown people. Carmen and Arturo are united in their shared loathing, and they both get a whole lot more productive when they're angry. It's like they each know how to take their temper out on the forces of entropy, instead of other human beings. "You want me to help out?"

"Two people is enough to work on this," Arturo says. "But someone needs to make a Costco run. The diapers this kid goes through!"

I don't want to go to Costco by myself. Not only will I have to fight my way through the hordes of people who somehow need to buy televisions and economy-size bottles of hot sauce at the same time—but I'll also be alone with my thoughts. That's the last thing I need today. "I'd rather stay here," I say, like it's no big deal. "Why don't I take crib duty while one of you guys heads out to Costco?"

Arturo gets this hopeful look on his face. "I haven't seen the sun in forty-eight hours."

I can't help laughing. "So go. See the sun. And give me the screwdriver."

This is how Carmen and I wind up sitting together on the nursery floor, surrounded by soft yellow walls and approximately one zillion crib pieces. "I had no idea these were so complicated," I say.

"My thesis is on point set topology with an emphasis on separation axioms." Carmen scowls at the junk around her. "This is harder."

If I ask what any of that actually means, I'm going to get a lesson in mathematics I really don't want. So I stick to the main subject at hand. "Do they have another crib ready?"

"Yeah—got one off Craigslist cheap. The seller's being super cool, dropping it off later on today. Mostly assembled, thank God."

I'm relieved to hear it. Arturo and Shay are still undergraduates. While they're both way more responsible with money than most people their age—more than I was, for sure—they don't have much. Every piece of furniture in this town house is thrifted or freecycled. It doesn't look it, thanks to Shay's mastery of "hipster chic," and the sheer love and care they've poured into their first home. But even small financial setbacks could hit them hard.

For an instant I remember Chloe e-mailing me photos of Libby's nursery. They'd found out the gender first thing—which Chloe said was good, because it let Anthony "get over the disappointment" of having a daughter instead of a son. She'd had her decorator paint the walls seashell pink and hang soft lace curtains over every window. At the time, I could only think of the impending arrival as more Anthony in the world, so I wanted to hate the nursery. To find it tacky. Instead I thought it was the sweetest place I'd ever seen. And when I saw the tiny crib for the first time, I could imagine the baby lying inside. That was the moment Libby became more than simply the proof my fate was shackled to Anthony Whedon's forever. That's when I realized this baby would be my niece—a part of my family, a part of me.

I waited along with my parents on the day Libby was born. I held her in my arms, took pictures like any proud aunt, even tolerated Anthony trying to stick a cigar in my mouth. If only I could say I had tons more memories like that, countless cherished moments I spent feeding her, taking her out in her stroller, or singing silly little songs.

But spending lots of time with Libby would mean spending time with her father. I'm a strong person in many ways, but relaxing in my rapist's presence—that's beyond me. So all the good times I've had with Libby have come in short bursts around the holidays and the occasional Skype call. She adores me as much as I adore her. God knows why. I'm grateful the little time we spend together is enough to kindle love in the heart of a child.

Libby won't be a kid forever. Soon she'll have dance recitals, school plays, graduations, and she'll expect me to be there, in the same row with her parents. Either I'll have to get used to sitting shoulder to shoulder with Anthony, or I'll have to let a little girl down.

And of course she can never know what her father did to me.

No child should ever have to know that about her dad, even if it's the truth.

"Hey," Carmen says, bringing me back to the here and now. "If you're not going to use the screwdriver, hand it over."

"I'm working." And I get back to it, focusing my entire attention on taking the crib apart.

That way I can stop myself from wondering whether I'm hours away from making love with Jonah again—or finding out I've lost him for good.

I don't know if Jonah will come to me tonight. I don't know what he'll do if he does; the nature of my ultimatum means he'll have total control over the scenario, if we do return to our games.

However, I know some things he absolutely *won't* do.

When Jonah and I first agreed to do this, before we knew anything about each other but our names and our desires, we laid down extremely clear boundaries:

- He can never threaten me with a weapon.
- He can slap me around, even hurt me, but not to the point of serious pain or injury.
- He will not take photographs or video of his "attacks."
- He will not come on me.

That last one seems so mundane, I know—but Anthony did that when he raped me, and the horror of that moment has stayed with me always. Initially I had other boundaries for Jonah as well, but as our games continued and he earned my trust, I let those boundaries fall. He can tie me up now if he wants. He can even fuck me in the ass.

(Jonah's the only man who's ever done that to me, and we only got around to it once. I wonder if he'll take my ass again tonight.)

I have to obey certain boundaries too:

- I can fight back, but can't leave marks or injuries he'd have to explain later.
- If anyone ever sees part of what's going on and misunderstands, I have to put aside my embarrassment and defend Jonah if necessary.
- And I may not call him *daddy*—a rule I thought was funny when he first laid it down. Now that I know the truth about Carter Hale, Jonah's need for that rule sickens me, makes me bleed for him inside.

Of course we have a safe word. *Silver.* I've had to use it with him twice so far. Tonight won't be the third time, I feel sure. Tonight I think I could take anything, if only Jonah will come to me.

I know he might not. Yet I'm already aching for it, the heat between my legs as tight as a clenched fist. As I park my car in front of my little house, I think, *Please, Jonah, don't make me wait much longer.*

Even though I know Jonah would never show up early for one of our games, my heart leaps into my throat the minute I walk inside my house. Every rustle of the wind through the trees outside makes me imagine him walking closer. Every creak of the wooden floorboards brings back the memory of him walking toward me in the night, dressed in black, ready to take me down.

Two and a half hours until I unlock my door.

I make myself a simple omelet for dinner, eat it at my tiny table. It occurs to me I've never cooked for Jonah. Not that I'm some sort of master chef—anything but. Still, we've skipped over so many of the usual, gentler milestones of intimacy. I'd like to make up for that, if I get the chance.

Just not tonight.

I wash the dishes. I take a shower, slathering myself with vanilla-scented body scrub so every inch of my skin will feel like silk. Every place my fingers touch, I imagine being touched by Jonah. He's gripped me there, bruised me, kissed me.

Afterward I blow-dry my honey-brown hair, trouble I'd never take to just sit at the house alone. I'd usually change into a shapeless T-shirt and leggings after an evening shower; tonight, I slip into a silky white robe. Nothing else. It will be easy for Jonah to peel the robe off. Maybe he'll use the sash to tie me up.

Assuming he comes here at all, I remind myself. I'm trying to brace myself in case he doesn't come. Though losing Jonah would crush me no matter what, I want to at least be . . . prepared.

So I try to read, but while my eyes scan over the words, my brain refuses to make sense of them. I go over the same paragraph time and again, attempting to concentrate on the here and now. It never works. Netflix offers me a TV show I've been meaning to catch up on, but it's just colors and light projected from a screen. Meaningless. All I can think about is my ever-quickening pulse, and the progression of the hands around the clock.

9:59. One whole minute early, I walk to my tiny kitchenette, take a deep breath, and unlock the door. Then I cut off all the lights in the house except for one small lamp in my bedroom—the one farthest from the bed. Now I can only lie down and wait.

Will he come in? Is he out there already?

It hits me then: Of course he is. Even if Jonah has no intention of having sex with me tonight, he's still outside. Because I told him I'd leave the door unlocked for one hour. That means I'm a little bit less safe.

And Jonah—who has tied me, fought me, held me down, bruised me, had me at his mercy—would always want to protect me.

Our relationship is pure paradox.

Or it was. I'll find out within the hour.

But down deep, I had hoped he would come through the door almost as soon as I'd slid back the bolt. He hasn't. Jonah must be parked across the street even now, sitting behind the wheel of his car, listening to the radio and not coming in. On some level he wants to; I know that. Wanting isn't enough.

In the darkness outside, Jonah is fighting a battle inside his own head.

Fifteen minutes go by. Twenty. Arousal begins to fade into sorrow.

I roll onto my belly in the bed, the pillow cool against my flushed face. Now I feel foolish, even manipulative. *What do you mean, giving someone an order to fuck you or else? Jonah doesn't want to hurt you—he's uncomfortable with our rape fantasy. Shouldn't he be? Aren't you?*

Then my ears prick up. My breath catches. *You imagined that sound. Just like you've been doing all night. You only think that's the sound of the door hinges—*

And I hear Jonah's footstep on the floor.

FIVE

I sit up, hands still braced against the sheets, just before Jonah walks in.

He's dressed like he usually is—jeans, belt, long-sleeved red tee. No black gear, no mask. Jonah spreads his arms to brace them on either side of my bedroom doorway. The dim light outlines his muscled arms, and hides the expression on his face.

"You think you can play this any way you want," he says, voice low and rough.

Is this the game or isn't it? It is. I know it is. He wouldn't be in my house right now if it weren't. But Jonah is only barely playing a role tonight. I sense that his fury is directed at this fantasy, and our mutual need for it; he's going to burn it off the only way either of us ever could—in bed. The anger he's brought here is real.

So are our rules. I know that. If I say *silver*, it's over. *I'm safe, I'm safe, with Jonah I'm always safe.*

One deep breath, and I'm ready. Let the game begin.

First I feign ignorance. "I don't know what you—"

"Shut your mouth," he says. "Unless I tell you to open it for me."

Sometimes I fight him. Sometimes I submit immediately. Tonight

I submit. I scramble backward on the bed until my back hits the headboard, but I say nothing.

Jonah reaches down to his belt and unbuckles it as he walks forward. I shiver at the sound of metal and leather.

"You thought you could push me." His voice has lowered almost to a growl. "You thought I was yours to boss around. But that's not how this works, little girl. You belong to *me*."

He snaps the belt between his hands, and I jump. Adrenaline hits me like a drug injected into my heart—every nerve is on fire for his touch, every instinct telling me to flee or fight. My limbs tremble; my breaths quicken.

Jonah notices. "Panting for it already, you little whore? Maybe I ought to make you beg."

With his belt in one hand, he reaches for my foot with the other. Deep instinct makes me jerk back. That only ignites his anger. Jonah lunges across the bed, grabs my ankle so tightly it takes me to the edge of pain, and drags me down the mattress. My white robe rides up, baring me to the waist.

"I knew you wanted it," Jonah says, looking at my exposed body. "Look at you, just waiting for somebody to come along and fuck you. Because that's what you wanted, isn't it? To get used *rough*."

He lets go of my ankle only to yank open the top of my robe, exposing my breasts. His fingers knead them aggressively hard, enough that I whine in discomfort. And yet he must be able to feel my nipple hardening against his palm.

"Little slut," he whispers. "I'm going to use you now. And you're gonna take it."

Oh, God, I don't want to love this. But I do. I do.

Jonah thrusts two long fingers into my cunt—no warning, no preparation. Doesn't matter. I'm already so wet for him. He laughs, a low, wicked sound. "Oh, yeah. You'd beg me for it, wouldn't you?

Beg me, whore. Beg me to fuck you so hard you won't be able to walk tomorrow."

I want to. But that would shatter the illusion. Instead I turn my head, push myself back far enough that his fingers slip out of me. As I try to crawl across the bed, away from him, Jonah's hand fists in my hair, brutally tight. I cry out; he doesn't let go.

"When I tell you to stay," he whispers, "you'll stay."

He slips the leather belt around my neck. I freeze on my hands and knees, and my fear isn't feigned. This isn't a weapon, but it's closer. We're on the very border of our limits. Jonah's testing me.

But this is what I need. He pushes me to the brink, and slightly past it, the way no one else ever has.

I hear the purr of his zipper, the rustle of cotton. His free hand is busy taking his cock out. If I could turn my head to see it, I would—Jonah's body is so fucking beautiful. But the strap of leather around my neck keeps me frozen still. If he pulled it any tighter, twisted his wrist a couple of times, I wouldn't be able to breathe. Jonah has total control, which is just how we both like it.

He whispers, "Spread your legs, bitch."

"Please—"

"That's right. Beg me to fuck you." The belt tightens around my neck. "Beg or you'll find out what happens to girls who *don't* want it."

My voice sounds like he's choked me already. "Please fuck me."

"How do you want me to fuck you? Tell me. You know what I want to hear."

". . . Fuck me hard."

"Oh, yeah. Then open your legs for me, slut."

By now I'm reeling. The whirlwind of hormones and emotions makes my arousal indistinguishable from panic. If Jonah were a stranger, an intruder who had found his way in here, I would have to surrender. Slowly, I begin to part my thighs.

Not fast enough for Jonah. With a snarl, he uses his free hand to yank one of my legs over sharply. Now my cunt is laid bare before his gaze. Jonah reaches for me, but this time he buries a finger in my ass. I cry out in alarm that isn't entirely feigned. Feeling his finger in me awakens primal fear. Even though the one time Jonah did this I came so many times I nearly passed out, I want to pull back. This is all happening so fast, like tumbling over a waterfall—

But I gave him permission. I released him from that limitation. If Jonah wants to fuck my ass all night long, he's still within the rules of the game.

The only way to stop him is to say *silver*, and I won't. I can't. I want this too much—no matter what *this* is.

When the leather strap suddenly loosens, I suck in a deep breath. But Jonah's not showing me mercy. He's only changing his attack. One arm hooks through both of mine, pinning them behind my back. Then I feel his hand gripping my ass, and the firm hot pressure of his cock against my thigh.

"You feel that? Huh?" Jonah can sound like a demon when he laughs. "That's what you're going to take for me."

With that he shoves himself inside my cunt, in one savage thrust.

God. Jonah is so big—long and thick, so much that when I first saw him I didn't know if I could take him all. It feels like he's splitting me in two. I cry out in mingled pain and pleasure as he rocks into me, and my whole body bends and turns in the desperate effort to accept every inch of his cock.

My reward is Jonah's other hand gripping the back of my head, forcing it down onto the mattress. "You don't make a sound unless you're begging me for more. Are you ready to beg?"

"No—"

"Beg me."

Jonah slams into me, and I want to cry out again. But I stifle it somehow. By now, tears have sprung to my eyes. But God help me, I love it. "Please. Please."

"There you go. I knew you'd admit you were a slut as soon as I got my cock in you. You'd take any cock, wouldn't you? Now you're taking mine."

His thrusts are slow at first. Deliberate. Punishing. But the tempo increases as he starts to get into it. Jonah never loses his grip on me; my shoulders ache from being pulled back so far. The side of my face is pressed onto the mattress, and I can feel my tears pooling between my skin and the sheets. And he keeps going, rutting on me harder and harder.

The only sounds in the room are his guttural grunts of pleasure and the slap of our bodies against each other. Hearing this turns me on even more. By now, the shame and fear I should feel at being taken like this have been eclipsed by the arousal peaking within me. Every single goddamned stroke of Jonah's body sets me on fire a little bit more. The heat could consume me whole.

Jonah quickens his thrusts. I want to scream into the mattress, because he's getting me just where it feels best. Most women don't get off just from being fucked, but I can, as long as I'm imagining this fantasy—or living it, like I am now. He brings me here like nobody else ever has.

"This is what you need," he pants. His voice is tense; he's as close as I am. "You need to be treated like the worthless little bitch you are."

Jonah's moving even faster now, even harder, and I'm nothing but heat and pulse. Everything else is far away. Pleasure tightens me, blazes inside, and then I come so hard that the world is nothing but white light, white noise. My cry is muffled by the mattress, but I wail it out anyway, unable to hold back.

He laughs again as he presses my head down more forcefully into the mattress, and pulls my arms up more to remind me how powerless I am. But he's almost there, and just as I begin to be able to breathe and see again, Jonah slams into me once—a pause—then again. His entire body shudders as he spends himself inside me. His grip on me tightens. He never makes a sound.

When Jonah unhitches his arm from my elbows, I let my arms sink down to the bed in relief. Usually this is when the game would end, but he stands up and rolls me over. Dazed, I lie there in my rumpled robe, breasts exposed, as Jonah stands at the edge of my bed. His enormous cock is still half hard, and in the dim light I can see that he's slick from being inside me. Jonah pulls my legs open. He whispers, "Look at you. All red and open and wet for me. My come is inside you, all over you. That's how you ought to be kept. Legs spread and ready for me. Because you're a whore. Isn't that right?"

"Yes," I pant.

"Say it."

"I'm a whore."

"*My* whore."

"Yours."

For some reason, that's what finally snaps him out of the spell. Jonah's grip on my knees gentles, and then he lets my legs fall to the side. When he whispers to me, his voice is again his own. "Are you all right?"

I nod. "Are you?"

Jonah doesn't answer immediately. Instead he reaches down and strokes the side of my face with two fingers, infinitely tender, before he unties the sash around my waist. I sit up, and the white robe falls away. Even as he's tucking himself back in, so that he's again fully dressed, I'm sitting in front of him naked. Yet as soon as he's zipped up, Jonah sits on the edge of the bed and wraps his arms around me. I hug him back, pulling him down onto the bed; he responds by rolling us over until I'm on top—giving me back the power I let him take away.

"Was it okay?" I whisper.

"More than that. Perfect. You're always perfect, Vivienne. You know everything I want, everything I need. And you always give it to me."

His words melt my heart, though that's not the answer to the question I was asking. "I meant, was it okay that I asked you to do this? Are you okay with being—with our games?"

I want to hear him say *Yes, of course, my God, I can't believe I nearly let you go, we'll do this forever.* Instead Jonah wears the most rueful smile. "Don't worry about me. I can take care of myself."

That's still not an answer. At least it's not a no. "I never wanted to make you feel like this was the only thing about you that mattered to me."

"You didn't. You made yourself clear. This fantasy we share—we both hate it, but we both need it. We'll figure out how to make it work." His gray eyes search mine, somehow loving and lonely in the same moment. "You and I, what we have together, it's more than this. And yet this is a part of us. It always will be."

There was a time, before a whole lot of therapy, when I would've argued that he was wrong. Once I longed to believe that I could heal every single wound Anthony inflicted, that I could rip all the dark pages from my life and be just like any other woman. Untouched. Whole. But I've learned that's impossible. You wear your scars for a lifetime.

At least now Jonah is here in the darkness with me.

His hand trails up and down my back. It always amazes me how tender he can be. "I shouldn't have pushed you away," he says, and that makes me feel more hopeful. It's all right, really. We just have to settle back into it. Balancing our games with the rest of our relationship isn't easy.

"You just wanted to protect me," I whisper. "But this is the safest I've ever felt with anyone."

He folds me against his chest and kisses my hair. "I will always protect you," he swears. "Always."

Even when Jonah left me, he was trying to protect me from himself.

Next morning dawns brighter. Jonah wakes faster than I do—one of those people who passes from sleep to awareness as quickly as flipping a switch. Me, I'm the mumble-and-walk-into-furniture type in the mornings. At least he seems to find it cute.

Neither of us has to be on campus particularly early, so we can take our time with breakfast. He knows how to work my French press, so once I'm able to fully open my eyes, the delicious scent of coffee fills the air. I pad into the kitchen, robe slightly akimbo, to find Jonah scrambling eggs. English muffins slowly brown in the toaster oven.

"You're the best," I say as I pull two mugs from the cabinet. Jonah smiles at me, but I sense that he's still slightly uneasy. I can understand that; honestly, I am too. As much as I loved last night—and I totally loved it—the memories are fresh and raw: Jonah calling me a whore, forcing me to beg. Just because I get off on the humiliation doesn't make it easier to look at in the light of day. *Is that me? Could I have said those things, wanted it all?*

The answer to those questions is yes. It's just hard to integrate that knowledge into the person I am the rest of the time, and the relationship Jonah and I are trying to rebuild.

Step by step, I remind myself. Jonah's learning how to handle this just like I am. We'll get it right yet.

I'm an NPR listener on weekday mornings, but Jonah asks for music, and I oblige. I figure I'll hear alt-rock or maybe jazz; to my surprise, his first-choice Internet radio station is classical music—opera, to be exact.

"Didn't figure you for an opera fan," I say.

"Not a fan, exactly. But I like it. My mother used to take us even when we were kids. Most children would probably have thought of it as an ordeal, but I didn't." Jonah sits across from me, coffee mug almost entirely hidden within his broad hands.

"Why? You enjoyed the music?" It's beautiful, really. But I can't quite imagine this being a small child's favorite, especially after hearing Libby sing "Let It Go" about forty million times.

"Eventually I came to enjoy it a great deal." He falls silent. I think that's all the explanation I'll get, until he adds, more quietly. "Carter never went to the opera house. So I felt safe there. When my brother or sisters came, I knew they were safe too. Getting dressed up and sitting still for a few hours bought us one night of freedom. After a while, opera seemed like the most beautiful thing in the world."

Never before has Jonah volunteered something so intimate, so difficult, as part of an everyday conversation. This is a huge step for him; I want to acknowledge that, but making too big a deal of it would backfire.

So I simply reach across the table, holding my hand out to him. He takes it. When our eyes meet, I ask, "Which opera is this music from?"

"*Fidelio*."

I squeeze his hand, and that's all it takes. He knows I've heard him, that I understand how much each glimpse into his past matters.

"I'm expecting some important data in from the University of Tokyo today, so I'll probably be putting in extra hours for a few days," Jonah says. "But—next week—would you like to get together? Stay over at my place?"

"Of course." I can't help smiling. This isn't only an invitation to play; it's also another step toward turning our strange relationship into a normal part of our lives. "I can't wait."

Jonah breathes out, and the tension within him finally fades, replaced by desire. He wants me as much as I want him. Maybe everything's going to be okay after all.

After breakfast, I kiss him good-bye at the door, and he drives away—just like pretty much any other couple on an unhurried weekday morning. Maybe it's silly to take so much pleasure in feeling ordinary, but I do. That's one of the joys of being with Jonah; I don't have to feel like a freak with a secret all the time.

Just most of the time.

I take a shower, put on jeans and a fleece jacket, and decide to take a stroll along South Congress. There's plenty of time before I need to drive onto campus, and a second cup of coffee seems like a great idea. Of course I could make it at home, but then how would I get whipped cream or cinnamon sprinkles?

Come to think of it, I should probably hit a spin class again pretty soon . . .

Or so I'm musing as I turn the corner onto Congress, when I pass one of the forlorn plastic newspaper boxes—the ones everyone mostly ignores, including me. But then one word in black grabs me and holds me fast.

RAPE.

The headline reads in full: BRUTAL RAPE ON NORTH SIDE. With a shaking hand, I take one of the issues; the newsprint smudges against my fingers as I straighten the pages to read. Last night some guy broke into an apartment shared by two college students. One of them was out, and came home late to find her badly beaten roommate—who is in stable condition, the kind of thing you hate to have to feel grateful for. This unnamed girl will live. Maybe she won't even bear any physical scars. But she will live forever with the knowledge that she was raped.

All anyone knows about her attacker was that he was a Caucasian male in a dark ski mask. So far as this girl knows, she never laid eyes on him before he decided to attack her and change her life forever.

Sometimes I wonder whether it's worse or better, stranger rape. If I'd never had to see my rapist again, rather than welcome him into my family, that would have been easier—but at least I never feared for my life. As scared as I was that night, as completely as Anthony overpowered me, it never crossed my mind that he would kill me. Nor his, I feel sure. That's not his brand of evil.

Fearing for your life has to be so much worse.

My throat tightens with a sob I can't set free. I wish I could go to the hospital and offer to talk with this poor girl. Just so she could be with someone else who understood a little. Yet I'm not a part of any support groups; I don't volunteer to work with other survivors. To do that, I would have to publicly identify myself as someone who has been raped, and I have never done this.

Besides, do I have any right to proclaim myself healed or recovered? Hardly.

And it would take more gall than I possess to stand in front of a fellow victim now, when I spent last night playing at being raped, for fun.

SIX

The shadows of that crime stretch over the next few days. UT Austin may be one of the largest universities in the nation, but news travels fast over any campus. Proximity to the victim holds a morbid sort of cachet—as if it both guaranteed genuine information and yet provided protection. Because lightning never strikes twice in the same place—or so people prefer to think.

Whispers in the library tell me what sorority the girl belongs to. A half-overheard question before our weekly departmental meeting informs me that she was in Art History: From the Neolithic to the Renaissance, but has now dropped out of this and all her other classes for the semester. During a grocery run, Carmen lets slip that the girl lived in the same apartment complex Shay did last year. The mere thought of this happening to sweet, bubbly Shay nauseates me.

Not that anyone else is a better victim. It's just . . . too fucking close.

I even contemplate calling Jonah to say, *Let's not play this week. Not so soon.* But I don't. Our reunion is too new, too fragile, for me to pull back right now.

And even though I hate myself for it, I *don't want* to pull back.

The real-world crime isn't enough to drive out the psychological need.

It makes me feel dirty. And helpless. So on Thursday morning, when I have no tasks ahead except a few hours of studio time, I treat myself to a lazy start. I take my time with my coffee. Luxuriate on the sofa with a book for an hour, then take a long, luxurious shower—complete with the vanilla-scented oil. By the time I've changed into leggings and a soft violet hoodie, I feel ready to take on the entire world.

Except my mother.

Calling home is rarely pleasant. The list of topics my mother and I can easily discuss comprises only two items: Dad's health and Libby. Only one of those topics is actually enjoyable, and even though my mom and dad are very involved grandparents, Libby doesn't visit every single day. Still, since Dad's heart attack, I've made a point of calling at least once a week. However strained my relationships with my family might be, I love them and always will; above all, I want to remain a constant part of Libby's life. That means maintaining some kind of truce.

Of course, it also means sacrificing my newly restored tranquility on the altar of preserving twisted family ties. But I've learned it's better to let my mother dull a good mood than let her make a bad one worse.

So I sit on my sofa, brace myself, and hit the phone logo beside her contact. To my surprise, she picks up on the first ring. "*Vivienne*?"

"Ah, yeah, hi."

She sounds so surprised that it's me. My mom might not keep up with current technology, but I thought she'd at least gotten used to seeing the name of the caller on her mobile phone screen.

"Have you talked to Chloe?" Mom's voice is sharp.

Fear plunges into my gut. "No. Oh, my God—did something happen to Libby?"

"Of course not. Libby's *fine*." She says it as if there could be no possible reason for me to think otherwise. "I just wonder if you talk to your sister once in a while. It makes me sad to think that two girls who grew up with bedrooms next to each other would be so distant as adults. Of course Chloe's busy as a young mother, but it seems like you at least could make the time to reach out."

Mines lie buried just beneath the surface of every sentence my mother says. It's my fault Chloe and I aren't best friends. My fault that my mother worries about our relationship. Chloe, who has no job, a housekeeper, a part-time nanny to help with anything Libby needs, and virtually no events on her schedule more pressing than her Bikram yoga class—she's the one who is too busy to call. Whereas I, a grad student heading into finals, am supposedly swimming in free time. You have to hand it to Renee Larroux Charles: She doesn't just dabble in guilt. She's the master.

But to call her on any of this would be to step on the tripwires, send the mines blowing sky-high. Worst of all, it would lead to another round of denial about the real reason Chloe and I don't have much to do with each other any longer.

So, instead of defending myself, I say, "You're sure there's no special reason you thought Chloe might have called me?"

Mom makes a huffy sound. "Honestly, Vivienne. There's no need to overreact to a simple question. I suppose that's the one thing you and Chloe have in common. Your endless tendency to overreact."

Hmmm.

I know better than to pry further. For now I simply ask after my father (still feeling pretty good, already eating burgers again despite doctor's orders) and about Christmas plans. The second topic seems even safer than the first, especially since my mother has not changed our holiday schedule one jot since Libby's birth. Chloe and Anthony have "Santa" at their house, early in the morning, then drive to my parents' house before noon. We have a big lunch, then exchange gifts, all while the stereo plays the most old-fashioned carols imaginable, mostly sung by the Mormon Tabernacle Choir. Really the only question is whether we're having turkey or ham, or maybe what to get Libby, so we don't accidentally buy her the same present.

But Mom doesn't want to discuss Christmas. "It's too early to think about that yet."

"It's the first week of December."

"Exactly. That's a whole month away. We have to think about your father, after all."

"You said Dad was doing fine."

"Which he is, but I think we might take his preferences into account. Don't you think he deserves to have some say in his own Christmas?"

That would make this year the first time Dad has ever had any say in how we spend Christmas. Again, I let it slide. "Sure. Right. We'll figure it out."

Mom's tone turns crafty. Hmm. "You *are* coming home, aren't you?"

"Absolutely." This is true. I wouldn't miss Christmas Day with Libby for anything. But I'd rather be set on fire than spend more than seventy-two hours in the same city as Anthony.

Mom tells me about a few former classmates of mine who have gotten engaged, married, or pregnant, with the suggestion that at age twenty-five I've already wasted my childbearing potential. I let this slide, get off the call as smoothly as I can, and hang up. Then I sit on my sofa for a few long minutes, cell still in my hand.

If I phone Chloe, there's no guarantee she'll tell me what's up. Obviously something *is* up, but God only knows what. If I don't call her, maybe I'll never have to know.

Then it hits me—what if Chloe's pregnant again?

No. Oh, God, no. The thought of her having one child with

Anthony was revolting enough. Then again, Mom would hardly sound so sharp and strange if that were Chloe's big secret. She'd be totally happy, over the moon, and very coy about not being able to tell me. Instead, she sounded completely off-kilter.

Maybe Chloe's pregnant, but the pregnancy isn't a healthy one. They could've conceived triplets, and are considering reducing, a decision my mother would look on with horror. Chloe could be on the verge of losing the baby, or genetic tests might have come back with some awful diagnosis.

I can't take it anymore. As angry as I've been with Chloe these past many years, she's still my sister. I don't know whether she's in serious trouble, but if she is, I want to help. So I call.

Chloe picks up so late that I first assume it must be her voice mail. "Vivienne," she says faintly. "I wasn't expecting to hear from you."

Forget the small talk. "When I spoke on the phone with Mom this morning, she sounded really weird. Are you okay? Is everything all right?"

"Well." Chloe remains silent for a long time. "I suppose you might as well know. Anthony has— I've asked Anthony to move out."

Did she really say that? Did I just hear it?

Anthony is gone?

I bite down on my lower lip to keep myself from laughing out loud for joy. What do I say? How do I sound supportive without sounding *delighted*? "Whoa," I manage. "I didn't expect that."

"Things fell apart pretty quickly," Chloe says in an absent tone, as if she were checking her manicure instead of confessing something that must be intensely painful for her.

"Are you going to tell me what happened?"

Her voice sharpens. "I would've thought you already knew."

She could only be referring to one thing. A month ago, right after my father's heart attack, Jonah confronted Anthony about what he'd done to me—and Chloe overheard. At the time I thought she still refused to believe that Anthony had raped me, but she did at least finally know that what happened went well beyond his version of events in which we were only "flirting."

Yet now she's thrown Anthony out. Does that mean Chloe has finally accepted the truth?

If I press her on it, I'll only alienate her. That's the last thing I want to do—especially now, when for the first time in more than ten years, I feel like I might actually get my big sister back.

"Are you okay?" I ask, as gently as I can.

Chloe makes a sound that doesn't quite count as a laugh. "I'm miserable. But I know I've made the right choice."

"Is he still in the house?"

"He hasn't found a place of his own yet, but for the time being he's staying with his brother."

That counts as progress. "I, uh—I'm glad you've done what you wanted to do."

"I suppose I will be too, someday."

Then I hear another voice, high-pitched and more distant. "*Who is that? Is it Daddy?*"

Libby. As always, when I hear her voice, I can't help but smile.

Chloe answers her daughter. "No, sweetie, it's Aunt Vivi. Would you like to talk with her?"

"Put her on," I plead.

Then I hear Libby say, "Hi, Aunt Vivi."

"Hey there! How are you?"

She answers with more honesty than any adult would ever show. "I'm sad."

That catches me short. The best news I've had in forever is, to this little girl, a disaster—the kind that leaves scars for a lifetime. Remembering that doesn't make me any less thrilled that Anthony's been thrown out, but it does remind me that one person, at least, has a reason to be sad he's gone. "I'm sorry, honey. What are you doing to help yourself feel better?"

"Well, Daddy is staying with Uncle Richie right now, but he comes to see me pretty much every day after school, and he says we'll spend all of Saturday together." I can tell she's brightening at the very thought. "He's going to take me to Chuck E. Cheese!"

Singing animatronic rodents. Better him than me. "You guys will have fun, I bet."

"Daddy always helps me with the games at Chuck E. Cheese." Libby even giggles. "He's really good at Whac-A-Mole."

For all of the wretched things about Anthony Whedon—for all that he brutalized me when I was less than ten years older than Libby is now—he is not only my rapist. He is also Libby's father, and he loves her. I think he'd try to kill any man who treated her the way he treated me. His adoration of his daughter may be the one truly pure part of his soul.

Even the best of us isn't purely good. And even the worst of us isn't purely evil.

How am I supposed to get any work done up here on cloud nine?

Yes, I'm worried for Libby, and I know this is difficult for Chloe—but once the call is over, all I can do is luxuriate in my delight. I've waited too long for this moment not to enjoy it. So I text Jonah the whole story. He doesn't reply back right away, no doubt because he's neck-deep in research. Once he reads it, I know he'll understand completely what this means to me.

(How often must he have longed for his mother to announce she was divorcing Carter Hale? Jonah has waited more than thirty years for his deliverance, and it still hasn't come.)

Then I change into my sloppiest, paint-striped jeans and a ratty old hoodie. It's time to make some art.

I share studio space with a number of other local artists, most of them also affiliated with the fine arts program at UT Austin. We have our designated stations, though when the studio is mostly empty, we feel free to spread out a bit. When I walk into the broad, concrete-floored former warehouse, with its high ceiling and exposed metal beams, I see I'm by myself today except for Keiko, one of my fellow TAs. She's sitting at the pottery wheel in the corner, her hands slathered in clay, and can spare only a quick glance at me to smile hello. Although her art is something I've only dabbled in, I know very well the dangers of looking away while you're throwing a pot.

My own station is much more dangerous, actually. See, I work a lot with acid. Although I sketch, and even paint a little, my first love is etching. This means I draw an image on a plate, burn that image into the plate with acid, and use it to make prints. Depending on the acids, inks, and printing techniques used, the final etching can express many different shades of meaning—while the plate remains the same, each print has its own unique identity.

Today, I want to work on creating a new plate; I'll need to broaden my range of work for my final portfolio review next semester. But what should I work on first? The problem isn't that I don't have any ideas. It's that I have too many. Whenever life offers new people and experiences, new artistic inspiration arrives—and no matter what else you might say about Jonah Marks's influence in my life, he has definitely provided inspiration of every kind.

Wait. What if I created an etching that symbolized Jonah himself?

I've never done that before—tried to personify anyone in my life as a symbol in my work. Yet the idea immediately catches fire in my mind. Jonah has challenged me, frightened me, freed me. He's brought me from despair to ecstasy. Portraying those complex emotions in one single image . . . now that would be a challenge.

And the different roles he plays in my life, those could be shown with new inks, new papers, new techniques. My mind goes into overdrive even as I start setting up my station. *I could use thick, black, blotchy ink on stained fabric—or even on burlap, maybe. Then something silvery on dark gray paper, good stuff, the same stock as top-quality formal stationery—*

I catch myself. Thinking about all the creative ways I'll print this is putting the cart in front of the horse. First I have to choose the image, and create it.

And yet—*one* image that could capture everything Jonah has meant to me? What on earth would it be?

For ideas, I pull out one of my sketchbooks. This is the one I took along when Jonah swept me off to the Scottish Highlands for a week. Every night we made love in a little inn on the rugged coast of the Isle of Skye; every day, he went out on the water for his research, and I was free to wander, see, and draw. Maybe something here will spark my imagination . . .

My phone rings; the song it plays is the ringtone I assigned to Jonah. Smiling, I answer, "Hey. I was just thinking about you."

"That son of a bitch is gone," Jonah says without preamble. "I'm so happy for you, Vivienne."

"I feel like throwing a ticker tape parade," I confess. "Or drinking champagne, or dancing in the streets. It's like a hundred New Year's Eves rolled into one."

"You'd like to celebrate?"

The low tone in his voice as he says it sends electricity crackling inside me. "I would." I try to sound innocent. "Do you have an idea?"

"I do. Would you be in the mood for something a little more . . . elaborate than usual?"

I remember our would-be weekend at the cabin, where Jonah kidnapped me, tied me up, and used me as savagely and perfectly as I could ever have dreamed. We would have spent three days like that, instead of three hours, if not for my father's sudden crisis. I've never stopped longing for those days back. "Oh, yeah."

"Give me another three hours," he says. "Then come to my apartment. I'll explain the scenario then. Lay down the rules."

"Yes." I can't imagine what the rules will be. I like not knowing. Mystery invites that frisson of fear that makes everything more tantalizing.

After we've hung up, it occurs to me that celebrating with one of our games is possibly not the most mentally healthy way to commemorate my rapist's expulsion from my family.

But to hell with that. Healthy left me behind a long time ago. Tonight I feel powerful, overjoyed, and invincible.

That will make it so much sweeter when I surrender to Jonah completely.

SEVEN

Jonah's apartment complex sits downtown, very near the lake. This is the most desirable location in the city—at the very heart of Austin, secure, luxurious in a low-key way.

He's given me the security code to punch in at the ground level of the building's parking garage, so I drive in without any fuss. My heart thumps hard in my chest as I maneuver my Honda Civic into one of the spots marked with the yellow, spray-painted word *Visitor.* My palms are sweaty against the gearshift as I put it in park, on my keys as I pull them from the ignition. I can feel my pulse between my legs, steady and insistent, already longing for him.

When I changed out of my studio clothes, I made sure to put on one of the little dresses I've bought at Goodwill for the express purpose of being destroyed, if Jonah so chooses. This one is dark blue, bandana-patterned, with skinny straps and a hemline that stops several inches above the knee. Both the cooler fall weather and local style would call for a cardigan on top and cowboy boots on my feet. I go without. Warmer clothes are in the large backpack I'll carry in, so I can change into them before I leave hours from now—once Jonah's done with me. For now my shoulders are bare, as are my legs all the way down to the ballet flats I wear. Small gold hoop earrings are my only jewelry.

No bra. It only gets in the way. Panties, yes—because both of us enjoy it when he tears them off.

The elevator's heavy metal doors slide shut around me. I punch in the numerical code that allows me to travel to the penthouse floor. That space belongs to Jonah alone.

When the doors open, I blink in surprise. No lamps are lit anywhere in the apartment. As I step out, however, my eyes adjust to the darkness and take in the city lights beyond the broad windows, and the shadows in front of them. One of those shadows is Jonah.

"Put your things down," he says. His voice is still his—we aren't yet in the game. But that wasn't a request; it was a command. Jonah's as impatient for this to begin as I am. "Take off your shoes."

I slide my foot out of one ballet flat, then the other. A nearby chair provides a place to ditch my bag. Slowly I walk forward. Jonah stands still, waiting, forcing me to come to him.

More details take shape. Something is dangling from one of the high beams overhead—one rope, I think. Jonah wears solid black from head to toe, and whatever he's got on outlines his powerful form like a second skin. He's holding something soft and black in his hands.

My breaths are quick and shallow by the time we're standing face to face. Very quietly Jonah says, "I'm going to restrain your hands. And I'm going to shut you up. You remember how to stop me if you can't talk?"

In our very first conversation about the rules of our games, we devised an alternative to our safe word. "I snap my fingers."

"So I'm going to tie your hands. You show me you can snap your fingers even when you're bound. The minute you do—the game is on. And you belong to me."

Fuck. Just hearing him say that makes me dizzy with need. I nod, and hold out my wrists.

Instead of taking them, Jonah first turns his attention to the black cloth in his hand. When he tugs it on, I see it's a mask—not a ski mask. Just simple, flat, and black, like the sort of thing sold at Halloween. When even that much of his face is hidden from me, he becomes anonymous. More frightening. A shudder runs through me.

Then Jonah's broad hands grip mine, he pulls me over to stand underneath the rope. There's a second coil of rope on the floor by my feet, and Jonah forces me to kneel before him as he uses it to loop my wrists together in a complicated-looking knot, being careful not to cut off my circulation. When he's finished he drags me up and pulls my arms above my head, securing my bound wrists to the other rope. For one panicked moment I think he's going to haul me off the ground, but he doesn't. Instead, Jonah stops at the point where my hands are completely overhead and I can hold on to the rope and stand on my tiptoes. It's enough for me to support my weight, but not enough for me to feel sure of my balance. I couldn't kick him without pulling painfully on my arms.

His voice is low. "Now show me how you can stop this. Show me how you want it."

In this one instance, the safe word is the signal. Trembling, I bring my fingers together—and snap.

"Look at this." Instantly his voice transforms into a growl. His hand runs up and down my body as if I were something he had purchased, his to inspect. "Got you right where I want you."

He wants to know that I can call this off without words; that means he plans to muffle me. First I have to goad him into doing it. "Please, stop," I beg. "Let me go. Whatever you want—money, anything—I'll get that for you, I promise. Just untie my hands and let me leave."

"Anything I want?" he murmurs. His fingers trail down to the edge of my dress, which has been hiked so high that it now barely covers my crotch. I feel him tracing a line up my thigh. "You're gonna get me what I want? Yeah. I think you are."

"Please—" My words break off in a gasp as he yanks my panties away so hard they tear. My skin stings, and I try to writhe away from the sensation—but then I nearly lose my balance and have to still myself.

Jonah laughs as he makes a fist around my panties. Surely he can feel the dampness against his palm. He can smell how much I want him.

With his free hand he pinches my nose, forcing me to part my lips to breathe. As soon as I do, he lets go of my nose and stuffs my own panties into my mouth. I try to protest, but it comes out muffled nonsense, nothing more.

"What's that?" Jonah murmurs as his fingers trace the neckline of my dress, find the space between my breasts. I bet he can feel the pounding of my heart, the proof that he controls me down to my pulse. "What did you try to say?"

No. Stop it. I keep attempting to talk, because it seems to turn him on. And I allow myself to believe it—that I am held captive in the dark by a stranger, and that I want to plead for my safety even though I know it's too late. *Stop.*

"Still don't understand you."

Both of Jonah's hands go to the fabric bunched between my breasts. He tears it in two, ripping it nearly down to the hem. Now my body is all but exposed to him. Jonah makes a satisfied sound, almost a hum, like he's pleased with what he's caught.

"I'll have to guess what you want," Jonah murmurs as he tears one of the fragile spaghetti straps of my dress. The cotton slides away, now dangling only from one arm. "Let's see. Are you telling me you want to get fucked?"

No! No! I try to scream through the panties in my mouth. The sound is slightly muffled, but my desperation is clear.

Jonah laughs. "Sounds like you want to get fucked bad. Don't worry. I'm gonna take care of you."

He tears the other strap; the remains of my dress flutter to the floor. I twist my body away from his, but the bindings on my wrists pull so tightly that I can't get far. The struggle only seems to amuse Jonah more as he walks around me, squeezes my ass.

"Are you scared I won't fuck you hard enough? Because trust me, I'm going to pound you senseless."

Jonah pulls apart my legs. I scream again, but he ignores me. Although I can still balance, the muscles in my arms and shoulders are burning from holding the stretch now. My face is flushed and hot as his fingers push inside me.

"Feel how wet that is," he whispers. His breath is warm on the back of my neck. "No wonder you're begging me to fuck you."

I hear him open his zipper. *No, no, don't,* I attempt to shout into the gag of my own panties. It means *God, yes, now.*

Then I feel his cock against my ass. One of his hands grips me at the pubic bone, fingers spreading the lips of my cunt. By this time my whole body is shaking, but he's still merciless—teasing me with it, rubbing the head against my cunt, slipping in just barely before pulling back again.

"Are you ready to get fucked?" he growls into the curve of my neck as he lifts and tilts my pelvis to angle me just right. "You better *get* ready."

And then he shoves inside.

I gasp, or try to around my panties. Jonah pushes in all the way and hooks his other arm around and under my hips, forcing my back to arch as he holds me up. Even so I'm at the limits of my flexibility. He's keeping me exactly where he wants me, and there's absolutely no way for me to break free. He starts moving in and out, slowly at first, but quickening with every thrust. Growing stronger too—my breasts jiggle with every slap of his body against mine, and

I have to fight to keep my balance, though the angle of his muscular arm is bearing enough of my weight to make that possible. Each stroke kindles yet more of the fire building inside me.

"Is that not what you wanted?" Jonah is thrusting into me savagely now. "You didn't want to get fucked?"

My moan sounds desperate even through my gag.

He only laughs again. "Too bad, bitch."

Then he lets go completely. The illusion of force is complete. I close my eyes; every muscle in my body trembles, and I'm hanging on every way a person can. It's like he gets deeper every time, though it's impossible—his enormous cock splitting me in two. And he fucks me, and he fucks me, and then I know nothing but the pleasure swelling inside me, tightening my cunt around him, until I come.

It hits me like a tidal wave, and I scream so loud and long that even the gag can't hold it all back. Jonah's thrusts speed up even more. Limp in the aftermath of orgasm, it's all I can do to hold on for those final moments. Then he goes tense, makes an animal sound that seems to come from his gut, and slams into me one more time. When he comes, his fingers grip me so tightly they dig into my flesh, as if he were trying to claw his way inside.

But then his fingers relax. He pulls out, and I feel hot wetness begin trickling down my bare legs. "Stand up," he whispers. Shaky as I am, I can pull my legs back together; he quickly unties me from the rope overhead before freeing my wrists. Letting my arms fall to my side again is a relief. Only now do I realize they're tingling. Soon I would've been numb. With cool, clumsy fingers I extract my sodden underwear from my mouth and let them fall atop the remnants of my dress.

Jonah pulls off his mask and braces me with an arm around my shoulders. "Are you okay?"

"Yeah. I'm good." My arm and shoulder muscles are a little tender from having been stretched upward like that, but the soreness I'll feel will be more than worth it.

"Did you like this game?"

"God, yes. It was so intense." I smile crookedly. "I *loved* it."

Jonah pulls me into his arms, and for a few minutes we make out like crazy, as if we'd only started having sex instead of having just finished. At one moment, while he's kissing my throat, I glimpse my etching on his wall. The image of two masculine hands cradling a bird is eclipsed by our reflection in the glass—me naked, Jonah fully clothed. He still grips his mask in one of the hands circled around my back.

I want to be so happy now. Completely reassured that Jonah's okay with our games, and that we've fully reclaimed our gloriously twisted, utterly satisfying sexual bond.

But he still hasn't let go of that disguise.

"Did you need it?" I whisper, pulling back enough to look him in the face. "The mask? Did you have to wear it to play? You—you couldn't look me in the face last time either."

His eyes meet mine; he's steadier than I would've thought. "The mask made it easier. That's all."

"You're sure?"

"Anything that brings me back to you is worth it," Jonah says. Then he sweeps me up in his arms like Rhett with Scarlett, takes me to bed, and kisses me until I fall asleep from pure exhausted satisfaction.

"You've had too much coffee," Geordie says, the next morning. "Or too much sugar."

"Just because I'm more cheerful in the morning than some people—"

"You *aren't*." He gives me a dark look across the table at Moonshine Patio, where our half-finished huevos rancheros sit on brightly colored plates. "If memory serves, you normally awaken in the sort of mood one associates more with grizzlies roused from hibernation."

"I'm not that bad," I insist, though Geordie has a point. But it's not like I can explain why I'm so elated right now. That has to remain secret. I made sure to wear bangle bracelets that will cover the rope marks on my wrists. "Besides, it's not that early."

"Normally any time before noon is too early to approach the awakened Vivienne in her natural habitat."

I laugh, though his jokes are getting too close for comfort. Phoning Geordie for an impromptu brunch this morning felt a little weird, especially since I was still at Jonah's when I made the call. But Jonah had already headed into his labs to study the Japanese fault line data, or whatever, and I know it's important to keep checking on Geordie during these first stages of his recovery.

Still, it can be a little inconvenient hanging out with someone who knows you this well. I try to cover. "It's just that I—um, woke up on the right side of the bed this morning. Finals are nearly over, I had a great day in the studio yesterday, what's not to like?"

Geordie sighs, and it hits me how forlorn he looks. How worn out. He's lost even more weight since his release from Mullins, probably because he's now drinking more water, fewer margaritas. But that wouldn't explain the uncharacteristic stubble on his cheeks, or the dullness in his eyes. I realize he's not picking on me because I'm overly cheerful this morning. It's because he's down. When you're depressed, no one is more irritating than an optimist.

I dial it back. "What are you doing for the holiday? Going home to Boston?"

"Going *really* home, actually. Mum and Dad want us to visit Gran. So it's across the pond to Inverness for me."

"That sounds lovely." Again I imagine the inn Jonah and I visited in Scotland, on that wild and beautiful coast. What must those craggy hills look like when they're covered in snow?

"I suppose." Geordie pushes his huevos rancheros around his plate with his fork. Even though he doesn't look up, he seems to sense my staring at him. "It's just—the culture over there, they drink more than Americans do. If you want to hang out with your mates or your cousins, you go to the pub, right? It's bloody everywhere."

Oh, no. "You can explain, though. Can't you? You don't have to tell them the whole story if you don't want, just that you're not drinking right now."

Geordie shakes his head and laughs. "In America, that works. People assume you're in a twelve-step program, or giving up gluten, or being the 'designated driver' or whatever else. But Scotland's not received the memo. Someone's going to put a pint glass in my hand for me, sooner or later. And I want to think I'll put it down, but I don't know if I will."

"Hey." I reach across the table to take his hand. From the way he looks at me when I touch him, I worry that I might've done too much—but hopefully he understands this is from one friend to another. "You can do it. I know you can."

"Right." He couldn't seem less convinced.

If he believes he won't make it, then he won't. "Are you going to your meetings? They probably have them in Inverness too."

"Christ, they're enough of a pain here. Alcoholics Anonymous is the last place I want to spend Christmas Eve."

I think fast. "Do you have to go to Scotland?"

Geordie looks up at me. "My parents and Moira already bought their tickets."

"Your sister will understand. Your parents will forgive you."

"But they don't know."

"You still haven't told them?" I don't know why I'm so surprised. He can't be the first person to have hidden his substance abuse treatment from his family. "You could, you know. Moira would listen." I've never met his parents, but Geordie's big sister is feisty, funny, and down-to-earth. She came to Austin last spring when we were still together and was pretty much nonstop terrific.

"I'm going to, all right? But not now. Not before Christmas, and not while I'm still—" He sighs so softly the sound is almost drowned out by the clatter of plates, the murmuring chitchat of brunch. "I want to tell them once I know I've got it together. Then they don't have to be scared for me, you know?"

"But then they don't know to look out for you."

My father's the only one in my family I never told about Anthony because after Mom and Chloe didn't believe me, I couldn't take another letdown. So he's never realized that I try to avoid Anthony. He'll suggest that we make a run to the store together, or leave it so that I have to sit next to Anthony at the dinner table. My mother and Chloe, for all their denial, at least wanted to keep the two of us apart. Ignorance can harm you as surely as malice.

So I keep thinking up solutions. "If you're not ready to talk to them, then remain in the U.S. this Christmas."

Geordie raises an eyebrow. "Are you inviting me home with you?"

"Umm, I think Jonah might be coming with me." Not that we've worked this out in detail, but it seems possible. Certainly Jonah has no desire to spend the holidays in Chicago.

"Awkward, then," he says, easily enough. "Best avoided."

Inspiration strikes. "I know. You should spend the holidays with Arturo and Carmen and Shay. I bet they'd love to have you!"

"Ahh, come on. It's baby's first Christmas and all of that. They won't want some loudmouth Scotsman in recovery hanging around."

"Of course they will. And they already understand the whole story, so you'd be with people who can help you stay strong, right? You might even get to play Santa Claus."

"Father Christmas," he insists. But I can see a small, unwilling smile.

"I'll check with them to make sure it's okay." Volunteering

friends for Christmas hosting would be a leap if I weren't as close to Carmen and Arturo as I am. But they care about Geordie too, so I'm sure they'll agree. "Tell your parents you're sticking around to help some friends who have a new baby and need their support system around them. It's true enough."

"Guess so."

"Great," I say, hardly able to stop grinning. He needs human connection if he's going to truly recover. I'm doing my part—but the ex-girlfriend can't be the only one involved. Otherwise he's doomed. Getting Arturo, Shay, and Carmen involved might make all the difference.

Geordie tucks into his brunch again, humor still uncertain. "What's got you in such an ungodly good mood today, anyway? Don't tell me. Big plans with Jonah later?"

I remember everything Jonah did to me last night. We don't have immediate plans, but there's so much more he could do to me. That he *will* do to me. Heat rushes to my cheeks, and I can't look at Geordie any longer.

"Thought so," he says, and turns back to his food.

When I had sex for the first time—consensual sex—I walked into high school the next day feeling like everyone would know. As if a neon sign floated overhead, glowing letters reading *Vivienne Went All the Way with Derek*. Of course, nobody did, and Derek was a good guy, not the type to brag in the locker room. At the end of the day, when my secret remained undetected, I felt silly for having worried about it in the first place.

Nearly ten years later, that feeling is back.

I make my way through campus that afternoon, backpack on my shoulders and portfolio case under one arm, wondering if the neon sign has returned. Geordie definitely figured out something was up, and it seems as if everyone should see rope marks on my wrists despite the bracelets. My body remains mostly unscathed; Jonah takes such good care of me. The sting I feel on my skin is purely psychological. But every time someone passes me on the sidewalk, I can't help feeling like they should guess. If nothing else, the bone-deep satisfaction I feel ought to tip them off—the way my walk is still loose, the way I blush every time a memory from last night fills me with mingled shame and delight.

Then again, today I could dress like a rodeo clown and nobody at UT Austin would notice. Finals are upon us. Professors wear a harried look, no doubt surrounded by endless begging for deadline extensions or better grades. Students shamble around even sloppier than usual. They're cramming until dawn, then showing up for the tests almost brain-dead. To judge by the number of cardboard-sleeved paper cups I see clutched in people's fists, the campus coffee shop is doing record business.

I hurry upstairs to the fine arts department, where Kip sits at his desk. The sweet old lady who preceded him as secretary used to put out a glass dish of peppermints every Christmas season. Kip, however, goes all out. His work area is draped with silver tinsel and blue lights . . . and the dish of peppermints, which he proclaimed a worthy tradition.

"You never struck me as the kitschy type," I say as the lights begin blinking in some sort of synchronized pattern.

"How little you know me. I'm wounded." Kip never looks away from his typing; his painted green nails seem to fly along the keyboard. "I'll have you know an actual vintage black-velvet Elvis painting hangs on my wall at home."

"I take it back. You're the king of kitsch." I laugh as I grab a peppermint. "You don't dress like it, though."

"Ugh, no. Only hipsters dress ironically. *Decorating* ironically, however, is another matter. That's what you do until you can afford the good stuff. Better hilariously tacky than some sort of pitiful Ikea-catalog concept of style."

I guess I won't mention my Ikea table and chairs.

Kip gives me an up-and-down look. The clicking of his keyboard ceases. "Aha. I see things are heating up again with Lava Boy."

He pronounces it to sound almost like *lover boy.* "I told you we were trying to work things out."

"Not that you *had* worked them out, apparently to your glorious satisfaction."

Now I'm flustered, though I try to cover it as well as I can. "What's my tell?"

"That ponytail. Messier than your usual—it practically screams, *I had to drag myself out of bed after being sexed up this morning.* Now tell me of your adventures with the volcano scientist. Describe the most recent eruption."

"*Stop* it." I laugh to cover my discomfort.

I remind myself that Kip only knows I slept over at Jonah's. He doesn't have any idea what I let Jonah do to me, or why. So there's nothing to be embarrassed about.

But bringing Jonah into my life—making him more than my dirtiest secret—it's been tricky.

"Seriously," Kip adds, "there's a glow about you. That's more than sex, darling. Either the two of you are falling in love, or Jonah Marks does something for you in bed no other man has ever done. In which case, spill."

The best defense is a good offense. "I'm not the only one glowing these days. Speaking of lover boys, how's Ryan?"

Kip lights up. Sometimes I forget that he's only a couple years older than I am; at this moment he might be a teenager in love for the first time. "He's a revelation to me. Ryan's not what I used to think of as my type. You know, he's so *butch.*"

Ryan's muscled like a bodybuilder. "But you like him? His personality matches that hot bod?"

"Oh, we have our little disagreements, but who doesn't? I'm learning to manage things for him."

"Manage things?"

"You know. Learning his pet peeves and avoiding them, so on, and so forth." Kip looks pensive for a moment, then sighs dreamily. "I've never been so . . . passionately wanted by someone. It's amazing to feel that way."

"Yeah, it is."

Then Kip frowns at his screen, leans forward, and puts one hand to his chest. "Oh, no."

"Oh, no, what?" Have they pulled our parking privileges? Is one of the professors ill?

But the truth is so much worse than that.

"Campus crime alert," Kip says. "There's been another rape by an intruder. Last night. They think it's the same perpetrator—same creepy ski mask and everything."

So what happened to that one girl a week ago wasn't an isolated incident. It was part of a pattern—a pattern that has only just begun.

Which means there's a predator on the loose, right now.

EIGHT

"I'm not upset," I insist next Monday during my session with Doreen. "My house is secure. I have pepper spray on my keychain and a baton under the bed. Plus I've taken self-defense classes. I know how to look out for myself."

Doreen isn't distracted by my personal array of armaments. "You're not upset by this at all? Most women would be. Hell, I am."

I fold my arms in front of my chest. "Obviously it's terrible for those women. And the sooner the police catch this guy and lock him up, the better I'll feel. But I don't think I'm in more danger than any other woman in Austin. Less than most."

"Fear is a natural reaction, but sometimes our responses to things like this are more complicated than pure fear."

The best and worst thing about Doreen? She can see right through me. "Volunteers will have reached out to both of those girls by now," I say. "Other survivors, who have come forward and told their stories. I'd like to help too. But I can't, because I've never told the world the truth."

Doreen nods. "After your mother and Chloe responded so

badly, nobody could blame you for being hesitant to tell anyone else."

"Jonah reacted badly at first too. Not like Mom and Chloe—he believed me, stood up for me. He freaked out about his own damage, that's all. But it was weeks before he would touch me again, and even that only happened because I pushed him."

"What else happened after Jonah learned the truth?"

"He told me about his own past. He opened up to me in a way I don't think he's ever opened up to anyone else."

"Honesty is the foundation of intimacy," Doreen says. "When Jonah learned the truth of what you went through, it took him a while to come around. But he did. Do you think it's possible that other people in your life might respond as well as he did? Maybe even better?"

I try to imagine Carmen's face. Or Geordie's, or Shay's. It's impossible. "There's no point. None of them need to know anything about my sex life. But Jonah and I had to work through this together. We're . . . wounded in the same way. We share the same scars."

"Have the two of you talked about this man on the loose in town?"

"No. Not yet." I chew on my lower lip. "We were both busy this weekend. He basically lived in his lab on campus, and I had to proctor a test on Friday. Then I stayed at Carmen's all weekend, because she was scared to death. But we bought her some pepper spray of her own and installed a couple of extra locks. So now she's good."

Doreen doesn't fall for the distraction. "But you talked to Jonah at some point, obviously. Yet you didn't discuss this subject at all."

Oh, fine. Might as well admit this and get it over with. "I don't want to discuss it with him."

"Are you afraid he'll respond badly?"

"It's not that." How can I put it into words? Instead of meeting Doreen's eyes, I stare at one of her lush houseplants the whole time I speak. "Playing games with Jonah—pretending to be raped for my own pleasure—it feels so much sicker while people are really being hurt."

"You and Jonah have worked hard on consent. On establishing boundaries. That makes what you do very, very different from the reality of rape. You know this, Vivienne."

"Yeah, I do. So why do I need to *pretend* it's the real thing? Why do I need the fantasy every single time?"

Doreen sighs. "Well, that's the question."

It has been for years. I feel no closer to an answer.

In the end, I don't have to raise the subject of the unknown assailant TV stations have now dubbed the Austin Stalker. Jonah does it for me.

Not half an hour after I've left Doreen's, as I'm in the vitamin aisle at the drugstore, my phone vibrates in my purse. When I see it's him, I pick up right away. "Hey. What's up?"

"You should stay at my place tonight," Jonah says.

My cheeks flush hot. "You want me again so soon?"

A woman over by the gingko supplements gives me a look. Oops. Reminder to self: *Lower your voice in public.*

Jonah says, "I always want you. But I meant that you'd be safer here. My apartment's on the top floor, and there's security in the lobby. And you wouldn't be alone."

"My place is more secure than it looks. You always have the door left open for you; a real intruder wouldn't find it so easy to get inside."

"Still. Good locks are no match for an actual security system with cameras and a guard."

"I'm not worried," I insist.

After a pause, Jonah says, "I am."

This isn't about making me feel safe—at least, not only about that. Jonah has his own fears to contend with. What might have been stirred up within his soul because of this? So I relent. "Okay. I'm going to run home and pack an overnight bag. I'll get to your place around . . . six thirty?"

"How does salmon sound for dinner?"

Apparently he genuinely likes to cook. This is yet another new discovery—one more of the many things I still get to learn about Jonah. "Sounds fantastic."

By the time I arrive there, darkness has fallen, and the city lights glitter all around the penthouse. It's as if we were suspended just above the stars. Jonah's apartment smells of lemon and fresh bread, and when he opens the door for me, he's even wearing a black apron tied neatly, chef-style, around his waist.

"Good," he says, instead of hello. Jonah pulls me into his arms for a long, lingering hug. "You're here."

"Thanks for asking me." I kiss his cheek, revel in the feeling of being held in those strong arms. "My house is safe—really—but it's just nice to know you were thinking of me."

He looks at me, and though I can't quite read his expression, I think he might be surprised. "I'm always thinking of you."

And now I'm melting.

The dining area of Jonah's penthouse offers a great look at the city—or at the nearby exposed-brick wall, where he hung my etching. Now I can look at it properly, without erotic reflections getting in the way. Although it's from a series I created last year, well before we ever met, it captures the exact contrast in him that I find so compelling. It depicts a man's hands holding a bird, the strength and tension in his fingers all the more striking because of the care with which he's protecting something so small and fragile.

Jonah bid for this at a charity auction without even knowing I was the artist. Maybe he senses this contrast within himself too—the intertwined brutality and gentleness.

This reminds me of my next project, creating a new series of etchings that will symbolize Jonah and what he means to me. Can I ever do better than these hands, this bird? In my heart I feel sure I can, but the exact image still eludes me.

"So I actually have to teach next semester." He pours us each a little sauvignon blanc. The wine is the palest possible shade of gold. "Even research professors get pulled in once in a while."

"I'm guessing they didn't stick you with the Rocks for Jocks section."

"Why they do that to entry-level geology, I'll never know." This seems to be a sore point for Jonah. "It's one of the most accessible sciences for non-science majors. We shouldn't treat it as a throw-away class."

"Wait, you *are* teaching that? If so, you can change things."

He looks thoughtful. "Maybe I'll volunteer sometime. But no. I'm doing a graduate seminar. Tuesdays and Thursdays, afternoon class."

"That's pretty close to my schedule. We could ride to class together."

Jonah gives me an appraising look. "Yeah. We could."

His imagination must be showing him much the same visions mine is showing me: The two of us sleeping over at each other's places, our lives coming together more and more. This is where most guys would panic. But Jonah seems to like the idea. So do I.

Once we've finished our meal and loaded the dishwasher, I expect Jonah to make some suggestion for our evening—finding a movie on TV or Netflix, for instance. We're still learning how to be with each other in the quiet moments. There's a charm to just standing beside him in his kitchen, Spanish guitar playing from the sound system.

But instead he slides his arms around me and steers me into a dance. I laugh softly; he does too, and says, "Is it too ridiculous? Dancing with a guy in front of the sink?"

"I wasn't laughing because it's funny. Because it's beautiful." I look into Jonah's gray eyes. "Because you're beautiful."

He kisses me, a gentle, searching kiss. As I open my lips for him, he keeps us swaying to the rhythm of the sultry guitar music. His mouth tastes like wine. City lights gleam in the dark around us. His broad hands smooth their way down my back, bringing our bodies closer together. I love the feel of him, the scent of him. The knowledge that I'm completely safe in his arms.

"I promise I invited you over with no ulterior motives," he whispers between kisses along my throat. "But I'd love to take you to bed."

Of course he assumed we'd sleep together. I guess I did too, until this very moment, when I'm turned on and blissed out and yet unsure what to do. "I—I don't think I can play one of our games tonight."

"That's okay. We don't have to . . ." Then his voice trails off. "But you need the fantasy, to enjoy sex."

"Not to *enjoy* it—"

"I meant, you need it to have an orgasm."

"Yeah. I do."

I needed him to understand this. Now he does. Why hasn't it made things any easier?

Jonah begins, "You said—sometimes the fantasy alone made you come. You fantasized about that when we had sex before."

"I don't even think I can fantasize about it tonight," I confess.

"With that guy out there—I just feel weird about it today. I'm sorry."

"Don't apologize," he says, and his voice is firm. "You're allowed to feel weird about it. You never have to say you're sorry for not wanting the same thing I do in bed."

"I guess I'm not used to that. Because you're so good at giving me what I want." I brush my hand against his hair; it's grown a little longer, just enough for me to run my fingers through it. "Tonight is different, that's all."

"Okay." Jonah kisses my forehead.

"We can still make love," I offer. "Sex is still fun, even when I don't—"

"No. I don't want to . . . use you."

I know what he needs. "You need to learn to accept a gift."

With that, I push him back—not too hard, only enough for him to get the idea. By this time, we've danced toward the living room area of his penthouse, and so he topples back onto the broad, dark red leather ottoman. As he sits there, arms braced wide, legs slightly spread, I kneel in front of him and reach for his belt.

"Vivienne—you don't have to—"

"I know. But I want to. And so do you. So let me just this once, okay?" I caress the ridge of his quickly hardening erection through the denim of his jeans. "Relax."

I unfasten his belt, unbutton, unzip. Jonah's already so hard he nearly juts out from his boxers. With one hand I circle him, push his underwear out of my way; as I brush my thumb over the tip, I feel the slickness of pre-come against my skin.

There is nothing more perfect than Jonah's face right now—lips slightly parted, eyes desperate. He winds his hands through my hair as I open my mouth to take him in.

But I don't give him everything right away. Instead I lick him, tease the ridge at the head with my lips, nuzzle him against my cheek, kiss him—anything but suck him. Anticipation is sometimes the best part, and I intend to make him enjoy the wait. I luxuriate in the feel of swollen veins against my tongue, and the taste of salt.

"Fuck," Jonah whispers.

"Mmm-mmm." It's a negative, but it makes him groan, no doubt from the vibration of my lips against his cock. I pull back, and he slips from my mouth, blood-dark and glistening. "Not tonight. Tonight is all about you, baby."

Somehow, that was the wrong thing to say.

Jonah pushes back from me and sits up. "No. We're not doing this."

"Are you serious?" *A man turning down a blowjob? Who knew that was even possible?* But the stupid joke dies in my throat unspoken. "I don't understand."

"I told you. I'm not comfortable using you."

"You're not!" But he knows that, surely—at least, his rational mind probably does. I suspect we're dealing with a deeper level here. "Why isn't it okay for me to make you come even if you're not doing the same for me?"

"It's too close," he says shortly. "If I'm not giving anything back to you, it's too much like—"

His voice trails off. There's no need for him to say the rest. Carter took what he wanted from Jonah's mother without any thought for her pleasure, only her pain. To Jonah, any sex that isn't reciprocal must be suspect.

"It's always been so important to you that it's good for me," I say. "But that's not just because you're generous, is it? You *need* me to come."

"That's how I know I don't want to be like him," Jonah says quietly. "That's how I know that he twisted my mind, but he doesn't control it."

"No. He doesn't. You're your own man, Jonah. Always. Never doubt that."

He smiles crookedly. Since sex is off the menu tonight, maybe we can finally talk more about his side of this. I feel like I understand the issues Jonah has because of his upbringing in the home of Carter and Lorena Hale, but apparently there are dimensions to this I hadn't yet guessed. If he's finally ready to open up more about this, I'm ready to listen.

I lean down to kiss him. Jonah embraces me tenderly, drawing me down beside him—but we both jerk upright when the intercom buzzes loudly, announcing someone who's dropped by uninvited.

Who the hell? I look at Jonah, but he seems to be as confused as I am. So I climb off him, allowing him to tuck himself in and zip up as he goes to the intercom. "Who is it?" he calls.

A Texas-twanged man's voice replies, "We're with the Austin Police Department. We'd like to have a word with you, if you don't mind."

The polite words only thinly veil hostility. Jonah and I look at each other, and I see in his eyes the terrible realization of why the police are here.

They're looking for the Stalker. And they think it's Jonah.

NINE

Thank God I had one of Kip's peppermints in my purse. At least I can sit here at the table beside Jonah without the cops smelling sex on my breath from the incomplete blowjob.

That would be tacky at the best of times—and now, it could be disastrous for Jonah.

The two police officers sitting opposite from us could not be more stereotypically good cop/bad cop unless one wore a halo and the other had devil horns. Good Cop is about fifty, male, African-American, with a bit of salt-and pepper in his beard and a small but constant smile. Bad Cop is thirtysomething, white, red-haired, wiry, and permanently scowling. Both of them focus on Jonah; neither of them looks much at me.

"As you might know," Good Cop says, "we had another attack a couple nights ago. Young girl was grabbed in the parking lot of her apartment complex. Guy forced her into his truck."

"I heard there was another attack." Jonah is cooler under pressure than I think I could ever be. "But I didn't hear any of the details."

This is Bad Cop's cue. "We keep some particulars out of the papers. To eliminate false confessions, make sure we're only going after the right guy."

Good Cop gives Bad Cop an admonishing look, as if they hadn't rehearsed this a thousand times. "We'll start with the basics. Can you account for your whereabouts on Thursday night between seven and ten P.M.?"

"I was here," Jonah says. "At home."

Bad Cop raises an eyebrow. "Alone?"

I speak for the first time since they walked through the door and I said hello through a mouthful of peppermint. "No. I stayed here that night."

"Yes, ma'am." Good Cop sounds more deferential than he feels, I'd bet. He's trying to coax me off my guard. "When did you arrive?"

"Seven fifteen? Seven thirty? Somewhere around there." I didn't make note of it them; I was too excited by the thought of what lay ahead to pay attention to those kinds of details. Now I wish I knew the answer to the minute.

This may be good enough, though. Good Cop and Bad Cop exchange glances that tell me they've done the math and realized Jonah couldn't have attacked the girl and returned here in time to welcome me. So now they've decided one of two things. Either they know Jonah's almost certainly innocent—or I'm just another messed-up woman lying to protect her man.

So I try to offer evidence they can't disprove. "Jonah doesn't even own a truck. And you said the attacker had one, right?"

Good Cop patiently explains, "Trucks can be rented, ma'am. And Professor Marks here is a man of means. If he wanted to buy a used truck from someone off Craigslist, without any of the legal niceties in the way—to rent or purchase a parking space somewhere else—he'd certainly have no trouble doing so."

All true. I feel embarrassed to have spoken.

Bad Cop's Texas drawl is thick. "Now, tell me who you are again, miss?"

"My name is Vivienne Charles. I'm a graduate student and TA in the fine arts department at the university."

"What I *meant* was," Bad Cop says, as if it were totally stupid to respond to his question with my name, "who are you to Mr. Marks here?"

Jonah fields this one. "She's my girlfriend."

He's never actually called me that before. Maybe it's an old-fashioned word, in some ways, but hearing it in Jonah's voice gives me a tiny thrill of happiness his current predicament can't fully eclipse.

"How long y'all been together?" Good Cop asks.

"We met last August," Jonah explains. "Went out on our first date in September."

Good Cop makes a note in his little booklet. Maybe he thinks a relationship that's less than four months old isn't substantive enough to turn me into Jonah's go-to alibi. I wouldn't lie to the cops for anyone.

But it doesn't matter. We can never explain why we were so intimately bound from the very start, least of all to the police.

"And you two simply stayed in all night," Good Cop says. "Dinner and a movie, that kind of thing?"

Bad Cop chimes in before we even have a chance to answer. "Did you have sexual intercourse?"

"How the hell is that any of your business?" Jonah's gray eyes have turned stormy; this could be about to get ugly.

"It's all right." I lay one hand over Jonah's forearm and smile at Bad Cop. "Yes, we had sex. Right about where you're sitting, actually."

That wipes the smirk off his face. Bad Cop slowly takes his arms off the dining room table as if it has Fornication Cooties, and sits way back in his chair.

(Okay, I lied by a few feet. It's worth it to see this jerk look like he just bit into a lemon.)

I add, "Besides, this building has security. You guys had to sign in, right?" Maybe there's an exception for the cops. "I put in the security code when I entered the garage, and I bet there's a record. You'll be able to see exactly when I arrived."

"True," Bad Cop says. "But that doesn't tell us when Mr. Marks here left. See, there's a residents-only entrance on the side of the building. Uses a key lock instead of a security code."

"Security footage should clear me," Jonah interjects. The tension in his voice is tightening.

"It might," Bad Cop says affably, "if the camera on the side of the building were working. It isn't. Hasn't been for a few months now—as you might've known, Mr. Marks."

"Of course he didn't know that!" I protest. "And he wouldn't sneak out the front and leave me alone here."

"What about the night of November twenty-ninth?" Good Cop acts like he didn't even hear what I said. "Mr. Marks, can you remember your whereabouts on that night?"

Jonah takes a deep breath. "Yes. That night, I stayed at Vivienne's."

"And where do you live in town, Ms. Charles?"

"South side, between South Congress and First. Over by Elizabeth's, you know." I answer as calmly as I can, but I already know it would be better if at least one of Jonah's alibis could be independently confirmed.

Bad Cop seems pleased. "So we only have her say-so for your whereabouts on the nights of both attacks."

"And mine," Jonah says. "Cell phone records should back me up."

Of course! Cell phone records! I hadn't thought of that. Granted, I'm not exactly sure how they work in criminal investigations, because I've gleaned most of what I know from episodes of *Law & Order: Special Victims Unit.* But apparently the cell phone pings tell you which tower the phone was closest to at any given time. The evidence to clear Jonah is at hand.

Or so I think, until Bad Cop says, “Cell phone records only tell us where your phone was. Some people, they’re up to no good, they’ve realized they need to leave their phones behind. Or take a burner instead.”

A burner is a cheap, prepaid phone you can ditch at a moment’s notice, according to Mariska Hargitay and Ice-T.

“Why are you questioning Jonah?” I ask. That’s the part of this I don’t get. “He wasn’t anywhere near either of those attacks. So it’s not like anyone could have seen him there.”

Good Cop looks sorrowful. “A concerned citizen came by the station. Had some interesting things to say. But—you know, lots of people say lots of stuff. Doesn’t mean they know a damn thing. And sometimes folks carry a grudge. You can be sure we check everything out thoroughly.”

Jonah ought to look relieved. Even though Good Cop’s pleasant demeanor is only an act, he’s no doubt right about the cops looking into every possibility. That means Jonah’s bound to be cleared almost right away. It’s just bad luck that the Stalker has a build like his, or whatever it was that made some busybody suspect Jonah.

The police officers tell Jonah they’ll be in touch if they have further questions, then head on their way. As soon as the elevator doors slide shut, I turn to Jonah. “What the hell?”

I expect him to go, *I know, it’s insane.* Instead Jonah sinks down onto one of the bar stools at his kitchen island. He looks as bruised and weary as a boxer after twelve rounds.

“Jonah?” I walk to him, take his hand. “What is it?”

“I know who talked to the police.” His voice is low. “Her name is Sunny Harris.”

"Who is she?" Realization begins to dawn. "An ex?"

He nods, miserable. "We went out about two years ago. She's a tennis coach at one of the local high schools, or she was. Now, I have no idea. We had fun, she seemed game for anything, and so—after a few months together—I told her about my fantasy."

The first time we ever spoke about this, Jonah told me he'd tried to act out these games with a couple of other women. Then I was so flustered by his approach I couldn't think past the forbidden thrill that rushed through me when he said no other girl had ever wanted it rough. He thought that was exactly how I wanted it. He was right.

But now I have to think about this man I need so badly playing our games with someone else.

That was long before you ever met, I tell myself. *Snap out of it.* "So, um, I guess when you guys tried to play, Sunny freaked out."

"I don't know what she thought I meant." Jonah leans his elbow on the counter, his forehead in his hand. "That's one reason I wanted to be so completely clear with you. With Sunny, I believed she understood, and holy shit, was I wrong. It wasn't like I even—well. It wasn't anything that crazy, not by our standards. But I really wanted to play the scenario out fully, and Sunny believed it would be more of a joke. So as soon as we started, it turned into a total disaster. I stopped the moment she asked, but it didn't matter. She said she wasn't afraid of me, that she knew we'd just failed to work things out with the scenario in advance—but she didn't stay the night. Broke up with me the next day, which by then I was expecting."

"That was a consensual fantasy you tried to share with her. Why would she take that to the police?"

"Because Sunny thinks I'm a man who gets off on the idea of forcing a woman, and she's right." His smile can be angrier than any other man's frown. "No, I would never cross that line. I'd die first. But Sunny doesn't know that. All she knows is that she saw my dark side the day before she bolted. When she heard the news of the latest attacks, she put two and two together and got five."

I want to be furious with this mysterious woman who's put Jonah under a cloud of suspicion, but I can't be. Sunny was trying to protect other women. She doesn't know the truth about Jonah, only enough to cloud her judgment.

So I lean against Jonah. "They'll realize you're innocent. The real Stalker will get caught, and this will blow over."

"I know I'm not going to be convicted for this."

"Yes. Exactly. DNA evidence will clear you, if nothing else."

"The cops didn't mention DNA evidence," Jonah says. "The guy might've worn a condom."

"Or maybe they just haven't gotten the test results from the rape kits back yet." Some municipalities put off testing rape kits for months or years on end. It's disgraceful. "Either way, like you said, you'll be cleared. You'll be fine."

"Fine? That's the one thing I'm not going to be." Jonah pulls away from me to slide off the bar stool and pace along the wall of windows that look out on Austin at night. "This fantasy—I might not need it every single time, like you do, but I need it. I do. And I hate it. Even now, when you and I are able to share this the only way it should ever be shared, it's still so goddamned *sick*."

He's not saying anything I haven't thought, in almost exactly the same words. But I won't let him torture himself the way I do. "Hey. Remember what I said? You don't hurt me. You help me. Acting out this fantasy—sharing it together, openly, and understanding why—that's the least sick thing about it."

Jonah gives me a dark look. "It's sure as hell not healthy."

"My therapist says totally normal, mentally healthy people are as fictional as the unicorn. We're all bent. Just in different ways."

He laughs despite himself. "I think I'd like your therapist."

Should I recommend Doreen to Jonah? Or would that create some eternal ouroboros of dysfunction? I'll decide later.

For now, I simply walk to Jonah and put my arms around him. This time he doesn't dodge the embrace; instead he holds me tightly, tenderly, as I feel his warm breath against my hair.

"Thank you," he says. "For earlier. I didn't even get the chance to say that."

Only thirty minutes ago, I was trying to give Jonah a blowjob a few feet away. Just days ago, he had me captive—completely under his erotic spell. It all feels so far away now.

But Jonah doesn't. As confused as we might be about our sexual bond, we know how deeply we care for each other. What we feel will see us through.

I have to believe that.

"Hey," I whisper. "Got any plans for Christmas?"

The sudden switch in topic surprises him. "No."

"You won't be going back to Chicago?"

"That's out of the question. If Elise or Rebecca were going to be there, Maddox and I might try to do something on our own, away from our parents. But Rebecca is in Belize—"

"Belize? On vacation?" I guess there are worse places for an escape from Chicago's winter.

But Jonah shakes his head. "She's a botanist, which means she goes on field surveys from time to time."

Brother and sister both became globe-trotting scientists: At first I think that's adorable, and nearly say so, but then I realize—both Jonah and Rebecca chose a way of life that would take them as far from home as possible. They wanted to escape that badly. Instead I ask about his stepsister. "And Elise?"

"She's in New York. We did Christmas there together one year, right after she'd moved to the city, and it was . . . you know, it was good." The shadow of a smile passes over Jonah's face, too briefly.

"Then she started dating this total son of a bitch. He's bad to her, bad for her. I can't be around them when they're together, and every time one of us tells her to dump the loser, Elise just clings to him tighter. So New York's not an option either. Maddox has to stay in Chicago for his club, because the Orchid's New Year's Eve party has become a local legend. That leaves me here."

"No it doesn't." I caress his arm with my hand. "Come to New Orleans with me."

Jonah should have been expecting me to say that, but he wasn't. "I didn't think you'd go home."

"Anthony's gone this year, remember? Hopefully forever." For a moment, all my worries about police suspicion and the Stalker are eclipsed by the pure, shining joy of knowing I finally get to spend Christmas Day without my rapist.

"I remember. But your mother and sister—have they ever acknowledged they were wrong? I don't understand how you can be around them if they haven't."

"I kind of got in the habit after I had to keep living in that house for the next four years." When I slide around to the other side of the table to face Jonah, I see how hard and set Jonah's features have become. His anger would be intimidating if I didn't know who all that pent-up fury is for. "You lived in a house like that too, Jonah. You know what it's like."

"And I got the fuck out of it as soon as I could. I want you out of there too." Jonah reaches for me, splays his warm hand over mine. "You deserve better than that."

"Since when did life start giving us what we deserved?"

He gives me a look. "We could go anywhere, you know."

The offer is genuine. Jonah's late father cofounded Oceanic Airlines; we could fly to Fiji tomorrow if we wanted. Maybe Switzerland. For a moment I'm tempted by visions of Jonah and me spending Christmas Day beneath the palms on a South Pacific beach, or nestled in a chalet after playing in the snow. Never in my life have I had a white Christmas . . .

But no. "Dad's still recovering, and spending Christmas with him—just after I thought I might lose him—it's important to me." A thought occurs to me and makes me wince. "Do you think the police would think it was suspicious? You leaving town?"

Jonah shrugs. "They didn't tell me I couldn't."

Can he really be that unworried? No, of course not. But Jonah sometimes works through things like this, simply refusing to look at the obstacles in the way. If he's not going to worry about the cops' reaction, I won't either.

I say, "You know, this will be the first time in my life I'll be able to spend entire days with Libby without Anthony being around. If you're there too, this will be the absolute best Christmas of my life."

How can a man so fierce smile so gently? "Then I'll be there."

My final task before leaving town is proctoring an exam—which, of course, is scheduled for the very latest testing period on the last day of the semester. I reach campus about half an hour before the exam starts, so I decide to swing by the department office and drop off my jacket and purse. Besides, I want to grab a few more peppermints. Turns out you never know when you'll need one.

As I walk in, Kip whirls around in his swivel chair. "Oh—my—*God*. You're *here*."

"What?" He looks so shocked I expect him to tell me the dean died or something.

Kip glances around the office; apparently Professor Prasanna is in, because he glares at her door and turns up the radio, treating everyone within earshot to a country music version of "Away in a Manger." Then he leans close to me and said, "I thought you'd be with Jonah. Or have you run away? Are you safe? If you feel unsafe, just say so. Or nod. If he threatened you if you say anything, just nod."

At another time, I might be amused or moved by Kip's would-be rescue. As it is, I'm appalled. "Jonah hasn't threatened me! He hasn't hurt anyone."

Kip folds his arms in front of his chest. The fuchsia My Little Pony Band-Aids on his hand clash with his neon orange manicure. "That's not what the police think."

I want to scream. "Was it online? On the news?"

"What? No. He's not even at person-of-interest level yet. No chance the police would release his name to the public."

"Then how do *you* know?"

"Why do you still doubt my sources? Do you really want to know how high it goes?"

Usually Kip's secretiveness amuses me. Not today. "Yes. I want to know. If you're helping spread a really ugly lie about Jonah Marks? You're damned straight I'm going to find out 'how high it goes.' And if you won't tell me, I'll learn who will."

"Whoa, whoa, hold it." Kip holds up his hands in surrender. "I'm not spreading anything. All right? I heard what I heard, and I figured you either already knew or needed to."

"*Tell me who told you.*" I didn't know I could be this angry at Kip. It's not like I'd ever hit him, or anyone, but right now I feel like I could rip the blinking blue lights from his desk. Kick down a wall. Something, anything, that would vent some of the fury I feel at hearing Jonah slandered.

In a lower voice, Kip says, "Ryan's brother Tommy is a police officer working on the case. I was at Ryan's place when he came by last night. Tommy didn't refer to Jonah by name, but—he mentioned the ex who'd reported this mystery man was a tennis coach. Also he said the guy was a professor at the university, so he might've had contact with the students who were attacked. Also said the suspect was someone with enough money to get a legal 'dream team,' so the force wants to have an airtight case before they move. I knew from my contacts in the athletics department that a local tennis coach of the blond and comely variety briefly went out with a certain someone in earth sciences. So obviously Tommy could only have been talking about Jonah."

Small mercies: That wouldn't have been obvious to anybody less all-knowing than Kip, except possibly Jonah himself. At least foul gossip about Jonah isn't making its way around campus—but the situation's even worse than gossip. The police are focusing their attention on Jonah, hard, probably for lack of other leads. Not only does that mean more harassment in Jonah's future, but it also means the cops aren't getting any closer to catching the *real* Austin Stalker.

"It's not Jonah," I say. "I know that, absolutely, one hundred percent. Both nights attacks happened, he was with me."

Kip breathes out in relief. The cops might doubt my alibi, but he doesn't. "Last night I could hardly sleep for fear. I would've texted you, but Ryan wouldn't let me. Thank God everything's all right."

"It's anything *but* all right! You make it sound like the police have already decided he's guilty!"

"They said they wanted an airtight case, remember?" Kip helps himself to a Hershey's kiss wrapped in green foil. "They can't get that if he's not guilty. So he'll be cleared sooner or later."

"Ever seen a news story about someone getting out of prison after 30 years because DNA evidence finally cleared them? Innocent people can be convicted, Kip. It might not happen often, but it happens." I lean against his desk, weak with exhaustion and horror.

Kip, on the other hand, has cheered up considerably. "One truth of our justice system—usually a horribly unfair truth—works to our advantage in this case. Innocent people are indeed convicted from time to time. But innocent *rich* people? Not so much."

Okay, he has a point there. But while prison might be the worst potential consequence of this meaningless witch hunt, it's not the only trouble Jonah could face. "What happens if this spreads around campus, though? Just being a suspect could ruin his life. Rumors like that could keep him from getting tenure. Discourage top students from coming to UT to work with him. Alienate him from the few friends he has."

Kip reaches out with both hands to take mine; his manicure puts my ragged nails to shame. "I swear to you, I'm the only person on campus who knows anything about this. And if I hear any rumors—and believe me, I *would* hear—I'll stomp them like cockroaches. We'll make sure the record is set straight."

If anyone can do it, Kip can. The knot of tension in my chest loosens slightly, and I feel as if I can breathe again. "Okay. Thank you."

After all that, I need something to brace me. The department's new, top-notch coffee machine beckons, complete with its shiny foil packets offering me any number of caffeine options. A mocha sounds about right—the oomph of coffee and the comfort of chocolate. It's still eleven whole minutes before I have to be in the exam room; that's enough time to recharge.

As I stand in the tiny break room watching the machine brew my mocha, Kip walks in behind me. Although he picks up one of the paper cups, like he's here for coffee too, we both know better.

We stand there awkwardly for several seconds, staring at the stupid plastic stirrers, before Kip says, quietly, "Why do you think the coach told the police to suspect Jonah?"

"I—" What is the smallest sliver of the truth that will work? "They broke up badly."

"I'd heard they weren't even together that long. And making

your ex a suspect in a criminal investigation? That's pretty high-octane revenge. Like, one step removed from Jodi Arias."

"It wasn't about revenge, I don't think." While I don't want any creepy false rumors about Jonah to circulate around campus, I also don't want to slander this woman I never met, who almost certainly thinks her suspicions are legitimate.

Kip purses his lips. "Then why?"

The machine finishes making my coffee. As the last drops of mocha fall into my cup, I take it in both hands. Warmth radiates through my palms; until now, I hadn't realized how cold my fingers had become.

This is Kip's cue to start making his own drink, which he does. Nor does he press me for an answer to his last question. But just as I'm walking out of the break room, he says, "The hottest ones always have a dark side, don't they?"

"Not always," I say as I go. I'd like to think that's true.

And neither Kip nor anyone else needs to understand the truth behind Jonah's darkness.

TEN

"So this is the famous *Jooooooo-nah*," Liz says, subtle as a lightning strike. She shifts her white wine into her other hand so she can shake Jonah's. All around us, family friends and Chloe's pals mill around in cocktail dresses and suits; Christmas music plays just loud enough to be heard amid the buzz of the crowd. Liz's grin is brighter than the chandelier overhead. "I've heard so much about you, Mr. Marks! Can't wait to find out if it's true."

From anyone else, this would be unbearably obnoxious. But this is Liz Marceau, my friend since we were six years old. Our parents were in the same clubs, sent us to the posh Sacred Heart Academy, and lived only a few blocks apart in the Garden District, also known as the most enviable section of town. And Liz and I were both, always, *so* over it.

Thank God for her, because if I hadn't had one person in my life always confirming that this high-society stuff was bullshit, I'm not sure I could have remained sane.

Jonah glances at me, like, *How much did you tell her?* I just laugh. "Don't let Liz psych you out."

"I cull the weak ones from the herd," Liz says as she lifts her glass for another sip. "Only the strongest survive to date my friend."

"I'll do my best," Jonah replies, straight-faced. The glint of humor in his gray eyes tells me he can deal with Liz, which is a relief. Not everyone can. But that's exactly why I love her; she is boldly, unapologetically herself in a way few other people are. She had that talent when she was six. I hope I'll master it by the time I'm sixty.

Liz is nearly as tall as Jonah, and—*Rubenesque* is the euphemism my mother uses, though Liz is on a kick about "reclaiming the word *fat*" as empowerment. But it's hard to imagine her needing more power. Her hair is the most stunning red I've ever seen, and she's wearing a turquoise dress that stands out from the dark-clad crowd so vividly that it acts as her own personal spotlight. Right now, she's shining that hot light on us too.

Technically this is Chloe's party. She and Anthony have always thrown a holiday bash together, which I was always told was the "hit of the season." Happily I never had to find out for myself. Since she's throwing it alone this year, she decided to have it here at my parents' house. Some of the faces around me are unfamiliar—people she met through Anthony, no doubt. I guess they're not yet to the point of figuring out who gets which friends in the divorce. But she still hangs out with her high school set, who have become sleeker and harder in the last decade. What do they see when they look at me?

Then again, most of them aren't looking at me. I might be wearing my best cocktail dress—dark red, sequined, modestly hemmed near the knee but plunging in the front. I've done my hair, worn my highest silver shoes. But I'm standing next to Jonah Marks.

He wears a suit cut so closely to his body that I'd assume it was custom tailored if I didn't know Jonah doesn't give a damn about these things. But he's built the way designers wish every man would be. That's why the charcoal-gray fabric drapes perfectly across his wide shoulders and narrow waist. The shade of his suit turns his eyes almost blue. If Jonah's not the tallest man in the room, he's close, and certainly he's the most built. His unstudied elegance contrasts with his brutish strength, and the effect is magnetic. Men glance at him with envy, women with the white-hot longing I know so well. So I'm invisible. It's a little like being whatever painting hangs beside the *Mona Lisa* in the Louvre.

I don't mind; in fact, I'm relieved. After years of homecomings that felt more like cross-examinations, I can finally relax. Is this what it feels like to actually *enjoy* Christmas?

In the living room, my father sits in his leather armchair, holding court with his friends. He's not his old boisterous self again; after the heart attack, he might never again be as loud or carefree. But he's enjoying himself, telling some hoary anecdote his pals will have heard a dozen times before, and they'll laugh just as hard as they did when they first heard it. Near the fireplace, my mother shows off her granddaughter to her friends, a group of women who look as polished as their daughters. Not one gray hair has escaped being dyed. Libby seems to enjoy the admiration. She twirls so the skirt of her white velvet party dress flares out around her, and all the women laugh in approval.

Nearer us, in the foyer, Chloe stands at the foot of the long staircase, one hand on the wooden banister as if she were posing for a photograph. She's lost a little weight, and she didn't have any to lose—but I can't deny she's still the most beautiful woman in the room. She always was.

Her blond hair is pulled into a chignon; her strapless black dress flows almost to the floor. She smiles at everyone, hiding the pain she must feel behind a perfect mask of poise and grace. The glittering earrings that dangle almost to her shoulders are undoubtedly real diamonds.

Anthony must have given those to her.

"Oh, my God, did you hear about Jackson Overstreet?" Liz hasn't stopped talking the entire time, though mostly she's been telling Jonah crazy childhood stories about us. But old names have brought up new gossip. "He's going to seminary!"

"Jackson?" That obnoxious kid I used to hang out with in sixth grade wants to be *a priest*?

Liz laughs so loud half the people in the party turn to look. "Either the Catholic Church seriously lowered its standards, or we have witnessed a miracle."

I start laughing too. Surely Jonah can only vaguely appreciate the humor, but he smiles down at me with such warmth that I feel like I could glow.

Later, while Liz is getting another glass of wine, I whisper to him, "Thanks for being such a good sport about this."

"You don't have to thank me for enjoying a party." Jonah brushes his fingers along my cheek.

"Oh, come on. You can't enjoy hearing endless anecdotes about people you never met."

"I enjoy seeing you this happy."

I *am* happy—and he is too. Our fears and troubles seem as if they took place a hundred years ago, or in a bad dream that faded with dawn.

We're in the middle of a party, surrounded by a crush of people on all sides, and I don't even care. I stroke two fingers down the length of his midnight-blue silk tie. "I'm not having so much fun that I couldn't leave a little early."

His smile widens into a grin; his hand finds my arm and grips it just tightly enough to suggest what he'll do later. Not enough for anyone around us to understand. Just me. "You like the tie?"

"Mmmm-hmm."

He leans closer and whispers, "It would make a good blindfold." Oh, Merry Christmas to me.

Two hours later, I'm wearing my red sequined cocktail dress, a midnight blue silk tie around my eyes, and absolutely nothing else.

Jonah pulled off my underwear a few minutes ago. Used his belt to bind my arms to the bedpost, and the terry-cloth tie of the hotel robe to lash my ankles together. I still don't understand that, but he'll make me understand when he's ready. Not before.

Normally Jonah would be talking dirty to me around now. But tonight, he remained "himself" until he had me bound and blindfolded like this. Now that he's tied me up, he goes silent.

I can hear only my breath and his, and the footsteps coming closer. Then his hand goes to the neckline of my dress. His fingertips are rough against the skin between my breasts. The fabric is drapey enough for him to push it aside, baring my breast. As his thumb runs over my nipple, I suck in a breath—and then he squeezes, hard. I bite my lip to keep from crying out.

He grasps my other breast in turn, tugging and pinching until both of my nipples are swollen and tender. Right on the edge between pleasure and pain. I twist away from him, drawing my bound legs up to my chest, but Jonah's strong hands push me onto my back again. Not savagely—he's firm, inexorable, silent. An unknown force taking charge of my body and denying me even the knowledge of how I affect him.

It's distant. Almost contemptuous. But this works on me too. This powerful, unspeaking stranger will use my body however he wants. He erases my will. Now I'm his plaything, nothing more.

The mattress dips and creaks as he climbs onto the bed. His knees press down on either side of my shoulders; the fabric of his suit trousers rubs against my exposed, sensitive breasts, and I stifle a whimper. He rests enough of his weight on me to have me completely pinned down.

He unbuckles his belt slowly so I have to listen and wait. The purr of his zipper goes almost tooth by tooth. I even hear the soft sound of his fingers taking hold of his cock.

The head bumps against my cheek. His hand grips my face tightly, forcing my jaw open. I couldn't turn my head if I tried.

Jonah makes not one sound, even as he pushes his cock inside my mouth.

He's so goddamned huge. Not only long but thick, so thick that it's hard for me to blow him even when I can move my head, angle my throat. Now it's all I can do to take him in. Jonah rocks his hips forward and back—again slowly, so much so that I can tell he's determined to stretch this out. That he likes me struggling beneath him, mouth open obscenely wide.

Pre-come is thick around my tongue now, and I manage to swallow. The contraction of my mouth and throat is enough to make him thrust in deeper, almost choking me. But that's the only sign he gives of how turned on he is, that and the fact that I keep having to swallow, faster and faster, just to keep breathing. Jonah just keeps moving at this same maddeningly slow tempo, wordless, like some machine built to rape me.

I cough around him and feel his pre-come on my lips, on my chin. He pulls out then, pausing one long moment to rub the head of his cock around my messy face, like he's marking me as his own. Then he climbs off me and off the bed.

At first I just pant for breath. But before I've even begun to recover, his broad hand grasps the tie binding my ankles and pulls me down, toward the side of the bed. My arms stretch—not to the point of pain, but enough to make me gasp—and my ass is now at the edge of the mattress.

Jonah pushes both my legs straight up, toes to the ceiling. My cunt is exposed, and he slides two fingers inside. Still he goes slowly, inspecting me, testing me. But I know he can feel how wet I am.

Then he wraps one arm around my legs, clutching them against his shoulder so I can't move. He withdraws his fingers only to replace them with his cock.

When he does it like this—pushing in inch by inch, making me wait for it—I feel every single sensation. The way my cunt burns as he forces me wider to take him. The wetness around him, slicking my thighs. Even the heat of his body coming closer to mine until he's finally buried in me up to the hilt.

For one long moment he remains still inside me. But then his grip tightens around my legs and he *goes mad.*

I cry out as he begins fucking me, hard, fast, and merciless. He's so deep inside, like he's getting to the core of me with every single savage thrust. With my legs up like this, I'm totally vulnerable; it feels rougher than ever before.

And I love it. I love it.

Having my legs bound together also means there's tight pressure on my clit the entire time. Each time he pounds into me, my thighs pulse, and it's like I'm getting stroked faster and faster. I thrash my head to the side—it's the only way I can move—trying to fight it. Though really I just want to stay here in this moment when pleasure is welling inside me, flooding me, drowning everything else.

Jonah thrusts in one final time—the hardest of all. His body shudders against mine as he grunts in carnal satisfaction. Even as I hear it, I come too, and the world is swallowed by the power of it. The sounds coming from my throat must be savage, but I can't listen. I can't know. I don't care.

He remains inside, maybe still spending into me, for what seems like a long time. When he pulls out, he folds my legs to the side. He unties my ankles first, only then crawling up the bed to push the blindfold from my face. Only one dim lamp is lit in the far corner of the room, but I still squint against the light. Jonah is dark and indistinct to my blinking eyes.

"Okay?" he whispers.

"Much better than okay." I lick my lips, tasting his salt. "God, Jonah, that was incredible."

"That's how Vikings used to rape their captives. I read it once. Never stopped thinking about it."

Maybe I should find that fascination of his disturbing, but how can I, when I share it? "It's brutal."

"That's why I like doing it to you." His eyes are clear to me now. I see no hint of the unease that shadowed our game at his apartment, the last time he tied me. Then he was the one who hid his face.

But maybe we're getting back to where we were. Jonah learned my truth and came all the way back to me anyway. It feels like a miracle.

"Untie my hands," I whisper. "I want to hold you."

He does.

The strangest thing about Christmas Day is how strange it isn't—or, to be more accurate, how completely my family refuses to acknowledge that anything has changed. Chloe and Libby remain at my parents' house throughout as if they did this every year. When I kneel beside the tree to tuck my gifts into the pile, with a jolt I see Anthony's name on one of the tags, nestled between gold and silver ribbons. Did my mother buy them before Chloe threw him out, or did she simply refuse to admit they wouldn't patch it up by December twenty-fifth?

The pretense applies to my father's health too. He's recovered well enough to go up and down the stairs, which is better than I thought he'd be at this stage. But he still drives the car when he and Mom leave the house. Still eats terrible food and has a cocktail with dinner. I say nothing but stare pointedly at his glass, to no avail.

Dad's better at not seeing things than I thought he was. It makes me wonder how much he chose not to see, back when I was fourteen—

—but I can't afford to think like that. I clung to my dad so tightly in those months after the rape because he felt like the one safe person in my family, maybe the last person who really loved me. If I ever came to think of that as a lie, I don't know what it would do to me.

Jonah's presence here is both the strangest thing about this holiday and the best. It's like everyone but Libby remains in a perpetual state of surprise that he's here, that he's amazing, and that he loves me.

When my mother asks if I've gained weight, Jonah says nothing, but smiles at me and runs his hand along my waist in a way that's not blatantly sexual—yet makes it clear that he's happy with my body just the way it is. Chloe spends half her time ignoring him, half her time peppering him with cheery questions about Austin. (Never once has she asked *me* about our best local restaurants.) It's as if he's any other guy she met at the cocktail party, one she's subtly flirting with by giving him only small tastes of her interest. This doesn't mean she's coming on to Jonah; Chloe flirts with pretty much any man she meets. That's how she measures her inner worth.

Maybe, now that Anthony's gone, my sister can find a deeper source of self-respect. At the moment, though, she's still newly severed from the "perfect life" she thought she had two months ago. So I try not to judge her. And I don't ask about Anthony once.

But Jonah and I are doing some selective forgetting of our own. The threat of the Stalker feels like something we left behind in Austin—both the real menace he represents and the false suspicion directed at Jonah. More than that, the awkwardness that had haunted our games has faded away again. He and I have been set free.

By Christmas lunch, I'm as blissed-out as I've been in years. Carols are playing, my parents' house smells like candles and cinnamon, and my cream-colored cowl-neck sweater has long sleeves with holes for my thumbs. It hides the bruises on my wrists.

"Honestly," my mother sniffs as Libby unwraps the gift I gave her—the Lego science lab kit. "Do you have to give such *political* presents?"

"What's political about it?" I curl into Jonah's side and smile up at her in innocence. Mom is, of course, referring to the fact that this is the kit with female scientists, but she won't say so out loud. She sends messages with her own gifts too, always giving me kitchen items more appropriate for a bridal registry than the tiny kitchen in my rental home; last year it was a marble cookie jar that weighed at least ten pounds.

Happily, Libby's too delighted with her present to notice our comments. "This is cool. They have all these test tubes and stuff! You're a scientist, aren't you, Uncle Jonah? Do you have test tubes?"

"No." Jonah leans forward to inspect the set as seriously as he would a piece of equipment delivered to his own lab. "We use seismographs. This panel here—that looks a little like a seismograph. So your lab can have one."

"They can be volcano scientists!" Libby begins tearing into the box with gusto. "You can show me how to set it up, right?"

Jonah nods, ready to get to work, but Chloe cuts in. "Olivia, sweetheart, don't forget, you're leaving to go see Daddy in only an hour."

My entire body goes rigid. But Libby wriggles in anticipation. "Are my presents for Daddy all wrapped?"

"Of course they are." Chloe's smile is brittle. "Remember? You stuck the bows on yourself."

"How're y'all handling that?" Dad asks as he pours himself a Bloody Mary.

Chloe clutches her club soda like it's pure gin. "I'll drive her to the theater out on Clearview. Anthony's going to take Libby to a movie, that new animated one, oh, what's it called—"

"You could come too, Mommy. If you wanted." The hope in Libby's face tears my heart out.

"No," Chloe says, too sharply, then tries to soften it. "This is a special treat for you and your father."

Jonah hesitates for a moment before he says, "Do you want Vivienne and me to drive her there instead? That would give me a chance to talk with Libby about building her lab."

The kindness he's offering Chloe touches me. It would be a treat for me as well—a chance to watch my attacker wilt against Jonah—but if Jonah realizes that, he doesn't confront my sister with that. He's even worded his suggestion in a way that will make Libby feel like it's all about her. For the first time this entire holiday, Chloe's expression softens until her smile looks real. "That's all right. I can manage. But I appreciate the offer."

Once Chloe and Libby are gone, my father lies down for a nap and my mother begins an array of phone calls to friends and family. Jonah and I are left alone in the living room, on the long velvet sofa, to exchange our own gifts. I bought him a messenger bag large enough to double as a weekender, which seemed about right for a guy who might have to dash off to another country at a moment's notice—or head out to the cabin where he'll possess me for three days straight. The honey-colored leather already has the softness of a well-worn antique. When he runs his hands along the strap and smiles, I know I chose well.

"This is perfect," he says, leaning close to kiss my temple. His eyelashes flutter against my skin; even that small a touch makes me shiver. "You know me."

"Better believe it."

He kisses my mouth, hardly more than a brush. Even as I lean forward for another, Jonah pulls back and hands me my own gift, a small box wrapped in the kind of shiny white paper only used by good stores. Hmm, promising. I slide a fingernail beneath the tape, and unfold the paper, which is creased as neatly as an origami swan. Then I lift up the lid and see—

—you know, I'd guessed it was going to be jewelry. Small box, not particularly heavy, yadda yadda. So I'd envisioned a pretty chain, or a bracelet.

Instead I see a pair of earrings, square-cut sapphires that must be a carat each, if not more. Their facets capture the light; the vivid cobalt color is so deep it feels as if I could dive inside. "*Jonah*," I whisper. "They're—oh, my God, they're so beautiful."

He smiles, runs his thumb along one of my earlobes. "Glad you like."

Maybe I should be more sophisticated about this, but I can't help it. I blurt out, "These had to cost more than my *car*."

Jonah laughs out loud. "Do you enjoy them?"

"I *love* them. I've never had anything this beautiful."

"Then they're worth every cent." He leans closer and whispers, "I want you to wear them tonight. These and nothing else."

Oh, yes. I pull Jonah in for a kiss—but at that moment, his phone rings.

We hesitate, wondering whether or not to ignore it, until Jonah recognizes the ring tone. "It's Maddox."

The guy ought to get to talk to his brother on Christmas. Besides, I'll have Jonah to myself again later. "Better pick up then."

Jonah's smile gentles as he pulls me against his side with one arm and answers his phone with the other. "Mad! Merry Christmas. How's it going?"

That's the most animated I've heard Jonah with anyone besides me. Although he'd told me that he and his siblings were close, witnessing it for myself makes me so happy. At least something from Jonah's early life hasn't been poisoned. It feels like one more perfect moment in a nearly perfect day—

Before Jonah's face goes pale, and he whispers, *"Shit."*

"What?" I can resist butting in. "What's wrong?" Has his mother done something disastrous? Or has someone else in the family been hurt?

Instead Jonah says, "My stepfather found out about the—the situation with the police in Austin."

I don't understand how that happened, but I also don't understand why it's so disastrous. "Is he using that against your mother?"

He laughs, and it's a terrible sound. "Carter's using it against me."

What could Carter Maddox Hale do? What kind of power does he still hold over Jonah?

I realize I'm about to find out.

ELEVEN

"Chicago? Tomorrow?" Dad still can't wrap his mind around it. "Awfully late notice. You'll pay through the nose for the tickets."

Jonah gives me a look across the dinner table, through the red candles and glittery gold pinecones my mother considers a centerpiece. ". . . I see Vivienne never told you about my father."

"Is he a pilot?" Libby pipes up.

As Jonah begins telling the story of Oceanic Airlines—and Mom starts to glow like she swallowed the Christmas tree lights—my phone buzzes in the pocket of my sweater. I didn't even remember I'd left it in there instead of my purse. Bad manners to text at the table, but I decide to sneak a quick glimpse. It's probably a friend wishing me Merry Christmas, just something to bring a smile to my face . . . and make me forget about the dollar signs that seem to be appearing in my mother's eyes.

But the words on my screen have nothing to do with happy holidays.

It's from Geordie.

I'm sorry I know you're busy but I'm having a bad night, Viv, a really bad night and if you get a chance please call.

My gut drops. I tuck the phone back in my pocket, murmur, "Excuse me," and head for the guest bathroom.

Geordie picks up on the first ring. "Oh, God love you, Viv."

I let him get away with the *Viv*. "What's wrong? You haven't—"

"No. But—I'm so fucking embarrassed." He speaks so hoarsely that I realize, with a pang, he's been crying. "I spent the morning with Carmen and Arturo and Shay, and it was great. I mean, really great. And then I came back to my apartment complex, and the neighbors were having a holiday get-together, and they said, 'Oh, come on inside, have a drink with us!' And I thought, it would be shitty for me to blow them off on Christmas, wouldn't it? They wouldn't understand. So I went in."

I lean back against the bathroom door, free hand to my temple. "What then?"

"The usual. Novelty hats and that fucking chipmunk song and—bottles and bottles just lined up for the taking. And I saw a Pepsi can, and just blurted out that I wanted a Pepsi. I *loathe* Pepsi."

Choked up as I am, I have to laugh. "That's good, though, right? You were in a dangerous situation. You recognized it, took care of yourself, and when you needed help, you called for it. That's pretty frickin' great, actually."

"I left after only a few minutes." But his voice sounds weak. "The party's still going on, though. Music and laughter coming through the walls."

He can't stay there by himself; I can't get to him or stay on the phone for the next few hours.

"You need to call someone. Your AA sponsor? Carmen?"

"Carmen and company have already put up with me for hours today—"

"It's okay. I promise." His sponsor must be out of town for Christmas. "She'll meet you someplace, even come get you."

"They were going to go see a movie. Her and Arturo. The Alamo Drafthouse."

Then Carmen's phone will be off. Nobody texts at the Drafthouse, because management will throw you out on your ass. "Then get in the car and drive to Arturo and Shay's place. Shay is at home with the baby, right?"

"She's got one helpless person to look after. She doesn't need two."

"You *are not* helpless." Geordie has to believe me. If he thinks he can't make it, he won't. "You can help yourself by getting in the car and driving. I'll call ahead for you if you want."

"And then what, exactly?"

"Then you watch TV! Or you talk. Or, I don't know, you do some laundry and change some diapers so Shay can sleep for more than two hours in a row. It doesn't matter as long as you don't go to that party again. Okay?"

After a moment of silence, he sighs. "Stay on the phone with me until I'm in the car, all right?"

I do. When I catch a glimpse of my reflection in the bathroom mirror, I see how pale I look. How frazzled. Only the sapphires at my ears provide any hint of how happy this morning was.

Finally I hear the key turn in the ignition, and I let out a heavy breath. "See? You did it. Victory."

"Oh, is this what winning feels like?" Geordie's laugh is weak. "It sucks more than I'd thought it would."

But he hangs up to drive, which is when I phone Shay. As I'd known she would, she readily agrees to take him in. "We should've insisted he stay. Or I should've made Arturo take Geordie to the movies with them."

"No, no. You guys have been terrific. Just keep being terrific awhile longer." I think fast. "And don't make plans for New Year's. Tell everybody I'm going to throw a party without alcohol."

"Oh, sure, now that I've had the baby and can drink again, that's when you start having booze-free parties." But Shay's protest is good-natured. She's on board.

Once I come back to my seat, Jonah gives me an inquisitive glance. I simply shake my head, like, *no big deal.*

Only then does it occur to me that I haven't told Jonah about Geordie's drinking problem, or his decision to quit. Telling Carmen, Arturo, and Shay was one thing; they're Geordie's friends too, and needed to know so they'd be able to help him at moments like this. Jonah and Geordie have only met once, and while they were congenial enough, there was no mistaking the ex-boyfriend/new-boyfriend bristling between them.

Although I know Jonah would understand, in the end, this isn't his business. Geordie deserves some privacy, some dignity. There's no need to get into it with anyone else.

And it's not like Jonah and I don't have enough to worry about already.

We leave my parents' house as early as we possibly can, begging off to pack and get ready for the trip tomorrow. "Besides," I say as we head for the door, "We'll need to swing by the mall so I can get a coat. Jonah too, I guess. We didn't bring anything warm enough for Chicago."

"Exactly," Jonah says. Although he smiles, I can see the strain just beneath the surface. I wonder if my family can too. Certainly Chloe's eyes have taken on an avid gleam of curiosity. But it doesn't matter. They know nothing; there's really nothing for them to know; and this will all be over soon.

"It was so lovely to spend more time with you, Jonah," my mother fawns. Her avarice is so naked as to be humiliating. "Vivienne, you bring him back with you as soon as you can."

Dad's liking is more genuine. "Glad I finally got to talk with you. You have a good trip home now."

"Yes, sir," Jonah says. It touches me in a way I can't define to hear him call my father *sir*, to pay him that small respect.

I kneel at the stoop to hug Libby tightly. As she hugs back, says, "You'll come home for Carnival, won't you, Aunt Vivi?"

Normally I try to stay with Liz as much as possible during the Mardi Gras season, but this year I can endure a little more family time. "You know it. You think I'm going to let you get all the beads?"

Libby grins with the confidence of a child in the age range known in New Orleans as "bead bait"—cute enough to throw to, agile enough to catch. "I'm going to get them *all*. Could I catch beads on your shoulders, Uncle Jonah? You're so tall that I would be high above everybody!"

"Sure," he says. "Of course."

I don't think he actually heard a word she said. But he hugs her good-bye too.

Somehow, Jonah holds it together until we're in the car.

As soon he slams his door shut, though, he leans forward, hands braced against the dash. "Son of a bitch," he whispers. "Son of a *bitch*."

"What's going on? How did Carter find out you were, I don't know, a person of interest or whatever it is?" Kip swore almost nobody in Austin knew, so how could the news have reached Chicago already?

Jonah closes his eyes. "After the police questioned me, I contacted a lawyer with the family firm. If he discussed what I told him with anyone else, the information could've gotten back to Carter—if he didn't just go straight to Carter with it in the first place."

"But that's a breach of confidentiality, isn't it?"

"Yes. And if that's how this happened, I'm going to get that guy disbarred. That doesn't change the fact that the news is out."

I search desperately for a bright side. "Hey. This is upsetting, I know, but it's not like he can do anything to you. Carter Hale doesn't control the Austin police department." Then I remember how I learned about all Jonah's crazy family drama: CNN. Kip and Carmen already knew tons of details I didn't simply from reading the tabloids. "Oh, my God. Is Carter talking to the press about this?"

"No. Not yet, anyway." Jonah tenses his hands, like he wishes he could punch his way through this problem. "Carter's going after the only thing he really cares about—the money."

I think of the sapphire earrings, notice the heavy gold watch around Jonah's wrist. Although he leads a fairly normal lifestyle, a handful of his possessions and gifts hint at the incredible wealth he inherited. And yet, I've never believed the money meant very much to Jonah.

"You don't care about the cash," I said. "You just don't want Carter to get his hands on one more thing that doesn't belong to him."

Jonah nods without even looking at me. He took it for granted that I'd understand; we've built that much trust.

I put one hand on his shoulder. "How does that work, though? The money's yours. It's not like you'd lose it if you were convicted of a crime—much less just because someone somewhere suspects you."

He slumps back into his seat, as if the weight of three decades with Carter Hale just hit him all at once. Dully he replies, "My inheritance from my father is tied up in a trust. Usually trusts like that expire when the kids turn eighteen or twenty-one, but for some goddamned reason my father made ours contingent on the approval of the executor."

"Who's the executor?" I thought that was always one of the lawyers.

"My mother, who thinks we'd abandon her if we could access the funds ourselves. She might be right." Jonah looks over at me, as if he thinks I'll be horrified by that, and only slowly relaxes as he remembers that I know just how he feels. "So she withholds her approval, and Rebecca and I stay on the leash—at least, that's how Mom sees it."

The trap is laid so perfectly, poised to spring no matter which way Jonah and his sister jump. "If you maintain ties with the trust, your mother and stepfather get to interfere with your life. If you cut ties with the trust, your stepfather wins, and you don't want to give him the satisfaction."

"It's not that petty." Then Jonah catches himself. "When it comes to Carter, I *can* be petty—but this is important. If I cut myself off from the trust, or if I'm cut off legally, my share of Oceanic stock will be sold. Carter already owns a large block of the airline outright, and if he buys my share, he'll have authority over the entire company. And that means he'll effectively control Rebecca's money from now on. If I walk away, he steals one more thing that should never have been his. No, more than that. He *wins*."

I know very little about trusts, but what Jonah's already told me allows me to draw some conclusions. "Trusts sometimes have conditions, don't they? Certain things the recipients have to do, or not do."

He nods. "One of the things we can't do is 'engage in morally deviant and criminal behavior.' Once that was used to force women to hide their sexual activity, or to keep anyone from openly living with someone of the same sex. These days, no judge would rule that anybody who was gay or living together before marriage was morally deviant, much less criminal. But a rapist? That counts."

Carter wants to use the false accusation against Jonah as a way to grab Oceanic Airlines, the family money, and power over Jonah and his sister. And even without having met the man, I know he'll never, ever let go.

"He'll fail," I say, sure it must be true. "You haven't been convicted. You haven't even been charged, and you won't be."

At last Jonah looks over at me, and the desolation I see in his eyes is terrible. "We know I'm innocent. Carter doesn't."

That's when it hits me. Carter knows what he did to Jonah's mother; he knows what he made Jonah watch, over and over and over, for years. So when he heard that Jonah was suspected of rape—he believed he'd made Jonah in his own image. He thinks his conditioning worked. Carter looks at Jonah and sees the reincarnation of his younger self, no longer cruel only to one woman, but unleashed on the world.

To Carter, the mere accusation would have been confirmation. Proof is irrelevant.

I reach across the front seat of the car to take Jonah's hand. "Carter Hale doesn't know you."

"Oh, yes he does. He knows me in ways no one else does, because he made me what I am. He trained me. He *designed* me." Jonah's laugh is broken. "No, he's never made me attack an innocent woman. But he made me dream about it. Made me want it."

"Jonah—"

"I have to go to Chicago," he says. I'm not sure he even noticed interrupting me. Already, his mind has focused wholly on the fight to come. "Carter's going to press his advantage hard, and immediately. If I don't head him off now, in person, it'll be too late. I'm sorry."

That makes me frown. "Sorry?"

"That I have to leave you the day after Christmas."

"But I'm coming with you."

He acts as if I spoke in some unknown language. "We don't have to explain the trip to your family anymore. You can go home to Austin."

"And do what? Spend days panicking about you?" It never occurred to me that Jonah might believe I'd only promised to stay at his side to keep my parents in the dark. "No way. I'm going to Chicago."

When I say it, I'm braced for a fight. Jonah seems dead set on a course of action that won't involve me. He's plunging into a family drama so byzantine that mine looks almost well-balanced by comparison. All I know about any of this is what he's told me: I've never even been to Chicago. So I expect him to say, *You shouldn't get mixed up in this, you don't understand, I can do this on my own.*

Instead, Jonah tilts his head, his expression disbelieving. "You'd do that?"

"Come with you to Chicago? Of course I would. I mean, you came here with me."

"It's not the same thing. This is going to be—so much worse."

I try to envision what my life would've been like if Anthony had controlled my entire childhood. If he now possessed enough money and power to essentially hold my entire family hostage. Carter Hale has done that, has targeted Jonah and his siblings their whole lives. When I show up in Chicago by Jonah's side, I'll essentially be joining him in the center of the bull's-eye.

"That doesn't matter," I say. "Your battles are my battles, Jonah. I go where you go."

He pulls me close, a swift desperate movement, as if I were about to be torn away from him instead of sitting beside him in the front seat of the car. Rain has begun to patter down on the windshield. Christmas is being washed away.

"Thank you." That's all Jonah says. Just from the way he speaks the words, I know people haven't come through for him very often. I doubt he's given them the chance as an adult. He grew up being betrayed by the people who were supposed to love him the most, time after time, night after night.

Jonah doesn't yet believe someone could stand by him no matter what. I'd say that was the saddest thing I've ever seen—if I hadn't felt that way too, before Jonah.

Maybe we can make each other believe.

TWELVE

Holy crap, Chicago is cold.

It's not as if I didn't know it would be. Like everyone else, I've seen countless Weather Channel updates on the city being buried knee-deep in snow. Flying at Christmastime has taught me that if O'Hare gets closed for winter storms, the entire nation's air traffic becomes paralyzed. Yesterday we drove to the Canal Place mall, where I fought my way through postholiday bargain hunters in order to nab a long white puffy coat, lined snow boots and red leather gloves, all items of clothing rarely required in Texas or Louisiana. So I thought I was prepared.

Nope.

The chill bites into your flesh, gnaws your bones. Even after Jonah and I dash from the taxi into the sumptuous lobby of the Drake Hotel, I continue shivering until we're in our room. Immediately I grab the ornamental half blanket on the bottom of the bed and wrap it around my shoulders as a makeshift shawl. Jonah cracks a smile for the first time today. "Hothouse flower."

"Okay, buddy, come to New Orleans in July, and we'll see how fast you wilt."

"I've survived Texas in summer. I think I can handle New Orleans."

"Maybe." They all say that until they discover the humidity never goes below eighty-five percent.

The smile fades from his face almost instantly. "I only have an hour and a half until the meeting. We should get settled in."

"Meeting? Today?" He hasn't said a word about it.

Jonah doesn't look up as he begins unpacking with near-military efficiency. I wonder if this is a habit he's picked up through years of traveling for work, or whether this is just his way. "I e-mailed the lawyer I spoke to and told him I intended to have a conference with him today at four P.M., regarding his duty of confidentiality to me as a client. He knows he fucked up; more than that, he knows he could get sued or disbarred. So when he said he could make the meeting, I wasn't surprised."

I wonder if the lawyer had to cancel a ski trip or something because of this. It would be the least he deserved for betraying Jonah.

"Is that all there is to it?" I ask. When Jonah looks up from his suitcase, I say, "You're tense. Way more tense than you would be if you were just going to take this guy down."

"That might be all there is to it—but it could get more complicated."

Before I can even ask how, I know the answer. "Carter's going to be there."

"Possibly. Probably. This lawyer could've tipped him off. Or if the leak was someone else within the firm, they might have told Carter instead. And at this point, I wouldn't be surprised if my son of a bitch stepfather were having me followed." Jonah's jaw tenses, his frustration and anger boiling just beneath the surface. "I give him a seventy-five percent chance of showing up."

"What about your mother?"

"She's currently 'regaining her mental stability.' Which for most people would mean actually obtaining psychological help. In this case? It means Carter sweet-talked her into another reconciliation and packed her off to a spa in Arizona." He sighs heavily. "We don't have to worry about her, at least. Just Carter. But that's enough."

I take a deep breath. "Okay. We'll be ready."

"You don't have to come to this meeting."

"Do you think I flew all the way up here to sit in this hotel room? No way. I told you—where you go, I go."

Jonah takes a step toward me, and I see how concerned he is. As if I were the one about to face my worst enemy. "It's going to get rough."

"I can handle rough. You should know."

Chicago isn't a city you often hear described as beautiful—but it is, with a downtown as spectacular as any I've ever seen. With the river winding its way through the heart of the city, you get an astonishing view of the skyscrapers that line every one of the broad streets. And each building seems to be more awe-inspiring than the last, whether they're century-old structures made of white stone or asymmetrical buildings of metal and glass that look more like something from a sci-fi novel.

"When you're a kid growing up and you hear about the big city, this is what you imagine it looking like," I say to Jonah in the back of the cab. "Not like New York, where everything's piled up on top of you so you can hardly see. Like *this*."

Jonah shakes his head, but fondly. "Chicago has its moments."

Snow continues to come down, endless fat flakes that show no sign of stopping. Piles a couple feet deep line the sidewalks. Yet the streets are totally clear, no doubt thanks to salt trucks like the one I saw rattle by a few minutes ago. People trundle along the streets bundled in their thick coats and mufflers like the Michelin Man. The surface of the river has a dull quality—not frozen over, but slushy, threatening to turn. Yet it remains beautiful in its stark way.

The building we walk into is as imposing inside as out. Black granite lines the floors and walls; large silver letters on the wall spell out the name of the law firm . . . and the Hale Hotels Group LLC, and Oceanic Airlines. All of this belongs to Carter Hale and the Marks family. Every story, every stone.

On duty is a tired security guard, who perks up considerably when she sees Jonah's ID. We pass through a sleek metal turnstile before finding the walls of elevator banks, each one handling twenty stories. At first I'm slightly disappointed we're headed to a lower floor: Looking at a view would help me maintain my calm during the confrontation to come. Seeing a whole city splayed beneath you gives you perspective. Then I realize that of course the lawyers have to take the bottom of the building. They're only here to serve the more important businesses above. And I'd bet anything Carter Hale has nabbed himself an office on the top floor.

Jonah remains silent. But if the lawyers think that means he's unsure, they're in for a shock. I know this expression; it's the dark sky before the storm.

It doesn't upset me that he seems to have withdrawn. He needs to focus on his enemies, and I'm here because he *can* take my support for granted. As the red letters above the elevator doors go higher, however, Jonah takes my hand. I squeeze his fingers tightly, a reminder to stay calm—not to let Carter get to him too much.

We're met at the elevators by a secretary in a suit sleeker than any I've ever owned. Jonah and I are only in sweaters and jeans. She takes our bulky coats with the same care she'd use with a floor-length mink, then ushers us down a long corridor and into a meeting room, where four people await us.

Three are anonymous lawyers. One is Carter Maddox Hale.

"No dramatic entrance this time?" Jonah says. "You're losing your touch, Carter."

"We can discuss my losses some other time," Carter replies smoothly. "Today we're discussing yours."

Carter's face is familiar to me from CNN and the occasional Web page. His hair has mostly turned gray, but is still shot through with blond. The man's brilliant blue eyes are so arresting they disguise the wrinkles on his face, at least at first glimpse. If I didn't know what kind of monster he really is, I might think he'd been handsome when he was younger. Instead he turns my stomach.

Jonah takes the chair at the other end of the table, a full seven feet away from the others. I remain at his side.

Carter notices. "I'm going to assume you haven't hired outside counsel. This must be your . . . assistant." He pronounces the word as if it were a euphemism for *personal escort.*

"My name is Vivienne Charles," I say. "I'm a witness."

Witness to what, I don't know, but it's the first thing that comes to mind. Weirdly enough, that proves effective; a couple of the lawyers straighten, apparently convinced Jonah's about to deploy some legal gambit they hadn't anticipated.

Jonah gives me a look; he was ready to defend me. But he doesn't need to waste any emotional energy on my account. If he lets Carter begin baiting him this early, this confrontation will go downhill fast. Besides, I don't give a shit what Carter Hale thinks of me.

Maybe Jonah understands this. He turns his attention back to Carter, his tone as hard as steel. "You want to meet with the board of trustees and argue that I should be removed as a beneficiary. It's not going to work."

"You're committing a string of felonies," Carter shoots back. "That's more than enough to trigger the morality clause—"

"First, I haven't been convicted of any crime. Second, I haven't even been arrested. If your legal eagles are worth the thousands they're charging you each hour, they've told you that both of those things have to happen before you've got a chance in hell." Jonah smiles, thin and joyless. "Third, if you think I'm going to listen to any lectures on morality from you, think again."

Carter isn't fazed. "You haven't been convicted or arrested. But you've been questioned, haven't you?"

"Which you only know because somebody at this law firm committed a serious breach of professional ethics," Jonah says, briefly turning his attention to the suit-and-tie brigade at the table. "Hope you guys are getting paid enough to retire on. Because a lot of you are about to get disbarred."

One of the lawyers hurriedly adds, "The associate responsible has already been fired."

Happy holidays, scapegoat.

"But you're acting on his information, and you think that's acceptable?" Jonah laughs. "I doubt the bar association will see it that way."

Carter leans forward, folding his hands on the table. His confidence is all too clear. "You can't file a complaint without detailing the violation. Which means you'd publicly declare yourself a suspect in a series of rapes. I wouldn't be in such a hurry, if I were you."

"I never said I was in a hurry," Jonah shoots back. "I'm innocent. The police will clear me sooner or later, probably sooner. But it doesn't matter. I can wait."

Carter sighs, his expression mock sympathetic. "Innocent until proven guilty. Of course."

"Innocent," I say. "I'm not only the witness; I'm also the alibi."

A couple of the lawyers exchange glances; they're evaluating my trustworthiness, the strength or weakness of the case against Jonah they'd been told to build. Their doubt doesn't affect Carter in the slightest. His smile only broadens.

"Vivienne seems like a good woman," Carter says to Jonah,

like I'm not even in the room. "Good women are loyal to their men. They'll stand behind them forever. Lie if they're told to lie. We both know that, don't we?"

My gut drops. The son of a bitch is throwing it in Jonah's face—the knowledge that he's raped Jonah's mother literally hundreds of time and will never get called on it.

Jonah sits up straighter in his chair; he's gripping the armrests so hard his knuckles are white. I put one hand on his arm, half comfort, half warning. Because if he loses his shit completely in front of the lawyers, they're going to start thinking of him as guilty for sure and this nightmare will only worsen.

"I'm not lying," I interject, before Jonah can speak. "The evidence will prove that."

Once again, Carter ignores me.

His laser-intense focus remains only on Jonah. This guy knows all the buttons to push. "I'm not judging you as harshly as you might think. Men have certain instincts, don't they? But that's why we have to learn self-control. A mature man waits for the right time. For his own wife."

Jonah's eyes blaze, and he gets to his feet. *Oh, fuck*, I think. I tighten my grip on his arm. It's not to hold him back, just to remind him of who he really is: his own man, his own creation, not Carter Hale's. Maybe it works, because Jonah pauses before saying . . .

Whatever it is he would've said. I never find out, because Carter finally looks at me and smiles. He speaks to Jonah again: "They'll say anything once you have them in line, won't they?"

Shame flushes through me so fast and paralyzing that it's like venom injected into my veins. Carter *knows*. He knows what Jonah and I do together, though in his mind he must have twisted it into a grotesque mockery of our mutual games. This man doesn't believe in consent. He thinks I'm Jonah's plaything, his servant. Nothing more.

"You son of a bitch," Jonah growls, and I brace myself for what's to come.

But the door bangs open, startling everyone. I turn to see a man a couple of years older than me, as impeccably dressed as any of the lawyers, snow still dusting his camel hair coat and wavy blond hair. My first strange thought is, *Where have I seen him before?* Behind him, panting, is the secretary who showed us in; her calm is blown. "I tried to stop him—"

"It's not your fault, Yvonne," the newcomer says. His broad, seemingly carefree smile is at odds with his undeniable intensity. "Nobody was going to keep me away if Jonah's in trouble."

Which is when it hits me that I've seen the shadow of this man in Carter's face. This meeting just got crashed by Maddox Hale—Jonah's stepbrother, and Carter's son.

THIRTEEN

"Mad." Jonah's voice is heavy. "I'm not in trouble."

"Nor are you, Maddox," Carter cuts in. The sharpness in his voice could cut new facets in a diamond. "I realize you felt a . . . sentimental need to inform your stepbrother of this. I won't hold it against you. But this is no longer your concern."

Maddox pays no attention to either of them. "If you're trying to rob my brother and pretending it's on my behalf? It's my concern."

Carter must have thought he could buy Maddox's silence by promising him Oceanic Airlines as his inheritance. But it looks like he doesn't know his own son. Although it would be good to see the shock and anger on Carter's face, I can't bring myself to look at him. My cheeks are still flushed hot with the revelation that Carter thinks he has figured out something of what Jonah and I are to each other.

That knowledge appears so ugly when I see it through his eyes.

One of the lawyers wants to earn his exorbitant fee, because he clears his throat. "Gentlemen. If we could get back to business—business which I believe does not directly concern the younger Mr. Hale—"

"There's no business here," Maddox says. "What, are you planning on shaking Jonah down for something he didn't do? Or threatening to expose him? Because the last time I checked, that was extortion." His smile broadens. "Extortion carries jail time, doesn't it? Please, I'd love to hear legal opinions on the subject."

I thought Jonah was nearly as stubborn as a man could get, but it looks like his stepbrother can hold his own. In this family, he'd have to.

The most nervous lawyer says, "No one here has committed or threatened extortion."

"Far from it." Carter has regained his aplomb. I can tell that he's angry with his son, just like I can tell Maddox doesn't give a shit whether his dad's angry or not. But the man remains focused on his target: Jonah, or everything Jonah owns that Carter desires. "In fact, I hope to make Jonah a very generous offer. One he should consider carefully."

"An offer?" Jonah has regained some measure of calm—enough, anyway. He's pulling strength from me and from Maddox; we've got his back. "You don't have anything I want. Nothing you're going to give me, at any rate."

Carter actually seems surprised. Yet he continues, "If you're forced out of the Marks trust, Jonah, you'll get nothing. Not one dime."

Like Jonah cares about money. Today, however, I'm realizing Jonah *does* care about his pride—at least, when it comes to his wicked stepfather—and that's one of the weak spots Carter's going after, like a shark scenting blood.

"But I have an alternative for you, Jonah. A buyout offer." Carter looks pleased with himself. "You can accept a buyout with the executor's approval, and I think we both know your mother would sign on the dotted line as soon as we asked her."

One of the lawyers slides a deal memo across the broad table toward us. Jonah makes no move for it, so I pick it up. Maddox leans over my shoulder as we look at the sums offered, and the long string of zeroes involved.

Maddox says, "This isn't one-quarter of what Jonah's share is worth, and you know it."

"It's more than nothing, which is what he'll get if he's thrown out." Carter smiles, and it's the exact same expression I've seen on the cover of *Forbes* magazine. It's his mask, the one he wears to conceal the vicious snake within. "This is a sum of money that would support anyone very comfortably for the rest of his life, given a few prudent investments. Given the inevitable conclusion of this sordid affair, I think my offer is probably far beyond Jonah's expectations. And for all your protestations, you *were* expecting this, weren't you, Jonah? Otherwise, why would you be here in the first place?"

The first answer is only silence. I look up at Jonah, and despite all the darkness I've seen in this man—despite everything I've let him do to me—the fury I sense now chills me to the core.

If the hatred contained in a single look had the power to kill a man, Carter Hale would drop dead this instant.

Yet Jonah's voice is controlled and cool. "I didn't come here to collect whatever crumbs you're willing to scatter. I'm innocent, the facts will eventually prove that, and my share in the trust will remain exactly that—mine." Carter's eyes narrow, and he opens his mouth to say something sarcastic in reply, but Jonah doesn't give him the chance. "So why did I come here, if you don't pose a threat? Just to deliver one simple message: You'd better pray to whatever devil you believe in that you don't outlive my mother. I might not have a team of lawyers following me around like underlings, but I've read the trust and I know what it says. If the executor dies after both Rebecca and I turn twenty-five, the trust reverts to us in full. We inherit the remainder of our father's shares. And on that day—at that same *hour*—you're going to be out on your ass."

"Rebecca's twenty-fifth birthday is this year," Maddox adds, as blithely as if he were about to ask everyone to chip in on a gift. "October third. And Mom's not even sick."

Jonah doesn't acknowledge what Maddox has said, but I can sense how much he enjoys the two of them facing Carter down together. "So it comes down to this, Carter. I don't have time for your petty power grabs. But every single time you overextend yourself like this, you make my position stronger and yours weaker. Are you going to give me more ammunition or get the hell out of my life? I'd rather you got out of my life, because I've already got everything on you I'll ever need. It's your call."

With that, Jonah heads for the door, Maddox right behind him. It takes me a moment longer to follow because I have to scoot back my chair—a moment Carter takes to say, in a low voice, "Are you sure you know what your alibi's worth?"

Oh, my God. This guy wants to bribe me to turn on Jonah. How could he think I'd ever do that?

Then again, he thinks Jonah's guilty. If I were as victimized as Jonah's mother, I might grab at some cash to make my own escape.

But I am not a victim.

To Carter I say, "You don't know how to handle people you can't control. Well, too fucking bad. Because you don't control me, and you never will." And I walk out.

Jonah's nowhere to be seen in the hallway, but Maddox is standing there, a smile on his face. "I like you already."

The feeling's mutual. "Do I need to introduce myself?"

"You mean, do I know who you are? You're Vivienne Charles, the woman Jonah's told me so much about. I'm Maddox Hale, spawn of Satan."

I have to laugh, but I'm still angry with Carter, and worried for Jonah. "Is he storming out of here? We need to catch up."

But Maddox shakes his head no. "He'll be back in a second. Then we can all storm out together." Seeing my confusion, he adds, more quietly, "Sometimes, after dealing with my father—Jonah gets sick."

My God. Jonah is vomiting up his guts just from looking that man in the face.

Maddox sighs. "He's not the only one."

We get out of the building without being accosted by Carter or any of his legal goons. Jonah's gaze is distant, his expression grim. I only met Maddox a few minutes ago—and yet the three of us are a unit, a team. It's as if we'd rehearsed how to do this in advance, right down to agreeing not to talk to each other until we're on the street. At the moment we hit the door, Maddox says, "You know he's not done."

Jonah nods. "I know."

The sidewalks are free of ice, but gritty beneath our boots and lined on every side by snow that's no longer white. As cold wind whips my hair, Jonah slides one arm around my shoulders; the gesture is more protective than romantic, but in some ways that touches me more.

"Is there anything else we can do?" I ask. Carter might not be able to wrest Jonah's share of the trust from him, but even confronting this is putting Jonah through hell. I want this misery to end, now. "Any way to call him off?"

"Maybe," Maddox says.

Jonah stares at his brother; that's not the response he expected. I say, "What do you mean?"

"I mean that it's time to have a family conference." Maddox squares his shoulders like a man bracing for a fight. "I contacted Elise and Rebecca. Elise is flying in later tonight; Rebecca can't leave South America, but she's going to join us via Skype."

Jonah's face remains pale from the strain of confronting Carter; the light blue scarf he wears around his neck and the snow beginning to dust his dark hair create the illusion that he's turning to ice. "You shouldn't have dragged them into this."

"Please. We all got dragged into this as kids." Maddox says. "Anyway, the meeting's tomorrow night. We'll go to my place—I finally managed to buy the penthouse I wanted, you know. Just a few stories above the Orchid."

"That's your club, right?" I remember seeing it written about as *the* place to see and be seen in downtown Chicago.

"You've heard of it? Fantastic." Maddox beams with obvious pride. He's like a ray of sunshine on this cold city street—for Jonah as much as for me. I can tell by the way Jonah looks at him. "If my fame has spread all the way to Texas, this New Year's party ought to be our biggest yet. Tonight, though, it's going to be dead. So why don't you come by? We can hang out, have time to talk. Drinks on the house."

I glance up at Jonah. "Pretty good deal."

Jonah probably wants to go into total-silence mode. He broods too much when he's as angry or upset as he is now. But he won't say no to his brother, I realize—and Maddox has intelligently, tactfully, made sure Jonah won't spend the next two days beating himself up. "Okay. We'll be there."

We hail a taxi, say our good-byes. Jonah continues holding me in the cab, the side of his head resting against mine, but he doesn't say a word. I don't try to draw him out either. Until we're alone, I couldn't do anything but make small talk, which at this point feels trivial. Even childish. Only after we return to our room at the Drake do I speak. "Are you okay?"

Jonah shrugs as he yanks off his blue scarf, tosses it down on the desk. "I'm fine."

I don't argue. Instead I sit on the small sofa in our room, shaking the snowflakes from my hair and simply look at him.

He sighs. "I'm as fine as I'm going to get, considering."

"What do you need?"

Jonah might need solitude, a few hours by himself to pull his thoughts together, in which case I'll investigate the high tea they're advertising in the lobby. Or maybe he'd rather be distracted for a while—watching a movie, talking about anything but what just took place. Whatever it is, I can handle it.

And then I see the way he's looking at me—the sudden heat behind that ice. My body responds powerfully, instinctively; it's like the sheer force of his desire is enough to quicken my pulse. To make my skin tingle with the expectation of being touched.

"I need to be angry," he says, his voice low. "I need to let it out."

Slowly I kick off one boot, then the other. "Then take it out on me."

Jonah pulls off his sweater and lets it drop to the floor. The intensity of his stare only increases. "Tell me something that will make me mad. Something that could make me completely fucking furious."

Does he want a lie or the truth? I don't have a truth that would drive him over the edge—but there is one small secret that might get under his skin. Eventually I knew I'd tell him about it. Might as well go ahead now.

"I talked to Geordie on Christmas. When I left the table for a few minutes. Remember?"

Jonah wasn't expecting that, but it works. "You're still talking to your ex? To the guy who screwed you before me?"

Is Jonah actually threatened by Geordie, or is he simply creating the scenario for what we're about to do? Doesn't matter yet. "Yeah. He's still fucked me more than you have too."

That does it. Jonah lunges toward me, pulls me up by my arms. I stumble into him, unable to get my balance before he shakes me. His voice is a predator's growl. "You belong *to me*."

He throws me onto the bed. Gasping, I try to crawl across the mattress to escape him, but Jonah grabs my leg and pulls me back down toward him. I twist my body around to push him away, but he shakes me again and shoves me onto my back.

As his hands unfasten my jeans, pulling them off, he says, "Your body is for me. Your cunt is for me. Nobody else. If you don't know that already, you're going to learn it today."

The rage I sense from him is so fucking real. I don't know if it's for Carter or for me, or if Jonah could even say where it all comes from. And it's scary as hell.

He rips my underwear away with my pants. Somehow the fact that I'm still wearing my sweater makes my nakedness beneath more obscene. Jonah shoves my thighs apart and thrusts two fingers inside me. I'm so unprepared it makes me gasp. "What, you like that?" Jonah pushes in deeper, working me roughly with his hand. "How much do you think you can take? How about my whole fist, huh? You want that? You want my fist inside you?"

Oh, fuck. I don't know if I can do that. I've never tried, never wanted to try—never even thought to tell Jonah whether it was forbidden or okay. The terror rising inside me is now very real. *Silver*, I remind myself. *He'll stop if you say silver.* And I believe that completely. But my voice still shakes as I beg, "No, please, no, don't do that."

"I just told you, your cunt is mine." Jonah's face is a mask of rage. He doesn't look like himself anymore. It scares the hell out of me and still—*still*—turns me on. "You don't tell me what to do with what's mine."

"Oh, God, *please* don't." The sob that rises from my chest surprises me. And I really don't want him to fist me. Yet I know my limits. I *want* to lose control. If he does it, I won't say the safe word unless the pain is unbearable. My fantasy is about my own powerlessness. Whatever Jonah wants to do to me, I have to take. "Please, I'll do anything."

"That's right. You'll do anything I want you to do."

Three fingers now, or is it four? My cunt burns with the stretching—and yet the burn is only half pain. I begin to realize what it might be like to have that much of him inside me. Even if it made me scream, the intensity could bring me over the brink.

Jonah pushes harder. "You don't want my fist in you? You want something else? There's a wine bottle on the minibar. You want me to fuck you with that?"

"No!"

It's so hard to keep from screaming. But if I scream, other hotel guests in the hallway might hear, and they'd call security. This would end. As scared as I am, I don't want this to end.

"Are you crying? Good. I like it when you cry," Jonah rasps. He's breathing so hard, his body tense with the effort of holding back. "What do you want inside you? My cock?"

"Yes." I'm sobbing now, not even trying to hold it back. "Please, nothing else."

Jonah pulls out his hand, his fingers slick, and then drags me from the bed. I fall on the floor, flat on my belly, and immediately he presses down between my shoulder blades to keep me there. His thighs are between mine. I hear his other hand fumbling with his zipper—

—then he's on top of me, spreading my legs further, his weight pinning me down as he shoves his cock inside.

He has me so opened up, so wet, that it's effortless. But I can't stop crying. My sobs only get louder as Jonah starts thrusting.

"Did it feel like that when Geordie fucked you? Was it this good?"

I swallow my tears. "No."

"My cock's bigger than his, isn't it?"

"—Yes—"

Jonah pounds into me harder, and I think I'm going to start sobbing again when I realize the rush building inside me comes from somewhere else within. I sink deeper into myself with every thrust, deeper into pure instinctive sensation, and I shudder beneath him. Like an animal shot through with an arrow, trembling as it dies beneath the hunter's gaze.

When I come, my cry of pleasure is indistinguishable from my weeping. Jonah keeps on, pumping into me in what seems to be thoughtless rage. He could keep fucking me for an hour and I'd have to lie here—I can't escape—

He shouts out, plunges in deep, and bites the soft flesh of my shoulder. It's not a brutal bite—the skin wouldn't break—but I moan from the delicious ache of it anyway. Jonah hangs on with teeth and hands until his long, powerful orgasm finally subsides. When he rolls off me, we both remain on the floor for a few moments, struggling to catch our breath. My tears finally stop, but I feel like I couldn't get to my feet, or even turn over.

At last Jonah says, "I'm sorry. That was too much."

"No. It wasn't." I wipe my cheeks as I look at him lying next to me. "Trust me to say the safe word when I need it. Okay? You can trust me to do that, always."

He nods slowly, accepting that. "Did you—"

"Come? Yeah." And it felt totally fucking incredible. So why am I still sniffling?

Jonah rolls over and gently puts his arms around me. That titanic anger had nothing to do with me, nothing at all, because he has completely let it go. "Here. Let me help you."

We get to our feet, remove our remaining clothing, and curl up in bed together. Through the gauze curtains I can see snow still blanketing down; Jonah's body spooned behind mine feels like the only warmth in the world.

He murmurs into my hair, "Did you really talk to Geordie on Christmas?" Jonah doesn't sound jealous—only curious, and maybe confused.

"I did. But it wasn't anything remotely romantic." How can I put this? "He's going through an extremely difficult time. He needs all the support he can get. I'm not the only person he leans on, but I was the only one he could reach out to at that moment."

"Why didn't you tell me?"

"Because it's his problem, and it's private, and I'm trying to respect that."

"Okay," Jonah says. He believes me; he accepts Geordie's need for privacy. All this even though I know some small measure of his jealousy is real. My heart expands at being so deeply trusted.

I add, "Also—*nobody*'s cock is as big as yours."

He laughs once, his breath soft against my neck. "I don't need that much reassuring."

Of course he doesn't.

The rough handling of my body has faded into pleasant afterglow. Even the tender spot on my shoulder isn't painful. Jonah's arm is wrapped around me, he's worked out that tension, and everything should be perfect. Yet I can sense the cloud still hanging over Jonah, the darkness we can't quite escape.

FOURTEEN

The snowfall stops for an hour or so in the early evening, allowing Jonah and me to walk to the Orchid. Cold as the weather is, my coat is warm, the wind has died, and the city has been newly frosted white—erasing the metropolitan grime so that Chicago almost gleams. Besides, I'm a Southern girl. I can't help feeling a little excited by snow.

When I tell Jonah this, he smiles down at me. "I doubt you'd like it as much if you had to deal with it for four months straight."

"Probably true. But I don't have to, do I? I can just enjoy today."

He squeezes my hand. The affection I sense is real. He's happy to be here with me in this moment, maybe enjoying the familiar sights of this city. But his sadness and strain linger.

I wish I could lift his burdens from him, but I can't. All I can do for now is stand by his side.

Once again I think of the etching I want to create, the one that will symbolize what Jonah is to me. But what single image could encompass a man so complex? I envision a stone tower—no. Too Freudian. But a stone wall, maybe, or a castle. Strong even though it's endured so much, but with cracks in the mortar to show the punishment it's taken. Maybe even moss or ivy growing on the edges to show a sense of life, vitality, harmony?

Still not right. No matter how mighty something like that stood after all its centuries, the image would still suggest inevitable collapse. My etching would portray something at the end of its strength. Jonah's strength is far from giving out—I have to believe that.

The Orchid is located in another of Chicago's skyscrapers on the river, on one of the highest floors. For the occasion, I changed into wide-legged pants and a silky top, both in inky black; Jonah replaced his jeans with charcoal-colored trousers. Despite this, the minute we walk into the club, I feel drastically underdressed.

Before us lies the city, brilliantly lit in the nighttime. Headlights along the streets below look like strings of fairy lights. The enormous space of the club is largely broken up into smaller enclosures—some for ten or twelve people, others cozy little nooks for two. Although the dividers slope in modernistic waves from a couple feet high to taller than Jonah's head, they're made of lustrous burled wood as richly striped as a tiger's pelt, so the overall effect is warm and organic. Couches and chairs are low, plush, in muted earth tones. Yet beyond all the private niches, I can see a wide expanse that must be the dance floor on wilder nights than this one. Tonight the only music is soft R&B. The dark walls are almost unornamented, save for a few crescent-shaped sconces carved of mica and one enormous photograph of a glorious yellow orchid. The color of the petals is so vivid that looking at the picture is like staring straight into flame.

As Maddox predicted, the club's not crowded tonight; a couple dozen patrons murmur and laugh in their enclaves, no more. Which no doubt is why the host is able to greet us right away.

"Jonah, Vivienne." Maddox strides toward us from the broad semicircular bar. "You made it."

"I flew to Antarctica a couple months ago, you know," Jonah

says as he submits to his brother's enthusiastic hug. "I can handle a trip along three city blocks."

"I think it's colder here than in Antarctica." Maddox lets go of Jonah to buss me on the cheek. "Come on. Saved you guys the best table in the house."

Despite the warmth between them, nobody could be fooled into thinking Jonah and Maddox were blood brothers. Where Jonah is dark haired with haunting gray eyes, Maddox is golden from head to toe—blond wavy hair, hazel eyes, and a tan complexion that is obviously completely natural. Maddox isn't a short man by any means, but Jonah has a couple inches on him. And their body types are different too. Jonah's frame is powerful, aggressively masculine, but with his distinctive proportions—the broad shoulders, the incredibly narrow waist. Maddox, however, is more solid, more square, even more muscled. If they were both athletes, Jonah would be an Olympic diver, Maddox a wrestler.

Also, while Jonah dresses well, Maddox is clearly the clotheshorse of the two. The creamy silk shirt and navy blue trousers he's wearing look like he walked straight off a designer's runway. Combined with his unruly, longish hair, the effect could almost be feminine, were it not for the undeniable power of his build. As it is, the contrast only makes him more attractive. Several women lift their eyes to watch him walk by; at least one man does as well.

Of course, they're probably looking at Jonah too. But I hope my hand in his sends a clear message. *Sorry, this one's taken.*

Maddox leads us to a little nook that offers a perfect view of the skyline; we're just far enough back to glimpse the edge of the river too. As we sink down onto the welcoming curved sofa, a waitress appears with a tray of cocktails.

"Sazeracs," Maddox says, smiling at me. "Jonah told me you were from New Orleans. Thought I'd make you feel at home."

Most tourists leave New Orleans believing Hurricanes are the city's signature drink. I don't think a local has touched one in years. Obviously Maddox knows his mixology. "Thank you. And cheers."

"Cheers." Jonah joins in the toast, takes a quick drink, then sets the glass down. "Is Elise in town already? Will she be here tonight?"

Maddox's expression falls. It's like watching a cloud pass in front of the sun. "She flew in a couple hours ago. But of course she can't go out because Griffin needs her on the phone for whatever reason."

Jonah leans back, grimacing like a man with a headache. "In other words, she's going to spend a few hours propping up his already enormous ego instead of seeing the people she flew halfway across the country to see."

"Got it in one," Maddox says.

"Only Jonah and Rebecca are in the trust, right?" I venture. This situation is a minefield, one these men have learned to navigate over the years. I have to tread more carefully. "So Elise is coming for—moral support."

Maddox seems to take it for granted that I have a right to discuss this with them. How much has Jonah told him about me? "You're right about the Marks trust. But Elise and I had a trust of our own from our mother, one that was structured more sanely, thank God. We inherited significant ownership in the Hale Hotel Group when we each turned twenty-one. No, we can't outvote Dad's shares. He retains control. But we can make his life a lot more difficult if we have to. It's starting to look like we do."

Jonah shakes his head no. "You guys shouldn't put yourselves on the line for me."

"That's not your call to make." As congenial as Maddox is, there's a vein of true strength in him, enough to match Jonah's. If Jonah is stone, Maddox is fire. "It's ours. And this is the lowest Dad has ever sunk. If we don't find a way to stop him now, who knows what he'll try next?"

There's a moment when I think Jonah will argue, but then I see realization setting in. "You're afraid he'll turn on Rebecca."

"We can't let that happen," Maddox says, his voice harder, harsher, than it's been before. "Anything else he dishes out, we can take. She can't."

Why is Rebecca more vulnerable than her brothers or sister? But I sense this is the one question I can't ask—that this secret belongs to Rebecca, and they keep it for her. Whatever it is, it's enough to make Jonah reconsider.

He always wants to endure his pain alone, I realize. *He doesn't think about protecting himself, only protecting others.*

"Give me a minute," Jonah says, rising from the table. He heads toward the restroom, or wherever; all three of us know he simply needs a break, a chance to think, before diving back into this conversation.

And that leaves me alone with Maddox.

"So," I begin.

"So." He smiles. "We've hit the awkward-small-talk portion of the evening. I'll start. How did you meet Jonah?"

"He fixed a flat tire for me." That is completely true, and yet not the complete truth. Apparently Jonah keeps at least one secret from his brother. Thank God. "Do you remember meeting Jonah?"

"Nope." Maddox's expression is fond. "In my earliest memories, I recall knowing that he and Rebecca hadn't always been there. But I don't actually remember life without them any more than I do without Elise."

"Tell me a good story. Something about Jonah as a little kid." That should be harmless enough. Besides, on Christmas, my mother went on and on to Jonah about how I wanted to be a baton twirler in middle school. Turnabout is fair play.

I'm expecting an anecdote about tricycles or T-ball games. Instead, Maddox's smile fades. The warmth he exudes doesn't cool—just the opposite. Instead I realize that his inner fire could rage out of control if he ever slipped, for even a moment. But Maddox remains steady. In control. "When I was four years old, my sister Elise and I were playing on the first floor, which was used mostly for guests. Receptions. That kind of thing. It was the part of Redgrave House the public was allowed to see."

Redgrave House is more than Jonah's childhood home. It's also one of the oldest and grandest private homes in the city of Chicago, quietly famous in its own right. At the airport, I saw it pictured along with several other landmarks on a postcard. Of course there would have been countless charity fundraisers and society events held there. Maybe that's one reason Jonah's so fiercely private; he grew up in a home that was never entirely his own.

Though of course he has other reasons.

"We were roughhousing," Maddox continues. "Chasing each other around, that kind of thing. We weren't supposed to go downstairs alone, but I ran down the stairs, Elise came after me—and she crashed right into a table. Knocked a vase to the floor, where it shattered into a million pieces. I mean, there wasn't a shard as big as my thumb, and I was only five."

"Let me guess," I say. "Ming Dynasty?"

Maddox laughs, but the sound is hollow. "Not *that* priceless. Honestly, it wouldn't have mattered if the vase were worth ten dollars or ten thousand. We'd broken one of Carter's rules, and we couldn't hide it. That was enough."

How much abuse did Carter heap on the children outside his bedroom door? I've never seen any scars on Jonah, but his need for violence—to be more powerful than someone else, to glory in taking dominance at the most primal level—

"We weren't beaten often," Maddox says, as if reading my mind. "He only struck me once or twice, ever. I'm his 'favorite.'"

The way he pronounces the word *favorite* makes it clear Maddox considers this more curse than blessing.

He continues, "It's not violence Dad craves. It's the humiliation of anyone and everyone who ever stood up to him. And with us kids, he always knew exactly where to strike. He knew the words to say to make you feel like you wished you'd never been born. Sometimes you'd do anything, say anything, to try to get him to stop. So when that vase fell, Elise and I knew we were in for it. And we knew it would be bad. We ran upstairs. Elise locked herself in her room, and I hid under my bed. I was that little." His attempt at a smile is more of a grimace. "By now you're probably wondering where Jonah comes into all this."

I'd forgotten about everything but the story Maddox was telling. This warm golden club with its soft light and sultry music—it seems more like a vision, a dream. We seem to be back in a house as grand as it was cold, its majestic exterior concealing the cruelty within. "Did Jonah come to your defense when Carter went after you?"

"No. He told our parents that *he* broke the vase. And he took all the punishment Dad could dish out, without flinching." Maddox takes a swig of his cocktail, as if it could brace him against the memory. "My father has always tried to turn us against each other. But that day, I knew I would do anything for Jonah, and that he would do anything for me."

"He's good at that. Taking care of people."

"Yeah, he is." One deep breath and then Maddox asks, "When did Jonah tell you the whole truth about Dad?"

"He only told me after we'd been together a couple of months and—and I'd told him some difficult things about my life too." I can't match Maddox's fearless candor, but even this veiled allusion startles me. It's more than I've ever admitted to Carmen, Geordie, or my own father. Is it that I trust Maddox so much already, or because I know his secrets so well that I feel obligated to share in return? "How did you know I'd heard the whole story? Did Jonah tell you?"

Maddox nods. "Which I couldn't believe. I'm not sure any of us have told the entire truth about our family to anybody before. Jonah trusts almost no one. So if he trusts you, I assume you're worth it."

Maybe I ought to thank him for the compliment. Instead I remember what Jonah told me, about how he and Elise fought hard to protect Maddox and Rebecca. About how their younger siblings never, ever had to go into their parents' bedroom and witness the act of rape. "When did *you* know the whole truth?"

Maddox hesitates. Despite the honesty he's shown so far, the question I've asked is so intensely intimate that he'd be within his rights to throw me out of this nightclub. I open my mouth to take it back and apologize, but that's when he speaks. "It sank in slowly. Bruises on Mom's body. Blood in places it shouldn't have been. Hearing Jonah and Elise coming back to bed at two or three in the morning; sometimes Elise would cry the rest of the night. They wouldn't talk about what happened. And even if Dad never dragged Rebecca and me into the bedroom, he couldn't muffle the sounds. So there was no one moment of revelation. I remember not knowing; I remember knowing. In between was a lot of fear and doubt." His smile is crooked. "You know, we totally blew the awkward-small-talk thing."

I laugh despite myself. "Ah, this Sazerac is perfect. Kudos to your bartender."

"There you go."

And just like that, I feel as if I've known Maddox my whole life. From the way he's smiling at me, I think he feels the same.

By the time Jonah returns a few minutes later, Maddox and I

are laughing. Although Jonah smiles at us, his expression is wary. "Do I want to know what's so funny?"

"*The Big Lebowski*," I explain. "Turns out we both love that movie."

Jonah shrugs. "Never saw it."

Maddox's jaw hangs open in mock horror. "What? Oh, we have to change that, ASAP."

Although Jonah smiles at his brother, his dark mood remains all too visible. This night out might have brought Maddox and me closer together—but Jonah remains angry, desolate. Lost.

The rest of our evening is a blur of cocktails and anecdotes—funny ones, this time. Maddox tells me about the four children running wild at Navy Pier right after the maze was built. I volunteer the time Liz and I tried to use the least convincing fake IDs ever at Tipitina's our junior year of high school, and got busted by a bouncer who couldn't stop laughing. Jonah comes up with the story of the first time he ever got drunk at a party, sneaked in late at night, nearly got caught, and only escaped by hiding in Rebecca's closet until dawn. He laughs along with us as he talks about sitting on her light-up sneakers and having them blink for hours, but the laughter never reaches his eyes. I make excuses for us fairly early. Maddox is too wise to argue. By the time we get downstairs, it's snowing again.

"Taxi?" I ask Jonah. It's the first word between us since we got in the elevator.

He shakes his head. "I need some fresh air. If that's okay with you."

"Sure." Yeah, it's cold as hell. But Jonah's arm is around me again, providing some shelter from the chill.

We walk in silence, side by side. Only when Jonah's body begins to feel less tense against mine do I say, "I like Maddox a lot."

"Most people do. He's got—charm. Charisma. I've never had that." He says this without resentment. To him, it's simple fact.

"Sometimes charisma is a mask." Anthony Whedon taught me that. "But your brother's actually a good guy."

"Yeah. He is."

Yet hours spent with this brother he loves, enjoying drinks and laughter, haven't been enough to restore Jonah. I hug him around his waist. "Is there anything I can do?"

Jonah doesn't answer at first. His profile is stark against the night surrounding us; snow has begun to dust his scarf and coat again. He doesn't look at me. "You've gone there once already today."

It's not that I don't know Jonah gives in to his inner darkness every time we play our games. I do too. But I hadn't realized how much more he would crave that release during this time of confrontation.

Maybe I should have. Hadn't I asked Jonah to brutalize me that night in New Orleans, after I'd had to deal with Anthony all day? Our demons are much the same.

"I'm ready," I tell him. "Let's play."

FIFTEEN

Although it's Jonah who needs this so badly, the scenario we choose is one of my fantasies. Jonah took me hard and rough this afternoon. As much as I loved it, the aftermath still lingers in my body—carpet burn on my knees, soreness in my inner thighs where he pried them apart. So we need something less rigorous. Something I can endure, and enjoy.

"This blurs the lines," Jonah says as we sit in the Drake's lobby, my fourth cocktail of the night in front of me. "You're going to be all right with it?"

"Definitely." I've gotten off on this fantasy dozens of times. "I know what I want."

"But you're getting drunk. I only do what you've given consent for—no more, ever. And you won't be able to tell me yes or no."

"I'm consenting now," I promise. "And I'm not going to get so messed up I can't tell you if we're going too far. Okay?"

"Okay."

I'm just going to get drunk enough that I can pretend to be completely helpless, and almost believe it myself. Then Jonah will do the rest.

Why is this one of my favorite scenarios? For a long time I thought it was "less violent," that I steered my imagination that way as a way of weaning myself off the more brutal visions that sometimes got me off. But force is force; violence is violence. Now I believe I gravitate toward this as a way of almost completely erasing not only my will, but also my consciousness. In this version of the fantasy, I am nothing but a body. Nothing but sensation. A thing to be used.

The Sazeracs we drank at the Orchid, we nursed over a period of hours. Maddox treated us to luxury-style bar snacks too—shrimp skewers and soft cheeses that were practically a second dinner. So when we got back to the Drake, I had no more than the faintest buzz.

Now, though, I'm knocking back a double, fast. No more food. This will take me over the brink for an hour or so. Should be enough.

I tilt my head back for the last swallow, and feel my head spin. "Mmm." Setting the glass back down, I take a deep breath. My lips are slightly numb from the Drambuie. "There we go."

Jonah says nothing, though he's watching me avidly. His caution is at war with his desire. And his desire is spiking higher and hotter as he watches me get a little sloppy. He could take me down, now, and he knows it. But he says, "Last chance."

I get to my feet, wobbling a bit as I brush my hair from my face. "Give me five minutes."

He nods once. I won't see him again until he enters our room, and the game begins.

In the elevator, my face is flushed with warmth. I lean heavily against the side wall; the elderly couple riding up with me exchange a glance. *Look at that drunk girl. She should be more careful.* That's what they're probably thinking. You're right, old guys. I should.

Not tonight.

When I reach my room, I slip off my clothes—ought to hang them up neatly, but I'm just messed up enough not to want to, and pretending to be even more messed up than I am. So I let them fall onto the chair. Take my hair down from its messy bun so that it falls across my face. The bra goes atop the clothes, and after a moment, I ditch my panties too. Those things are always in the way. Who's to say how I sleep?

I tug on a tank top, nothing else, and flop into bed. Although I pull the edge of the sheet over my exposed ass, I don't make any other moves. My head spins; the bed seems to float above the floor. It's easy to imagine that I'm far drunker than I am. That I can't even move . . .

A metallic click, and the door swings open. I'm facing away from it, so I only see a rectangle of light against the curtains, Jonah's blurry shadow in the center, before he seals us back into darkness. As his footsteps come nearer, I close my eyes.

Jonah brushes his hand along my shoulder. I don't react. He strokes more firmly this time, edging the strap of my tank top almost off. With a whine, I wriggle once, then go motionless again.

The illusion closes around us both: I'm helpless. Too drunk to move or fight, maybe even too drunk to say the word *stop*, but not completely unconscious. Just awake enough to feel it.

He pulls the sheet down. Cool air ghosts along my back, my exposed lower body. Jonah groans slightly to see me naked from the waist down—he likes that.

Two fingers trace a line of heat along my leg, from the back of my knee all the way up to the hip, where he finds the crest of my pelvic bone. Back down again, closer to the cleft of my ass—and then his touch curves in toward my cunt. His rougher skin brushes against me, just enough to get slick.

Then I hear him lift his hand to his lips to taste me.

Oh, fuck, if I wasn't wet before, I am now. I wonder if he can actually see it welling between my legs. My pulse has quickened, and every inch of my body is newly, sharply sensitive—and yet my head still reels, the alcohol making everything slightly surreal.

The next sound is the sound of Jonah stripping off his pants and sweater. I want to look up and see him, his magnificent body pale in the dim moonlight through the gauze drapes. But that would betray the game. So I lie there, pliant and helpless, awaiting his pleasure. His will.

Jonah rolls me onto my back, the motion taking me to the edge of the bed. My arm spills over the side. He tugs down the scoop neck of my tank to expose my tits, then begins to play with them—fondling, squeezing, jiggling. Arousal spirals through me, down to my core, as he kneads me, teases my nipples, presses my breasts together tightly. There's none of the punishment he's sometimes inflicted on my body. It's more as if he's exploring. Testing me to see how much I feel, how much I'll allow before I start to struggle.

I writhe beneath him once, with a whimper. No more.

Then he nudges my face sideways; my eyes remain shut. When I feel the head of his cock brush against my lips, I pull back—the room tilts—and he catches me under my chin with his fingertips. More firmly, he works my mouth open and slips his cock inside.

My only reaction is a groan, which he seems to like. I do nothing with my lips or tongue, simply allow him to rock in and out. But he's not aggressively fucking my mouth the way he sometimes does. He's just proving he can do this, that I'm so out of it he can violate me without my even turning my head.

What would I do, if I were drunker than this—so drunk a man I barely knew could get in here and work me over? Clumsily I push at him as I pull my head back. My resistance is useless—it's meant to be—but it's also meant to turn him on.

It works. Jonah breathes out sharply. Through my half-shut eyes, I see him moving to the foot of the bed, his hand around his cock as he gets himself harder.

A thought flickers through my head—that it could be hot to watch Jonah get himself off. Not sure how that would fit into one of our games, but I might mention it some other time. For now it's enough to watch his hand stroking the length of his shaft and to know every inch of him is for me.

He pulls my legs apart. By now I'm so wound up that I have to stifle a moan of pleasure from that sensation alone—the air against my cunt, the grip of his fingers on my thighs. Jonah shoves one knee to the side, then tugs my other leg up so that it's almost bent upon my chest. I realize he's enjoying the ability to manipulate my body. Twisting and turning me makes it even clearer that, for now, I'm only his plaything. Nothing more.

Jonah flips me over onto my belly and positions himself between my legs. Even the pressure of the mattress against my clit is enough to send a thrill through me. My powerlessness is getting me even hotter than it's getting him.

His cock bumps against me. Then into me—only a couple inches, to see what I'll take. I whimper and try to twist my body to one side, but Jonah leans over me, a broad hand on each of my arms, holding me flat on the bed as he starts shoving himself all the way inside.

The burn as he opens me—the way my entire world narrows until I perceive nothing but this inner blaze—only Jonah gives me this. Only Jonah, ever.

Immediately he starts thrusting fast, like a man trying to get off as quickly as possible. If this scenario were real, he would be. He'd want to do what he needed and get the hell out before I could come to enough to stop him, or identify him. So he's going for it, all out.

Doesn't matter. I'm right behind him, arousal arcing higher inside me until the world goes dark and fuzzy around the edges. The alcohol makes every sensation more overpowering. When I feel the inevitability of orgasm—that exhilarating moment before the fall, when you have to let go—I can't keep myself from crying out. Because then it's on me and I'm coming long and sweet and good, until I think I might faint.

If I weren't already lying down, I probably would.

Jonah pays no attention. He stays on me, thrusting for forever, as I lie beneath him limp and weak. Finally his hands tighten on my arms, and he pumps into me deeper and harder than before. A low, primal grunt—and then his hands relax.

As he straightens, I feel his cock slip out of me; his hot come spills onto my skin and the sheets. For a moment all I want to do is lie there and feel it.

"Vivienne?" he whispers. "You're—you have to be awake."

"I am," I mumble. "Just happy."

With that I summon my strength to crawl further up the mattress. At least the wet spot won't bother either of us tonight. As I curl onto my side, I hold a hand out for Jonah, who still stands at the foot of the bed, staring at me.

I whisper, "C'mon. Come to bed."

Jonah spoons behind my back and hugs me so tightly that at first I think I won't be able to fall asleep like that—and then I do.

In the morning, Jonah's still sound asleep after I've emerged from the shower. He must be exhausted; I wonder how much rest he's really had since this whole nightmare with the police and Carter began. Not enough, it seems.

Amazingly, I've avoided the hangover I so richly deserve. Although I feel a little dehydrated, it's nothing some orange juice won't cure. We didn't order one of the in-room breakfasts because there's a sumptuous buffet downstairs, but I don't want to wake up Jonah when he's finally getting some decent sleep. However, I also really want that orange juice, like, now.

Best of both worlds—I'll sneak out of the room, have some OJ and cereal, then bring Jonah breakfast in bed. Okay, this breakfast is going to be bagels and a cardboard cup of coffee instead of the traditional elegant French toast on a tray, but it's the thought that counts. So I put on jeans and my thickest gray sweater, grab my key card and cell phone, and tiptoe out the door.

My cell phone rings just as I'm pouring maple syrup onto my waffle. I manage to put down the bottle in time to answer. "Carmen! What's up?"

"Just wanted to check in on you. Normally this is the point in your visits home when it stops being merely crazy, and the deep crazy sets in."

She's not wrong, except for the part where I haven't kept her updated on where I am. "Actually, Jonah and I left New Orleans the day after Christmas. We're visiting his family in Chicago."

"Oh, my God. You're in the *deep, deep crazy.*"

"Pretty much," I admit as I slide into a chair at an empty table. "But mostly we've hung out with his brother Maddox, who's awesome."

That's true without being the whole truth. It's as much of Jonah's personal business as I feel comfortable sharing. There might come a time when I could confide more to Carmen, who I trust as much as I do anyone on Earth. But it's not now, while I'm sitting in the middle of a hotel's dining room surrounded by other drowsy travelers.

She says something that surprises me. "You guys are really going to work it out?"

"Um, yeah." I would've thought the trips home to meet each other's families made that clear. Her reluctance comes through too strongly. "I thought you liked Jonah."

"I do, I guess. It's not like I know him that well, and he's not, uh, talkative, but he seems like an okay guy."

"Wow. Don't know if I can handle that much enthusiasm."

"I didn't mean it like that! Jonah's hot. He's smart. He's crazy rich. He may have the single greatest arms I've ever seen on a man. What's not to like?"

I finish chewing a bite of my waffle. “You tell me.”

“This isn’t about Jonah,” Carmen insists. I can hear the tinkling sound of the baby’s mobile in the background; she must be babysitting Nicolas so Shay and Arturo can go out to brunch, or just sleep in. “It’s only that—well—I was wondering whether you and Geordie were back on again?”

“Geordie?” Oh, no. “He didn’t—Geordie hasn’t said—”

“Oh, no, he hasn’t mentioned anything. But you talked about picking him up at the clinic, and you helped make all these arrangements for Christmas, plus I know you guys went out to eat a couple times—”

“It wasn’t candlelight and roses! I mean, one time we went to *Torchy’s*.” Don’t get me wrong; I love Torchy’s. But its indoor location isn’t high on ambiance.

“You also mentioned throwing an alcohol-free New Year’s Eve party,” Carmen continues resolutely. “So it just seems to me like you’ve been thinking about Geordie a lot.”

“Yeah, of course I have. He’s my friend, and he’s going through a rough time.”

“You two were way more than friends a year ago.”

Not this again. Carmen seems really, truly unable to let go of the idea of me and Geordie. “We’ve moved on. People do.”

“Really?”

“*Really,*” I insist.

“Are you sure Geordie has moved on too?”

“Of course he has.” Though I wonder. While I feel sure Geordie has no illusions about our getting back together, and accepts our breakup is for the best—he’s still a little raw about my being with Jonah. It’s a topic I talk around when we’re together.

Then again, everyone sort of hopes to be the one who finds someone new first, don’t they? If Geordie had fallen for somebody else already, I admit, I might be . . . wistful. But that doesn't mean I'd want Geordie back, and I'm pretty sure he isn't longing for me.

"We're fine," I say. "He's just reaching out for support right now, which is exactly what he *should* do while he's in recovery."

"Ohhhh-kay." Carmen gives up the subject, but obviously remains unconvinced. We make some small talk about Nicolas's first Christmas, and how proud his *abuelos* are, before I hang up and finish my breakfast.

As I sip my long-awaited orange juice, I think more about what Carmen has said. It's not that I doubt my conclusions about what Geordie feels, and certainly I understand my own emotions about him. But Carmen's continuing worry strikes me as odd in some way. If she doesn't object to Jonah, and she understands the reasons for our breakup, then why is she so fixated on this?

It hits me just as I'm taking the last bite of my waffle. What if Carmen's thinking so much about Geordie not because she thinks I'm still in love with him, but because *she's* fallen in love with him?

I start to smile. If I'm right . . . this would be *so perfect*. Two of my best friends, together? Carmen's so steady and grounded that she'd help anchor Geordie, and his sense of humor and fun would keep her from wearing herself down with responsibility. It could work.

Not right now, of course. Geordie needs to be a whole lot healthier and stronger before he attempts a new relationship.

But that day will come.

My matchmaking plans keep me amused as I pour Jonah's coffee and fill a bag with bagels and danishes. By the time I'm back on our floor, sliding in the key card, I'm humming the song "Call Me Maybe," for some reason—

"*Vivienne.*" Jonah grabs me almost at the door. He's naked, his hair rumpled. But what strikes me is the tension in his whole body. His arms go around me tightly, like he expects someone to tear me away. "Christ. I thought you were gone."

"I *was* gone. Downstairs. See? I brought you breakfast?"

Jonah doesn't let go. "I mean, I thought—maybe last night took things too far, you wanted to say no and you couldn't, and then you left."

"Hey, hey. Remember what I said? You have to trust me to speak up when it's too much for me. It almost never has been."

"Last night was all about you *not* being able to speak up."

"I was pretending to be drunker than I was. Seriously. Not even hungover today." Mentally I cross this fantasy off the list. While I'm confident in our ability to handle it as beautifully as we did last night, Jonah doesn't share that confidence yet. This one is a step too far, for now. "I'm okay, I swear. Last night was great. And I brought you coffee."

Jonah finally lets go of me and accepts the coffee. But his face remains ashen. Haunted by the thought of the harm he could do without knowing.

SIXTEEN

Normally, if I had an unexpected few hours to spend at the Art Institute of Chicago, I'd head straight for their etchings collection. It would be incredible to soak in the details, study the techniques close up.

But we're here primarily to distract Jonah. My geeking out over beautiful etchings will only isolate him and push him deeper into his thoughts. So instead I lead us on the greatest hits trail—past the Georgia O'Keefe, the classical Indian sculpture, the Impressionists. None of it has much impact until we finally find Hopper's *Nighthawks*.

Most people know this painting more as kitsch—the posters that show James Dean and Marilyn Monroe at the bar instead. As we stand before it today, though, we're able to drink in the painting's true resonance: these strangers drawn together in the night, the unexpected brightness of their clothes compared to the outside gloom, the way this one corner bar seems to be the last source of light in the world. Jonah connects to this one even more than I do, I can tell.

"I always thought of this as a sad painting," Jonah says. His arms are folded across his chest, his gaze locked on the image before us. "You know, barflies getting drunk, all alone. But now I see they're connected to each other. Even if they never met before, they're speaking now. Bitching about . . . I don't know, whatever you'd bitch about then. Dewey versus Truman, maybe."

I smile despite myself. "Yeah. They've found a place not to be alone."

Are these people forming friendships, sharing jokes, truly bringing some brightness to the dark? Or are they sharing one fragile moment before sinking into isolation and despair? You can read the painting either way.

I don't suggest the darker version to Jonah, however. For once, he should get to focus on the light.

One of the reasons I want to be an artist is because art has the power to restore people. If they'll look—*really* look—one simple image can fill their minds with new thoughts, fresh emotions. A piece of art that speaks to you can open windows in a room you hadn't even known was dark.

Nighthawks does this for Jonah. His mood improves as we keep wandering through the exhibitions, and by the time we sit down to our overpriced museum café lunch, he seems like himself again.

"I should've brought you here long ago," he says. We're at a small plastic table, surrounded on every side by tourists from half a dozen countries. "Let you browse to your heart's content. You could show me all the nuances I've been missing."

"Don't sell yourself short. You see a lot on your own." If he hadn't seen so much in my etching of the man holding the bird—would we even be here now? This is the first time it's struck me that if Jonah didn't have an artist's eye, our first split would have been final.

Jonah leans onto the table with both arms. "We could go on a great museums tour sometime. Spend a month of the summer in Europe, going to the Louvre, the British Museum—"

The Reina Sophia! Topkapi Palace! my mind cries. I feel as gleeful as a little kid running around with sparklers. And yet next summer feels almost impossibly far away, on the other side of a long and treacherous journey. Even getting past this afternoon will be a challenge. Then again, Jonah knows that. I lean my elbow on the table, rest my chin in my hand. "You're giving me something to look forward to, aren't you?"

"And me too. With you as my guide, I'd have a whole new way of seeing . . . not just the art. The world." His hand closes over mine, warm and strong. It doesn't matter that we're sitting in a huddle of tourists, wearing the same gray sweaters and blue jeans as half of the other people in the room, surrounded by the clink of cheap silverware and a dozen discarded museum maps. Candlelight and a symphony couldn't make this moment more romantic.

Softly I say, "Then it's a plan."

Neither of us hesitated; we both believe we'll still be together this summer.

This relationship began within a very strict, specific set of boundaries. Now it seems like we're knocking the last of those walls down.

We can get through anything if we're together—even the next few days.

In the early afternoon, we walk back to the same building that houses the Orchid. The snow clouds have finally moved along, leaving behind a flawless blue sky that doesn't seem to belong above the ice-crusted city below. In the sunlight, the metal and glass of the skyscrapers sparkles.

"Looks so much warmer," I say to Jonah as we go inside. "Feels so much colder."

"Just Chicago playing tricks with your head. It loves to do that."

This time, we take a different bank of elevators to go to the residential levels of the building. Maddox has chosen to live only stories from his club. Does he ever feel closed in? No, I realize, he can't. Not with the views from the Orchid, and probably from this apartment too.

So I'm looking forward to getting a look around—until Maddox opens the door, letting us into an argument.

"You're judging me," says a blond woman, voice strained as she paces in the background. "I thought you promised not to do that."

"I'm not judging you," retorts Maddox. "I'm judging *him*."

"Stop calling Griffin *him!*"

Maddox sighs and looks at us like, *You see where this is going.* I don't, but Jonah obviously does. Already his lips are set in a firm line, a small wrinkle between his eyes the only evidence of the frown he's trying to suppress. He says, "Elise? It's me."

"Jonah!"

Elise stops pacing and hurries toward him, arms outstretched, almost like a little kid would. Maybe on some level we always remain childish with the people we knew at the beginning of our lives. Jonah bundles her up in his hug, more openly affectionate than I've ever seen him, except with me.

When he lets go of his sister, I'm able to get a good look at her. She's a couple inches shorter than I am, voluptuous for her height and weight—the kind of woman who probably curses the day the hourglass figure went out of style. Yet her clothing swallows her, pastel drapey stuff that turns her pale, china-doll complexion almost ghostly. Although I know she's older than Maddox, in her late twenties, Elise looks almost like a girl in high school. Her style contains only one element of pure chic—her blond pixie cut frames her round face to perfection. The part of my brain programmed by Mom and Chloe whispers, *Any girl who realizes she can pull off that hairdo ought to know how to dress better.*

Weirdly, I feel like I'm looking at . . . a costume. She wants the world to see her as a fragile child, though I don't know why. My first assumption would be that it's for her own comfort, but I don't think that's the case here. No matter how perfectly this look has been assembled, Elise seems ill at ease within it.

Then again, the situation they're all in is reason enough for discomfort.

"Who's this?" Elise says, looking me up and down.

Jonah's hand brushes against my shoulder. "Elise, this is Vivienne Charles. Vivienne, my sister Elise Hale."

"You're going to love Vivienne," Maddox promises. His mood seems to have lifted with the change of subject. "She's great."

"Thanks," I say. "Pleasure to meet you, Elise."

She smiles, but the expression is stiff. I realize Maddox didn't say I was going to love *her*.

"When is Rebecca phoning in?" Jonah says as we step into the living room.

"About—ten minutes? Let me put out some wine and cheese." Maddox sighs. "We could use the wine, at least."

Unsurprisingly, Maddox's house is as spectacular as his nightclub. While the view beyond the windows dazzles, it's the interior I like best. I see the same sort of earthy colors as in the Orchid, but paler—more sand than stone. The furnishings look to be made of reclaimed wood, or are restored antiques recovered in modern fabrics. Everything looks classic and yet comfortable too. On the floor is a batik rug; on the walls are bookshelves, laden with well-loved novels. This is the home I'd expect for a novelist or a scholar of means, not a nightclub owner. "Your place is gorgeous, Maddox."

"Thank the decorator." He points toward Elise. "She did the club too."

I'm startled. Elise looks like she's deliberately divorced herself from any sense of style—and she's a professional decorator? Then again, this apartment is proof that she knows her stuff. I guess a talented professional always tries to think like her client. "You translated Maddox's spirit," I say. "That's amazing."

"Oh." Her smile gentles. Only then do I realize some of her reserve is insecurity. "Thank you."

"Just wait until she opens her own design business," Maddox says as he puts a large cheese board on the coffee table in front of the taupe suede couch where we're all sitting. "Soon she'll be a decorating star. Maybe we can wrangle you one of those HGTV shows."

I laugh. "You know, I could see it." Certainly Elise is beautiful enough for TV. She just needs an injection of glamour.

Elise ducks her head, runs her hand along the bare nape of her neck. "I'm not in any hurry."

Sounds normal enough, but both Jonah and Maddox stare at her. After a moment, Jonah sighs—disappointed, but not surprised. Maddox is the one who's angry. "You said this year. Which is only a couple days from being next year, but I figured, hey, it takes some time—"

"I have certain advantages at Chapel and Associates, you know?" she says. Each word sounds brittle, on the verge of breaking. "Corporate accounts, health insurance—"

"Come *on*," Maddox snaps. "You're a millionaire, Elise. What the hell are you worrying about insurance for?"

It's not Elise who answers; it's Jonah. "She doesn't need it. Griffin does."

As soon as Jonah pronounces the name *Griffin*, Elise snaps. "How many times do I have to have this conversation today? Don't we have other priorities?"

Maddox looks like he's ready to argue, but Jonah speaks first. "You're right. This isn't the time."

Normally Jonah wouldn't back off so quickly, especially not

when he feels as strongly as he seems to feel about Elise's significant other. But I think he actually backed off because they have so much other family business to deal with. The longer I look at Elise, the more I understand her look. She doesn't try to hide her fragility; she demands that the world see it and acknowledge, on some level, that she has been broken.

"Fine, fine." Maddox surrenders. "It's almost time anyway." He opens his laptop and sits on the sofa on the other side of Jonah. As soon as he signs in to Skype, we get the signal for an incoming call. Maddox hits the key to answer, then grins. "There you are."

"Here I am," says Rebecca.

My first, uncharitable thought is that Jonah got the looks in the family. Not that Rebecca's hideous or anything: *Plain* is the word my mother would use. Her features strongly resemble Jonah's, only more delicate—long face, strong cheekbones, dark hair contrasting with fair skin and pale eyes, though hers are blue instead of gray. She wears a simple white tank top, her hair in a messy bun, no makeup, and a rose-gold pendant around her neck, in the shape of a crescent moon. There's absolutely nothing about her that would make anyone look twice.

She's a botanist at work in the field, you ass, I remind myself. *Probably she's been digging in tropical heat for hours by now. Should she have worn Versace for the occasion?*

Then Rebecca returns Maddox's smile, and in that one instant I realize—when she chooses, Rebecca Marks can be *radiant*.

Her voice is shaded with static; it's not a great connection. "Hi, everyone. Who's the newcomer? You don't look like a lawyer."

"She isn't," Jonah says. "This is Vivienne."

"*Oh*. Hi, Vivienne."

"Hey there."

So, Jonah told at least one of his sisters about me, and she must have liked what she'd heard. Rebecca's eyes shift between me and Jonah knowingly, but she doesn't derail the conversation to tease him. Instead, her smile fades as she says, "All right, let's go ahead and spoil our day already. What's going on with Carter?"

"Short version," Maddox says, "Jonah was questioned in regard to—some crimes in Austin. He's innocent, which we would know anyway, but Vivienne here can absolutely confirm for us and for the police, since she was with him across town at the time. But Carter doesn't believe Vivienne, or he doesn't want to, because he thinks he can use this to his advantage."

"You mean he wants to use the morality clause to rob Jonah of his part of the trust," Rebecca says.

Elise nods. "Precisely."

"He's doomed to failure, obviously," Maddox continues. "However, he could cause a lot of trouble for Jonah in between."

"What else can he do?" I ask. "Legally, I mean." Other than offering Jonah the buyout, it seems like Carter has nothing else to try.

"Not much, but he can feed the story to a tabloid or TMZ," Elise says. "He's done it before. There's not one of us he won't rake across the coals if it earns him a few lines of sympathetic press. If he went public with this? Jonah would have to live with all the shame of a conviction, even though he's done nothing."

Maddox swears under his breath. "Basically, he's blackmailing Jonah for something Jonah didn't do."

"He thinks I'm guilty." Jonah's expression is grim. "Doesn't matter. The point is, I'm innocent. In the end, nothing's going to happen to me. I'd rather this were kept secret, but I don't want any of you putting yourselves on the line to protect me from—harassment, nothing more."

"And show Dad he can divide-and-conquer us?" Maddox retorts. "No way. We stick together no matter what."

"That's the only thing he ever taught us," Elise says, too lightly.

"And it's the only lesson he never wanted us to learn. I love it when we prove he doesn't actually control our entire lives."

Jonah shakes his head. "Carter controls the board of trustees. That's enough."

Rebecca leans forward, her oval face filling the laptop screen. "You guys aren't thinking strategically."

They all stare at her, genuinely taken aback. I can believe that this soft-spoken, no-nonsense scientist doesn't get into the family drama often—and I've already heard them talking about how hard they try to keep her out of it. Right now, however, her blue eyes are bright, and the flush in her cheeks testifies to the emotion pent up inside.

Jonah finally asks, "Strategy?"

"The best defense is a good offense," Rebecca says. "We have to go after him. Screw with *his* head for a change, and see how he likes it."

Elise sighs. "As much as I like the sound of that—and I like it a lot—what are we supposed to go after him with? Say he made up all the stories about Mom? We know he didn't."

"We could come up with something," Maddox says. A frown line appears between his eyes. "Say he—he came to us with some plan to go around the board of directors? Like he's screwing with the business? There's a meeting of the Oceanic board tomorrow; he's planning to fly out of town immediately afterward. Instead we could go in there, bust it up, turn them against him."

"I don't know enough corporate law to make that convincing." Jonah's voice is heavy. "You're more of a businessman than I am, Mad, but I doubt you could pull it off either."

In disbelief, I look from one to the other. Why isn't anyone suggesting the obvious? Then it hits me—to them, it isn't obvious. It wouldn't have been obvious to me either, until very recently. Not until I fell for Jonah and learned this painful, precious lesson: Honesty is the only way out. No matter how deep it cuts, no matter how much you bleed, the truth can still save you. It's the only thing that can.

"Guys?" I begin. They all turn toward me; obviously nobody expected me to chime in, but nobody tells me to butt out either. "If you want to take Carter down, you can't use his methods. You have to be better than that. More fearless."

"What do you mean?" Elise says. Jonah straightens, no doubt realizing what I'm about to say. I give him one second to stop me if I'm going too far—and I might be. But he doesn't say a word.

So I take a deep breath and finish. "Carter's prepared to go public with a lie? Then we tell him you're prepared to go public with the truth."

It's as if a lightning bolt crashed into this room. All of them gape, and my hair stands on end, as if charged. Maddox manages to speak first. "When you say the truth—"

"She means the truth," Rebecca says. Her blue eyes blaze through the computer screen. As quiet as this woman first seemed to me, now I see the steel in her. "We tell the world what he did to our mother, what he did to us. We tell everyone what really happened inside Redgrave House. All of it."

Elise starts shaking her head no, but she looks toward Maddox for guidance. Maddox says, "You realize there's no taking that back. Ever."

"That's the point, Mad." The fury in Jonah's face is close to joy. Closer to danger. This is Jonah the predator, the one who gets off on power, domination and control. I've only ever seen him like this in bed. It scares me as much as it turns me on. "That's exactly what Vivienne is saying. If we want to defeat Carter, half measures won't do. No temporary fixes. No, we have to go nuclear. We have to *destroy* him."

SEVENTEEN

We walk back into the Hale Hotel Group building the next day, barely pausing at the security desk. "We're going up," Maddox says to the guards—not unpleasantly, but in a tone that doesn't allow for argument. I'm alongside Maddox, while Elise brings up the rear. Her deliberately childlike appearance is even more strikingly odd in this building, where she contrasts so strongly with the polished black stone around us.

Jonah's three steps ahead of everyone else. The nearest guard only manages to unlock the turnstile in the moment before Jonah strides through it. His shoulders are braced like a boxer preparing to go back into the ring.

I hope that's a metaphor. I'm not sure. The scarcely bottled tension within Jonah is clearly on the verge of exploding.

Only after the elevator doors shut around us does Maddox mutter, "I'm not as sure about this as you guys."

Jonah looks at him, his eyes like steel. He doesn't want anyone to get in his way—not even his beloved brother. "If you're having second thoughts, say so now."

"I'm not going to back down," Maddox insists. The glowing numbers over the doors mark ever-higher stories; I swallow to pop my ears. "Just making sure we're all clear this is going to be the biggest shitshow any of us has ever seen."

Elise sighs. "I'm not looking forward to being hounded by the paparazzi either. But it's not going to come to that. Is it?"

Jonah turns toward them. "You both need to be clear on this: If Carter calls our bluff, we're going through with it." He emphasizes every word, like separate shots from a gun. "If either of you backs down, that's it. We're done. And once Carter thinks he can get away with this, he'll believe he can get away with anything."

"He *has* gotten away with everything." Elise sounds sharper, harder—more knowing. I think this is the first time I've heard her true voice.

"Until now. We stop it here." Jonah looks at his two siblings, whose uncertainty is far clearer in this small private space. Grandstanding for the crowd is one thing; facing down something harsh one-on-one is a hell of a lot harder. I watch his expression change as he finally remembers himself for a moment. "I realize you're taking this step only to protect me. Thank you for that."

"It's not just for you." Maddox's laugh breaks off, awkward and unfinished. "Like you said, if this doesn't work, we're all done. You're just the first one on Dad's chopping block. He still means to break us eventually. Each and every one of us. So we stand up now."

A silence falls. They're going ahead with this—I know that—but I also know how completely freaked-out they all feel. Even Jonah. His fury masks deeper, less obvious emotions, but by now I understand this man enough to realize what he's enduring inside. I felt some shadow of it when Jonah confronted Anthony—the first time anyone confronted my rapist about exactly what he'd done to me. I felt exhilaration, yes, and power too, but also a sick kind of fear. Before that I knew the boundaries of my suffering as well as a longtime prisoner must know the dimensions of his cell. When the truth came out, I realized everything would change. Sometimes it's hard to let go of the pain you already know.

As it turns out, things seem to have changed for the better. Yet I didn't know it when we stood on my parents' lawn, my heart pounding as Jonah finally saw Anthony for what he really was. Then I felt as if I had just been pushed over a cliff.

And even I have never had the strength to confront Anthony myself, in my own voice, the way they're about to confront Carter Hale.

"Sometimes—" I begin, and they all three stare at me. "Sometimes there are secrets we keep to protect other people. But sometimes there are secrets we have to tell to protect ourselves."

Maddox nods, but absently. He's so focused on the confrontation ahead that he can't really hear me. Elise, however—it's like she's on the verge of anger, asking me where the hell I get off, lecturing her on how to deal with this. I couldn't blame her if she felt that way. But even as she opens her mouth, I see comprehension sink in. Elise might not have discovered exactly what happened in my past, but she knows we share enough for me to understand.

Jonah's gray eyes meet mine. I expect to see the same empathy there, maybe mixed in with his anger for Carter. Instead what I see is a fury that goes so deep it frightens me. It's as if, in this instant, Jonah has forgotten how to feel anything but hate.

I used to think he was so cool, so untouchable. But now I wonder whether Jonah is like one of the dormant volcanoes he studies—solid as stone, proud as a mountain, seemingly implacable but with a fire deep within that could erupt at any time.

I reach for his hand—his touch would reassure me—but that's when the elevator stops and opens the door with a chime. The show is on.

We can hear Carter's voice from the boardroom as we walk down the hallway. Various scurrying interns and secretaries part to clear our way like the Red Sea around Moses. "If we call a shareholder meeting, within the—" Carter's drone shifts up an octave as he sees us walk in. "What are you doing here?"

"Final negotiations," Jonah replies.

Carter laughs. "You're in no position to negotiate."

But Jonah isn't so easily baited. "We'll see. Ladies and gentlemen of the board, I apologize for the intrusion. This won't take long."

A dozen people in polished business suits stare at us like we just spilled out of a clown car. Clearly most of them know who Jonah, Maddox, and Elise are, but none of them have the slightest clue why we've shown up today. Carter looks down at the tablet in front of him, like some data for review is more important than anything we could possibly say.

Jonah addresses the room. "Mr. Hale has made a buyout offer for my share of the trust, which would give him a controlling interest in Oceanic. Although he'll deny it, he intends to release false information about me if I don't accept the offer."

Carter looks up then, squinting at Jonah. He believes in Jonah's guilt so deeply that he can't comprehend the confidence he sees.

As for Jonah, he sounds . . . reasonable. Measured. He has banked down his anger so that he can get close enough to deliver the killing blow.

"Should Mr. Hale take this step," Jonah continues, "my siblings and I will feel obligated to release some completely true information about Mr. Hale. It will be personal. It will be graphic. If it weren't for the statute of limitations, it would be criminal. And it will be, without question, the biggest scandal this company has ever seen. We are all prepared to sign affidavits, to speak to the press, and to testify in court if necessary. You should understand—if it comes to that, there is very little question that this board would be compelled to ask Mr. Hale to step down as CEO."

"What the hell are you talking about?" Carter says.

"You *know*, Dad." Maddox bunches his fists in the pockets of his camel hair overcoat. "Don't pretend not to get it. This one time—you don't have to admit it—just don't pretend you don't know what we're talking about. Could you give me that much honesty for once in your life?"

The naked plea there breaks my heart. Maddox is the unluckiest of the kids, I realize. He's the only one who still wishes his father were someone he could love.

Carter doesn't give his son that small sign of respect, but he hesitates one moment too long before answering. "This is nonsense. You're disrupting this meeting for no purpose."

Everyone else sitting around the boardroom stares at Carter. None of them can guess what's going on, but by now they've all realized Jonah isn't bluffing. Our threat may be veiled, but it's real.

"We'll all testify to this," Elise stresses. She has found her strength at last. "In court, in affidavits, or even to the *National* fucking *Enquirer* if it comes to that. Just know this, Dad. If you fire the first shot—we'll fire the second. And the second shot will be the last one you ever hear."

Jonah keeps going, as smoothly as though nobody else had said a word since we walked into the room. "Finally, if Mr. Hale does seek retribution for my rejection of his offer, both recipients of the trust are prepared to sign over all proceeds of the trust to charity, effective immediately."

Carter blanches. "That's not—"

"It's a clause in the trust, as you know," Jonah says. Only now does he look directly at Carter. There's no hint of the depthless contempt he feels on his face; it's all in his voice, in every word he speaks to his stepfather. "We're legal adults. So if both Rebecca and I choose, we can surrender the entire trust—including all our stock in Oceanic Airlines—to any mutually agreed-upon, legitimate charity. We spoke earlier today and agreed we especially like Carbon Cull."

Carbon Cull is an environmental group specifically targeting the enormous air pollution caused by jets. The first thing they'd do with such a massive interest in the airline is slash into profits in order to save the world. Not a bad plan, really. But to judge by Carter Hale's ashen face, he doesn't agree.

"You can't do that," Carter says. At first he sounds hoarse and weak—like someone punched in the gut—but he regains some strength as he keeps going. "Rebecca would have to be here in person to register her vote on that, and she shows no sign of returning from the jungle anytime soon."

"Nope," Maddox says. "But according to the trust, Rebecca can designate a legal proxy to conduct business for her in the United States during her absence, if she fills out the proper forms and e-mails them to us—and as of ten minutes ago, she has."

Carter's face has turned red with rage, or maybe embarrassment at his total powerlessness. "A *proxy*?"

I raise my hand and wave. "Hi."

One of the executives seated around the table glares at Carter over the rims of her eyeglasses. "Mr. Hale, is this situation likely to arise? Because I needn't explain how . . . problematic that would be for Oceanic Airlines."

That's corporate-speak for *Shut up about Jonah*.

Carter turns toward Jonah, and when I see his face, I shudder. The anger within Carter now is worse than the fury I saw in Jonah while we rode the elevator. It's vicious, contemptuous—almost reptilian. This is my one glimpse of the true Carter Hale. This is what he looked like when he dragged a young boy into the bedroom to watch his mother being raped.

"This is merely a hypothetical," Carter says. His answer is for the executive, but his gaze never leaves Jonah. "We won't be dealing with that situation anytime soon."

The executives are relieved. Maddox breathes out heavily, and

Elise sags against his arm. They think that because the confrontation is over, the danger has passed.

But I see the way Carter and Jonah are looking at each other. Under his breath, Carter says, "This isn't over. It hasn't even begun."

Carter Hale will want revenge for this someday. Soon.

For now, though, Jonah has won.

"You're sure you won't come with us?" Maddox holds open the taxicab door, while Elise smiles out at us, like we might all four pile in the back. "Dad backed down! His tail was practically between his legs. You don't think that's worth a bottle of champagne?"

"No," Jonah says. His expression is unfathomable. The gray winter day seems to have claimed him—his pale skin, his eyes, the light blue of his muffler reflecting the metal city and frozen river around us. "Vivienne and I need some time."

I don't need any time. But if Jonah does, okay. "We'll see you guys again before we leave town," I promise. "Besides, I bet the two of you can murder a bottle of champagne all on your own."

Elise laughs. "I won't mind trying!"

Maddox wraps me in a one-armed hug, which I return. He smells like sandalwood. Then he turns toward Jonah, and his gaze betrays how worried he is. "Sure you're all right?"

"When have I ever been?" Jonah says. It's not a joke. "Go have fun, Mad. We'll talk soon."

Although Maddox clearly remains unconvinced, he nods. Silently he hugs Jonah, embracing him a moment longer than he did me. "Good-bye," he says against Jonah's shoulder. Then he turns back toward the cab, giving all his attention to Elise as brother and sister take off to celebrate.

After the car pulls away, I slide my arm through Jonah's. "Now what?"

"We're going home."

"Okay." His decision is sudden, but I want to support him. Besides, the novelty of the snow is wearing off. "I doubt we could catch a night flight back to Austin, but there's got to be one tomorrow."

"I didn't mean Austin." He begins walking forward, pulling me alongside him.

"Then what—"

"Like Maddox said, Carter's flying out right after the board meeting. His fucking helicopter's on the roof, pretentious bastard." Jonah glances up at the skyscraper behind us, as if his gaze were a missile that could shoot the copter down. "Mad and Elise will go to his club. Mom's still swaddled in her luxury spa in the desert. So that means the house is ours."

"Redgrave House," I say. "We're going there?"

"Now."

For lots of guys, inviting his girlfriend to see his childhood home would be a sweet gesture. The kind of thing you see in cheesy television ads for engagement rings.

For Jonah, this is a journey to the scene of the crime.

EIGHTEEN

We walk to Redgrave House. It's located close enough for me to endure the chill that long, despite the icy air that creeps in at my coat's sleeves and collar.

If Jonah even feels the cold, he shows no sign.

His family home is one of the few private residences remaining in downtown Chicago, a building listed on the National Historic Register. I knew what the front of the house looked like before I ever met Jonah; it was featured in the art nouveau section of a Decorative Architecture seminar I took.

Yet this knowledge hasn't prepared me for the impact of seeing Redgrave House in person.

As we walk closer, the house slowly takes shape in the snowy night. First I make out the grayish stone stretching up for four stories, so skillfully designed that even the enormous skyscrapers nearby don't make it any less imposing. Then I see the famous caryatids, statues of women nearly two stories high. They wear classical drapery that clings to their muscular forms, and they each seem to bow their head under the weight of the cornice they support. Snow and ice have crusted on the statues' faces, as if someone had wanted to blind them.

Jonah's hand grips mine like a lifeline, but he doesn't look over at me once as he punches in a security code at the gate. The lock clicks and falls open, clearing our path to the enormous red doors.

From his pocket, he takes a key—not one he carries on his normal chain. It's brass, I think, larger than keys are made today, complete with an ornate fob. As he slides it into the keyhole, I find myself remembering fairy tales. Mysteries. The kinds of stories that would begin with such a key.

Nobody ever starts a horror story that way. Which is strange, considering what happened in this house.

Inside it's completely dark. When Jonah finds the light switch, an enormous chandelier glows bright, revealing the interior to me. I see—perfection. Or what my mother would call perfection, because everything from the hardwood floor to the Aubusson rugs to the pristine white furnishings is expensive, designer, and flawless. My mother wouldn't care that this place feels utterly emotionally cold.

Not one picture on the walls reveals any sense of artistic taste or emotional connection. They seem to have been chosen merely to match the paler-than-pale color scheme. No photos of Jonah or his siblings are displayed anywhere. Not a single houseplant blooms from a pot. I'm grateful there's no pet, for the animal's sake. Instead everything is laid out with the sterile precision of a surgeon's operating theater. A marble-topped coffee table displays a fan of decorating magazines that probably were never read; the floors shine so brilliantly that I hesitate to step off the smaller rug near the door, thinking the surface might be slippery and wet.

Jonah answers the question without my even having to ask it. "We spent most of our time upstairs," he says, as he pushes the heavy door shut. Then he slides a heavy dead bolt lock into place; it feels like he's sealed us off from the rest of the world.

"Upstairs. Okay." I tug off my knit cap and tuck a lock of my hair behind one ear. "Why?"

"These rooms are like the façade. They're meant to impress the outside world—for receptions, dinner parties, their 'charity' events where they show off." Jonah's stare is remote. "The upper stories served as our cage."

A shiver runs along my back. But when Jonah grips my hand in his, I let him pull me onto the stairs—steep and dark. These weren't built to enhance the grand spectacle of the ground floor. Their narrowness suggests that nobody would ever want to walk up, or perhaps that nobody could easily get out.

"Where's the butler?" I meant it as a joke to defuse the tension, but then I realize it's a valid question.

"None of the staff lives in," Jonah says, his gaze locked on the landing above us. "Carter never wanted that. He wants to be waited on hand and foot, but he also wants silence. Secrecy. He doesn't want extra witnesses."

The landing on the second floor is clean but nondescript. Hunter green paint on the walls darkens the space and makes it feel smaller. Although there's no visible line, I can sense the division between Carter and Lorena, the way they've split their house in two. There's a distinct lack of any furnishing or clutter on his side, while a stack of old newspapers rests in her corner beneath an oil painting of racehorses, which hangs askew on the wall.

"We slept on the third floor," Jonah says, as he stares up the next flight of steps. "We had a playroom, which was supposed to be a privilege. Really Carter didn't want us in the rest of his house or his life, except when and how he chose."

"Did they keep your room the way it was?" I know the answer is *no* before I ask. But I want to learn how Jonah will respond. What does he need from this house? What does he want? Surely not nostalgia . . .

"I haven't been upstairs once since I left home at eighteen." He shows no sign of wanting to go up now either. "Come on."

Jonah opens Carter's door. The word *trespassing* flashes through my mind, but that's ridiculous. While I was talking through legal stuff with the family on the Skype call, Maddox mentioned that the trust guarantees that Jonah will always own a share of this house. You can't trespass on your own property.

Yet my nerves jangle. My heart races. We aren't breaking the law; we're breaking a taboo. That's more frightening by far.

Carter's rooms are almost empty. The furnishings are antique pieces, ornately scrolled, but set so far apart from each other that this could be a showroom. Heavy, dark drapes seal out whatever light could shine through the windows. No photographs. The only sign of modernity is a top-of-the-line sound system, which lines most of one wall. Jonah snaps it on, tunes it to satellite radio, and turns from droning business reports until he finds classical music. Opera.

"*Don Giovanni*," Jonah says. He doesn't look at me. He doesn't let go of my hand. Instead he turns the volume up so loud that the house seems to vibrate around us. "Very near the end."

I wince against the thunderous bass voice that seems to fill this room. At this decibel level, the opera seems less beautiful. More aggressive.

Jonah pulls me away. At first I'd thought he was going to vandalize this space, and that I'd have to talk him out of it. Destruction of property would be a crime, one Carter would surely prosecute. But Jonah simply drags me along until we reach an inner door, one that leads to a completely bare room.

Wooden floor. Golden walls. And on the longest wall, an enormous fireplace—one with a green marble mantel, held up by two columns.

We can only be passing through. "That door—" I point to the one opposite us. "Does that lead to your mother's side of the house?"

"Yes." But Jonah doesn't walk toward it. He's breathing faster.

"Nothing to see there. Unless you were wondering what Miss Havisham's house would look like in the twenty-first century."

I wasn't. "Jonah, what are we doing here?"

"This was the only room." Jonah lets go of my hand to pace around the octagonal room, like a panther in a cage. "The only one he never used. He'd drag her out of her bedroom. Up to our rooms, sometimes, when Rebecca and Mad weren't home. In the hall, on the fucking stairs. But for some reason he never did it here. I guess he just never got around to doing that."

I know, now, what Jonah wants. "The one room he kept clean," I say. "You want to defile it."

He doesn't even look at me. "Take off your clothes. *Now.* You don't leave here until I say so. And you don't get to leave without being fucked."

We've gone to some troubling places together. Wrestled with our most intimate and shameful demons. But something about this moment, this scene, feels more dangerous than anything that went before.

If that's what Jonah needs, I can give it to him.

I let my coat fall to the floor, toe off my boots, step on the toes of my socks to ditch them too. When I unbuckle my belt, Jonah grabs it from me. The leather slithers hot and fast against my palm.

"Come on," he says, his voice shaking in . . . impatience. Need. Something else I dare not identify. "Come on."

Sweater. Now panties. Jonah's eyes darken as he sees me bare from the waist down, or the pale pink traces of my nipples through the lace of my bra. As soon as I've unhooked it, Jonah wheels me around so he can yank my hands behind my back. He winds my belt around my wrists, a binding that won't give. Only once I'm naked and tied does he push me to my knees.

"You're all whores," Jonah says as he comes toward me, unfastening his pants. "Every single one of you. Do you think you're different? Do you think you're better? You're not. I'm going to teach you what you are."

His words lash me, though in the way I want to be lashed. All our pent-up ugliness flows free at moments like this—when it's no longer our prison but our fuel.

Jonah takes out his enormous cock. The first time I saw the length of him, he intimidated me. I'd never been with a guy even close to that big, and felt like he'd break me in two. Even now, after all we've done, I find myself trembling. His thumb pushes between my lips as he forces my mouth open.

"Wider," he says as I struggle to accommodate him. "Take it all. I want you to gag."

I try. It's hard—he'll pull back just enough to get the friction, to feel me choke—but then he's in there, all the way in, and my throat convulses around him. Jonah groans in satisfaction.

"You're all like this." His voice is ragged as he rocks forward and back, the huge head of his cock filling my mouth and throat in turn. "You think you want it soft. You think you get to say when. But you don't. Not with me. I own you, do you understand? I fucking own you."

Will he come in my mouth? I'm ready for that. I like it.

And yet Jonah senses this. *Hates* it. He pushes me back so hard that I nearly fall. "You think you want it, don't you? But you don't want what I'm going to do to you. I'm going to find your limit, and that's where I'm going to break you, do you understand?"

"You don't get to break me," I retort. I can't get a handle on the scenario he wants. Submission didn't work? I'll try defiance.

That's closer. Jonah's eyes blaze as he hauls me to my feet. Leather snaps around my wrists as he rips my belt away. "Run," he says. "While you can."

I dash for the door, the one that leads to Carter's side of the house, and tear naked through these nearly empty rooms. The opera music swells louder, until it's almost deafening—and the melody has shifted into a minor key. The chorus sounds ominous. Whatever this opera is about, it's no love story.

Scrambling, I find my way into Carter's bedroom and slam the door behind me. There's a lock, but I hesitate before turning it. Would Jonah kick the door down? Is that something he wants discovered?

My hesitation lasts too long. Jonah shoulders through.

He says nothing, merely grabs my shoulders to push me into the wall again. I wriggle free and lunge through the nearest open door—the one that leads to an enormous, opulent bathroom in marble. This takes me nowhere. Then Jonah's arm closes around my waist, and his hand fists in my hair.

As I cry out, he says, "You can't get away. Fight all you want. But you can't. You're mine."

I thrash in his grip, to no avail. Jonah picks me up and slings me over his shoulder. Dizzy, upside down, I can only dimly see that Jonah's opening all the drawers, in search of something. What? A hairbrush to spank me with?

He turns and strides out with me dangling on his shoulder like a caveman's prize. At first I think he'll throw me on Carter's bed and take me there—Freudian revenge—but instead he marches us back to that one bare room. The only place in this house where he hasn't witnessed a rape: That's where he wants to commit one.

Jonah drops me back onto my feet. I try to spin away from him, but he slaps me across the face. Hard.

I stagger into the wall, my back pressed against the carved wood. It's all right for Jonah to hit me during one of our games; that's in our rules. As long as he doesn't intend to injure or scar me, I'm his to smack around. But actually having him do it, that hard, shocks me more than I'd realized it would.

"You don't think it can get worse?" Jonah mutters. I realize what he's holding in his other hand; it's a tub of petroleum jelly. "It's about to."

With that he shoves me so hard that I fall, knees jarring against the floor. My cry of pain is genuine. He's still within our boundaries, but only now do I realize how comfortable I'd become within our games. Not since the first time he took me has this fantasy felt so dangerous. So real.

"Brace yourself." Jonah gets down on his knees behind me and grabs my hair again. "Find something to hold you up, or else I'm going to fuck you through the floor."

I'm only a few paces from the fireplace, so I crawl toward that, grabbing the marble pillar with both hands. My breaths are coming so deep and fast that I'm panting, and the marble feels good against my sweaty hands.

"Spread your legs. Wider," Jonah commands me. I obey. The plastic clatter of a lid hits the floor—and then I feel Jonah's slicked fingers at the entrance to my ass.

Oh, God. He's only ever fucked my ass once. It scared me beforehand, during, and ever since. I came so hard, but with a vibrator, something we don't have now. This time, it's enough for Jonah to humiliate me. To subject me to something I've always found frightening and shameful. Maybe he even wants to hurt me.

Silver, whispers the voice in my head. But I don't need the safe word. Not yet. This scares me, but it excites me even more.

Two fingers inside me now. Three. My body stretches around him, and my face flushes hot as I imagine how he must see me in this moment. The cheek he slapped burns, and tears are welling in my eyes.

He notices. "Cry for me again. Cry all you want. Doesn't do a damned bit of good."

I don't feel the need to weep. It's shame coming over me now, deep primal shame. That's enough to turn my face scarlet and scramble every thought in my head. Enough to drive me wild.

Silver, I think. I say nothing. Because shame is something else Jonah gives me, something I enjoy so much more than I want to.

Jonah's pants slip further down his body with the rustling of wool, the clinking of his belt. The head of his cock presses against the entrance to my ass, firm and insistent. "Don't you want to beg me? Even just to use your cunt instead?"

"Would—" My throat closes around the word. "Would it make any difference if I did?"

"No," Jonah says, and he pushes inside.

Fuck. My jaw drops. The aching burn is so intense it's as if I'm being turned inside out. Jonah's enormous cock presses deeper into me—slowly, but without ceasing. I moan in defeat, and yet also in pleasure. Jonah has erased every objection, every coherent thought. Now I am nothing but his vessel.

Then Jonah starts fucking me in earnest, his strokes going deeper and faster. The petroleum jelly slicks me enough that the friction doesn't hurt; that doesn't change the fact that I feel split apart. Speared. As he speeds up, my joints rock and I have to brace myself harder against the mantelpiece. My hair swings around my face, tendrils sticking to my sweaty, flushed cheeks.

"I'm using you." Jonah's growl is one of animal triumph. "You're only in this world so I can use you."

He grabs my hair again, tighter. Again I shout in pain, but Jonah doesn't even hear. He's slamming into me now, the slap of his body against mine echoing obscenely in the small room. Through the haze of arousal I can see only the empty fireplace in front of me, the ashes left behind. It's like I can't feel anything in the world but his cock, the way he's taken me over completely—

The pleasure swells inside me. It has little to do with the way

Jonah's abusing my body, everything to do with my twisted satisfaction in that abuse. All I know is that the more savagely Jonah fucks my ass, the more desperation in my wordless cries, the better it is for us both. Jonah has set his demons loose, all of them, and we are holding absolutely nothing back.

A thrust, and my arousal peaks. Another, and it goes higher. Jonah pushes me, and pushes me, and even as my body has begun to burn, the world has gone dark and sparkly around the edges. The next time Jonah buries himself balls-deep in my ass, he pushes me over the edge. I scream the raw sound of orgasm, hands shaking against the marble pillar, Jonah's cock still pumping inside.

If Jonah knows I came, he doesn't acknowledge it. He just keeps going. "You bitch," he pants. "You fucking bitch. You think this is as bad as it can get? We're not even close. Wait until you find out what I have for you."

What next? I can hardly think. I want to collapse into postorgasmic jelly, but instead I have to keep bracing myself against his assault. Will he use me until I collapse? I shouldn't want that as much as I do.

All right, I think. *All right*. Complete surrender can feel so sweet.

"Just wait. Then we'll know what it takes to break you." Jonah slams into me again, so hard I wince. "What it takes to destroy you."

Yes, Jonah, yes, do whatever you want with me. I have no choice. I'm yours to do what you want with—anything you want—

Suddenly he jerks back. His cock slides from my body. Despite my exhausted shaking, I try to remain braced. God only knows what he'll do to me next. But when he remains quiet for a few moments, I dare to glance over my shoulder at him.

Jonah is rising to his feet, his still-hard cock jutting from him. His eyes are glazed like a man in a trance, and he's started shaking even harder than me.

"Silver," he says. "Silver."

It takes a moment for this to sink in. "You—*you* need to use the safe word?"

He nods as he takes a step backward from me, then another, until he thuds against the wall. Then he slides down it and curls into a ball, drawing his knees up until he can lean his head on them, hiding his face.

Jonah gets to have limits too. Whatever we found in this house—whatever primal scene he was reenacting—it finally took us to his limit, and past it.

Slowly, still naked and glistening from the Vaseline he used, I crawl toward him on trembling limbs. He doesn't acknowledge me until I sit beside him and gingerly slide one arm around his shoulders. Then Jonah leans against me, burying his face in the side of my neck. His breaths catch in his throat, and I wonder if I will finally see this strong, implacable, unbreakable man start to cry.

I don't. He holds it together. But we have to sit in this nightmarish house, in this barren room, for a very long time before either of us can move. Even then, we do not speak.

NINETEEN

"You're sure you're okay?"

"I'm fine. Can we just not—"

"Okay, Jonah. It's okay. But you'd tell me if I needed—if we needed—"

"Just *come here*."

We're back in our room at the Drake Hotel, Jonah's half-dressed in his undershirt and socks as he crawls into bed and holds his arm out for me. Despite the muscular strength evident in every sinew of his body, I see only the vulnerability in him. His gray eyes have never looked so haunted.

I slip under the covers beside him, still in my jeans and bra. Jonah wraps his arms around me, both giving comfort and seeking it. My body's soreness matters little compared to the tension I feel in his every limb.

This should feel like sanctuary. A place of rest. Instead all I can think is that, at Redgrave House, I saw Jonah begin to shatter—and that process is still taking place. What happens when he's totally fallen apart?

He won't. Jonah's stronger than that. You've both faced terrible truths, alone, for a long time now. You have the ability to face them together.

So I tell myself, and so I believe. Yet the person who needs to believe it most is Jonah, and right now, I doubt he could even hear me say the words, much less acknowledge their truth.

Finally I understand more of what Doreen was trying to say to me back when Jonah and I first reunited. She warned me about our limits, about how much more difficult a relationship becomes without them. I thought she was warning me about intense games like the one we just played out in Redgrave House, but that wasn't what she meant at all.

She meant that when people push beyond their boundaries, we have to discover what lies on the other side.

What hides within Jonah's darkness? I know it, roughly; I recognize its shape. But the full dimensions of his pain remain murky, perhaps unfathomable.

As I hold him tighter and close my eyes, I find myself remembering antique maps I've studied. In the margins, upon seas no Westerner had ever traveled, the calligraphy reads: *Here be dragons.*

We don't sleep well that night. Jonah's bad dreams jostle me awake, again and again. When I gently shake his shoulder, he regains consciousness just enough to put his arms around me once more. That helps him for a while.

But never for very long.

Jonah's solemn silence continues the next day, all through our checkout from the hotel and our ride to the airport. I'm exhausted and worried, and I keep biting my ragged lips, which are chapped from the unfamiliar cold. Elise has drawn back into herself; she sits in the front passenger seat, the collar of her white leather coat turned up, staring into the distance.

Thank God for Maddox. "Like I'd make you guys take a taxi," he says as he steers his McLaren sports car through the salt-crusted streets. "You're my family. Why would I turn you over to some Uber driver?"

"I hear some of those drivers are dangerous," Elise murmurs, without glancing toward her brother.

"You'd be fine with us," Jonah says. He's staring out the window at the cityscape around us, which grows less spectacular, more humdrum, as we get farther from downtown and into the burbs. I'd worry Jonah was upset with me if it weren't for his leather-gloved hand over mine. He holds on tightly, never letting go for a moment.

Some guys with luxury cars freak out at the slightest hint of damage or even wear. Maddox, however, obviously understands that cars are for driving. Sludge and spatter don't deter him as he darts in and out of traffic, determined to get us there in plenty of time. Yet he has enough attention left over to detect the strange, flat silence in the car, which he combats by turning up the satellite radio. Latin piano music cascades through the car, rippling like sunlight on water.

Jonah's murky temper makes sense to me. Yesterday he found his breaking point, and it's going to take him a while to pull back from that. I'm quiet mostly because I'm worried about him, and tired. Maddox has to drive. It's Elise's silence I don't understand.

I mean, yesterday, we *shut down* Carter Hale. Embarrassed him in front of the airline's board of directors, and made it clear that he can't dominate his children one day longer. Shouldn't she be elated? At least, you know, *happy*? Maddox seems cheerful enough—

Cut it out, I tell myself. *Elise's mood is her own business. You're only thinking about her because that doesn't hurt as much as worrying about Jonah.*

We get to the airport and say our farewells to Maddox in the usual jumbled line of cars and suitcases. As taxicabs crawl past us, Maddox embraces Elise, then Jonah, who wraps his arms around his little brother as if Maddox were the one who needed protection. When Maddox turns to me, I'm pleasantly surprised at how natural it feels when he hugs me too.

"Be there for Jonah, okay?" he whispers into my ear. "He needs to let someone take care of him for once."

"I'm figuring that out."

I kiss Maddox's cheek, and he rewards me with a smile.

After the usual tedium of airport security, we sit down in what passes for a decent restaurant in O'Hare and have the most awkward family lunch ever.

"You'll be okay in Texas?" Elise asks Jonah. "The police aren't—they won't give you any trouble?"

He shrugs. "They don't have anything new to give me trouble about."

"They didn't have anything in the first place," she points out. "That didn't stop them."

"It's going to be fine, sooner or later," I interject. Hopefully sooner.

Jonah finally snaps into focus as he turns his gaze on his sister. "And you're going back to Griffin?"

She freezes—seemingly literally, with her entire body going stiff, and her skin turning pale. "Are we going to have this conversation again?"

"So that's a yes." Jonah sighs heavily. "Does he still make you live in that slum hole of an apartment?"

Elise lifts her chin. "Griffin doesn't want to be supported by my money. I think that's honorable."

"Fine. Great. He can pay for his own place. But he could let *you* live somewhere decent, or accept that living with you isn't the same thing as mooching off you."

"He's proud, okay? It's not the worst thing."

"He can't handle the reality that you're richer than he is and always will be. So he controls you. Is he still picking out your clothes?" Jonah's eyes narrow. "Is he still picking out your friends too? How long before he demands that you cut one of us loose? Or maybe he wants to push your entire family out."

Elise goes very still. I think Jonah believed he was exaggerating, but he hit it exactly. Griffin wants Elise to separate herself from her family, and she must be considering it.

Elise whispers, "You don't understand. You never will."

Jonah's cool anger cracks, and once again I see the raw pain he usually hides so well. "I'll be back," he says as he gets up and wanders in the general direction of the restrooms. Really I think he's going to walk out of sight and simply stand there for a few minutes, regaining his composure.

Now Elise and I are alone for the first time ever, and I have no idea what to say. *So, tell me about Griffin!* Yeah, no. And what else do we have to talk about? Maddox, I guess—though as I recall, Maddox wasn't fond of Griffin either. But just before I start spouting some inanity about the cold weather, I see a single tear well in Elise's eye, then trickle down her cheek.

"Hey," I murmur, offering her a Kleenex from my purse. "It's okay."

"Is it?"

My instincts tell me to despise Griffin just because Jonah does. Still, I know what it means to share a bond that the majority of people could never comprehend. Maybe Elise and Griffin understand each other in ways the rest of us can't see. "If Griffin makes you happy, then nobody else's opinion about your relationship matters. Not even Jonah's."

Elise looks up at me, and after a moment she smiles. Yet that slight hesitation has told me the one thing she doesn't want anyone to know, the fact that vindicates Jonah completely: Griffin doesn't make Elise happy.

"Brothers are always overprotective," she says, trying to sound blithe. "Aren't they?"

"Never had a brother." I often wished for one. A big brother might have believed in me and kicked Anthony Whedon's ass.

"Well, they are." Her china-doll face finally dimples as her smile turns genuine. "I have to say, growing up the way we did—it's just so surprising that Jonah turned out to be so traditional and . . . uptight."

Say nothing. Don't meet her eyes. Eat your breakfast.

"Good for him, I suppose." Elise sighs. "We all have to find our own ways out."

Here, at least, we completely agree. "Yeah. We do."

Our flight passes with hardly a dozen words exchanged between Jonah and me. Again, he's not freezing me out; when his arm isn't around my shoulders, he's holding my hand. For now, however, he's wrestling his inner demons in silence. I want him to open up to me about it, but a crowded airplane is hardly the time.

After we land, every phone onboard is in its owner's hand, being snapped back out of airplane mode. Texts cascade in front of my eyes, most of them from Carmen.

I just realized your trip to Chi-town probably means you won't have time to get ready for the New Year's party—

Oh, shit. I agreed to throw the booze-free party for Geordie, didn't I? What with the Marks-Hale family turmoil, I completely forgot.

Before I can groan, however, Carmen's next texts come through.

I decided I'd throw one instead. Arturo and Shay are in, and they're inviting a few friends.

All you have to do is figure out WTF we're supposed to drink. Gotta be something more festive than ginger ale, right?

Geordie says he's looking forward to it. We took the tree down for Arturo & company today—super fun.

I bite my lip to keep my smile from becoming too unbearably smug. Looks like the field is ripe for a little matchmaking. If Geordie and Carmen even need it.

"We have New Year's plans, by the way," I say to Jonah as the plane taxis toward the gate. Men in fluorescent orange vests hurry around on the tarmac outside our small oval window. "Sedate, but good. Does that work for you?"

"Why wouldn't it?"

"You might have been planning to surprise me with tickets to something swanky."

He glances at me, and the faint glint of humor in his eyes heartens me. "Do you really want to go to some big fancy party?"

"Nah. I can do that anytime." Maybe I should explain Mardi Gras balls to Jonah before I invite him to one in February. "But I expect the unexpected from a guy who once swept me away for a romantic fling in *Scotland*."

Jonah kisses my temple. I thought leaving Chicago would help a little, putting some space between Jonah and his worst memories. Yet I still sense the weight pressing down on him. Last night he gave in to his most brutal demons. I can forgive him for that—there's nothing to forgive. Jonah can't forgive himself. He said the safe word because he was scared of what he was becoming, or what he might do.

I'm not scared. If Jonah could pull back at that moment, when he was fucking me senseless, surely he can control the beast within him. It feels safer, not more dangerous.

To me. Not to him. Do I trust his instincts or my own?

When Jonah remains quiet the entire drive back to my place, I know a conversation is brewing. I suspect it's not one I'm going to like. But I wait for it, asking no questions. The old Lenny Kravitz song on the radio fills my mind as I focus on the lyrics like never before. I tap the beat out on the dashboard of Jonah's sedan. If he even notices, he gives no sign.

We get home. Jonah leaves his suitcase in the trunk, and my first impulse is to say nothing. Let him go pull himself together. We can deal with this later.

But "dealing with it later" often turns into "dealing with it never." I hate suspense. And Jonah and I are working hard to get to a place of deep, radical honesty. Biting my tongue now is a form of lying.

"Why not bring it in?" I venture. "Stay the night."

He hesitates, but he takes the suitcase in. I guess that's a win.

As soon as we've put our stuff down and shucked our coats, I force myself to say, "Something's weighing on you. What is it?"

Jonah looks at me incredulously. "How can you ask that after yesterday?"

"Okay, it got rough. And I know it was—worse than rough, for you. If you're worried about me, don't be. I'll *always* tell you when it's too much for me. Okay? If you're worried about yourself, just remember, when you needed to stop, you did. The safe word is for both of us."

"It's not that. Not only that, anyway." He walks to the corner farthest from me—not that far, given the tininess of my living room. After one deep breath, he finally comes out with it. "We can't play the games any longer."

Oh, no. "We've been over this, remember? You said you could stop seeing me as fragile—as a victim—"

"I can, and I have. But I'm not doing this to protect you, Vivienne. I need to protect myself."

Jonah gets to have limits too, my voice echoes inside my head. It still feels like I'm watching something precious and irreplaceable being stolen.

"What I turned into yesterday—what I felt the entire time I was in Chicago—it proved to me that Carter did make me in his image. No, not entirely. But enough to treat you like an animal. Enough to want to hurt you."

"You've slapped me before. Thrown me down. This wasn't so different."

"The hell it wasn't."

I catch myself. Our honesty is precious; I can't let it slide. "Okay. It was different, but it wasn't too much to handle. At least it wasn't for me."

"For me, it turned into . . . horror." Jonah visibly shudders. "I can't go there anymore. I *can't.*"

I feel seasick. As I flop onto my sofa, I close my eyes. "You have to do what you have to do," I manage to say.

No more games. Like anyone else, Jonah has the right to draw his own lines. But the line he's drawn cuts me off from any sexual satisfaction. "You know why I need it, don't you?"

"You can come without that fantasy. We both know it has to

be possible. You're more responsive than any other woman I've ever been with—hell, you don't even need me to touch your clit. Your body's so ready for this."

"No shit. My mind is the problem. Whatever you need to do, we'll do."

Jonah studies my expression for what feels like a very long time, before he abruptly says, "Are you in love with me?"

It catches me short, the realization that I've never said those words. Never even asked myself if they were true. Jonah Marks has dominated my thoughts for months now, taken possession of me in every way one person can possess another. How could I not have known?

But I did know, of course. I always have. I knew it on a level deeper than words.

Jonah glances away, unsure what to make of my silence. Before I can say anything, though, he begins, "I tried to dislike you, at first. To feel contempt for you. The anger that fueled our games—some of it was real. Because I believed that to you this was *only* a game. To me it was something so much darker, and I needed it so goddamn much."

That part I understand completely. Our shared craving torments us as much as it unites us.

Jonah seems to fill this small room; his raw masculinity changes it. The white slipcovers and piles of paperbacks, the Tiffany-style lamp with its rosy shade—usually I find these surroundings so comfortable, so steadying. He is a stark black line slicing my haven in two.

He continues, "At first I told myself that was all I needed. I tried to deny I needed you, but I did. I do. And I love you, more than I've ever loved any other woman."

Other guys have told me they loved me. Probably they all meant it at the time. But in the moment I know that no one has ever offered me his soul like Jonah just has.

My throat tightens with unshed tears, and I can't quite speak. Jonah misinterprets my silence and says, more quietly, "So if there's anything I need to hear, or know—if you can't accept this—tell me now. Show some mercy. Spare me the hell of losing you by degrees."

He's brave enough to lay himself bare before me. I have to match his courage. It's time to find the words for all the things we've left unsaid.

"You scared me at first," I say hoarsely, as I curl my legs beneath me on my couch. "Not enough for me to walk away, but I kept asking myself what kind of man would get off thinking about rape. It took me so long to realize I was angry with you for wanting this because I was angry with myself for it too. Every day I thought about you, every time I closed my eyes I imagined your face, but I still didn't see the real you."

Jonah looks down at me so sadly that I'm taken aback. I realize the only other time I saw Jonah like this was the day he confessed to me about his childhood, and how his twisted stepfather tried to corrupt Jonah's mind into the mirror image of his own.

Do we always have to revisit our deepest wounds to be fully open to each other? We have to make this easier. We have to clear a path that will always connect us, with or without our rape fantasies. We must become more than that.

But why give the games up forever and ever—?

Because it's what Jonah needs.

What about what I need?

Try. At least try. This man is worth it.

Slowly, I say, "I see you now, Jonah. I know you. And you're so much braver and better than anyone else can ever understand. I wanted you, and then I needed you so much that . . . I didn't even think of it as love, because love is something we feel for other people. But you're a part of me, or I'm a part of you. That has to be true, because you're the only one who's ever made me feel complete." My voice has begun to tremble. "If that's not love," I say, "what is?"

Jonah sits beside, pulls me into his arms, and hugs me so tightly I can hardly breathe. I don't care. Never have I been so fully honest, so fully *myself*, with anyone else.

"I love you so much," I whisper against his cheek. "More than I knew I could love anybody."

He responds by taking my face in his hands. One teardrop escapes my eye and trickles down my cheek; Jonah brushes it away with his little finger, then leans in for a kiss.

Sometimes our kisses are fierce and wild. Even savage. This is pure tenderness. We sink down onto the sofa, Jonah atop me, our bodies pressed together from knees to shoulders. He slides one thigh between mine, buries his face in the curve of my neck. I kiss his eyelids, arch my body so that we lock together even more perfectly. Yet this isn't about sex—only about being as close as we can possibly be to one another. To bring our bodies as near as our hearts.

A wish, a longing, grips me so overpoweringly that it forces another few tears from my eyes. If I could only make love with Jonah right now like other people do—without violence, without roleplaying, without games—and still know that I'd find it satisfying. Right now I can imagine nothing sweeter than to come in Jonah's arms, or from the sweet pressure of his mouth between my legs.

But there's still a boundary no one can cross, not Jonah, not even me. It's ringed in barbed wire and flame. It will stand forever. Anthony built it and he made it strong.

Don't think that man's name. Don't bring him here. Don't give him one second of this.

And, for now, I don't. I cast out the shadows of the past, my fears for the future. This moment is the only time there has ever been; Jonah and I, the only people. My heart has always been this full, this perfect, this whole.

TWENTY

Our high school guidance counselors, our parents, and a zillion cheesy public service campaigns have all told us that we don't need booze to have a good time. Which is totally true! While I enjoy a glass of wine, and sometimes find a few sips calming during a fraught situation, on the average day I'd just as soon have a cup of coffee. If I could have only caffeine or alcohol for the rest of my life, caffeine would win that contest hands down.

But as we get closer to midnight on December 31, I have to admit—a little bit of bubbly does a *lot* for a New Year's party.

"You must loathe me," Geordie says as we stare forlornly at our glasses of "sparkling white grape juice," aka Satan's champagne. "You could be enjoying a lovely Veuve Cliquot if it weren't for me."

"Don't be silly. This is fine. Better than fine, because, hey, no more hangovers." Not that I often drank to that point, but I don't bother bringing that up.

Jonah walks up then and slides his arm around me, and I smile at him as he says, "Why start off a new year feeling miserable? Full of regret? Better to start fresh."

"Exactly," I agree, and even Geordie manages a grin. While he and Jonah are still very, very far from being friends, they're finally getting past the caveman-jealousy bullshit.

As for the rest of the party—well, everybody's doing the best they can. Carmen turned the lights down low, got a few candles going, and even figured out how to make a nonalcoholic sangria that tastes pretty good. I'm going back to it after I finish this grape juice mess. More people showed up than I would have thought, given that this evening is dry. And we have the perfect music playing, a mix of classic lounge tunes from the fifties and sixties together with contemporary neo-soul with everyone from Adele to Pink Martini.

Yet a miasma of pure awkward settled over the party after the first cheerful hour. Maybe it's the fact that two of the principal guests brought along a very tiny infant; Nicolas is adorable to fuss over, but he also means we have to keep the music down, and Arturo continually asks us to reapply hand sanitizer anytime we get near the baby. (We all smell like artificial strawberry scent.) Or maybe it's the fact that a few of the guests know exactly why this event is alcohol-free, and their eyes keep raking over Geordie as if he were a grenade primed to blow at any moment. They're better than the clueless ones, though, who always joke about having a flask at the very moment Geordie's walking by.

Also, it's like every single person dressed for totally different occasions. I put on a party dress—shell-pink sequins, slim straps, and a hem that falls a few inches north of the knee—which matches Jonah's beautifully tailored suit and Carmen's pencil skirt and glittery red top. But Geordie simply went for shirtsleeves and tie, and most people wear jeans and sweaters. Carmen's friend Nicole wore pajamas with a plastic tiara, which is at least festive, and Arturo's old roommate Mack came in his Longhorns jersey. I'll excuse Shay and Arturo for going casual, because merely getting out of the house with a newborn baby is a feat. Everyone else, though—do they not even *like* special occasions?

I whisper as much to Jonah at one point, which makes him laugh. "Most people prefer dressing down. You didn't strike me as the kind of girl who's addicted to her high heels."

"Not even. Still, why wear the exact same thing to every single occasion? It just . . . turns the world gray."

Jonah shrugs. "Turns it comfortable, I'd say."

True enough, I guess. My mania for dressing up—that's probably the New Orleans girl in me. And that reminds me: "Hey, what are you doing in mid-February?"

"No scheduled trips. Why?" Jonah's eyes crinkle at the corners, not quite a smile. "Is this where you tell me I'd better put together a huge surprise for Valentine's Day?"

"What? No." Jonah would hardly be the balloons-and-teddy-bear type anyway. "That's Carnival time. Usually I try to get back to New Orleans for at least a couple of parades and one of the balls. Want to come with?"

"A Mardi Gras ball? What's that like?"

"Only one way to find out." I grin as I take hold of the dark blue silk of his tie. "But I should warn you—dressing up is mandatory."

"I've got the suits." When I shake my head, Jonah frowns. "I'll need a tux?"

"Even tuxedoes are too casual for a proper Mardi Gras ball. If you're not in white tie and tails, they won't let you through the door."

"It's worth it if you'll wear that green dress again."

Jonah's seen my floor-length gown before at a charity benefit where he pretended to rape me behind the red velvet curtain of a stage. Just remembering that starts to get me wet. I whisper, "I'll put it on if you'll take it off."

The fierceness returns to Jonah's grin. "Then we have a deal."

And yet this reminds me of the final reason tonight's party isn't working for me. I can't stop thinking about our New Year's resolution.

No more games. Ever.

I feel as confined by this as I did when Jonah first drew this line, with me on the other side. Yet I have to admit the situation has fundamentally changed. Before, Jonah pulled away from me because he thought it was for my own good; he saw me only as a victim, which wounded me deeply.

Now, however, Jonah's decision is rooted in what *he* needs. The side of him he showed me in Chicago was dangerous, even frightening—but nothing I couldn't accept, or even enjoy. For Jonah, however, it was unbearable. He's not being selfish; he's being honest about a limit he must draw for his own sanity.

If I love this man—and I do—then somehow I have to learn how to accept this.

But I feel so cheated, so deprived, and even angry . . .

Come on. You wanted to move past the fantasy at some point. Shouldn't you be able to have an orgasm without it? You only need to learn how, and you can't learn without trying.

Finally I have a partner, a lover, who truly understands. Jonah will help me every step of the way. That has to make a difference. We can do this, together.

Besides, this is about Jonah. *For* Jonah. He met me halfway when I needed him to, stood up for me the way nobody else ever has. This man is worth working for. Worth sacrificing for. I'm in for a long dry spell—but so what? I'd cross a literal desert for this man; I can cross a metaphorical one too. It's my turn to be the protector.

I take another sip of the grape juice and grimace. Jonah laughs softly at my face. "The sangria's better."

"Definitely."

"Let me get you a glass." He kisses my forehead before he moves toward Carmen's kitchen. I'm tempted to follow him in there and brush up against his chest; that's what was happening when Shay introduced us to each other. A little nostalgia is always fun, particularly when it's sexy—

But that party, in this same house, is also where Jonah first learned of my fixation on a rape fantasy. Where he approached me and dared me to live out those fantasies with him.

I don't want to dwell on what we've lost—and it is a loss, no matter what we might gain later. We need to make new memories, not dwell on the old ones.

"Global warming," says Shay, who's suddenly at my elbow. "I figure that explains it."

"Explains what?" The melting of the Arctic ice sheet? True, but not exactly lighthearted party chatter.

Shay smiles at me coyly. "How you managed to defrost the famously chilly Professor Marks."

"He's not that chilly. Not when you get to know him." I can hardly explain Jonah's true reasons for his silent, guarded nature, but I still feel the need to defend him.

But Shay's not on the attack. She'd never attack anyone, with her cheerful spirit and warm heart. "I just can't reconcile the guy I know from the earth sciences department with the one who cuddles with you at parties and kisses you good-bye before he even goes to fetch you a drink."

"Same guy, I promise." I glance over her shoulder to see Arturo sitting crisscross on the floor, Nicolas in his lap. He's talking to his infant son, exaggerating his facial expressions, as if that will help the tiny wriggling boy in a blue sleeper understand what's going on. "Arturo has turned out to be just the kind of dad I imagined he would be."

Shay nods, though she looks wistful as she stands there in her thrift-store patterned shirt and oversized jeans. "Sometimes it's hard to shut that off, though. To stop being Nicolas's mum and dad, and remember we're husband and wife."

"When you guys are ready for a romantic night out, just let me know. I can babysit!" Honestly, the thought of caring for a newborn unnerves me. They're so—little, and floppy, and how are you supposed to know what they want? But I'd like to have kids of my own someday, so I guess I'd better start figuring that out.

"I might take you up on that in a few weeks." Shay sips her ginger ale. Her eyes are bright behind her thick-rimmed glasses. "Don't misunderstand. I love Nicolas more than I knew I could love anybody. I wouldn't change one single thing. But I feel like—like maybe Arturo and I missed out on some time to just have fun and be in love."

This is where my mother's training would have me spout platitudes about the Responsibility of Parenthood. She'd go the extra mile and make sure she forced Shay to feel guilty about admitting even the slightest drawback to being a mother—which is ironic, given that she's never stopped complaining about how much Chloe and I needed from her. I don't want to answer on autopilot, especially when my instincts suck.

So after a moment's consideration, I say to Shay, "You *did* miss out on that time. It's okay to recognize that. But you also gained so much more time being a wife and a mom. You've already found the love the rest of us have to search for throughout our lives." I nudge her shoulder playfully. "Besides, this way your kids will go off to college while you and Arturo are still young enough to enjoy your freedom. The rest of us are going to be gray and grumpy at our sixth graders' PTA meetings—"

Shay pushes back, but now she's grinning. "*Stop* it. You won't be searching for love your entire life." Her eyes flick over toward Jonah; he's at the bar, attempting to gracefully extricate himself from some interminable anecdote Mack is telling. "Looks like you might already have found it."

Jonah and I—forever?

Shay's only joking. To her, or to anyone on the outside, Jonah and I are a very new pair. We only met five months ago. While we've met each other's families and spent the holidays together, conventional wisdom would suggest that it's far too early to start speculating about the altar.

Yet we know each other more intimately than most people do after years. I have shown Jonah the deepest part of my soul, and he didn't flinch. He revealed himself to me just as fully. Whatever we are, it's not "conventional." We could never walk away from each other in a break like any other couple. Either we will go up in devastating flames, or we'll be together—always.

Those are the stakes we're playing for.

Jumbled visions crowd into my mind: mostly stupid, ring-commercial bullshit about white dresses and cakes decorated with complicated loops of frosting, the stuff I can barely stand and Jonah probably hates. I recognize this as more of Mom's programming and push it aside.

One image, however, refuses to fade so quickly: Jonah holding a child, our child, as tenderly as Arturo is holding Nicolas.

Could we be decent parents? It's not like we have the greatest examples to learn from. My parents insist on living life only on the surface, judging by appearances, and avoiding uncomfortable truths. As for Jonah—he'd have been better off being raised by wolves.

I take a deep breath and shake off my complicated thoughts. That cart is incredibly far before its horse. Besides, this is a party, dammit.

A limp, tepid party, but it still counts.

Glancing around the room, I see Carmen in her pretty dress. She's weaving through the crowd distributing silly paper hats and plastic tiaras. Jonah simply shakes his head no, but her next target is more appreciative. Geordie smiles, checks out the silver top hat, then insists on taking a purple glitter tiara. Carmen laughs—she has the most amazing laugh, one that lights up a room—and Geordie looks more cheerful than I've seen him in months. I wonder what might happen at midnight . . .

"Here you go," Jonah says. He hands me my glass of faux sangria as he nods back at Mack. "That guy doesn't know when to stop."

"Tell me about it. What was he going on about this time?"

"One of those jokes where you're not sure whether it's racist, but it's definitely stupid. I'll spare you the details."

"Forget about him." I take my glass and hold it up. "Shouldn't we make a toast?"

Jonah does the same, but his expression is wary. "Superstition says it's bad luck to toast with anything but alcohol."

"You never struck me as the superstitious type. Besides, aren't we already tempting fate?"

"In so many ways," he murmurs. "All right. I'll propose a toast. To this year, one of the strangest of my life—but worth every problem and every pain. Because this is the year that brought you to me."

"To this year." We clink our plastic glasses against each other, and I laugh at the silliness of it. Jonah takes a drink first; I'm interrupted by Carmen.

"All right, Jonah, you're determined to be a spoilsport"—she sticks her tongue out at him, which he takes with good grace—"but I know you'll have fun with it, Vivienne. Which hat do you want?"

I take the silver top hat and place it on my head. It slides slightly to the side, off-kilter, but that seems about right for New Year's. "Finally, it's a party. Thanks, Carmen."

"You're welcome—oh, look at the time!"

This is exactly when Arturo calls out, "One minute to the new year. Get ready!"

We all gather around the television, which is on silent but

displays the thousands of revelers in Times Square. The ball begins to shimmer with countless tiny bulbs, and confetti begins spiraling down from the sky.

The chant begins. *"Ten! Nine! Eight!"*

"I can't wait to spend this year with you," I whisper to Jonah.

"I can't wait to spend tonight with you," he answers, even more quietly.

My gut clenches. We haven't made love since we decided to put the games aside. Will I be able to come? Can Jonah accept it if I don't?

"Seven! Six! Five! Four!"

Jonah frames my face with both his hands. "If you could see yourself like this—this dress, your eyes, even the damned shiny hat—Jesus, Vivienne. You're the most beautiful thing I've ever seen."

We'll be all right. We have to be.

"Three! Two!"

"I love you," I whisper.

"One!"

"I love you too." He pulls me in for a kiss just as the cheers go up, and in the first moments of the new year—our first year together—I forget about everything except the feel of his mouth against mine.

TWENTY-ONE

We go back to my place. It's closer to Carmen's, and besides—even if we haven't been drinking tonight, other drivers will have been. As we walk through the door, I find myself thinking, *We're safe. Everything's fine.*

It was easier to worry about the traffic. Now I'm alone with Jonah, and the moment of truth has come.

Jonah slides and turns all the locks, sealing us inside. I slip off my cardboard top hat, then hold it out for his inspection. "Would you rather I kept it on?"

"Interesting idea." My little joke doesn't fool him, though. "You're nervous. Don't be."

"Easy for you to say." Jonah may share the same dark urges I do, but they've never been the only way he could get off.

He pulls me closer to him; the silver hat falls from my fingers onto the sofa, where it shines softly in the dim light. "Hey. You've never been with anyone who knew the whole story. That changes things. Doesn't it?"

"I hope so."

"It's going to be okay." Jonah's broad hands stroke the length of my back. The pale pink sequins on my dress make a silvery sound against his palms. "I'll take good care of you."

The sound of his voice melts me, every time. If any man can do this for me, Jonah can. I caress the side of his face with my hand, then go on tiptoe for a kiss.

We've kissed less than most couples. Our foreplay hasn't been sweet or gentle; our aftermaths have been as much about soothing bruises as touching lips. That's a shame, because the way Jonah kisses drives me wild.

He buries his hands in my hair as he opens my mouth with his. We kiss long and deep, sharing one breath. Jonah slides his tongue in and out of my mouth—once, slowly—inviting me to think of the way he'll push his cock into me later tonight. In response I lean against him so he can feel my breasts rising and falling with my quickening breath.

Jonah likes that. His fingers trace the strap of my dress and push it over my bare shoulder. "No bra," he murmured. "I like that."

"You like thinking about me naked under this dress?" I flick my tongue against his earlobe. "Is that it?"

"I always like thinking about you naked. Tonight, I'm glad nothing else is in my way." He bends me back slightly, drops a kiss on the hollow of my throat, then slides his hands down my body to the hem of my dress. I gasp as his fingertips catch the edge of my underwear. "I could just push those panties to the floor and fuck you right here."

"Show me," I whisper.

Jonah tugs downward until my nude-colored panties slip down my thighs to puddle around my ankles. He slides his fingers between my legs, first tracing the heat of my skin, then parting me, probing me—

"Oh." The sound escapes my mouth as he gently pushes two fingers inside me. A gush of wetness welcomes him—so much it would embarrass me if it didn't clearly turn Jonah on.

"You like it when I use my hand?" he asks, his voice maddeningly calm, as if he were merely observing this, controlling it, instead of wanting it as much as I do. Only the long, thick swelling down the leg of his pants betrays his arousal. "Then I know how to start."

My head swirls. Dizziness mingles with lust. *It's going to be okay!* I think, my excitement peaking. *We'll be all right. Jonah changes everything, I should've known he would—*

Jonah pulls his hand back, but before I can protest, he sweeps me into his arms and carries me the few steps to my bedroom. When he tosses me on the bed, I feel a thrill—he's begun like this so many times, throwing me down before holding me down—but this time, he alters his approach. He curves his hand around my thigh, savoring me for one moment, before he backs off to strip.

My *God*, this man's body. He could've been sketched by Leonardo, with this perfect symmetry, every muscle of his powerful form shown in tantalizing detail. Who could have sculpted him? *Michelangelo*, says my art-student brain, but I reject the idea almost as fast. Jonah's unique proportions—his elongated torso, the unbelievable contrast of his broad shoulders and slim waist—they wouldn't match any of Michelangelo's hulking mesomorphs. Jonah Marks is a masterpiece unlike any other.

And he is mine.

He finishes undressing, shedding his boxers. His cock, already hard for me, springs free from the elastic. As always, I can't believe all that is for me. I slide my legs around to get on my knees and crawl toward the edge of the bed. Smiling, I look up at Jonah and lick my lips before saying, "Come here."

Jonah steps forward, brushing back my hair with one hand while using the other to guide his cock into my mouth.

Usually he's so forceful with me—shoving deep into my throat, fucking my mouth, pulling my hair. I love that. But this is good too, because I can really give him the attention he deserves. I run my tongue along the length of his shaft, tease the ridge with my lips, suck the head once or twice before pulling back to make him groan. When I finally take him in all the way, Jonah breathes out as sharply as if he'd been struck. I smile around his cock and start working him with my hand too.

Pre-come slicks my tongue. He could get off like this. He's so hard, so flushed, that it wouldn't take much to bring him over the edge. Maybe that's how I ought to do it.

And then maybe he'd just want to go to sleep, maybe he wouldn't insist on trying to get me off too, not tonight—

Jonah pulls out of my mouth, takes one step back, and shakes his head. He caught himself right on the brink. "*Damn*," he breathes.

I wipe my lips with the back of my hand. "Hey, I wasn't finished."

"I'd ask how you got so good at that if I didn't think the answer would make me completely fucking insane with jealousy." He visibly struggles for control, and wins. As a slow smile spreads across his face, he pulls me from all fours to my knees and tugs my dress away. Now I'm naked too. The snow-white sheets make my skin seem darker by contrast, an almost dusky pink. Whatever Jonah sees, he likes. "Stand up for me."

I get off the bed, willing but uncertain. Then Jonah drops to his knees in front of me, and I barely have time to gasp before he gets his face between my legs.

Reeling, I brace myself against his shoulders. He grips me at the hipbones as he works, his tongue parting the soft folds of my cunt before finding my clit. Then Jonah goes for it, caressing me in spirals until I'm seeing stars. I don't think it can get any better than that until he starts to suck. After that I can't think anything any longer.

This is it. This has to be it. I'm so close—so fucking close—my heartbeat has sped up, the muscles of my inner thighs have locked, and my body is poised right there, right there . . .

Any moment now . . .

But I don't come. All the pressure and tension is there, but it's not enough to break the walls down.

Fuck, I think in frustration, then decide that's the answer. "Fuck me," I pant as I run my fingers through Jonah's short hair. "Please, Jonah, I want you to fuck me."

Instantly he pulls back and climbs onto the bed, tugging me down alongside him. First he's distracted by my breasts, caressing them roughly, rubbing my already-hard nipples with his thumbs until I writhe. But it's only moments before he slings one of his legs between mine, the hard muscles of his thigh spreading me wider.

As Jonah crawls over me, he whispers, "You won't—you promise not to—"

Not to fantasize about him raping me. I want to so bad, because it would get me off. And the way I feel now, helpless and overwhelmed, would work so well . . .

But I promise. "I won't. I won't. Just fuck me."

It's going to be enough this time. I know it.

Jonah covers my body with his and starts rocking back and forth; I'd say he was dry-humping me, except that this is anything but dry. The wetness between my thighs is all over his legs, his mouth and his hands, and his pre-come only makes this slicker. His cock slides over my clit, between the folds of my cunt, teasing the entrance but never quite sliding in. The friction is just enough to make me start panting again.

Then I realize—the head of his cock is penetrating me, just barely, but slightly more with every stroke. Jonah is working me open as slowly and deliciously as possible.

Maybe this is what it's like between two virgins, I think in a daze as the whole head of his cock dips inside, only for a moment. *Moving from foreplay to intercourse without even noticing the boundary line. Pure and perfect.*

I'd like that sometime—if I pretended to be a virgin again and Jonah took my virginity by force, but in some completely unexpected way—

No. He asked me not to have those fantasies. I can resist, even now.

Jonah's cock finally penetrates me fully, and we both moan in mutual bliss. He takes his time, moving us in slow spirals. I clutch his waist as he straightens his arms, separating our bodies enough for us to see his cock sliding in and out of me.

"I want to fuck you like this all night." His voice is tight with strain. He's just barely holding on, waiting for me.

And as good as this feels—I'm still not able to come.

Why not? The voice in my head has become insistent now. Almost a shriek. *Why can't you do this? The hottest man you've ever seen is making love to you with all the strength and technique and tenderness you could ever want. You can come just from feeling a cock inside you. So why not his cock, right now? Come on. Come on!*

My arousal fades, rubbed out by frustration. My cheeks flush in humiliation and useless exertion as I try to match Jonah thrust for thrust. If I could bring him off, maybe he—wouldn't notice?

Stupid idea. Worthless too. Because as Jonah slows down, then stops, his expression clouds over. "You don't like this."

"I do! I *love* it." He feels so incredibly good inside me. It's just not enough. "But I can't quite . . . get there."

"We'll keep going. I can hang on for a while." Jonah smiles unevenly. "And if I jump the gun, that just gives me an excuse to go down on you again."

Most women would be singing the "Hallelujah Chorus" right around now. What else could you ask for in a man? But all I can imagine is minute after minute, hour after hour, of Jonah watching me, working me, all the while needing me to come. Feeling observed like that—judged—that only makes sure orgasm remains completely impossible.

"Please don't," I say. "Please."

"Why wouldn't you want to—"

"I don't want to disappoint you!"

"You couldn't, Vivienne. Not ever."

He sounds so sweet, but now there are tears in my eyes. "I'm disappointing you right now, and we both know it."

Jonah sighs. His head droops against my shoulder, and then he pulls out to flop down by my side. "Okay," he says heavily. "Okay."

"You don't have to stop." I curl along his side and slide one thigh invitingly over his groin. His cock is still half-hard; he must be aching from the release he's denying himself. "I don't mind. Like I said, it feels amazing just having you inside me."

"I can't use you, without at least trying to get you off too."

"You did try. You're not using me."

"I'm not, because this is over."

"Jonah—"

"Please, don't." He grimaces, then covers his face with one hand. "Besides, at this point, we've killed the mood."

He's right. What had been so passionate, so glorious, now feels like nothing but failure.

A few tears escape, and Jonah must hear me sniffle, because he gathers me into his arms and kisses my hair. "So we didn't get there on our first try. We have a long time to work it out."

Those words are meant to be kind. Instead they make me feel even worse. "How long is too long? I can wait—I can work on it—but you don't want this, Jonah." No man could. I've gone from being Jonah's wanton fantasy partner to the endlessly dissatisfied woman out of a thousand sexist jokes.

"I want *you*. What you're going through—it can't be forever. You deserve so much better than that. So much more."

"Some scars last forever, Jonah. You ought to know."

He goes quiet then, but he holds me even more snugly against him. It helps.

There's a bleak symmetry to this, I realize. A kind of poetry. Once we believed we shared nothing but a sexual fetish. Now that fetish is the only thing keeping us apart. It is beautiful to be so tied to someone. It's terrible to know that's not the only way you're bound.

After a while, once I've calmed down and I think Jonah must be on the verge of sleep, he says, "What have you done about this? In the past."

"Fantasized inside my own head. Said yes to your offer to live out our fantasies."

Jonah smiles, but his gaze remains worried. "That's it? You never saw a specialist?"

Like I'd take this to a sex surrogate. "I go to therapy."

"Did you tell your therapist the truth about what happened to you?"

"I tell Doreen the truth about pretty much everything. Even us." She'll be proud of me for trying this with Jonah. That's my only consolation, and it's a pretty minor one.

"What *don't* you tell her the truth about?"

"Usually? The same stuff where I find it hard to be honest with myself."

"She sounds good."

"She is."

And yet she hasn't been able to help me over this line—the one between me and Jonah, even as we lie in the same bed.

He hugs me closer, resting his head against mine, and I know he doesn't want to talk any longer. Or he can't. I don't want to either. Sleep seems like the only escape from this evening gone so horribly wrong.

It won't seem so bad tomorrow, I tell myself. But that's another platitude. Words people say and don't really mean.

Sorrow hangs over us like a canopy as we try to sleep. I think of my resolution—to create a single image that would symbolize Jonah Marks, and everything he means to me. Before tonight I always thought it would be something majestic. Something powerful. But now in my mind's eye I see nothing but shattered glass. I fall asleep imagining us lying there among the shards.

TWENTY-TWO

Jonah and I had to do something. This seemed like the sanest solution. Doesn't change the fact that it's awkward as hell.

"So," Doreen says, her gaze moving from me to Jonah as we sit side by side on her couch. "You both understand that couples' counseling isn't part of my standard practice."

"We understand." Jonah's tone is brusque, and he doesn't meet Doreen's eyes. She must think he's a total asshole.

Then again, what must it be like, meeting someone for the first time and knowing they've already heard the most intimate facts of your sex life, and the deepest wounds of your past?

("Should I not have said anything?" I asked him when I explained how much I'd disclosed to Doreen in our therapy sessions—including the abuse he grew up with, something I don't think he'd willingly shared with anyone but me.

Jonah didn't look happy, but he didn't let go of my hand. "You weren't—gossiping. Being careless. You told your therapist about your life, which is exactly what you're supposed to do."

"I told her about your life."

He smiled then, a cool, remote smile like a winter sunrise. "We're intertwined now, you and I. Our lives aren't separate."

"No. They aren't."

Doreen doesn't appear offended by Jonah's attitude. She's as unruffled as ever, relaxed in her overstuffed beige armchair. Her flowing red cardigan warms the sheen of the wooden beads hanging around her neck. Scattered around the room are her potted ferns and her African sculptures, all of them lit by the ample sunlight flowing through the windows. This room feels less like a therapist's office, more like a sanctuary.

Hopefully Jonah feels safe enough to speak.

"The first question we need to tackle is—where to begin?" Doreen folds her arms in her lap. "Let's start with this: What made you two decide to come to me?"

"We have enough reasons," Jonah says. "Don't you think?"

She nods. "But I want to know what *you* think."

I bite back a smile. There's no getting around Doreen when she wants a straight answer, as Jonah will soon learn.

When I begin to reply for us both, Doreen's eyes briefly meet mine. I recognize the signal immediately. She doesn't want me to answer, because she already knows that I can dig deep when I have to. What she wants to know now is whether Jonah can and will do the same.

Silence stretches out, going from uncomfortable to nearly torturous before Jonah finally can't take it any longer. "I need to stop, ah, acting out this fantasy with Vivienne."

"Not because he's worried about me anymore," I add. "For himself."

Doreen nods. "What triggered this realization?"

Jonah takes a deep breath. "The last time we did, I went to a dark place that I never needed to be."

Patiently, Doreen draws more and more from us. Although she works harder with Jonah than with me, I tell my share of the story too. Before long, I'm spilling my guts. "The sex was great—I mean, it should've been great. The way Jonah made me feel . . ."

"You didn't lack stimulation," Doreen says. "But you couldn't let go."

At the word *stimulation*, Jonah leans his forehead into his hand. If this moment weren't so fraught, I'd be amused at the sight of someone so self-possessed giving in to total embarrassment.

I nod. "No. I couldn't. It's not something I have conscious control over, you know?"

"I know," Doreen says. "Jonah, Vivienne says that she offered to give you the sexual satisfaction she couldn't find herself. Why did you refuse?"

Jonah looks like he'd rather set himself on fire than answer. But he doesn't flinch. "Because I don't want to *use* her."

"If you could bring Vivienne to orgasm without this fantasy, would you insist on finishing every time she did? Or might you do something for her, oh, just because?"

He sees what she's getting at, but shakes his head no. "We're not talking about a one-time thing. Vivienne doesn't put her own needs first, not often enough. If I let her . . . 'service me' once, we could fall into a pattern that isn't fair to her."

"What if you let Vivienne decide what's fair for her?" Doreen asks.

But I hold up my hands in the time-out symbol. "Hold on. I know when to put my needs first."

"You've spent decades coddling your family instead of making them face what they did to you," Jonah says.

Like that's so easy? "How long did it take you to stand up to Carter?"

"I graduated from high school a year early and got a scholarship to a university halfway across the country. When I was walking out of Redgrave House, Carter followed me to the door—mostly to slam it after me, I guess. But it gave me a chance to spit in his face instead of saying good-bye." Jonah looks insufferably proud of himself.

"Well, bravo for you," I retort. "But it's not the same for everyone."

"No, no, I realize that," he says, sounding stricken. Only now do I understand his smugness wasn't because he was braver than me; it was merely glee at the memory of spitting on his worst enemy. "I do. That doesn't change the fact that you sometimes let people take advantage of you."

In my mind I hear the echo of something Kip said to me once: *You're not good at conflict.* Jonah may be overstating his case, but he's not entirely wrong.

I admit, "Maybe, sometimes. Still, Jonah, we aren't talking about some random person taking advantage of me. We're talking about you! I trust myself to draw the line, and I trust you too."

That stops Jonah short. "How am I supposed to feel, though? Having sex knowing you're not enjoying it? That's too close to—no."

How many guys never even give a shit whether or not the girl in their bed is having a good time? Jonah's both too sensitive and too proud for that. He needs to know he's made me come. Normally this is one of the things I'd like best about him. At the moment? His generosity is only getting in our way.

I start counting off points on my fingers. "First of all, not having an orgasm during sex isn't the same as not enjoying it. It feels good anyway, you know? We kiss. We touch. What's not to like? And it makes me happy to do that for you."

Jonah doesn't get this. Most guys don't. To them, sex without orgasm is like breathing without air: useless. "You shouldn't have to—"

"Excuse me, but I wasn't done." If he genuinely thinks I can't stand up for myself, it's time he learned better. "Second—and I think this is the critical part—if you insist on my having an orgasm, and also insist on my not indulging in the fantasy that gets me off—Jonah, do you realize how much pressure that puts on me? It's like I have to perform or else. How is *anybody* supposed to get off like that?"

He pauses, taken aback. "I hadn't thought of it that way."

"Good," Doreen says. I'd almost forgotten she was there. "This is the kind of dialogue that can move you forward. You've identified a goal now—a means of sexual communication that lets Vivienne explore without pressure, but doesn't make you feel as if you're abusing her generosity and trust."

That sounds amazing. But I can't help asking, "So, any chance you'd tell us exactly what that is?"

Doreen has a magnificent laugh, a deep belly chuckle that makes me smile every time. "If I had a magical wand that fixed everybody's sex life, do you really think I'd still be paying off a mortgage in Austin, Texas? I'd be queen of the world, honey! Fact is, I can't define that for you. Nobody else ever could. The two of you have to discover it for yourselves."

Jonah looks unconvinced, but he says, "I see why Vivienne speaks so highly of you."

"Oh, really?" Doreen raises an eyebrow. "And why is that?"

"You don't let anybody get away with an easy answer."

She nods, satisfied. "I think we're going to get along just fine."

The soft chiming of the grandfather clock in the hallway signals the end of our session. As we rise to get our coats, I sling my satchel over one shoulder just in time to hear my cell phone chirp. I fish it out to see a text from Geordie: Are you around? Not having such a great afternoon.

He wouldn't text me like that just because he got a speeding ticket or something like that. Geordie has to be feeling low. By now I'd hoped he would call Carmen instead of me—but maybe he isn't yet ready for her to see him at his worst.

"I should go," I say. "A friend isn't doing well."

Jonah looks at Doreen. "Putting her own needs first again."

I'd like to argue this point; to judge by the way Doreen's searching Jonah's face, she'd like to hear the discussion that would follow. But that would mean revealing it's Geordie I'm going to see, and justifying a mad dash to my ex-boyfriend's side would mean revealing secrets that aren't mine to tell.

"We just spent an entire hour focusing on our needs," I say instead. "Time to get back into the world." And I go on tiptoe to kiss Jonah's cheek before I leave.

I wind up meeting Geordie at Kerbey Lane, a diner that's just a little bit too schlocky for hipster appeal. They serve huge helpings of pancakes and eggs, though, and nobody can deny the psychological comfort offered by having breakfast at any hour of the day you please.

Opposite me in the booth, Geordie leans his face into his hands, tugging at his own floppy brown hair. "I'm so fucking embarrassed."

"Hey, come on. Don't be embarrassed. You were put in a dangerous situation. You recognized it, and when you needed help, you called for it. That's pretty frickin' great, actually."

Geordie won't look at me. "A bloody law school mixer. Plastic cups and bottles of wine fit only for use as an emergency antiseptic in third-world disaster areas. Dull as dirt and I still wanted to run in there and get plastered as fast as humanly possible."

"But you didn't," I say firmly. "One day at a time, right? Well, you just made it through one more day. A tough one."

"I know. I'm just sick of tough days. They're outnumbering the rest."

The waitress shows up with my omelet and Geordie's waffles. Although it could have been an awkward moment, the break in the conversation turns out to come at the perfect time. Geordie tucks into his pecan waffles with such gusto that I first wonder whether he's eaten today. Then I realize—this is a treat. An indulgence. If he can't give in to one craving, he can at least revel in another.

"More syrup?" I ask, as innocently as I can manage. Geordie's mouth is full, so he simply nods.

As soon as I've drenched his waffles, my phone buzzes in my purse. I pull it out to see a message from Jonah: Everything OK?

It will be, I send back.

Today was good. Thanks for that.

I can't believe he handled our session so well. He must have resisted the idea of therapy, to have lived through what he did without ever turning to a counselor before. Maybe it's hard for me, still, to wrap my mind around the concept that someone as powerful and strong as Jonah Marks could really need *me*.

His next text reads, Something just came up we ought to talk about.

I resist the dirty joke that instantly comes to mind. OK. Should I come by later?

Definitely. Can't wait.

This, despite the fact that we only parted ways half an hour ago. I smile softly at the screen, reveling in the knowledge of Jonah's love for me.

My smile wavers, though, when Geordie says, "Want to go to a movie after? Something loud and stupid with explosions—that sounds like just the ticket. No pun intended."

"Actually, I'm headed over to Jonah's later tonight."

Geordie's expression clouds. Oh, no. Is he still hung up on me after all?

But that's not it, I realize. The fact that I'm going to see Jonah has hardly even registered; Geordie simply doesn't want me to leave. He's that afraid of being alone.

"Hey," I say, trying to smile for him. "This is where you could talk to your sponsor, right?"

He shifts awkwardly, as if the booth's padded seats had suddenly become uncomfortable. "It takes a while to find a sponsor, usually."

"You don't even have a sponsor yet?"

"Someone else in the program usually connects you to a person they think would work well with you. They say you have to find the right fit."

"Are you going to the meetings? Getting to know people?"

"Ah, not as much as I should." Geordie winces. "I know. I know. But first it was bloody finals, and now my thesis—if I've not reviewed the South African immigration laws by the end of the week, I'll never get the damned thing done in time."

"And then what?" I ask.

"And then—then I won't get the LLM I've been working toward for eighteen months now."

"And then what? You'll wind up unemployable? Sick? Dead? No. You just won't have an LLM. Big fucking deal." I lean forward. "Your recovery has to come first, always. If you don't take care of yourself, the extra law degree isn't going to matter."

Geordie nods, though I think it's less in agreement, more him showing he's at least heard what I'm saying. His smile is uncertain. "At least I have friends who can help take care of me."

"Always," I promise. "But I can't always be there. You need a whole support system around you, and a sponsor's supposed to be a big part of that. Right?"

Since I have exactly zero direct experience with twelve-step groups, I'm kind of talking out of my ass here. So it's a relief when

Geordie says, "Yeah. It is. You can't just grab a sponsor at random—but if I don't go to the meetings, I don't meet people who could become my sponsors, et cetera, et cetera. Fuck me, I'm even a failure at being an *alcoholic*."

"No way. You're turning your life around. Just because it's a rough process doesn't mean you're not doing it right." I remember something I read online, which might resonate for Geordie, with his love of video games. "They say if everything suddenly becomes more difficult, that means you've leveled up."

It works; he laughs. "That shouldn't make as much sense as it does. All right. Leveling up."

"Is there a meeting tonight? Maybe you could ask about a sponsor then."

"It's more complicated than that, but—yeah, there's a meeting. I'll go." Geordie smiles at me with something of his normal panache. "Thanks, Viv."

He knows I hate that nickname. "*Vivienne*."

"Just making sure you were listening."

I briefly touch his hand. "Always."

This is the last time I need any curveballs, which is why Jonah throws one at me over dinner.

We're sitting at his table, Franklin's BBQ spread out before us to be enjoyed as God intended—with a couple cool bottles of beer and the freedom to lick the sauce from our fingers. I feel more relaxed than I would've dreamed possible just over a week ago, on New Year's Eve.

"Maybe I'm looking forward to the school year starting again," I say. "Is that weird?"

"Given the holiday break we had? No."

True. Grading papers and herding undergraduates seem tame

compared to facing down Carter Hale in a Chicago boardroom. "It's actually going to feel good to get back into some of my old routines. And to make some new ones too." Jonah and I can figure out what nights would work best for me to sleep over here, or for him to come to my place. Although I'm still not sure exactly what we're going to do in these shared beds . . .

It's not important, I remind myself. Not compared to Jonah's well-being. We can rebuild our sex life somehow. The harm that could come to Jonah if we don't figure out a new path—I'm not sure that's something we could fix.

"You don't have to go back to your routines right away," Jonah suggests. "Not if you don't want to."

"Is this about me staying over more often? Are you worried about me being at my place alone, still?" The Austin Stalker hasn't struck again. Already the tension in the city has relaxed a bit. People wonder whether there was no serial rapist at all, whether unconnected crimes were wrongly conflated by the police. Why these people think it would be more reassuring to have two rapists in town than one, I couldn't say. But I too am breathing a little easier. "It's safe, I swear."

"My apartment is safer, and I don't need extra reasons to want you over here more often. But that's not actually what I meant when I said you didn't have to go back to routine."

I look at him over the sticky rib I'm holding. "You research professors might lose sight of this, but the rest of us have to deal with this thing called an academic calendar. It starts again in two days."

"Research professors have to deal with unexpected requests for us to work elsewhere."

"Like Scotland?" I say. Sun-splashed memories of our time in the Highlands make me smile.

He nods. "Or Japan."

I pause mid bite. Did he just say what I think he just said?

Yes, he did. Jonah leans across the table, a spark in his gray eyes. "I know it's harder for you to get away than it is for me. But you said your schedule's more forgiving this semester. You'd only have to move a couple of classes to get a solid week off. We could spend that week in Kyoto together."

Japan! I've always dreamed of going there. Okay, I mostly want to see the ancient woodcuts, which is not the average tourist activity, but it still counts. The rest is a blur of cherry blossoms, kimono silks and Mt. Fuji—but if I go, I'll get to discover the real country. It would be such an incredible adventure . . .

"You need studio time," Jonah says, anticipating my objections. "But you also need inspiration, and Japan would provide plenty of that, right? You'd owe other people in your department favors. Well, okay, do a few favors. I'll help if I can. It's worth it."

I want to go so much it feels like I could scream.

And yet I can't bring myself to agree. Instead I set down my food, wipe my hands. "I'd love to. But I can't."

He doesn't fully believe me. "Are you worried about the expense? You can't be."

After seeing the luxurious sky-rise offices of Oceanic Airlines? Hardly. "It's not the expense. It's not *not* wanting to go—oh, Jonah, it sounds amazing. But this isn't right for us, not now."

"Getting away from it all? It might do us good to relax."

I smile sadly at him. "We'd be getting away from everything except the real problem. Sharing some tiny Japanese pod hotel room for a week would only intensify that. Don't you think?"

That finally makes Jonah pause. His hand curls around his bottle of beer, but he doesn't take a drink. Behind him, on the brick wall, is my etching—the strong hands cradling a fragile bird. For some reason the image looms larger now.

Finally he asks, "Are you saying you aren't comfortable with me?"

"No. I mean, look at us, Jonah." I gesture at this apartment, with my purse on his countertop, my coat draped over one of the hooks on the wall. "Of course I feel comfortable with you. But this seems like a moment when we need to—breathe. Take a step back. Come back to each other without so much pressure."

"That word again." Jonah doesn't dispute it; he simply sounds resigned. "I'll be gone for two or three weeks."

Three whole weeks? The thought sends a tangible pang through my body. I hadn't realized even that would make me feel bereft. He wouldn't have argued for me to come to Japan with him if he didn't think he'd miss me too.

However, I'm still certain that remaining in Austin is the best choice for us both.

Or am I?

Because if I'm being really honest with myself, I have to acknowledge this sneaky whisper in the back of my mind, the one that says, *Three weeks is a long time. He'll have some time to get over what happened in Chicago. He'll want me as badly as I want him. He'll stop worrying about our games. Jonah will come back ready to do everything to me—to do anything, no matter what—*

I shouldn't let myself hope for that. But that's one more reason I shouldn't go to Japan with Jonah; I'm still trying to twist this situation around. Attempting to wriggle my way out of it. Either Jonah needs time to heal, or I need time to accept. So Austin it is.

"Absence makes the heart grow fonder," I say softly.

Jonah reaches across the rough-hewn wooden table to take my hand. "Impossible."

TWENTY-THREE

The first e-mail has no words except for the subject line: *Missing you.* I click on Jonah's message to see a photograph of a temple, symmetrical and serene. Although I'm not familiar enough with Eastern religions to know which one this temple serves (Shinto? Buddhism?), the design alone communicates peace and harmony.

I'm glad Jonah felt drawn to a place like that, and I wish I could see it with him.

You did the right thing, staying here, I remind myself. And yet I can't stop looking at the photograph, imagining myself half a world away with the man I love.

"It's a miracle babies ever figure the world out, isn't it?" Geordie says that evening as he sits on Arturo and Shay's floor, next to the play mat where Nicolas kicks vigorously.

"Why d'ya say that?" Shay calls from the kitchen, where she's helping herself to a second serving of red beans and rice. I don't attempt to cook dishes from home very often, but this one seems to be a success.

"Think about it." Geordie points at Carmen, who's sitting slightly apart from the rest of us—dining in front of the TV even though there's room at the table. Maybe she's trying to get closer to Geordie? "What's the first thing you did when you came in, Carmen?"

She pauses, fork in hand. "Um, I said hi to the baby."

"Ah, but no. You leaned over him and went *wooby-wooby-woo* for about three minutes straight." Geordie cracks up laughing.

Carmen makes a face. "Oh, come on. Everyone likes to be silly with babies."

"Exactly! Their new little brains are trying to interpret this enormous new world around them, and what data do they get? Countless people leaning over them, chanting pure nonsense." Ruefully, Geordie leans over Nicolas and says, "Stick with me, kid. I'll talk to you with a proper Scots accent. Bring you up right."

"Don't even," Arturo says. "Between his grandparents' Mexican accents and his mother's Australian—"

"I'm not the one with the accent!" Shay protests as she comes back to the table. "You are."

Arturo ignores this, though he can't help a smile. "—the last thing Nicolas needs is another accent in the mix."

"What about another language?" I've been curious about this for a few months now. "Are you guys going to raise Nicolas to be bilingual?"

Shay and Arturo give each other a look, and I realize I've accidentally tripped over a marital debate. Too late—they each launch into overlapping explanations, with Shay saying she thinks it's important to speak two languages from the very beginning, while Arturo insists his parents were right to teach him Spanish first, then English, so he wouldn't get confused. Neither of them is angry about it, but it's pretty obvious extra opinions are totally unnecessary.

I glance over at the other two adults in the room to get their reactions. Geordie, like me, is stifling a laugh. He looks so much better the past couple of weeks; he's found a sponsor, a woman named

Kitty who's apparently been sober for more than two decades. Probably she hasn't had much chance to really work with him yet—just knowing someone in the same boat is committed to helping seems to have been enough to buoy his spirits. Geordie's resumed shaving every day; his clothes once again seem to be neatly pressed. He no longer looks like his own shadow. The guy I knew is coming back.

Although I'd like to think he's doing this for Carmen's benefit, she isn't responding in kind. Normally she chooses clothes in the brightest colors. Today, however, she's in slouchy jeans and a sweatshirt. She looks fine, but nobody would ever say she's dressed to impress a guy.

More than that, she seems oddly withdrawn, and has ever since I got back into town . . .

Oh, no. What if my matchmaking only worked on one of the two people involved? Did I only saddle Carmen with the misery of unrequited love?

Inwardly I groan. Why, exactly, did I ever think *I* was an expert on romance?

After we've finished dinner, Geordie and Shay find a marathon of Star Wars movies on some channel and insist they need to watch the whole thing with Nicolas, because it's "such an important part of American culture." Meanwhile, Arturo—the only native-born American of the three—takes his turn washing the dishes. That gives me a chance to walk out with Carmen and suggest we make an evening run to Amy's for some ice cream. Austin's having one of its occasional bursts of unseasonal warmth—while it's cool enough for me to wear my mint-colored cardigan, it's definitely not too cold for ice cream.

(Then again, I tend to believe there's no such thing as "too cold for ice cream.")

Amy's is another of the city landmark shops on South Congress Street. As good as the specialty flavors are, that's not why this place became one of the most beloved places in town. The people behind the counter don't stop at scooping your ice cream—they flip it in the air, almost impossibly high, and manage to catch it with the cone or cup every single time. During the day, the line of people often stretches out the door onto the sidewalk, and people clap for each successful landing. Amy's night hours get quieter however, so Carmen and I practically have the place to ourselves.

"So," I say over a scoop of chocolate chip. "You seem kind of down."

"Down isn't the right word." Carmen stirs her strawberry milkshake with a red straw. "Freaked out, maybe."

I frown. *Freaked out* doesn't sound like romantic trouble. "What's the issue?"

She looks over her frosted glass and bites her full bottom lip. "You have to promise not to tell anyone yet. Maybe not anyone ever."

"Oh, my God, what is it? Is everything okay?"

Carmen laughs as she lowers her head behind her hand. "It's fine, I swear. I'm making it sound worse than it is."

"So spill it."

"I got into the Stanford Ph.D. program."

I admit it; I squeal like a teenager who just found out Zayn's coming back to One Direction. "That's fantastic! Beyond fantastic. What are you moping about? We should be—setting off fireworks! Getting seconds of ice cream! I think I still have my New Year's party hat."

"Thanks, Vivienne," she says, but her smile doesn't reach her eyes. "But think about it. Stanford is in California. If I move out there, I'm leaving Arturo and Shay and the baby behind."

So what? I want to protest. *It's not like you could live with your little brother forever. You have to go where your career takes you!*

But I'm coming from a background where I couldn't wait to get out of my house. Carmen and Arturo had an entirely different experience growing up. Sometimes they feel like their parents are too far away in San Antonio, only a few hours' drive. For Carmen to decamp to California—it's an even bigger leap than it would be for most people.

Even that isn't the main issue on Carmen's mind, though. She's thinking of the young family we just left in their run-down rental town house, the one they furnished from Goodwill.

"They need all the help they can get," she whispers. "Arturo got married so young. Shay has to take fewer classes this semester—she won't even graduate until this December! When I think about moving away, ditching them, I feel so guilty. But it's Stanford. One of the best math programs in the world."

"Hey, let's toast your getting in, okay? No matter what, that's awesome." I lift my ice cream cone; with a smile, she raises her milkshake glass to click against the cone. "Last semester you were in a panic. Now? You're king of the world."

Carmen holds out her arms for a moment, like Leonardo DiCaprio. Her smile remains crooked, though. "Honestly, that's another factor I have to consider. If the pressure was too much for me here, what's it going to be like at Stanford?"

"It *wasn't* too much for you here. If it were, you'd never have gotten into Stanford in the first place."

She turns back to her milkshake, looking up at me only with her eyes. "If it were you—what would you do?"

"I'd go. But I'm *not* you." Wow, super helpful. I struggle to come up with something better for her. "You want to be there for the people in your life, but you have to do the best you can for yourself too. Striking that balance is difficult."

In my mind I hear Jonah's voice telling me I don't look out for myself enough. I think he's wrong about that, mostly because he's had to ruthlessly prioritize his own mental health to even survive his terrible childhood. Where I see roots, he sees chains. But he's right about examining choices from time to time. Carmen shouldn't sacrifice everything for her family, but she's someone who's happiest when she's *not* completely independent.

I start to tell her as much, but that's when my phone buzzes. Hoping for a message from Jonah, maybe with another beautiful picture from Japan, I steal a glance at the screen—and my gut drops.

"Carmen," I say slowly, "I know you're having a rough night, but I've got to go."

Within twenty minutes I'm on the other side of town, in front of an apartment complex I've never visited before. I'm supposed sit here in my car and wait—under no circumstances am I to walk up to the door and knock.

But to hell with that. If I don't see or hear something in another five minutes, I'm going in there with my lug wrench in one hand and my phone set to speed-dial 911 in the other . . .

Then I see movement, and shadows against the ground-floor windows. The figure approaching me takes shape with every step forward, though he looks hardly recognizable.

When he slides into the car, I tell myself not to overreact. But when I see his face, I gasp.

"Please," Kip says, his voice thick through his split lip. "Just drive."

The silence between us stretches over the jazz piano on the radio until I can't bear it any more. "Tell me this one thing. Was it the first time?"

"No."

I can't wrap my mind around it. Kip Rucker sees all. Knows all. He arranges every single thing at the University of Texas at Austin to his satisfaction. I've heard people from virtually every department on campus wheedling for favors, seen him handle crises for everyone from the cafeteria lunch crew to one of the assistant deans. But here he is on the front seat of my car, bruised and bleeding from punches delivered by the man he cared about.

Why should it be so hard to believe? I stood as a bridesmaid in my rapist's wedding. Jonah still owns part of the house his stepfather lives in. Sometimes we can't pull away from the ones who have hurt us, any more than we can from the ones who have loved us.

And when they're the same person—that's the hardest of all.

"It's done, okay?" Kip flips down the sunshade to check his face in the mirror. "I'm not going back to him. Deleting his number from my phone. Blocking him on Twitter. Et cetera. So you can skip the lectures."

The overstuffed duffel bag he's clutching suggests he's telling the truth about leaving Ryan behind for good. Yet I can't get over the fact that Kip got hit and he *stayed*.

We tell ourselves only weak people are victims. That the bad guys wear black and broadcast their evil intentions with every word and gesture, so nobody can fall prey to them except innocents and fools. We tell ourselves that because it gives us the comforting illusion of control.

It's so much harder to face that it could happen to anyone. That it *does* happen, all the time, and we hide it because we're ashamed of what was done to us. Meanwhile, the people who should be ashamed go on with their lives, mentioning us only to talk about how "hysterical" or "crazy" we are.

Why is the world so fucked-up?

"I wasn't going to lecture you, Kip," I say, keeping my eyes on the road. "Do you need anything?"

Kip tosses it off lightly: "Got any miracle concealer? I don't intend to show up bruised at the office."

"I'll check my purse when I drop you off."

If Kip doesn't want to talk, we won't talk. But I reach over to take his hand, and after a moment, he squeezes my fingers.

By the time I get home, it's nearly midnight. My head throbs, my eyes feel red, and I feel like I could sleep for a thousand years. Tomorrow I have to TA a class and try to get in some studio time. If only I could call in sick. Or comatose. *Sorry, can't make it today, in a coma. See you tomorrow.*

I flop onto my bed, kicking off my shoes. As much as I'd like to slip into unconsciousness, an unfinished memo to my advisor nags at me. I'll sleep better if I get the damned thing done. So I wake my laptop, prop myself on some pillows. The screen glows softly to life. Before I can open my word processing program, however, Skype blinks with a call from an "unknown number."

It's international. I grin. While I don't know the country code for Japan off the top of my head, I'd bet anything this is Jonah.

Sure enough, he appears in the window, brilliant daylight streaming around him like a halo. When he sees me, his stern face eases into the slightest, gentlest smile. "Vivienne. I thought I'd try—just in case—but I figured you'd already be in bed."

"Nearly. But not quite." The sound of his voice flows through me—tranquilizer, painkiller, and intoxicant all at once. My head sinks deeper into the pillow as I nestle the computer comfortably in my lap. "How's the trip going?"

"Incredible. Seismic activity is nearly constant in Japan, of course, but the recent activity we've been monitoring . . . you don't want to hear about tectonic plates, do you?"

Jonah actually looks disappointed; I have to laugh. "Sometime. Not right now, though. I'm too exhausted for scientific talk."

"Bad day?"

"Not for me. But for some of the people around me, yeah." When I remember Kip's bloody mouth, sympathetic pain slashes me inside.

Jonah nods. "Sometimes that's worse. Your own problems, you can handle. Someone else's troubles might be out of your control."

I love his confidence, how he takes it as a given that he'll defeat any problem that comes his way. Why did I think Jonah and I needed some time apart? It sounded reasonable at the time—maybe it still is—but at the moment, while I'm worn out and my heart is hurting for Kip, all I can think of is how good it would be to feel Jonah's arms around me. "I've missed you."

"I've missed you too, but—" His expression tightens, becomes unreadable. "—our work here is turning out to be more complicated than we'd thought. The university has asked me to extend my stay."

"For how long?" I sit upright, rocking the computer. A month? A semester?

"Another three weeks, I'm afraid."

"*Ouch.*"

"I know. But this is an opportunity that doesn't come around very often—the earth's mantle rarely cooperates. We've gotten lucky." Jonah lifts one eyebrow. "Sure you won't come over for a visit?"

My resistance is weak. If I could take a time machine back to his first invitation, I'd accept, even if it did turn out to be a mistake. But now—"I'm in the thick of the semester. Plus Marvin has mono, so I've got to cover some classes for him. No escaping now. *Dammit.*"

"It's okay." He attempts to be cavalier about it, though I can sense his disappointment. "We'll have other trips."

Quickly I tally the days. "Three weeks—that should get you back to the U.S. in time for Mardi Gras. Promise me you'll get back for that. When you come to New Orleans with me, I feel so much braver. So much stronger." I can't resist a smile as I imagine some of the wilder aspects of Carnival, and how someone as somber as Jonah could deal with them. "Besides, you promised to take Libby to a parade, Remember? No fair backing out now."

"Mardi Gras. I think I can manage that."

It's a relief—no, more than that. A gift. "Good."

"Have you been staying at my place?"

I don't have to ask why he wants to know; it's not like Jonah owns a bunch of plants that need watering. "The Stalker hasn't shown up. People are speculating he blew town to avoid getting caught."

"Hope so," Jonah says.

"That just means that guy is out there in some new place where the women don't know to look out for him." Though, of course, we do. We are told, again and again, to look behind us and lock our doors and walk with confidence and do a thousand other things that may or may not reduce the chances of being raped. Society wants us scared, but refuses to change in the ways that would actually make us safe.

Jonah grimaces. "I didn't mean it like that."

"I know you didn't. You just want me to be safe. But I am, I swear."

He doesn't fully accept that even now; I can tell. Jonah's overprotective streak remains strong. "Stop by my place once in a while anyway. I like the thought of you there."

"Okay." I've done worse things for a guy than stay in his gorgeous penthouse. Besides, if I have to do without Jonah for three more weeks, it would be comforting to spend some time surrounded by his things, the books he loves, sheets that still smell faintly of his skin. Briefly I touch the screen. "I need you. I love you."

"I love you too," he says, and for one instant, it's as if there isn't half a world between us. As if I weren't on the edge of one night while he's awoken to a brand-new day. We're together in every way that matters.

TWENTY-FOUR

Jonah keeps his promise—barely.

I wait inside the security gates at Louis Armstrong International in New Orleans, suitcase at my feet, overpriced bottle of water in my hand. My flight landed almost two hours ago, but I decided I'd rather hang out here. After six weeks without Jonah, I don't intend to let our separation last one more minute than necessary.

For six weeks, I've slept alone. For six weeks, I've fantasized about Jonah, reliving every one of our games in brutal detail. Oh, I've tried other fantasies too—particularly reliving our nights in Scotland, and trying to pretend I got off from the way Jonah went down on me. But in the end—always, always, my mind reeled back toward the memory of Jonah at his most dominant, even his most cruel.

And yet I haven't only missed Jonah's darkness. I miss the man entire.

Finally, passengers begin trudging out of his arrival gate, towing roller bags behind them. Jonah's one of the first out. He sees me instantly, and his face lights up—and for one moment, it's like seeing the Jonah who should have been, the one without so many scars.

"*Vivienne.*" He pushes his way through the thicket of people waiting to board the next flight and clutches me in his arms so tightly my feet rise off the ground. Laughing, I sling my arms around his neck and kiss him. When our lips part, he brushes my hair back from my face. "I'd started to think I only dreamed you."

"Same here." We kiss again, and then I finally recognize the shadows beneath his eyes. "How jet-lagged are you?"

"I feel like today has already lasted about thirty-six hours."

Given his flights from Tokyo and L.A., he really might have been up that long. "Come on." I pull him toward the exit. "Let's get you to Liz's place, so you can get some sleep."

He laughs. "I want to say I have better things to do with you and a bed than sleep—but Jesus Christ, a nap sounds amazing."

"So you'll nap." As we walk through the security gate, toward baggage claim, I snuggle closer to his side and whisper, "You're gonna need your strength later."

"I like the sound of that."

We still haven't settled exactly what he's going to need his strength for—what our new boundaries will be in bed. But right now I'm so happy to be with Jonah again that nothing else matters.

The trip into the heart of New Orleans takes longer than it usually would. We first see signs of the chaos at baggage claim, where three times the number of usual suitcases spill along the conveyor belt, and the crowd's energy is already percolating. Then, as soon as our taxi gets within a few miles of Uptown, traffic slows and snarls. "They've started rerouting everything for the parades," I explain to Jonah, who has leaned his head against my shoulder.

"Already?" he murmurs. "It's six days until Mardi Gras, isn't it?"

"The parades started three weeks ago, silly."

Most people don't understand the full extent of New Orleans' Carnival season until they experience it for themselves. They think it's all about getting drunk on Bourbon Street, when the reality is bigger and stranger. Dozens of parades in locations all around the city, each one of them miles long, with thousands of riders, dancers and band members. Grand balls for various krewes held everywhere from country clubs to the Superdome. Open houses with trays of chicken, pots of gumbo, and ice chests full of beer for all the homeowners' friends, any friends of friends, and a few random strangers who seem amiable enough and so are invited in.

I've always loved Mardi Gras, but this year already feels special. I imagine the entire city is throwing a party to welcome Jonah home.

How perfectly have our stars aligned? For one, we're not staying with my parents, and not even my mother expects us to. A bunch of her Chi Omega sisters come down every few years, including this one, which means the house is packed. So instead Jonah and I get to camp out at the Garden District home that once belonged to the Marceaus, currently inhabited by Liz and her fiancé. She welcomes us to the tiny carriage house at the back of their property, which is shaded by a vast oak tree. By the time we get there, Jonah's on the verge of collapse, so I tuck him in and hang out with my childhood best friend for a while.

The first thing Liz says once we're alone: "Please explain to me why that delicious man is lying in bed without you lying on top of him."

"Liz!" I pretend to be shocked, which makes her laugh with gusto. "He's worn out."

"Unless you're the one who wore him out? Not an adequate answer." She drapes herself across the porch swing as sinuously as a cat. Her lime-colored dress contrasts beautifully with the swing's vivid yellow paint. "Now, I want to make sure I've got this straight, so I don't screw up like I did last fall. If I see anyone from your family, you *are* or *are not* in New Orleans right now?"

I sigh. "This time I'm here. We're even going to the Krewe of Templars ball tomorrow night with my parents, Chloe, everyone."

Liz shakes her head in pleasant disbelief. "Renee Charles approves of a man who's actually good for you. Will wonders never cease?"

"She only approves because his family is rich."

"Honey, take your victories where you find them."

That night is one of the first big parades, so we meet up with Chloe and Libby along the route on St. Charles. Bleary as Jonah is, he willingly takes Libby on his shoulders so she can beg for throws from the women riding the floats in their crazy-colored wigs; between his height and Libby's cuteness, they make an effective team. By the time the tenth marching band comes by, we're all draped in so many beads that our necks are heavy.

"I want all the purple ones!" Libby insists as we divvy things up between floats. "Jonah, you can have these pink ones if you give me the purple."

Chloe raises her voice enough to be heard over the approaching bass drums. "He won't want pink, silly. He's a boy."

But Jonah contradicts her by sliding the pink beads over his head. He nods toward the guys near us—who are wearing tutus and tinsel wigs. "Looks like the usual rules don't apply."

Afterward we walk back to Liz's amid the sounds of laughter and jangling beads. Liz invites us in for a cocktail, but Jonah's brief nap hasn't fully recharged him. We go to bed early, chastely, though I take enormous physical comfort simply from the warmth of his body next to mine. From the heaviness of his arm around me, and the splay of his rough hand over my belly.

"I brought you a present," Jonah murmurs. Even though I just turned out the light, he's already halfway asleep again. "I kept trying to think of the right moment to give it to you today, but it never came."

"Whenever. I'm just glad you're here."

"Mmm." He's agreeing with me, but already he's too close to unconsciousness to form words.

I am glad. Elated, even. Tonight couldn't have gone any better, especially given how exhausted Jonah is.

And yet the great unanswered question still looms before us. Will I have to give up the fantasy that turns me on every single time? I want to think I can grow past the fantasy to enjoy sex on different terms, but it's so hard for me to believe that's possible.

But this is mostly about Jonah's healing, his ability to face his own demons. Can he once again come to terms with the darkness inside him, the same darkness that wove us together?

You'll make this work, I tell myself. *We love each other enough for that. For now, just be grateful that he's here.*

All true. Yet it takes me a very long time to fall asleep.

The next day is the usual happy blur of Carnival: unwrapping the silk robe Jonah brought me from Japan (a delicate floral pattern in shades of dark pink and mint green); standing in line at lunchtime for the best po'boy in town; fighting the crowds at the grocery store to stock up on beer, wine, and snacks; and picking up Jonah's formal wear at the rental place. Tonight is the Krewe of Templars ball, which means we have to dress to the nines.

"I owned a tuxedo when I was in high school," Jonah says as he works with his white waistcoat. "My mother insisted, so she could drag me to every charitable event and show off what a 'happy family' we were. In all those years, I don't think I wore white tie and tails more than four times."

"At least you don't need a top hat." I shinny out of my jeans and black sweater, then watch Jonah watch my reflection in his mirror. My nude-colored strapless bra and panties are translucent, so he can see the flush of my nipples, the narrow dark triangle between my legs. After the comfortable, easy way we've been together these past few days, it's exhilarating to watch his eyes darken while he looks at my body. To know that I ignite the same desperate passion in him that he does in me.

His voice is husky as he says, "Are you wearing your green dress?"

"Of course. I bought it for Mardi Gras balls like these."

My careless shrug belies what we're both thinking of—the last time I wore this dress. Jonah tricked me into walking backstage at a charity event, then pretended to rape me, savagely, on a nearby table. I remember his hand around my throat, the growl of his voice as he called me a whore.

You loved that, Jonah. You can't pretend you don't. We can have all that back again. The only thing you have to do is ask—

But he says nothing as I slip into the emerald-green satin, not until I turn to him pulled together—my hair held back on one side with a rhinestone clip, which matches the heavy necklace around my throat. The glittering choker reminds me of his grip, the way it tightened just as I came. I think it reminds him too.

As for Jonah—sometimes white tie and tails can overwhelm a man. If the fit isn't ideal, the waistcoats emphasize the belly, or the tailcoat makes him look like a penguin. But Jonah has the kind of body that fills this out to perfection. He might have strolled out of the Edwardian era; I can imagine a vintage Rolls-Royce waiting for us, or an ivy-covered manor in the background.

But nothing in my imagination thrills me as much as the look on his face as he steps closer to me. His hand curls around my upper arm, his fingers tighten, and my breath catches in my throat . . .

"We should leave," he says, and steps away.

Frustration sparks inside me, but I force it into the far corners of my mind. The night is still young.

The Krewe of Templars is one of the old-school krewes. That means we aren't attending one of the raucous megaparties with thousands of people screaming for each float as it rolls in to complete its ride. Instead, we're at a private club in a classic New Orleans–style mansion, along with another four hundred people in formal wear.

Jonah looks bemused as the traditional ceremonies begin—mummers dancing around with masks and banners, some of the city's wealthiest men wearing sequined satin costumes and feathered headdresses, and young girls in white dresses being presented as ladies-in-waiting, princesses, or the queen. While the queen takes her traditional turn around the room, waving her glittery scepter at us all, he says, "This is like something out of another century."

"It *is* out of another century. I guess this is how people had fun before cable."

He nods toward the queen in white, with her enormous sparkling ruff. "Did you do this?"

"I was one of the princesses. Chloe had been queen a few years before—they wouldn't pick a second girl from the same family so close together. Besides, I always thought it was kind of ridiculous." Meanwhile, Chloe hung a photo of herself as Templars queen in the foyer of her home.

"You hated it?" Jonah says, sympathetically.

Ugh, yes, awful, I begin to answer, but I stop myself. This is another chance to be totally honest. "No, I didn't hate it. Maybe I laughed at how seriously the others took the whole thing. Like, one girl kept crying because she hadn't been named queen. As if it could ever matter. Still, I got to dress up and hear everyone say I was beautiful. Every girl likes that, on some level. And for me—I guess this was one of the first times I remember feeling pretty without also feeling vulnerable. Where I started to regain some of the confidence that was taken from me."

He kisses my forehead and whispers, "You should've been queen."

Longingly I glance at the red velvet curtains hanging from the sixteen-foot windows. *We could find a private spot, you could drag me back there, Jonah, please—*

But of course he doesn't.

After the festivities comes the supper dance. A band swings into the usual reception-style hits: "She Loves You," "Stayin' Alive," "Celebration," "500 Miles." Enormous buffets of rich Southern food are placed along the walls so we can feast on biscuits and gravy, smothered chicken and creamy grits. Tablecloths are linen; the silverware is actually silver. From the bartenders flow endless glasses of wine. The lines at the bars are long, though, so when Jonah goes to get us a couple flutes of champagne, he's missing for a while.

"Libby will be eligible to be a lady-in-waiting in just three more years," my mother says. Her beige lace gown glints softly in the light from the chandelier above. "I can hardly wait!"

I frown. "*Is* she eligible? I thought that was only for girls whose fathers belonged to the krewe."

"Well, you know, we've been working on Anthony to join. I'm sure he'll want Libby to have this experience, so it can't be long."

As always, Anthony's name makes my stomach clench. "Mom, come on. Even if he did want to join, wouldn't that only make things more difficult for Chloe?"

My mother doesn't meet my eyes as she salts her grits. "Every marriage has its bumps."

Meaning my parents still hope Chloe and Anthony will reunite. Suddenly I'm no longer hungry. "Jonah's taking a while with the drinks," I say as I toss my napkin onto the table and rise to my feet. "I'm going to check on him."

I weave my way through the dancers, scanning the room. The multiplicity of bars means I don't know exactly where he might be. In one corner I see Liz laughing with her fiancé; in another, Dad is talking with old friends, no longer quite filling out the tailcoat he's owned for years.

At the doors to the veranda, I see a flash of cotton-candy pink chiffon—almost undoubtedly Chloe. She's been remarkably quiet all evening; I wonder if she's become sentimental about her glory days. It looks like she's near the outdoor bar, so I head that way.

A man in a red satin knight's costume holds the heavy door open for me. I hug myself against the cool air as I look for Chloe, who is standing next to Jonah.

With her hand on his chest.

"What's the rush?" She laughs, low and sultry. "I think there's a gazebo out back."

Jonah stands rock-still, staring past Chloe—no, through her. He holds a flute of champagne in each hand. "I'm taking a drink to Vivienne."

"Vivienne can wait."

Chloe leans in closer and slides her hand down his waistcoat, toward his pants. Jonah steps away, his face creasing into a frown. "Drink some coffee," he says, words clipped. "You've had too much."

"I'd say I haven't had enough." She lets her head fall to one side; a long blond curl, escaped from her chignon, brushes her bare shoulder. "Come on, Jonah. Not even a taste?"

"Excuse me," Jonah replies, and walks away. Within a couple of steps he sees me. He doesn't stop walking, merely slows as he whispers to me, "It's not worth getting into."

"Not for you. It is for me." I push past him and grab Chloe by the elbow. "Did you say something about a gazebo?"

I haul my sister off the veranda, down the steps. From the corner of my eye I see Jonah hesitating, wondering whether to pursue us; he's smart enough to finally decide he shouldn't. This is between Chloe and me.

"What are you doing?" Chloe protests. She has the nerve to be angry. "It's damp out here. I'm getting mud on my shoes!"

"To hell with your shoes. You were hitting on Jonah!"

I expect her to deny it; the words to prove her wrong hover on my tongue. Instead, Chloe sticks her chin out. "He's a free man. He can make his own choices."

"*What?*" None of this makes any sense. Chloe and I are standing on the club's broad lawn, beneath an enormous tree roped in fairy lights, in floor-length gowns—and yet I'm about two seconds away from starting an actual fistfight. "This from the same person who said I was 'flirting' with Anthony after he—"

"Exactly!" Chloe smiles, triumphant. "Turnabout is fair play. You went after my man once. Now I went after yours. See how it feels? If you got to make love with Anthony, shouldn't I get a turn with Jonah Marks?"

Make love. I could scream. I could vomit. "I didn't 'go after' Anthony! He came after me! Jesus, Chloe, you heard him admit that he raped me."

She flinches. The word *rape* isn't one she's had to face very often. "I heard him admit that the two of you slept together, yes. He made a mistake, and he lied to me about it, and I'm having trouble getting past that. But that doesn't mean *you* get to tell lies too. Get off your damned high horse and admit that I've never done anything to you half as terrible as you did to me when you had sex with Anthony."

Chloe still thinks I'm lying. She always has. Even hearing Jonah confront Anthony—even seeing Anthony shrink in front of the accusation—it wasn't enough to shake her belief in the man she married.

Or maybe the truer answer is that it wasn't enough to make my sister finally believe in me.

"I ought to feel sorry for you," I say, my voice shaking. "Because your whole fucking life is a lie. But you know what? That's your choice. So wallow in it, Chloe. We're done."

With that I turn and walk back into the club. If Chloe follows me at any point, she doesn't make it inside. Several feet from the door stands Jonah. While my glass of champagne is still full, I can see he's taken a few sips of his own. No doubt he needed to brace himself after my sister practically felt him up. "Hey," he says as he comes toward me. "Are you all right?"

"No."

Jonah studies my face. "You realize I didn't—"

"You did absolutely nothing wrong. That's not the problem." The revelry surrounding us seems to mock the misery crashing into my soul. "Chloe thinks I slept with Anthony of my own free will. She heard the truth and she still doesn't believe me. She wanted to hook up with you for revenge. Because Anthony raped me, she wants *revenge*."

He closes his eyes, only for a moment, feeling my pain as if it were his own. "God. I'm sorry."

"Let's leave. I want to leave, now."

"Of course." Setting the flutes of champagne on the nearest tray, he puts one arm around my shoulders. "We'll get a taxi."

On a Carnival night. Not likely. "We could walk there faster. It's only a dozen blocks."

"Okay. We'll walk."

Jonah puts his arms around me, and I hug him. Around us, the partygoers laugh and dance to "Don't Stop Believin'." The celebration roars on.

TWENTY-FIVE

Our walk home passes in a daze. Jonah keeps his arm around me as we take St. Charles most of the way back, walking beneath curtains of beads trapped by nearby wires and tree branches. The crews have already cleared away most evidence of the earlier parades, but a few people in feather boas stagger around, their giggling fading into the sounds of cars driving by.

"I want to go home tomorrow," I say, my voice thick. "I can't stay here until Fat Tuesday, I'm sorry—"

"Don't feel bad on my account. I'm here with you. For you." As Jonah says this, my heel catches in a sidewalk crack; only his steady arm keeps me from falling. "We'll fly out as early as possible."

I laugh brokenly. "It's Carnival, Jonah. Every seat on every plane has been sold out for months. We'll have to rent a car and drive." Assuming the rental cars aren't sold out too.

Jonah remains unperturbed. "Trust me. This is one of those times when owning part of an airline comes in handy."

Whatever. I don't care if we ride horses or roller skate. Nothing matters except getting the hell away from Chloe, and my entire family.

No wonder my mother assumes Chloe and Anthony will get

back together, I realize. As far as she knows, Anthony hasn't done anything so terribly wrong. She's treating this as a decade-old peccadillo, something better off forgotten. Chloe hasn't said one word to convince her otherwise.

But—even if I *had* wanted to have sex with Anthony, I was only fourteen! That's statutory rape by any measure, because the age of consent in Louisiana is seventeen. Shouldn't my mother care about that, if nothing else?

She doesn't, though. For Mom and Chloe both, this is a very simple story. Anthony was just "being a guy." It couldn't have happened if I didn't ask for it. The end.

Quietly Jonah says, "Do you want to go by the house tomorrow to say good-bye to Libby?"

Oh, God, Libby. She'll never understand why her Aunt Vivi left before Fat Tuesday. The thought brings me to the verge of tears. "I can't. I want to, but I can't."

"Shhh. It's okay. You can call her."

Will Chloe even put Libby on the phone? I doubt it.

Despair fills me. I've tried so hard to be good. To think healthy thoughts. To become strong inside and out. None of it has helped. None of it has changed one damn thing.

By the time we get back to the carriage house, my feet throb at the heels; when I slip off my heels, the strap marks stretch red across my ankles. Jonah turns on one lamp before taking out his phone. "I'm just going to text Liz and tell her where we are."

I ought to have thought of that. My mind is too crowded with memories of Chloe's words, my mother's callousness and always, always Anthony. With fumbling fingers I remove my heavy rhinestone necklace; it takes a few tries, because I still have just enough alcohol in me to make me clumsy.

And reckless.

Jonah has already shucked his tailcoat. He stands there in white shirt, waistcoat, and tie, the shadows outlining his perfect profile. The elegance of his attire can't fully disguise the raw power of his form. I know the savage beneath the surface, and only that savagery can help me tonight.

When Jonah takes me—when we play our games—he casts out every doubt, every fear. I become nothing but a body. Nothing but desire and delight. My mind forgets everything but how he tastes, or how he feels inside me.

I want to forget.

This carriage house is one large room, but a Coromandel screen separates the bed and bathroom from the small sitting area. Two cane chairs sit beneath a gilded mirror, across from a coffee table laden with tourist guides and a longer sofa.

It's velvet. Not leather like the one we had when I was a teenager. It's dark blue instead of tan. A couple feet shorter too. But it will do.

"Jonah?" I wait until he looks up, and we are face to face. "I need to—to live through this."

For the first split second, he doesn't understand. So I sit on the sofa, leaning back slightly, bracing myself against force that hasn't yet come. I lift my chin, exposing my throat. There's nothing deliberately sexual about any of this, but it is the body language of vulnerability. We both know that vulnerability turns him on.

Break me. Force me. Let yourself go.

He tilts his head slightly, eyes searching mine, as comprehension sinks in. "Vivienne—on a sofa—that's where he—"

"I *need* this. I need it now. I need you." Does he need me to beg? I'll beg. "Please. This one time. Just—shove me down. Push my dress up. Force me onto my back."

He hesitates. Although I can tell he'd like to argue, he doesn't. Instead his breaths quicken slightly, and I know he's imagining me under him. Pressing me down. Fucking me hard.

Jonah doesn't want to want our games—but he does. No matter how much he wishes otherwise, he will *always* want them.

And I'm desperate enough to make him admit it.

"Come on, Jonah." I remove the rhinestone clip from my hair, so it falls loose and messy around my face—the way it would if he'd already wrecked me. His gaze drifts downward, where the satin of my gown clings to my belly. The low neckline of the dress must reveal how my breasts rise and fall with each breath. And I'm breathing so fast and shallow now that I'm starting to get dizzy. I want him so fucking badly. "Come *on*."

He breaks. Jonah's on me in an instant, slamming my shoulders down onto the sofa so hard I cry out in involuntary surprise. His rough hands reach beneath the rustling green skirt of my dress, fingers digging into my thighs as he pries them apart. My panties stretch enough to allow his fingers to penetrate my cunt, just an inch or two. My wetness welcomes him, soaking through the thin fabric. Slowly Jonah smiles—the fierce hunter's smile I crave.

"See?" he whispers. "See what I can make you do?"

What did I do? When this happened for real—what did I try? I struggled so little. But I attempted to pull down my T-shirt; the closest I can get is to paw at Jonah's arms as if I could get him to let go. He's so strong I couldn't do it, ever. Not even if I really wanted to.

Jonah laughs and tugs me roughly down, so that not even my head rests on one of the pillows. I'm flat beneath him as he moves his hand to cover my mouth. His skin smells of my sex. "Shhhhh. Don't say a word. Don't say anything."

I make a small, despairing cry against his palm. His hand tightens.

"You know what I want," he says, grinding against me to make sure. He's rock-hard for me already, his cock pressing insistently against my belly. Still he wears his white bow tie and waistcoat, the elegant attire a vivid contrast to his brutality. "You're going to give it to me. You're gonna give it up."

Although I try to twist beneath him, it's useless. He rams his cock against me again, just as he would if he were shoving into me.

Jonah's stare has turned dangerous. Ravenous. He loves the sight of my frightened face half-hidden by his palm. Roughly he whispers, "Take it out."

I hesitate, like I would have then. I wouldn't have been sure what he meant, or how to proceed—

"Do it."

My hands shake with remembered fear and new arousal. Clumsily I reach for his belt, fumble with the buckle and zipper. His enormous cock juts out almost immediately, eager to be free, and inside me.

As I do this, Jonah uses his other hand to rub at my nipple through the fabric of my dress. The strapless bra I wear is so thin that it does nothing to veil the heat and friction of his thumb. Nor does it hide how my nipples are hardening into points, more and more obvious beneath the shimmering green fabric. "See?" he whispers. "You're figuring it out. This is what you're for."

Nothing but a body. Nothing but the way his bare cock feels against my trembling hands, nothing but the spiraling, dizzy yearning that has taken me over completely.

"Shhh," Jonah repeats as he draws his hand away from my mouth. As I lie beneath him, helpless, he bends his head down and does something he's never done during any of our games. He kisses me.

But this is unlike any of his other kisses, which have been tender, yearning, passionate—and always, always real. This kiss is meant to punish, insult, and bruise. He shoves his tongue into my mouth, almost down my throat, a deliberate violation meant to mimic everything else he's going to do to me. I whimper as he keeps thrusting his tongue into me, and as his hand moves to pull aside the crotch of my panties. The head of his cock brushes my thigh, leaving a streak of damp pre-come behind.

My whimper breaks into a scream as he shoves inside.

It didn't hurt. It only burns, the way it always does, the good hot ache of my body opening for the impossible length of him. And yet I keep crying out into his open mouth, then louder and more desperately as he buries his face in the curve of my neck.

They told me I would have screamed. I should have screamed. Now I can't stop screaming.

"Nobody can hear you," Jonah pants as he starts thrusting in earnest, hard enough to make my breasts shake, so that the thumping of our bodies against the sofa is loud in the room. "Nobody cares."

Oh, fuck, why did that make it better? My cries shift into a higher pitch as I feel myself starting to give.

Jonah recognizes my response, knows I'm close. He props himself onto his arms so he can pound me faster. I can see the base of his cock in the split seconds before his shaft sinks into me again, all the way to the hilt. His smile is feral now, his abandon obvious.

I knew you wanted it, I think. Is that his line or mine?

My cheeks flush. The wave starts to hit me. I turn my head from his as I come—pleasure rushing through me, ten times more intense after all these weeks without him. My climax makes me shudder beneath him, and Jonah laughs.

"Yes," he whispers as he pistons into me even faster than before. "Fuck, yes—"

Jonah groans as he spends into me, a deep guttural sound that comes from his core. His eyes screw shut and he grimaces as if he were in agony.

But it's good. I know it's good. He wanted this all along.

When he finally collapses atop me, we lie in silence for a few moments, breathing hard. Neither of us knows what words to use, if we even have the breath to speak.

He recovers first. "Are you okay?"

I have to lick my lips and swallow before I can speak. "I am now."

No, we didn't exactly copy what Anthony did to me—but this came close. Close enough. Why was that so completely fucking great for me? Why does it feel like the fresh wounds to my spirit are already bandaged and healing?

Doreen's going to have to put in some overtime. "What about you?"

"Let's go to bed," Jonah says as he pulls out. That's the only answer he gives. Hot come leaks from me onto the dress—but I was getting it cleaned after this trip anyway. I'll just have to avoid eye contact with the guys at the drycleaner's when I pick it up.

Together we stumble to the bed, help each other undress. We leave our things crumpled on the floor. This is one of those times when the aftermath of orgasm is so powerful that it drags you down into slumber almost instantly.

Only in the final moments before I fall asleep do I realize Jonah's lying with his face away from mine.

When Jonah said owning an airline would come in handy, I had visions of Oceanic punting two unsuspecting tourists so we could fly to Austin in their place. What he actually meant is that, if you're one of the owners of an airline, you know people who would be willing to loan you a private plane on short notice.

"Swanky," I say as we take our seats—lush, leather-covered, facing a small table. It's an attempt to lighten the mood, which fails. Jonah doesn't respond; he hasn't said much all day.

The pilots say hello before sealing themselves in their tiny cockpit.

We have no attendant, but there's a minibar stocked with sodas and snacks. I take a can of Diet Coke and look inquisitively at Jonah, who simply shakes his head no. Although nobody tells us to belt ourselves in for takeoff, I do it anyway. I tell myself this is for safety's sake. Really, at the moment, I'm grateful for anything that can make me feel secure, on any level.

It's not a long flight from New Orleans to Austin—maybe not long enough for the conversation we need to have. Still, about half an hour in, while neither of us can easily dodge the Talk. "Listen," I begin, "about last night."

"You don't have to explain why you wanted it." Jonah continues staring out the window, down at the clouds. "I don't have to understand, and you don't either. What we did helped you. That's enough."

If only I could reconcile my needs so easily. But my self-acceptance is something I can work on over time. The bleak expression on Jonah's face worries me more. "I violated a boundary I meant to respect. That wasn't fair."

His smile is grim. "Do you think you could have pushed me over the line if I hadn't wanted you to?"

There. At last he admitted that he still longs for our games, as much as I do. I knew it last night, when he took so much delight in pinning me down; what I wasn't sure of was whether *he* knew it. He does. Yet there's no release in this. If anything, Jonah is even more conflicted than before.

He continues, "It's hard for me to control myself, knowing you want me to lose control."

"I'm sorry."

"Don't apologize. It's not your fault. Do you understand? *None of this* is your fault." Jonah finally turns to face me. "I was the one who came to you. The one who thought we could live out opposite sides of a fantasy without any repercussions. What a goddamned fool I was."

"One of those repercussions was falling in love." I lean across the table, close enough to take one of his hands in mine. "Another was mind-blowing sex. Okay, we have some psychological issues to deal with. More than most people. That doesn't mean we can't handle it."

"We've had this conversation before. Every time, you nearly convince me. But every time, we go one more step over that line, heading somewhere neither of us wants to go." Jonah breathes out heavily. "I loved last night. I fucking *loved* it. I got off as hard and as good as I ever have. And this time, I wasn't just pretending to be a rapist. I was pretending to be *your* rapist. Where does this end?"

"I don't know," I confess. "Last night troubles me too. But it was good for us both, so let's not judge each other for that."

"Vivienne, I'd never judge you for how you've dealt with what happened to you. I judge myself."

How can I respond? But he isn't looking for an answer. Jonah's thumb brushes across my wrist, a gentle caress that I should find more reassuring than I do. We remain silent until my ears tighten, and the sound of the engine changes.

We've already begun our descent.

That night, we sleep in our separate apartments. Before we have sex again, we need to have a whole new set of negotiations, and neither of us is strong enough to deal with them yet. I go to bed early. After I climb between the sheets, I text Jonah good night, but I don't wait for his answer before putting the phone on silent and turning out the lamp.

When I hear the buzzing from my nightstand, my first groggy thought is that Jonah wanted to tell me good night himself—which is sweet enough to make me smile. Then I see that nearly an hour has passed; I drifted off without realizing it. And while there are a couple of texts from Jonah, it's Carmen calling. With a frown, I slide the bar across to answer. "Hello?"

"Vivienne?" She sounds strange. Tense. "Are you still in New Orleans with Jonah?"

"No, we came back today. My family . . . they were getting on my nerves, that's all. What's wrong?"

"Did you see the ten o'clock news?"

"Uh, no—"

"They were talking about the Stalker."

The Austin Stalker—I'd almost managed to forget about him. After two months of inactivity, the guy seemed likely to have blown town. "Oh, no. He's back?"

"He never left. Apparently there was a third girl—she was scared to go to the police, because he told her he'd come back and kill her if she did. This was right after New Year's."

Damn it. That poor girl. "Well, don't worry about me. I always turn all the dead bolts, and nobody could get through these windows without shattering the glass. Pepper spray on the keychain, as always. And remember that self-defense class we took together? 'You don't have to be stronger than your assailant. You just have to be strong enough to hurt him.'" I've never forgotten those words; they reassured me tremendously.

Carmen isn't reassured in the slightest. "That wasn't what I was calling about. Oh, God. This is difficult."

I sit upright, the quilt and sheets sliding down. "What is it?"

"Vivienne—a source told the news that the police suspect Jonah."

TWENTY-SIX

Apparently it is not libel to report on television that someone is a person of interest in a criminal investigation, especially if this is true. A person of interest isn't necessarily a suspect; it can be a witness, or merely a person who might be able to disprove an alibi. That said, Jonah's new lawyers swoop down swiftly and sharply enough to make sure the allegation is never repeated on the air.

Too late.

To the world at large, *person of interest* means guilty as hell, and after months of suspense, the fear and hatred is finally directed at a target: Jonah Marks.

Carmen calls me once more that night, twice in the morning. "Have you heard anything else? Did the police come by?"

"Why would they come here?" I'm having this conversation wrapped in a towel, postshower. The sooner I can pull myself together and get over to Jonah's, the better. He's answered my texts, but he sounded terrible on the phone. I can only imagine how torn up he must be. "They already questioned me once. I told them I was with Jonah on the nights of the attacks, but they didn't believe me."

When I first heard the news, I felt a brief flicker of hope that at least this might have happened while Jonah was in Japan. Even the baddest Bad Cop in the world couldn't argue with that alibi; the stamps on Jonah's passport would provide complete vindication. But no, the Austin Stalker struck the night before the trip—in the hours when I went to the studio so Jonah could finish packing. Home alone: the worst cover story in the world. Why didn't I stay over that night?

Then again, if the cops didn't believe my alibi for the first two evenings, the third might only have made them more suspicious. But how is it possible for people to be more suspicious of Jonah than they already are today?

At least I can convince Carmen. She sighs and says, "You told me that already. I'm sorry. I just wanted to make sure you were safe."

"I realize that." My temper is soothed by remembering that she's only looking out for me. "But there's no need to worry."

"That guy has gotten worse. Scarier."

This time the Stalker injured his victim far more seriously, strangling her long enough to terrify her and bring her to the brink of unconsciousness, but not long enough to kill. According to the forensic psychology expertise I've picked up via *Criminal Minds* reruns, that means the guy is "escalating." He's wondering whether he'd enjoy murdering women too. "Yeah. You still have your pepper spray too, right?"

"I gave mine to Shay. I'll pick up some more today, though, if they're not sold out. The entire town is in a panic."

Certainly the entire town feels the need to check in with me, or so it seems. Carmen's phone call is followed by one from Kip ("I'm telling *everyone* I know that Jonah's innocent, and commanding them to spread the word!") and a text from Geordie (I believe you! I absolutely believe you. Jonah's wrongly accused. All I'm saying is, if you're worried, call and I'll come over anytime). Like Geordie would last long in a fight against Jonah. But I suppose it's sweet that he would try. Shay sends a long rambling e-mail about how nobody who works in earth sciences thinks Jonah could've had anything to do with it, but these same nobodies all feel the need to repeat the scary stuff that someone *else* has told them. While I feel sure Shay's belief in his innocence is genuine, I wonder about his fellow professors. The department staff. His students.

Jonah is as strong a person as I've ever known. But he's proud too. Working with students who believe him guilty of the most despicable crime—that would be one of the few blows I'm not sure he could bear.

Ironically, the one person in Austin I don't hear much from is Jonah himself. He answered my call tersely last night, but I didn't blame him; he was already on the other line with his new legal representation. Today's he's replied to my texts, but only briefly, and never initiated any of his own.

> I'm angry but I'm handling it. / No, I don't think it was Carter—just the usual news leak. / Maddox and Elise shouldn't hear about this until I have a strategy for dealing with the situation.

Strategy? That was probably the word his new lawyer had used. But after months of slowly getting closer to Jonah—of our honesty and intimacy unfolding petal by petal—it seems as if he is suddenly far away again.

Don't take it personally, I remind myself. *When he's been hurt or when he gets angry, Jonah sometimes needs a while to pull himself together before he can talk about it. His feelings should be the priority today, not yours.* I text him about coming over to his place, and his OK is enough, for now.

At least he's not shutting me out completely. As hard as it is for him to admit it, he needs support and comfort. When I'm at his place, we'll have our chance to really talk.

Just in time for the Thoth parade to roll, I call home, knowing full well my parents and Chloe will be standing on the route with Libby, unable to hear their cell phones ring over the music and cheers. My text messages yesterday let them know the basics, but this is where I supply the longer explanation that should in theory keep my mother from guilt-tripping me about this for years to come. Jonah already agreed to have a "work emergency" to explain our absence. Chloe knows the truth, of course, but she won't admit it to a soul. Mom may favor her shamelessly, but she'd still be horrified to hear that Chloe threw herself at my boyfriend. So I make my apologies, lying without guilt.

No questions will be asked. They always prefer my fictions to the truth.

Afterward I somehow focus enough to review the lesson plans for the week, and to send a department e-mail letting everyone know I'm back early from Carnival and won't need them to cover those two days after all. I unpack the rest of my suitcase; I pull my hair back in a ponytail and put on leggings and a boho tunic. Jangly earrings too. But every bit of this—selecting my outfit, separating colors and whites for the laundry, even providing the best cover story for my family—it's all just noise I have to get through before I can go to Jonah's.

He's saved me so many times. I intend to save him too.

With one finger I punch in the security code for the garage of Jonah's building, my red nails shiny against the dull silver. No news crews seem to be milling about outside, waiting to ambush him. Maybe that's silly, to assume the local TV stations would be so bloodthirsty—especially after his lawyer's warnings. But it's still a relief to see the sidewalks bare of anyone but the usual weekend brunch crowd. At least the press is leaving Jonah alone.

Yet when the elevator doors open into his apartment, I see he's not completely alone.

"Ridiculous," says Rosalind. She's pacing the far side of his apartment, beside the longest wall of windows, so distracted by her wrath that she doesn't even notice me stepping into the kitchen. Jonah, standing at the kitchen island, looks up at me. His arms are crossed against his pale gray T-shirt, and his posture is slightly hunched, like a person trying to endure stomach pain. Rosalind continues, "How can they do that when they have *absolutely nothing* against you?"

"They have a citizen's report and some deputy with a loose tongue," Jonah says. "That's enough, apparently."

When Rosalind turns around to argue, she finally catches sight of me. "Vivienne. Thank goodness. We need to get Team Jonah together!"

Despite everything, I can't help laughing at the term *Team Jonah.* "It's good to see you too."

Dr. Rosalind Campbell entered my life in two entirely different ways—as Shay's obstetrician, and as Jonah's running partner and perhaps his closest friend in town. She wears white jeans and a pale pink sweater that set off her dark brown skin, even pearl studs in her ears, yet her usual elegant composure has been tested by this wretched day. Well, that makes all of us. At least Jonah has more than one person who'll drop everything to stand at his side.

"Threaten to sue," Rosalind continues as she walks toward the kitchen area of Jonah's open-plan apartment. I set down my purse and come to Jonah's side, though I don't attempt to hug or kiss him; that's the kind of comfort he'll be slower to accept. She keeps going, "It doesn't matter if you don't have grounds. They'd still have to pay their lawyers to get the suit thrown out of court!"

"We already did all of that." Jonah rubs at his temples; his pallor is so marked that the stubble on his cheeks stands out sharply. I don't think he's slept. "Which is why they're not repeating the story."

Rosalind retorts, "But you'd feel better if you yelled at them personally, wouldn't you?"

"Maybe." Jonah's smile is fleeting. "Today, I'd rather not."

She turns her attention to me. "You haven't come by the restaurant yet, Candace says. I've already given Jonah hell about it; now it's your turn."

"It won't be long," I promise. Apparently Rosalind's partner, Candace, is the head chef at one of the fanciest restaurants in town. We've been invited to enjoy a five-star dinner on the house, whenever we'd like, and the thought cheers me for a second. Then I imagine the two of us going there now, surrounded by whispers and suspicious glances. "Not *too* long, anyway."

Rosalind must have caught the wary note in my voice. Her eyes flick from me to Jonah and back again. Turning brisk, she says, "I should leave you two to it. Jonah, you'll call if you need me?"

"Of course," he answers, by rote.

She doesn't let him get away with that. As she slings her designer bag over one shoulder, Rosalind fixes him with her sternest stare. I can imagine her striking fear into the heart of interns. "You'll call even if you don't need me. At least once a day. And the final decision on whether or not I'm needed is up to me. Got it?"

Jonah is clearly torn between affection and exasperation. "Got it."

Rosalind's smile returns as she looks at me. "Watch this one, will you?"

"I'll do my best."

Why does that make Jonah go tense?

As soon as the elevator doors slide shut around Rosalind, I run my hand along his upper arm. "You look worn out."

"I am."

"Do you think you could nap? You need rest."

"I couldn't sleep." He leans back against his enormous fridge and stares up at the wooden and metal beams along his ceiling. "My landline number is unlisted, but somehow a couple dozen people got hold of it. They called all night—some hangups, but mostly death threats and warnings that I was going straight to hell."

"*Jonah*. Did you call the police?"

"The same guys who think I'm guilty? If anyone actually tried to murder me, they'd probably applaud."

"You're entitled to protection! They should never have put you in danger like that."

Jonah shrugs, maddeningly unconcerned. "This building is pretty secure. And I don't think any of my neighbors even know my name. It's fine."

"You could stay at my place for a while," I offer. "Until things blow over."

He doesn't seem to hear me. "The department head wants us to have a 'conference' tomorrow morning. Probably he's going to suggest a voluntary leave of absence. He can make that sound like he's looking out for me, when really he's putting as much distance between me and the department as possible."

What happened to loyalty? Don't these people know Jonah at all?

Then I realize—no, they don't. Jonah's taciturn nature, his stubborn independence, and cool temper keep him from making friends easily. Most people misunderstand him at first, mistaking his silence for contempt. I did too. Few would guess the scars behind that quiet façade.

The injustice of it makes me want to weep. Jonah keeps to himself because Carter Hale taught him to distrust the world. Now the world distrusts Jonah in return.

"We'll get past this," I swear. "No matter what happens, I'm here with you. Okay?"

He ducks his head. "Vivienne, we have to talk."

Uh-oh. This sounds bad. Like, fleeing-the-jurisdiction bad—but no, Jonah's smarter than that. "What is it?"

He walks across the room, into the living room area with its long sofa, brick wall, and the red leather ottoman where he once tied my wrists behind my back . . . but I can't think about that right now. Not while Jonah looks so haggard, even distraught.

"There's no telling how long this will last," he says. "Or how bad it will get. While I don't think Carter is behind this, he'll try to take advantage of it if he can."

"Then you guys go nuclear on him, right?"

Jonah shrugs again. "The nuclear option felt better when Carter was the one being attacked. I don't like being on the defensive."

True. Still, there have to be actions we can take. Things we can do. And the fact of Jonah's innocence has to come out sooner or later. "It's going to be okay, Jonah. In the long run, at least, and hopefully a lot sooner than that."

"It's going to be hell. And I'm not putting you through it."

His meaning hits me, as physically and emotionally shocking as a slap to the face. "You—are you saying—you're breaking up with me until you're cleared?"

"No," Jonah says evenly. "I'm breaking up with you for good."

I sit down on the nearest chair so I won't fall. "What? *Why*?"

"I'm bad for you. This fantasy of mine—it's the whole reason I got reported to the police in the first place. It's like this . . . *poison* that seeps out of me and ruins everything. Doesn't matter how hard I try; it's never going away. That wanting will always be a part of me. I finally learned that in New Orleans."

I knew he had, and I was fool enough to be happy about it. Now it's like I'm trapped inside some terrible car crash, watching the metal buckle and glass break in excruciating slow motion. "It's my fantasy too. And it's even worse for me than it is for you."

"No. You've done the hard work, Vivienne. Bared your soul to a therapist for years, drawn lines that let you stay in touch with your family without being overwhelmed by them. You've surrounded yourself with friends who would do anything for you, and have made you a part of their lives." The terrible longing I hear in Jonah's voice breaks my heart. "Maybe you aren't completely better yet—but you will be. You're on that path. And I never have been."

"You came to counseling with me—Rosalind's your friend, and your sisters and brother—"

Jonah interrupts as if he hadn't even heard me. "We're both in danger of drowning. But you're doing your damnedest to swim, and I'm nothing but the weight dragging you down. So I'm cutting you loose."

Tears and anger war inside me. "That's not your call to make! I'm the one who gets to decide what I can take. Don't you realize what this relationship has meant to me? I *love you*, Jonah. How could you ever believe losing you wouldn't destroy me?"

"You're more indestructible than you think," he says quietly. "This isn't a debate. A relationship ends when one person says it ends. We're over. That's it."

He thinks he's being so fucking noble and strong. Instead he's torn my heart in two.

But he's right about one thing. It will do no good to argue. For today, at least, Jonah can't hear anything I have to say.

"We'll talk about this some other time." That's about the best I can do. "When you're thinking more clearly."

"I'm thinking clearly right—" Jonah at least has the decency to fall silent when I hold up my hand. I can't take any more of this at the moment. If I hear him give his reasons one more time, I might start to believe him.

Wiping at my eyes, I pick up my purse. I never got around to taking off my jacket. I haven't been in his apartment fifteen minutes.

When I look back at Jonah, I don't say good-bye. The only words I speak are, "I love you."

"I love you too," Jonah says. His voice breaks, and that nearly destroys me. But he doesn't falter. Not even this moment will change his mind.

Behind him in its heavy frame is my etching, the one he won at the charity auction a few months ago. Jonah didn't understand what the image meant until I told him. He thought the man with his hands around the captive bird was keeping it only to protect it. I explained that the man was about to set it free for good. At the time, I had no idea that image was prophecy.

The elevator doors slide shut behind me. Leaning against the metal wall, tears hot on my face, I remember my resolution to come up with a new etching, one that would symbolize everything Jonah meant to me. But I never found the right image. As hard as I tried, I never figured him out.

TWENTY-SEVEN

The entire city of Austin seems to fall under a dark cloud. Normally we're friendly here—the type to wave or say hello to a stranger on the sidewalk. Laid-back, easygoing. Sunshine and warmth figure largely in both our weather reports and our outlook. Most people in the world would find a bat colony vaguely creepy; we cheer them on.

In late February, though, the bats have migrated elsewhere for the winter. A cold front blows in and stays put, bringing temperatures lower than any Texas has seen in a long while.

But that's not the main reason for the chill.

Women stop walking the sidewalks alone after about three P.M. Displays go up beside gas station and grocery cash registers, hawking pepper spray, retractable batons, and those keychains that look like a cute kitty face until you use the pointed metal ears to gouge out an attacker's eyes. At homes and apartment complexes around the city, workmen can be seen installing security cameras and motion-sensitive lights. This being Texas, gun stores and firing ranges are already plentiful, but they step up their advertising. Their billboards and flyers now sometimes have pink borders, because that's what we ladies think about when we consider buying a gun: Which store has the most pink?

I've never bothered with a gun. The way I see it, a firearm could just as easily be turned against me. But I'm newly aware of the pepper spray in my purse, and the path from where I park to my door seems longer than it did before.

My landlords install some extra lights without my even asking.

Arturo insists on taking precautions too, as I discover when I come over for dinner one week after Jonah and I . . .

(I won't say *broke up*. That means forever, and I still refuse to believe that.)

. . . after he pushed me away.

For the first few days, all I did was work and bawl. Once I scarfed an entire pint of chocolate ice cream while watching *Empire* and getting overly emotional about the rift between Cookie and Hakeem. That's the closest I've come to fun since I left Jonah's building last Sunday. But now Saturday night has come around again, and I'm determined to pull myself together. I arrive at Arturo and Shay's town house with a six-pack of 7-Up in hand to see Arturo and Mack at work in the yard.

"This is stupid," Mack says as he thrusts the point of a solar-powered yard light into the ground. "Nobody's breaking in here."

"You don't know that." Arturo's on his knees too, spading the earth where the next light will go. "Nobody can know. I have to work nights, sometimes, but I don't like leaving Shay on her own with the baby, not like this."

Mack rolls his eyes, then sees me. He gives me his usual smarmy grin, which I acknowledge only with a nod before turning to Arturo. "Hiya. The landlord said you could put these in?"

"I didn't ask her," Arturo says as he jams in the last of the lights, then peers at the slowly darkening sky. "My guess is she'll be cool with it. If not? I've lost security deposits for worse reasons."

My mouth twitches, like it wants to smile but hasn't fully

remembered how yet. "Like that time you tried to hang a picture in your dorm room and put a hammer straight through the wall?"

Arturo laughs. "Damn, that dorm was crappy."

Inside, I find another few friends milling around, Shay readying the plates and napkins for when the pizza arrives, and Geordie and Carmen sitting on the floor with Nicolas. In the past couple of weeks, it's as if he's transformed from this sweet pink blob into an actual baby; Nicolas can lift his head and chest, and he'll hang on to the toys we give him, shaking them forever if they rattle or chime. And today, it seems, he finally got the hang of babbling.

"Ba ba ba BA *BA!*" goes Nicolas, smiling in delight at his own loudness.

"Yes, that's the core issue Brussels has to deal with," Geordie answers in all seriousness, as he play-walks a toy giraffe toward Nicolas's eager hand. "But if Greece leaves the eurozone, what does that do to their long-term economic recovery?"

Nicolas yells "BA!" again, and Geordie nods thoughtfully. This entire performance reduces Carmen to giggles. Hmmm.

When food arrives, the gathering finally swings into party mode. They turn up the radio, people start joking and laughing, and soda cans are cracked open with a pop and a hiss. Although I'm still not really in the mood, I can at least listen to other people having fun. Being with friends is always one of the best sources of comfort.

A few times I see Arturo or Shay stealing a glance at me. They're worried, even if they won't say so. I know I look like hell, with my hair pulled into a messy bun and no makeup. I'm wearing my oldest jeans and an even older plaid shirt. Wryly I think I might as well have hung a sandwich board around my neck. *Recently Dumped. Prone to Weeping. Do Not Taunt.*

I'm okay, though. I feel like hell, and every time I think about Jonah I want to cry—but I refuse to let myself slide any lower than this. After what I've been through in my life, it takes more than a breakup to destroy me. I'll keep going no matter how long my lonely heart keeps repeating Jonah's name.

The party breaks up early, mostly because Mack and his friends want to head out to a bar. Carmen takes Nicolas upstairs to take care of his stinky diaper while Geordie and I clean up. As I stuff the latest pizza box into the cardboard-recycling can, Geordie says, "Hey, mind if I catch a ride back with you? Shay picked me up so I could help her with the heavier stuff at the grocery."

"Uh, heavy stuff?" I'm just stalling. Wouldn't it be better if Carmen gave him a ride home?

But this idea doesn't seem to have occurred to Geordie. "You know. Hefting those twelve-packs of Coca-Cola and ginger ale—it's a man's job."

The slight vibration in the pipes reveals that Carmen's running Nicolas's bath now, so she won't be coming downstairs anytime soon. "Okay, sure. I'll give you a lift."

In the car, Geordie again syncs his phone with the sound system, this time bringing up Sharon Jones and the Dap-Kings. She sings about how it takes a hundred days to know a man's heart, and against my will I feel myself getting emotional again.

Did Jonah and I have even a hundred days?

Geordie clears his throat. "As long as we're talking about subjects that are none of my business—"

"We weren't."

"I take it you and Jonah Marks are still on the outs."

Oh, shit, the last topic I want to talk about. "My love life is not your concern anymore."

"*Ouch.*" Geordie makes the sound you hear from most people when they see a really bad sunburn. "I'm only asking as a friend. Okay? No grabby hands will be stealing toward your knee at any point this evening."

This guy always gets me to smile at some point. "I realize you're not trying to—that you're only looking out for me. And I appreciate it. But I'm really not ready to have a conversation about this with you or with anyone." Not even Doreen: Our last therapy session was mostly me crying, and Doreen handing out Kleenex after Kleenex.

Geordie nods, and for almost a minute more, we drive along without speaking, accompanied only by the music. As I turn onto the road that leads to his apartment complex, however, he blurts out, "I've got to ask you another question about Jonah. Last one ever, probably."

I wince. "I'd rather not."

"Sorry, Vivienne. This one's a must." His tone is unexpectedly firm.

Whatever this is, he expects it to upset me. So I pull over into a lot for the shopping center a few blocks from Geordie's place, put my Civic in park, and say, "Fine. Ask."

"You don't have to give me any details. I understand if you don't know anything for sure, and you don't want anyone to take action based on—on a suspicion, or a fear—but—" His eyes meet mine, stricken. "Did you split up with Jonah Marks because you thought he might be guilty?"

Fuck. Is this what all my friends are thinking?

Geordie continues, the words spilling out of him. "Because if you're afraid of this man, on any level, we can switch apartments, switch cars, whatever you'd need to feel safe."

"No. No, Geordie, that's not it. I *know* Jonah's not guilty, absolutely. What I said about being with him during the Stalker's first two attacks—that's one hundred percent true. Please, you have to tell people that Jonah didn't do this."

"All right." He only looks more worried. "But one question's been worrying at me. If Jonah's innocent, and it appears he is—then why the hell are the police after him? He's a bloody professor. A *millionaire*. That's the sort of person they usually suspect last."

"I know. It's this ex-girlfriend of his—she named him to the police back in December—"

"What, like, for revenge?" Geordie's jaw drops. "That's *awful.* What kind of a bitch does something like that?"

"She's not a bitch. I mean, I guess she isn't. I never met her." I'm stumbling over my own words now, becoming emotional again. "She had her reasons for worrying about Jonah, okay? But she's wrong. Can we leave it at that?"

The dashboard lights illuminate Geordie's frown. "Her reasons? Forgive me, but that doesn't sound good."

"It's not what you're thinking."

"Then what is it, Vivienne?"

I'm not the type to tell one lover too many details about my sex life with another. This subject is too intensely personal to share with anyone but my therapist. Given how far over the line Geordie is here, I'd be well within my rights to tell him to shut up and let it go.

But Geordie's one of the only other people in the world who knows about my rape fetish. He is my friend, and he genuinely cares about my safety and happiness. And more than anything else, the sheer force of these unspoken fears has been pent up inside me so long that I can't hold it back any longer. The dam finally breaks.

Which is why, half an hour later, I'm sitting on the floor of Geordie's apartment, still spilling the whole damn story.

"And he says we'll never get over this fixation if we keep acting it out together. But I felt like acting it out was the only way I ever got any better." I blow my nose in the wad of toilet paper he fetched for me a few minutes ago. "It was *my choice* to get tied up! My choice to be blindfolded! My choice to—"

"Slow down," Geordie says faintly. He's leaning back on his sofa, one hand on his forehead like it hurts. "Fewer details."

Whatever. My personal dignity is already pretty much shot. "You understand now, right? There's no way Jonah would ever rape anyone. That's not how he dealt with the shit that happened to him." I've remained vague about Jonah's past—that part isn't mine to tell. But that's all I've held back. "We were working through that together, until he broke up with me 'for my own good.' Now he's alone during all of this, and I feel like—both like I'm some kind of monster sicko for wanting this, and like I'm going to die because I've lost it forever."

"You're not a sicko," Geordie says.

I give him a look. "Earlier you said your ears were bleeding."

"I apologize. Bad joke." He manages to sit up and meet my eyes. "Listen. First of all, okay. I believe you about Jonah. The story makes sense now, somehow. Poor bastard's caught in the perfect storm of kink and suspicion."

"Yeah." If nothing else, at least I've completely cleared Jonah to one person's satisfaction. It's not much comfort, but it's all I've got.

"Second—this part is hard. Vivienne, you never said this outright, but what I'm hearing is . . . you were raped once, long ago. By your sister's husband?"

I'd always felt like I'd die if any of my friends knew. But now it's almost a relief. "When I was fourteen. They were only dating then."

"And she married him anyway. Jesus Christ. I'm so sorry."

No one else has ever said that before. Not even Jonah. *I'm sorry.* I needed to hear that simple empathy more than I'd ever realized. The only answer I can give is a nod.

Geordie leans forward, forearms on his knees. "You know you could've told me. Either to explain why you wanted—or just, you know, to tell."

"Almost nobody knows. Not Carmen, not Arturo and Shay, not

even my own dad." I brush back the strands of honey-brown hair that have escaped from my bun. "It's not that I don't trust you guys. But I never wanted anybody to look at me and see a victim. It felt like—like I'd be dragging my rape with me into my future, when all I wanted to do was leave it in the past. Do you understand?"

He nods too fast, unabashedly concerned. "Right. Sure. You get to choose who you tell and when. Only you."

In the past, Geordie hasn't been so great about keeping my secrets, but that was before he was sober. His mistakes were never intentional. Now I feel like he'd keep this safe for me forever.

So I can tell him the rest too. "The fantasy was only one thing Jonah and I shared. We're compatible in so many other ways too; I think we would've been drawn to each other no matter what. But admitting this to each other, sharing it, that's why we became so close so quickly. We only started going out six months ago, but the relationship we have goes so much deeper than the time makes it seem. Losing him is killing me. I don't want to think it's permanent, but if *he* thinks it's permanent, then we're done."

"Give the man some time. He's in the middle of some serious insanity right now, yeah? Might take him a while to get his head together."

"I know that. I do. Still, I keep wondering—what if he's right? What if we prevent each other from ever getting better? If we live this out together over and over, how do we ever move past it?"

Geordie does the last thing I expected; he laughs. "You don't." I frown in confusion, and with a sigh, he comes to sit on the floor beside me. His smile is crooked. "Usually you're the wise one. Not hard, if I'm the competition. But these past few months, in treatment—I finally learned something that it sounds like you should learn too."

"What?"

"Nobody ever gets all better. *Ever.* No one." He takes my hand. "In the past, whenever I'd think I was drinking too much, I'd say—well, I'll taper off for a bit. Clear my head. Make new friends, new habits. Then I can go hang out at the pub again like before. But now I know I can never do that. I'm an addict. An alcoholic. I don't get to hang out at the pub. No civilized glasses of wine with dinner. No New Year's champagne. Doesn't matter how long I live, or how many years I stay sober. I will never be able to have those things. Sobriety is partly about learning to accept that fact."

The serenity to accept the things I cannot change—isn't that how it goes? "I'm not an addict. Not in that way, I don't think."

"No, you're not. But the principle's the same. We don't get all better; we don't fix everything that's broken. We just learn how to work around the broken bits. How to do the best we can with what we have, and who we are."

This is something Doreen's tried to say to me a few times, though I only fully understand it now. Always, before, I've careened between feeling as if I had to put the past behind me completely, or surrender to it and accept defeat. But there's a middle path too. One where I own what happened to me and do the best I can anyway.

And finally I realize how close I got to that, with Jonah, only to have it snatched away.

"Thank you," I say to Geordie. "I've needed to hear that for so long."

He shrugs, embarrassed by own his earnestness. "Guess I jumped ahead to step nine." When I look at him in confusion, he elaborates: "The one where we make amends."

"You never had anything to make amends for. Not with me." One time he blabbed my secret—but if he hadn't, Jonah and I would never have found each other.

We clasp hands, fully friends in a way we never were before, but always will be from now on. This doesn't fill the void left by Jonah's absence; maybe nothing ever can. But for this night, this hour, it's enough.

TWENTY-EIGHT

Geordie insists on following me home in his car, and asks me to text once I'm sure everything's safe inside. No sooner do I send it than I get a message from Carmen saying, Hey, just got home, wanted to check in!

I sigh. Every woman in the city is on red alert, as is any guy worth a damn.

But I dedicate myself to my friends as well, because it's something constructive to do. Keiko and I arrange to carpool to the studio, taking turns driving. She's struggling to master raku glazing, and I need to fill the empty hours, so we wind up going virtually every day. Creating new images feels beyond me right now—the unfinished Jonah project still haunts me. Instead I devote myself to printmaking, experimenting with different inks and surfaces. I reprint the man's hands around the dove at least three dozen times on everything from cardboard to concrete. I print them in black glittery ink, and a gray almost too pale to be seen against white, in shining gold, and in a red as deep as blood. Maybe I'll hang them all together in one enormous installation that would show how many interpretations of one image there can be.

Marvin drags himself into the studio to install a dead bolt lock inside the door, so the female artists can feel safer working late. We even assemble a chart with the name and security answer of every artist renting space here, and Marvin hangs it beside the door so women can feel confident about who they're letting in before they slide that dead bolt open again.

Shay, Carmen, and I shop together for everything from groceries to clothes. Geordie and Arturo are both completely unsubtle about volunteering to run errands anytime after about three P.M.

Even so, I'm unprepared for the most audacious attempt to protect me.

It comes not quite a week after my huge confession to Geordie, on a night when he's suddenly expressed this enormous, unprecedented interest in my "artistic process," and wants to come along to the studio.

"You're actually going to guard us against the Stalker," I say with my hands on my hips. "Right?"

"And against any ninjas that might happen to stop by. Potentially also Bigfoot. I'm ready for anything, is what I'm saying."

"Fine, but bring something to read. Because the 'artistic process' is duller than you'd think, and I doubt Bigfoot will put in an appearance."

Sure enough, after a few hours, Geordie's ignoring both my printmaking and Keiko's work with her clay. He buries his nose in one of his law books and jots down notes for his next paper as an old Fiona Apple song plays on the radio. As I check out my latest print—deliberately messy, the sepia-colored ink gloppy enough to obscure a few details—my phone buzzes with a text. I check the screen with no expectations, but then my gut drops when I see the sender's name: JONAH MARKS.

Are you free? There's something I'd like to talk about.

He wants to get back together! No, he's going to leave the country on a research trip, maybe going all the way to Japan or Antarctica for months. Or something's happened with his family and he needs to open up to somebody who understands . . .

Don't get ahead of yourself, I remind myself. *Deal with the facts.*

So I send: I'm at the studio, actually. Getting some work done.

Can I meet you there?

Oh, my God. Jonah can't wait. That has to mean good news—right? When?

I'm in the neighborhood, actually. I can get there in 5 minutes or so.

OK.

Heart pounding, I slide the phone back into my purse. "Uh, Geordie?"

He doesn't even look up from his legal textbook. "Hmm?"

"Jonah's going to drop by."

That makes Geordie sit up. Even Keiko looks up from her vase-in-progress, then swears as it wobbles off-center and collapses. As she heads to the work sink area to wash off wet clay, Geordie says, "What do you want us to do? Stick around or get lost?"

"I have no idea."

In the end, Geordie stays put until Jonah arrives, which is only a couple of minutes later. I slide back the dead bolt, take a deep breath and open the door. But my efforts to prepare myself are useless. When I see Jonah for the first time in almost two weeks, my heart and my body both melt.

"Hi," Jonah says. He's wearing a leather bomber jacket the color of good whiskey over a cream-colored sweater he bought on our trip in Scotland. His jeans hug him as sexily as ever. Yet what draws me to him the most is the quiet sorrow behind his eyes. I think he's lost weight; I have too. He continues, "Are you here alone at night?"

"Nope," I say. This time, I'll be the one who skips the hellos. "See?"

With a gesture I point out both Geordie and Keiko. Geordie waves as I shut the door behind Jonah and slide the bolt shut again.

Jonah doesn't seem to know what to do with this. "Well. Okay. I guess we can talk here just as well."

Geordie, for once in his life, is visited by the Spirit of Tact. "Oh, you know, Keiko, we ought to run out for some—baklava!"

She frowns at him. "Baklava?"

"Yeah! A craving just hit me. We can run by Phoenicia, and the coffee's on me. What do you say?" Geordie claps his hands together, too cheerfully. "We won't be long. Fifteen minutes, at most."

Keiko looks from me to Jonah and finally catches on. "Right. Totally. Besides, I need some—things—that are, uh, not here."

It takes all my strength not to facepalm. These two are subtle as a Category Five hurricane.

Jonah's gaze settles on Geordie as Keiko ducks into the bathroom to change out of her grubby pottery clothes. "So," he says heavily, to Geordie. "You're back."

This earns him a raised eyebrow. "What, as Vivienne's boyfriend? You ought to know her better than that, mate."

"That's not what Jonah meant," I interject. "We've spent a lot of time together, and—you know, forget it. It's not important anymore."

Geordie takes a deep breath. "She keeps secrets well, doesn't she, Jonah? Personally I think she's been asked to keep too many. So

Jonah, you ought to know that I've recently accepted that I—I have a drinking problem." He hasn't said that aloud to people outside the program very often; the words are still awkward for him. "Thanks in part to Vivienne, I'm in treatment. And she's been putting in some friendship overtime, for which I'm profoundly grateful."

Obviously Jonah's taken aback, but he manages to nod. " I'm glad to hear it."

Geordie grins and nods toward me. "That your girl's still your girl? Aye, but you'd better stop acting like an enormous git soon, or she's likely to find someone better than either of us."

"Hey." I appreciate what Geordie's trying to do, but this is going too far. "I already have a relationship counselor. Who is an actual licensed counselor." Geordie holds up his hands in mock surrender.

Jonah says to him, "I meant, I'm glad to hear that you're—that things are going better for you."

"Thanks." Geordie's expression gentles slightly; I think this might be the first moment he's liked Jonah at all.

Keiko hurries out in a fresh T-shirt and jeans, Geordie grabs his keychain, and the two of them hurry out to Phoenicia. As soon as the dead bolt clicks into place, Jonah says to me, "You could've told me that, you know. About Geordie."

"I try to respect people's privacy." I hug myself, not caring about the multicolored ink stains transferring from my blue smock to my arms. "How are you, Jonah?"

He shrugs as he slides his hands into the pockets of his bomber jacket. "I've had better months."

The master of understatement strikes again. "Do you feel safe? Are the police harassing you? What have your lawyers said?"

Jonah doesn't quite meet my eyes. "I'm following legal advice. Although I'm not on a leave of absence from the university, I'm working from home for a while. Documenting my whereabouts via webcam and my phone camera. Other than that, there's not much to do. Listen, that's not what I wanted to talk about."

So, he didn't come here to unburden himself. The wall between us still stands. "What, then?"

"Where you're living—I know you feel safe at your place, but it's hardly secure. You don't have a security system, or any neighbors close enough to hear if you called for help."

You used to like that, I think but don't say. "This is, what, you offering advice?"

"I can do better than advice." Jonah takes a deep breath, then holds out an envelope.

Hesitantly I take it and open the flap. Inside is a Northstar Roadside Assistance membership in my name, a card for a limo service, another for some movers, and—"Jonah, is this a *lease*?"

"Another apartment building downtown, a few blocks from mine. Their security is even tighter; if I lived there, I wouldn't be a suspect now. You'll be completely secure. The movers have been prepaid for their services, including packing, so all you have to do is name the day. Since the lease is also prepaid for two years, you can keep sending rent checks to your landlords as long as necessary, until they let you out of your lease."

I'm so agog I can't even come up with words.

He continues laying it out, using the same demeanor his lawyers probably coached him to use with the police: unemotional, professional, and succinct. "I have an account with the limousine service; the number is written on the card. It would be better if you took that everywhere, but I realize you probably won't, so—Northstar. Because you never got around to getting a roadside assistance service, did you?"

"No." My mouth twists into an unpleasant smile. "So. These are my parting gifts? The payoff so you don't have to feel guilty about leaving me?"

Jonah's eyes widen. He hadn't even considered that, though on some level I suspect he recognizes it's partly true. "I just want you to be safe. It's been impossible to sleep, worrying about where you are, or what could be happening to you. When I think that you could be hurt . . . Christ, it drives me insane." He's almost pleading with me. "Don't you see? This is the only way I can still take care of you."

"No, it isn't. You could take care of me the way I actually *need* you to take care of me—by being in my life, and loving me, and getting through this together."

He turns his face away from me, and I realize he's struggling for composure as hard as I am. Maybe harder. "I walked away for your sake, Vivienne; I couldn't have done it for anything less. You're the only one I'd suffer like this for. Nobody else, ever."

"I don't need your suffering, and I don't need your guilty conscience. I need you." I laugh, though my throat is so tight the sound comes out all wrong. "Jonah, when I look at this stuff, I realize you're trying to protect me. That you still love me. You thought of everything, and for what's in your heart, thank you. But I can't accept the apartment, or the limo, or any of that."

"Just for your own safety," he insists. "Forget about me."

As if I ever could. "You're substituting control for love, Jonah. It's a bad road to travel down. I won't go that way, and you shouldn't either. Besides—in this world, no one's ever safe. Not really. Haven't we both learned that by now?"

Jonah leans heavily against the nearest worktable; a ceramic cylinder filled with colored pencils rattles against the wood. "You won't take any of it?"

I look down at the paperwork in my hands, extract the Northstar card, and put the rest back on the table in front of him. "I'll pick up the membership when this year ends. Thanks for that."

Wordless and resigned, he nods. After he tucks the envelope back in his pocket, he casts his eyes around the studio. We are surrounded by copies of the etching on his wall, in endless colors and variations. What must he think I'm doing? Maybe he believes I'm obsessed.

Jonah says only, "It haunts me too."

Staring down at the Northstar card is easier than trying to meet his eyes. "Is it hard for you to look at the etching now?"

"Yes."

"Have you taken it down?"

"No. I see it every day." With that, Jonah walks out.

I follow him to the door only to lock it behind him. We do not say good-bye.

TWENTY-NINE

By now, Kip no longer needs foundation and powder to cover any bruises on his face. His lips are fuller than usual, and redder, though he informs all of us in the fine arts department that this is due to Sephora lip plumper, which is a steal at the price. Certainly there's no further sign of injury. Kip said he would never go back to Ryan, and it appears he's told the truth.

But Kip's sparkle hasn't returned. He remains efficient, eerily well-informed, and as stylishly turned out as ever. Anyone who hadn't met him before now would probably think he seemed cheerful. Only those of us closest to Kip can sense the weight he's still carrying around.

The day after Jonah's attempt at relocating my entire existence, I bring half a bag of leftover baklava and set it on his desk. "The delicious baklava can be yours, if you agree to have lunch with me today."

Kip pauses in his typing. His fingernails look oddly naked without their polish. "Is this from Phoenicia Bakery or some other, lesser source of Greek pastries?"

"Phoenicia."

"You know my weakness," he sighs. It's supposed to be a joke, but strikes too close to the bone. After a half second too long of silence, Kip continues, "Lunch, then. Twelve thirty?"

"Got it."

With March come midterms and the resulting frenzy of student activity, so neither of us has a lot of free time in the middle of the day. This is how we wind up at the cafeteria, a place I feel sure neither of us has willingly eaten in at any point in the past four years. The pizza slices seem safest; once we're at our plastic table, insulated by the hubbub of undergrads around us, all we have to do is use extra napkins to dab off the grease.

"Thank God I still have some of the baklava left," Kip says as he tears the paper from his drinking straw. "Nothing less would ever get this taste out of my mouth."

"It's not that bad." I take a bite of the pizza to prove my point. Of course, it's not that good either, but I don't want Kip to derail this whole lunch by bitching about the food. I swallow and venture, "How are you doing?"

"Oh, I'm fine. Taking some 'me time.' The men of Grindr will still be there when I return." His green eyes study mine. "What about you?"

Never had it occurred to me that Kip might think he was the one who should be more worried. "I miss Jonah. I'm afraid for him. But I'm doing okay."

"Is that all there is to it?" He raises an eyebrow.

These days, my ability to deal with bullshit is at an all-time low. "Basically, yeah. Because I'm being brief, but I'm being honest, which is more than I can say for you."

Kip sets his pizza back down. He stares down at the table instead of meeting my eyes. "I'm done with Ryan. He's done with me. But I still feel so fucking stupid."

"You weren't stupid! How could you have known?"

"When I met him at that bar? I couldn't have. After he slapped me the first time? Which by the way was for complaining when he woke me up for sex. Yes. I could have known I was in a bad situation. I could've walked out the door with my pride. Instead I stuck around for a storyline straight out of *Mary Worth*. If Mary Worth had gay people in it."

Is *Mary Worth* that comic strip with the meddling old lady? Not worth asking. I say only, "It's easy to write stuff off, the first time. To think it's—an aberration. An accident." Or to tell yourself that the other person didn't understand how you would feel, the way I decided, the morning after my rape, that Anthony must've thought I wanted to have sex with him.

"He'd had a bad night at the bar. A bunch of frat-boy shitheads got drunk, and one of them vomited in the john, and Ryan had to clean it up. Once we'd calmed down he said he'd just been relying so much on my comforting him when he got home. He had all this pent-up anger and didn't mean to take it out on me." Kip singsongs this as he uses his straw to fitfully stir the ice cubes in his plastic cup of soda. "I *believed* that, because I wanted to."

I remember how built Ryan is. The first time I saw him, I wondered whether he might be a bodybuilder. Even a slap from him would've hurt terribly—and this didn't end with a slap. Kip could've been injured far worse if he hadn't left when he did. "You got out in time."

"Time for what? To rescue my dignity? Not quite."

"You still have your dignity. Come on, Kip. You're not the one who should feel ashamed. That's Ryan."

Kip shrugs and leans back in his plastic chair. Above us, wall-mounted monitors play a mixture of school announcements, music videos, and celebrity trivia—obviously designed to appeal to "youth" by some group of marketing executives. "What I'm ashamed of is not learning my lesson the first time."

Never would I have imagined that someone as confident and

in control as Kip could wind up in multiple abusive relationships. Never. And yet I have no doubt that's what he's just told me.

As I sit there in mute disbelief, Kip stares out at the sea of students eating, talking, and playing with their phones. "Oh, I've never been smacked around before," he says, too carelessly. "But when I was young, I ran into a man lots of young gay guys run into. The one with plenty of money, plenty of charm, and plenty of secrets. He wants you, but he also wants you to stay hidden, and he knows just how to gild the cage."

Admittedly I've never thought about this scenario much, but I instantly see how often it might arise. "I guess it's tough being with someone closeted."

"Not necessarily. Well, I mean, yes, ducking behind booths at restaurants gets old. So does pretending to be 'roommates.' That's only trivia, though. Most of us go through that phase, honestly; sometimes it lasts months, sometimes decades. You understand it. What destroys the spirit is being thought of as someone's dirty little secret."

I never felt that way with Jonah, in the era when we told no one. But that's the difference, of course—he was my secret as much as I was his.

For a moment I remember him whispering to me outside a downtown bar, threatening and promising to back me against a brick wall and take me then and there . . .

Kip's voice brings me back to the here and now. "I got tangled up in that for a long time. When I escaped, I told myself, never again will I let anyone control me. But I did."

"He didn't control you," I say. "You walked out. You drew a line."

"I suppose." He shrugs. "Nonetheless, as Austin Powers would say, my mojo is missing."

"It'll come back." After a few moments, I venture, "This

Christmas, when we were talking about Jonah—you said the hot ones always had a dark side. You were thinking about Ryan, and how he treated you."

"It wasn't an SOS signal. So don't beat yourself up about it." Kip probably needs to talk about this more, but he makes it clear he doesn't intend to. "Can we talk about something less tiresome than our love lives? What else is going on with you?"

I'm creatively blocked and refusing extravagant gifts from my ex. "Well, let's see. Uh, I've been playing matchmaker, but I don't know whether it's working."

He perks up. Sometimes people need distraction more than introspection. "Really. Tell me, who are the two lucky people? Or if you're trying to link up more than two people at a time, points to you for both polyamory acceptance *and* ambition."

I blow the paper sleeve of my straw at him. "Carmen and Geordie always seemed to get along, and they'd been spending more time together, so . . ."

Kip snorts soda up his nose, then sputters and laughs until he can manage to speak again. "Carmen Ortiz and Geordie Hilton? Are you kidding me?"

Stung, I say, "They're hanging out a lot these days!"

"Because babies have the same inexorable pull as black holes. Honestly, Vivienne. Those two have no chemistry. They have—anti-chemistry. Like matter and antimatter! If they touched, they'd explode."

"I don't think that's real science."

Kip ignores this. "You'd have better luck setting up Neil Patrick Harris and Ellen DeGeneres. At least those two have something in common."

"Carmen and Geordie have plenty in common," I insist. But—do they? Although they've always been friendly, and enjoy hanging out . . . Carmen loves silly comedy movies, while Geordie goes to see every pretentious foreign drama that exists. She's politically almost conservative; Geordie will probably wind up in the Green Party. She's an observant Catholic, he's agnostic, he hopes to move back to Europe in a few years but she can hardly imagine living as far away as California—

And now I get why Kip is laughing. I've been fooling myself this whole time.

"Okay, maybe not." My blush feels warm on my cheeks.

Kip actually has to wipe tears from his eyes. "Whatever gave you the idea? Did you experiment with hallucinogens? Take a blow to the head?"

"I thought I'd picked up on a vibe. Guess I was wrong."

He puts his chin in his hand. "Remember how I said you hate conflict? Related issue—you often try to fix things that aren't yours to fix. You probably thought one or the other was lonely, and your imagination folded reality like an origami swan to try and give them both a happy ending. But even origami doesn't fold up that neatly."

"I've been worried about Geordie," I admit. Although we haven't discussed Geordie's recovery, I feel certain Kip knows the details. His omnipotence may be in doubt, but not his omniscience. "He needs all the love and care he can get."

"Don't we all?"

It was supposed to be a joke. But the last word catches in Kip's throat, and for the next few minutes, every tall man I see could be Jonah. *Is* Jonah, in that initial, cruel folly of the mind.

That night neither Shay nor Carmen needs groceries, so I'm shopping alone for once. I make sure to run to the store well before dark. One pound of turkey, one loaf of bread that might go moldy before I finish it: Groceries for the single are slightly depressing.

But hey. When you're single, wine and cashews make a *perfectly good* dinner. So I'm just going to roll with that.

I get home just before twilight and cast an appraising glance up at the security lights. The sky hasn't darkened enough for them to activate yet. Any second now—

The impact against my waist knocks the breath out of me, making me stumble. One of my grocery bags goes flying, plastic ripping against the stone walkway and scattering pasta on the pale spring grass. *A branch*, I think at first, dazed with surprise and distracted by the pain lancing through my skinned knee. *From the bushes?*

Then two hands stretch a cord across my throat, and I realize what's happening.

"Walk into your house," the Stalker says. "Don't say a word."

I remain kneeling on the stones for a second longer, paralyzed by a thousand colliding thoughts. *Shit, oh shit, oh shit! Do I know that voice? I have to be dreaming this. Please don't let him kill me. Not again! Don't let this happen to me again!* One idea begins to loom larger than all the rest. *Get the pepper spray.*

When I reach for my purse, though, the Stalker tightens the cord against my larynx. "Leave it."

"The keys." The words come out raspy. "I can't open the door without the keys."

He hesitates. "Let me see them."

Will he recognize the tiny pink canister dangling from my keychain? Maybe. That just means I have to work fast.

I fumble in my leather hobo bag a second longer than necessary, not only finding the keys but also hooking my fingers into the pepper spray. He's behind me, but on his feet while I'm still on my knees, so if I spray upward and back that might work, up and back, up and back—

Now! I spray the stuff overhead, and the cord slips away as he stumbles to the side, coughing. Instantly I lunge to my feet and run to the door, purse still dangling around one wrist. *Please let him run for it, or be overcome just long enough for me to get on the other side of this door!*

Key in lock, turn, push, turn, slam. That's the plan, and I get as far as the second turn. But when I wheel around to shut the door, he barrels through it so hard he knocks me across my tiny kitchen. The small of my back hits the porcelain rim of my sink, and my head thuds against the cabinets. Dishes rattle, and he's inside, the Stalker's inside my house, and he's closed the door behind him.

He's big. Not that much taller than me, but bulky, like a football player. He's wearing the most nondescript blue jeans and white T-shirt, plus a dark brown ski mask that barely covers his thick neck. Somehow his mouth and eyes are more horrifying glimpsed through that mask, as if the disguise reveals just how inhumanly gleeful they are. He has me where he wants me, and he likes it.

"Nobody's getting in here," he says. "So you better be nice to me."

I do know that voice.

For one split second, despair closes over me, suffocates me. I'm trapped. I'm facing my worst nightmare yet again, and this time there's no guarantee I'll even walk away alive. The Stalker is stronger than me and we both know it.

But thanks to that self-defense class, I know something else too. I don't have to be stronger than he is. I just have to be strong enough to hurt him.

And I am.

I had to let go of the pepper spray to grab the key. But I fumble with the keychain anyway, as if to get at it again. The Stalker lunges for that hand, as I knew he would. That leaves my left hand free to go for the wooden block next to the sink, the one where I store my knives. The cool plastic handle feels good in my hand, and then there's the rasp of metal on wood as I pull the blade free.

With one stroke I slash across the Stalker's chest, tearing open his shirt and spraying a fine mist of hot blood across my hand and chest. I stab at him again, but he brings my arm down against the counter so hard that—in the first flush of pain—I think my wrist might be broken. I don't care. I can still fight.

Quickly I swing my knee up into his groin; he doubles over and loses his grip on my left hand. Thank God I'm wearing high heels, because they call 'em *stilettos* for a reason. I stomp down on his foot as hard as I can, and I feel the seams of his cheap tennis shoes give away. He howls, a primitive baying sound that sends a chill through me.

By now the Stalker must be almost as desperate as I am. He sounds like an animal going in for the kill.

But I'm the one with the knife.

This time I don't slash. I stab. He wheels out of the way, so the blade doesn't go into his chest like I'd hoped—but the point sinks into his upper arm. His flesh resists more than I thought it would, but I push hard. Blood streams over my hands; I must've hit a vein.

The Stalker's fist slams into the side of my face, so hard it knocks me into the cabinets. Dazed as I am, I don't lose my grip on the knife. When the blade pulls free of his arm, the blood begins to gush from him in earnest. He grabs at the wound, and in that instant I know he's not sure whether to continue the attack or get the hell out.

That instant is the one I need to let go of the knife, and grab my marble cookie jar with both hands. With all my strength I swing it upward and smash it into his jaw. My reward is a scream, and the sound of splintering bone, and the sight of him sagging against the wall, then sliding onto the floor, semiconscious.

Blood makes my fingers slippery, but I'm able to open the door and I see my phone lying on the welcome mat where it must've fallen from my purse. "Somebody help!" I shriek as I dial 911. I'm in the doorway now, neither in nor out, able to be heard and seen without taking my eyes off my attacker. Across the street, I see someone come to their window; I've drawn attention.

Through the phone come the tinny words: "Nine-one-one, what is your emergency?"

"A man broke into my apartment. Ski mask. The Stalker. He's down." I'm panting so hard, I'm not sure the woman on the other end of the line has heard me. "I've got him down. The police need to get here, now."

"Down?"

Are people stupid or am I just too out of it to understand? "The Stalker tried to rape me! I beat the shit out of him! Will you come arrest him already?"

"Give me your name and address?"

I do. By now the middle-aged man who lives across the street is headed this way with a fireplace poker in his hands; I wave him over, then lean in quickly to grab my keys and pepper spray, which lie on the floor atop my purse. The Stalker has pushed his way into a seated position, but he seems unable to get to his feet. Good.

The 911 operator says, "You believe your attacker is the Austin Stalker?"

"I think so. What I know is that his name is Mack."

Mack startles. He hadn't realized I'd caught on.

"I think his last name is Lahane. He roomed with a friend of mine a couple years ago." Shay lived in the same apartment complex as one of the victims last year; Mack would've been Arturo's roommate then, would've ridden over there with him several times. And through my friendship with Carmen, Mack spotted me. I bet none of the attacks were random; he's had his eyes on all of us for a long time. "He drives a pickup truck. White. It should be parked near here."

"We're on our way." I hear the operator typing. Right now everything I'm saying is probably being filed under "allegations." The proof will come soon enough.

As I remain on the line, tasting blood from the cuts in my mouth, Mack says, "How'd you—"

"I recognized your voice. And your thick fucking neck. I always thought you looked like a canned ham in a shirt."

The ski mask doesn't disguise Mack's sneer. Even with him lying at my feet, bloody from my attack, the hatred in his voice gives me the shivers. "I know about you. I heard what Geordie said at the party. You fucking *wanted* this."

"I think your knife wounds prove I didn't want it—ever—you piece of shit." Slumping against the door in relief, I welcome the approaching footsteps of my first rescuer, and the distant wail of police sirens.

Unconvinced, Mack says, "I thought we were going to have some fun."

"I'm having fun right now, Mack."

And somehow it's true. I beat the shit out of my attacker and I *fucking loved it*. This might just be the most fun I've ever had.

Either this is the best day of my life, or I've finally cracked.

THIRTY

Good Cop and Bad Cop were wary at first. I'd provided Jonah with an alibi for two of the Stalker's earlier attacks; was this only my next attempt to cover for him, by framing an innocent man?

But even they couldn't ignore the bleeding guy in a ski mask lying on my floor, and when they found duct tape and some belongings from the other victims in his trunk, they became believers. Mack asked for a lawyer. I don't have to see him again.

At the hospital, as a doctor shines a light in one of my eyes, then the other, Good Cop shakes his head. "It's just a hell of a coincidence. You knowing the guy *and* our other suspect."

"College towns, I guess."

The thing is—it's not a coincidence at all. Mack was at the party where Geordie blurted out my rape fantasy; so was Jonah. They each heard it. Jonah came to me and asked to fulfill my fantasy in a way that would make me feel both safe and satisfied. Mack stored it in his head along with all the other twisted visions of what he wanted to do to unwilling women, and targeted me for later. Every single woman he attacked is one he had encountered in the past few years.

Did I push Mack over the edge? When he heard about my fantasy at the party, did it give him ideas? My logic rejects this almost instantly; the fuse that led Mack to explode would've been a long one, lit before I ever met him. Yet this goes deeper than logic. I'm still fighting to reconcile everything that happened tonight, everything I felt.

Always, because of my fantasy, I've questioned myself at the deepest level. Why would I wish for something so hurtful? Would I desire someone who really tried to harm me? That was the part that haunted me the night I met Jonah. Well, now I have the answer: No. I wouldn't desire that. I would in fact beat the living hell out of anyone who attempted it.

Or I would've tried. Mack had only attacked three other women, ever, none of whom had my self-defense training. If he'd been more experienced, or caught up with me at a weaker moment, this might not have ended as well.

"You don't show signs of a concussion, but the blow to the head—we'll want to keep tabs on you." The doctor begins taking notes on a clipboard.

"I don't want to stay in the hospital," I plead. "Please. I want to go—"

Where? Home? Blood will still be drying on my floor. Tonight I feel like I can't deal with that gore, even if it is proof of my victory.

The doctor doesn't look up from her notes. "Any nausea or dizziness? Vomiting?"

"No." My guts feel as if they're churning, but that's not physical. I can tell it's emotional.

"Okay. If you develop those symptoms—or any visual changes, even a headache, you need to get back in here ASAP. Otherwise—you're good to go as soon as we bandage that knee." The doctor finally looks up, her smile uncertain. "Would you like to speak with a counselor?"

"I have a therapist. I'll talk with her soon." However, I haven't texted Doreen yet. I only called Carmen and told her the basics; she's supposed to be taking care of everything else. She'll have to break it to Arturo that his former roommate, a guy he trusted, is the Stalker. God, that's going to kill him . . .

Why are you worrying about Arturo? You're the one with a black eye and blood drying under your fingernails! But my brain and my heart are still spinning, jumbled, unable to decide what to think and how to feel.

Bad Cop leans his head around the ER curtain. "Hey, we got news media out front. Somebody needs to stall them."

"Like hell," I snap. "Somebody in your department leaked the name of an innocent man. The least you can do is clear Jonah Marks at the first possible opportunity, which is *this second*."

Good Cop and Bad Cop look at each other, mumble sheepish good-byes, and walk out of this examination area, hopefully out of my life. The doctor pats my shoulder and asks me to hold on for someone to bandage my knee, then goes on her way, leaving me alone.

I shift position on this table, paper crinkling beneath me. Blood spatter stains my skirt and sweater so heavily it will never come out. Should I burn these clothes or frame them? My tongue searches for the tiny cuts in my mouth, even though they sting. With filthy hands I fish around in my purse and grab my phone. Through the blood smears on the screen I see texts scrolling all the way down my screen.

From Carmen: Are you okay? Are you upset? What am I saying, of course you're upset. Holy shit, I can't believe it was Mack!

From Shay: Come stay with us tonight, please, we'll feel so much better if you're not on your own. We love you.

From Arturo: If that motherfucker makes bail I'm gonna kill him myself. V, I'm so sorry I brought that guy into your life. I never saw it.

From Kip: Hail the conquering heroine! My God, you're like Sarah Connor and Sydney Bristow and Michonne all wrapped into one! You're FURIOSA!

From Geordie: It's over, OK? It's all over. Be proud of yourself, luv. Let me know whatever you need.

There are a handful of other texts from people I don't know as well, including some I feel sure Carmen wouldn't have reached out to. News is spreading fast, then. If there are news crews in front of the hospital, they've probably staked out my house as well. Another reason not to go home.

But I see no message from the person I wanted most.

It hasn't been an hour, I remind myself. *Just keep moving.*

Simple, concrete tasks would be best right now. Okay, wherever I sleep tonight, I'll need clothes and toiletries, and I don't want to go back into the house even to pack a bag—not until daylight. Is Target open this late? I could ask Geordie or Carmen to swing by, pick up a couple basic things . . .

In the hallway, someone official-sounding says, "Excuse me, are you cleared to go in there?" I look up just in time to see Jonah pull back the curtain.

His eyes search my bruised, ragged form, but it's like he's the one bleeding. His fist tightens around the hospital curtain; his face goes pale. Behind him appears an intern, ready to pull the intruder away. I find my voice. "It's okay. He's here for me."

The intern shrugs and walks off. Jonah steps inside, just far enough for the curtain to swing back into place behind him, but says nothing.

Instead he lowers himself, carefully, onto a chair near the examination table. His entire posture has altered—shoulders down, head ducked—and I realize he's making himself smaller. Taking a position beneath me. He sees that I've been hurt; always, before, he's responded to that by protecting me. Sometimes to the point of trying to control me. Now this powerful man is folding himself double to make me feel strong.

And I do. Tonight I proved to myself and to Jonah that I truly am strong enough to stand alone.

"It's all right." The rasp in my voice makes it sound like I've been awake for days. "He didn't hurt me."

"Your eye." Jonah lifts one hand, as if to touch the side of my face, where the swelling is already tender. But he stops himself long before we make contact, unwilling to force even the gentlest touch.

My puffy lip twinges as I give him a crooked smile. "Hey, you should see the other guy."

"Vivienne—"

I can hear every word he's going to say: the apologies for not knowing what Mack really was, the praise for my courage, and none of it matters. The only thing that matters is that he's *here*.

So I slide off the examination table and into his lap, his arms around me and his face next to mine. Jonah kisses my forehead and my cheeks, swiftly and fiercely, yet careful even now not to cause any further pain. When I rest my head on his shoulder, I exhale, and the swirling dark tumult inside me falls still. The pent-up tension of the last hours—the days without Jonah, the months of the Stalker's attacks—finally it all melts away. Only now does the Stalker's attack truly end.

"I left you when you needed me," he says.

"No. You came back when I needed you." This is the only truth I care about any longer.

When they show up with bandages for my knee, I'm still in Jonah's embrace. I never want to leave.

This isn't the day of the week when Doreen and I usually meet, but she makes exceptions for emergencies. This more than qualifies.

"You could be a media darling, you know." Doreen is teasing me; she knows there's nothing I'd hate more. "The woman who took down the Stalker. The avenger. That could get you the cover of *People* magazine, if Jennifer Aniston doesn't finally get married this week."

I make a face. "My life is weird enough already, thanks."

Although some reporters camped out in front of my place last night—according to Carmen, who did a drive-by—they've focused anew on Mack this morning. On TV and radio are the usual clips of old fraternity brothers and neighbors saying they never suspected a thing. Even some national news outlets have picked up the story, but without any information about the woman who finally fought him off, they don't have much to go on. Later today, a political scandal or celebrity divorce will knock this off the national radar. Austin will talk about it longer, but in college towns, it only takes a semester or two for memories to fade.

From the town. Not from the first three women Mack targeted. They'll endure the scars forever. But maybe today they at least feel a little safer.

The only good thing about the media flurry is that it definitely confirms Jonah's innocence. This morning the department head e-mailed about a meeting, which will no doubt involve the end of Jonah's informal exile from his university offices and hopefully an apology too. Jonah says he doesn't want apologies; he wants to get back to work on the latest data from Japan. Deep within that hot exterior, there's a science nerd trying to get out. I'm just glad he's been vindicated at last.

"How are you feeling?" Doreen says. "Usually I don't have to ask that question, but you've been dodging it today. Any idea why?"

"Because—I'm not sure how I'm feeling." I struggle for the right words. "Last night, I stayed over at Jonah's. And I was so *happy*. Completely at peace. Like the rest didn't matter as long as we were together."

"Is that the only reason you found peace?"

"No." Which I didn't fully realize until she asked me. "I faced my worst nightmare and I won. That was . . . incredible."

"Why did you win, do you think?" Doreen asks.

"Because attackers expect you to try to get away. They don't expect you to turn on them." But that's only a partial answer, isn't it?

Doreen studies my face, no doubt sensing my inner confusion, but waits it out. Her silence often clarifies things for me faster than anything else.

"Partly it's just luck," I finally say. "I was older and stronger than I was the first time someone attacked me. Mack didn't have a gun. I wasn't sick, or injured. He came after me at home, where I knew my surroundings. Neighbors were around. What happened to me when I was fourteen prepared me for the reality of what he was trying to do. All of that. It helps."

As much as I'd like to believe I'm some sort of superheroine, I need to remember that chance plays a role. Rape is all about stealing our power to control our own bodies and fates. Strong women are raped every single day. Men too, as little as we admit it. My escape doesn't prove I am better, smarter, or more virtuous than the ones who didn't get away. It's not a merit badge from God.

"Okay, it's good to acknowledge that," Doreen agrees. "But I want you to give yourself your due. You drew from a kind of strength you worked hard to build for years. Mack tried to take away your control. You took it back."

That's when it hits me. I don't know if this is what Doreen was leading toward—whether she herself even realizes it—but finally, I do.

My rape fantasies *helped* me.

The fantasy is the exact opposite of rape. When Anthony pushed me down on that couch, he controlled everything; I controlled nothing, not even my own body. But when I'm fantasizing inside my own mind, I have *absolute* control. By taking the scenario that frightened and hurt me the most, and owning it, I was reasserting my own power.

And with Jonah—even at his most brutal moments, he has always, always respected my boundaries. He has frightened me, dominated me, made me ache and weep. But I've always known beyond the tiniest sliver of doubt that all I had to do to stop one of our games was say the word *silver.* I control him as much as he controls me. With his help, and his love, I mastered my nightmares.

All these years, I've beaten myself up for my rape fantasies. Told myself I was sick or strange. I've carried around this tremendous weight of shame. No longer. Never again.

I lift my chin as I say to Doreen, "It wasn't about taking back my power. It was about realizing I'd had the power all along."

THIRTY-ONE

A few days later, Jonah and I return to our favorite hotel lobby bar for a new round of negotiations.

The outfit is more casual this time: black maxi skirt, heather-gray tank, cropped denim jacket. No jewelry except the sapphire earrings Jonah gave me for Christmas—paired with this outfit, they'll be written off as costume jewelry by anyone who notices. They could be, for all it matters; Jonah gave them to me, so they'd be precious to me whether they were rhinestones or the crown jewels. My hair hangs loose, which disguises the remaining bruises near my eyes.

(When I left the department office today for my "hot date," Kip wordlessly gave me a concealer stick to cover the remaining shadows. When I tried to return it, he told me he wouldn't be needing it any longer.)

Jonah's as comfortably dressed as I am—jeans, long-sleeved black tee—but his expression is wary. He's more uncertain about our next moves, but that's okay. I'm sure enough for both of us.

After the bartender has vanished, leaving behind two glasses of pinot noir, it's time to begin. "Okay," I say. "The first thing I want to say is—I don't want to give up our games. But it's not only up to me."

"You said the role-playing helped you," he admits. We already discussed the revelation I had in my last session with Doreen, so he's had some time to process this. But Jonah remains wary. "Maybe there are ways it helped me too. I think we need new limits, but . . . I'm willing to consider the possibilities."

"Thank you." I squeeze his hand. "There's one main thing I want to change, Jonah. I don't want the games to be the *only* kind of sex we share. It seems like that's healthier for you, and besides, I don't want that to be the one way I can find pleasure."

"I want that for you too. How do we get there?" His expression is rueful. "It didn't work so well the last time we tried."

"No, it didn't. But the way we handled it put a lot of pressure on me to respond or else. I should've been clearer with you from the beginning. Let's just—hang out for a while, okay? Play around in bed. Make me feel good, and don't worry if it doesn't get me off."

Jonah sighs. "That's the exact opposite of how good sex is supposed to work."

"Not for us. Not for now." I lean closer and playfully whisper, "You know it still feels really good even if I don't come, right?"

"Right. I just wish—" But he stops himself. Jonah is accepting that we can't beat ourselves up about our progress, or the lack of it. We have to take each other as we are. "I won't worry. I promise."

"Good. Because what I need is time to explore. To find out what else might work for me. When I know that, we can go back to the games—but for now, I want to take a little time for discovery. What do you want?"

"The rougher scenarios—like the cabin, or what happened at Redgrave House—I can't go there again, Vivienne. I just can't."

"Okay." I'll miss those, but I've still got my memories and my imagination.

He continues, "But some of the games, I think I could still

handle. The stuff that's less violent, more—coercive. Where the roles are more clearly fictional."

I think I understand what he's talking about; we'll definitely be able to figure it out when the time comes. "If that works for you, it works for me."

"And it's not like we can't try a few new tricks along the way." He brushes his fingers through my hair. The flickering light from the nearby fireplace burnishes his skin, darkens his gray eyes. "I was thinking—I only used a vibrator on you once. You liked that."

"A lot." The memory brings a blush to my cheeks, even with Jonah. That was the first time I ever experienced anal sex, and with the vibrator I wound up coming repeatedly, hard, so much so that it was one of the greatest sexual experiences of my life. "Yeah, we could try that again."

"Maybe some other toys too. You don't have anything except that ludicrous pink thing Geordie gave you. High time we changed that."

He refers to Geordie's past role in my life without any sign of jealousy. While I think he's still getting used to our closeness as friends, Jonah understands that relationship better now.

"Other toys?" I'm not an idiot—I know what's out there—but I want to hear exactly what appeals to Jonah's imagination. "Like what?"

Jonah's fierce smile sends the usual thrill through me. "Let me surprise you."

"Hmm. I like surprises."

"I know you do," he murmurs, drawing me close again. The soft R&B music playing in the bar flows around us, and I sigh in anticipation.

But there's no rush. We have to get used to taking our time.

"There are other games we could try too," I suggest. "Other kinds of domination, or other power fantasies?"

"What, like a French maid thing?" Jonah raises an eyebrow.

I laugh. "If you think that's hot, sure."

I expect to hear him scoff, but he doesn't. Maybe he's unwilling to rule anything out at this stage. Or who knows? Maybe he actually likes the idea of me in a French maid outfit. Interesting. "I find you hot in pretty much anything. Or out of it."

"Then feel free to come up with some possibilities." Does he have a lingerie fetish, or could I inspire one? Would being wrapped in all that silk and lace do something for me? Or maybe a corset . . . "While I'm still learning to get there—I kind of don't care what we try, you know? As long as it works, and it's good for both of us."

"Okay," he says. "I can see that. Let me think of a few suggestions."

I can't wait to hear this, but I also want to give him plenty of time to consider the options. Jonah's been so endlessly inventive with our games so far; who knows what he might come up with when we expand the playing field?

That line of thought has me so titillated that I decide we'd better talk about something less sexy, before I start drooling on the man in public. "Um—you know, Jonah, I wanted to ask—I've been feeling so guilty—were you able to get a refund on that apartment?"

He laughs. "No. So I turned it into a 'scholarship,' gifted it to a student and her husband who were having serious financial troubles. Anjali and Arun are moving in next weekend."

"Next best thing, I guess." Better, really. Jonah and I maintain the independence I still need, while two people in genuine need get to enjoy a great place to live and some peace of mind. "And did you ever get around to calling Carter and letting him know he has absolutely nothing to hold over you any longer?"

"Didn't bother. Talking to Carter always ruins my day. I let Maddox share the news—he'll enjoy it more, anyway. By the way,

Maddox wants us to come back to Chicago around spring break. Says this time he'll throw us a real party."

"Spring break? Will it be above freezing yet in Chicago?"

Jonah grimaces. "Maybe?"

"You know, I think summertime would be perfect for a trip to Chicago." I trace the line of Jonah's shoulder, the slant of his throat. "For spring break, how about—the mountains? Tennessee, or maybe Colorado. Someplace where we can nest in a little cabin and look at the beautiful scenery and make love in the woods."

"Remind me to let you plan all my future vacations."

"Got it."

We grin at each other, relieved and happy almost to the point of silliness. But the intensity swiftly returns to Jonah's gaze. "Speaking of making love—"

My breath catches. "Yeah?"

"Let's go back to my apartment," he whispers. "Take a little time for discovery. No games. Just fun."

I'd be lying if I said I didn't feel some uncertainty. If I didn't hope for some magical sexual recovery that grants me multiple orgasms on demand. But mostly I feel hopeful, and happy, and sure that Jonah and I are finally on the right path. With a smile, I say, "Let's get out of here."

Jonah and I work together to get my clothes off. Muscles are still sore; bruises still linger. He's gentle as he removes my jacket, and lifts up my legs, one by one, to slip off my shoes. I have to take it slow as I peel off my tank top, because otherwise my arm will twinge terribly, but the good side of it is that I get to show off for Jonah. To know that he's watching the swell of my newly exposed breasts, barely contained by the creamy white lace bra. As soon as I tug it free of my arms and toss it aside on his bed, Jonah grabs me at the waist and bends to plant a kiss in the hollow between my breasts. I respond by lying back and arching my hips, silently urging him to slide my skirt down my hips—which he does.

He kisses me again on the soft flesh just below my navel, then steps back to start stripping in turn—though much more urgently. Yet his voice remains laconic as he says, "I'd like to shower. Want to join me?"

"Absolutely."

As much as I love my little house, I do not love the tacky plastic bath-and-shower stall inside its tiny bathroom. Jonah's shower, meanwhile, is the latest in luxury—marble tiles, a walk-in two-head shower, and a simply carved teak mat just above the drain. The other times I've stayed over here, I've indulged with soaks in his equally enviable stone bathtub. So I'm overdue for a turn in this shower . . .

I take a moment to admire the sculpted lines of Jonah's naked body as he steps in and think, *So, so overdue.*

He turns the knobs until gentle twin streams of steaming water begin to spray, then holds his hand out to me in invitation. I step into the mist and into his embrace.

Our lips meet as Jonah pulls me near. Rivulets of water flow between my breasts while I snuggle closer to his chest. His broad hand strokes my belly, then cups my ass to bring me even closer. I feel his semi-erect cock stir against my upper thigh, and I laugh into his kiss.

"You said you were going to be patient." I grab his ass too, squeezing to relish the firmness of his muscles. "You don't *feel* patient."

"The spirit is willing, but the flesh is weak." He keeps pressing kisses against my forehead and throat.

"Weakness is not your problem," I insist, taking his cock in one hand.

Jonah whispers, "*Fuck.*" Although he half turns, as if to stop me, he doesn't go far enough. Not that I'd let him get away if he did.

Just because I might not have an orgasm for a while doesn't mean Jonah has to be deprived too.

Slowly I start working him with my hand, using the flowing water to slick every touch. My thumb runs around the sensitive head, teases the slit; I chuckle softly as I'm rewarded with the first drops of pre-come. Jonah groans as I start with my other hand too. That lets me cover almost the length of his shaft, to feel just how thick he is, to relish every ridge and vein.

"Wait," he says hoarsely, and then his fingers find me too.

My first impulse is to tense up. *I don't know if I can come like this, I don't think I even want to try yet!* But then I breathe out and force myself to relax. Jonah's thumb begins making circles around my clit, a touch so deliciously tantalizing that I can enjoy it even if it leads nowhere.

Jonah, however—I'm leading him straight to the brink.

We kiss again, open mouthed and sloppy, as we each quicken our movements. Little sparks of pleasure ignite inside me as Jonah works—never enough to start a fire, but more than enough to provide a warm glow. His other hand strokes my back, palms one of my breasts, and then cups the back of my head to hold me in place as he kisses me deeper. I go on tiptoe, inviting him to slide even lower with those long fingers of his. They'd feel so good inside me.

Just before I pull back to tell him so explicitly, Jonah gasps. More pre-come flows onto my fingers only to be washed away in an instant. But he's close now. *Really* close. And there are few things I enjoy more than watching Jonah come.

"Back up," I whisper. He's in no mood to argue. Instead he lets me back him against the tile wall. Jonah breathes in sharply as I start pumping him with my fist; his ab muscles flex with every desperate exhalation. I want to watch the dark head of his cock sliding in and out of my closed hand, but I can't tear my eyes from the sight of his face—skin beaded with water, mouth open, eyes screwed shut as the sensation overtakes him . . .

"I'm gonna come," he gasps.

"Come for me, baby."

"But—on you—"

I realize, suddenly, that it will be okay. Never could it have been all right with anybody else, but tonight I can say, "It's all right. Do it. I want you to."

Jonah cries out, long and ragged, as he comes. He spatters all over my hand and my belly, hot and thick for the split second it takes for the shower to rinse it down my body. The sight isn't erotic for me, but it doesn't turn me off the way I always thought it would. Seeing Jonah shudder in his throes is hot enough to eclipse the rest. I work him all the way through it, every last spasm, every last drop. Finally he slumps forward, leaning on me so hard I almost have to hold him up as we kiss again.

When our lips part, I can't stop smiling. "Good?"

"God, yes." He brushes my damp hair away from my face. "Will you—Vivienne, let me try—"

"No." I have to be firm about this. "We can go to bed. We can play around. You can keep touching me, because it feels completely fantastic. But don't try anything tonight that's mostly about getting me off."

Jonah laughs, disbelieving but willing to go with it. "You don't want to come?"

"Of course I do. But—it's a marathon, not a sprint. We're not dashing for the finish line tonight. This is more like a quick practice run on the treadmill."

"Please, stop with the metaphor."

That makes me giggle. "Okay. No more metaphors, I promise."

"And no more sprints. Let's just go to bed and have a good time, okay?"

"Okay," I whisper, and my reward is yet another kiss.

The next morning, I am awakened by Jonah rising to make us breakfast—but only barely. After he kisses my naked shoulder, he pads into the kitchen to get started on our omelets, and I drift into a pleasant, half-conscious haze where I possess no thoughts. No worries. Only the softness of Jonah's sheets around me, and the distant, delicious smells of food.

At the moment when I might nod off again, my phone chimes. My eyes open as I realize the sound is Chloe's ringtone.

We haven't spoken since the Templars ball. Nor have I felt any desire to talk to her. My name never appeared in the media stories about the Stalker's capture, so nobody in New Orleans ever learned about my escape. (Well, besides Liz, but I told her myself, and she's under strict orders not to inform absolutely anyone else.) So why would Chloe be calling me?

Dad, I think, and I grab the phone. "Chloe?"

"Hello, Vivienne." Her voice is coolly polite. "I would've thought you'd be in class by now."

So she was hoping to get my voice mail. Not surprising. "My first class isn't until the afternoon. Is Dad okay?"

"What? Of course he is."

Chloe sounds offended I even asked. Both my sister and my mother have settled into a state of denial where my father's cardiac arrest and subsequent open-heart surgery were no more than mere inconveniences. Dad likes that state of affairs, because it lets him eat and drink the way he likes. I'd change this about him if I could, but I can't. Maybe Chloe and Mom are smarter with their denial than I am with my resignation.

I'm relieved to hear my father's doing well, but that raises the question of why Chloe would call. "So, what's up?"

"Well, it won't be long before Easter. Mom wants to know if you'll come home this year. Not that you've ever made much of a point of coming home for Easter before, but for some reason, she's highly interested to know your plans."

This means that my mother hopes I'll bring Jonah, under her apparently unshakable belief that shared family holidays have the power to bring about a speedy marriage proposal. "I'm not coming home for Easter," I say. "It overlaps our spring break. Jonah and I want to head out west for the week, maybe visit the mountains."

Chloe, who views the outdoors as something to be avoided at all costs, merely sniffs. "Just as well. We wouldn't have had much room, since Anthony and I are hosting the lunch at our place—and, of course, I'm hoping we'll build an addition with a larger formal dining room, but for now space is limited—"

She keeps going on and on about home renovation plans, knowing full well that I don't care. She probably even understands I can hardly hear her anymore. Instead I am overcome by the dawning horror of the realization that Chloe and Anthony have reconciled.

My rapist has rejoined the family. Probably for good. I will never be rid of Anthony Whedon, never in my entire life.

"—though of course Libby always gets so excited about the Easter egg hunt." Chloe laughs, almost fondly. "It's a pity you've never bothered to come for Easter. You'd enjoy watching her."

"I bet she's adorable." My voice sounds hollow. I push myself into a seated position, holding the sheets against my bare chest. Jonah's bed feels like an island where I float far away from the rest of the world.

"We got her the prettiest dress! Yellow cotton, smocked—did

I tell you?" As if we've spoken once since she tried to jump Jonah's bones.

I wonder what Anthony would say if he knew about *that*? Well, I'll have to keep wondering. To tell him, I'd have to speak to him, something I intend to avoid even more than I did before.

"You'll have to send me pictures," I say.

Chloe pauses. She's baited so many hooks for me in this conversation. By now you'd think she'd have caught on that I know better than to bite. Still, her disappointment is all too obvious. "I suppose so. Well, you probably need to get to work."

"Yeah. Talk to you later." I hang up without waiting for her good-bye, and bury my face in my hand.

By the time Jonah walks in a couple minutes later, my breakfast-in-bed on a tray, I've dried my few tears. But he stops in his tracks. "What's wrong?"

"Chloe took Anthony back."

"Christ." In three swift strides, Jonah is beside me, carefully nestling the tray at my feet as he gathers me into his arms. His terry-cloth robe is soft against my cheek, and the warm scent of his skin reassuring on a deep, wordless level.

"I should've known," I say as I snuggle deeper into his embrace. "She'd never give up the status, much less the meal ticket."

"Is she that shallow?"

"Maybe."

Not entirely, though. Chloe may have chosen to believe Anthony over me, but she *does* believe him. She thinks he's telling the truth, that he and I willingly slept together as teens. Who would wreck their marriage over a one-night "mistake" more than a decade in the past, years before the wedding day? Besides, Chloe truly does dote on Libby, and watching her little girl miss her daddy would've been difficult.

It doesn't excuse her blindness to what Anthony's done, or her lack of belief in me. But it does make me recognize that Chloe's not just a spoiled rich-bitch. She's screwed-up in her own way, by the same weird parenting I grew up with too. Maybe if Anthony hadn't victimized me, I would've grown up not so terribly different from her.

No. I won't believe that. I refuse to feel grateful for what happened to me on any level.

But I can't write Chloe off so easily.

"I pretended for so long," I say, leaning back against the headboard. Jonah takes hold of my hands. "I sat across the table from Anthony at all those family holidays, and I can't do it anymore."

"You don't have to. If we go to your family's, I'll run interference. If not, you always have somewhere else to be. You'll always be with someone who loves you."

My smile is crooked. "I don't think I can go that often. But that means letting Libby slip away."

I have to choke back a sob. The little song she sang to me, the one I still have in my voice mail, plays softly in my memory: "*Happy birthday, Aunt Vivi—*"

"Hey," Jonah says, wiping away one escaped tear with his thumb. "That little girl adores you. She's not going to forget you. Even if you're not as close to her as you'd like the next few years, you have to trust her. Libby's intelligent. She has a big heart. Sooner or later, she's going to find her way back to you."

Is he right? I hope so. Still, I know our relationship is about to take damage that will never be fully healed.

Then I think of what Geordie said to me not so long ago: Nobody ever gets better for good. We can only take one day at a time, doing the best we can. *Damaged* is the natural state of most relationships in this world, and every single person alive.

We just learn how to keep going anyway.

"Do you really believe Libby will come back someday?" I say, as Jonah settles the breakfast tray in front of me.

He brushes his hand through my rumpled hair. "It doesn't matter whether I believe it. It only matters that you do."

And to my surprise, I realize—I do believe it. Or I want to. For now, that's enough.

THIRTY-TWO

A few weeks later, the entire city of Austin goes completely, totally insane—just like it does this time every year. We have our bats, our live music in grocery stores, our nude bike rides, and all the rest, but absolutely nothing electrifies this town like South by Southwest.

SXSW began as a small music festival a couple decades ago and has since exploded, turning into one of the biggest showcases in entertainment. Although movies dominate the entertainment schedule, highly anticipated TV pilots air here as well, and major musical stars sometimes show up in random nightspots, ready to perform new singles a few days before they drop. Downtown Austin turns into a crush of celebrities, wannabes and sightseers. Paparazzi appear on random street corners. It's partly a pain in the ass—seriously, you do not want to try to drive downtown in that mess. But it's mostly incredibly fun.

"Fresh sightings news!" Kip crows as I walk out of my office. He's back to his old self, organizing his annual SXSW celebrity road map. "I can hereby confirm that Solange, lesser of the two Knowles, is attending the next showing at the Drafthouse, and reliable sources indicate that Lucy Liu has just strolled into Book-People."

"You're sending out the e-mails, right?"

"E-mail, *please*," Kip scoffs. "You and all the others are on my MMS list, which means you'll be texted an updated version of the map on the hour."

"How many subscribers do you have this year?"

He smiles in satisfaction. "Let's just say certain global wire photo services have joined the fray."

I can't help laughing as I tug on my navy blue peacoat. "You should start charging for this, you know."

"My payment comes in the form of gratitude, a currency far more valuable than most." Kip leans across his desk and steeples his hands together; he's finally given himself a fresh manicure, this one in glittery gold. I'm not fool enough to believe he's completely over the train wreck of his love affair with Ryan—but the recovery has definitely begun. "So whom will you be stalking this evening? Lupita Nyong'o? James McAvoy? Or maybe even Brad Pitt? Though the Brad sighting is *not* confirmed, so don't start hyperventilating yet."

"None of the above," I admit, buckling my leather portfolio case. "Jonah and I are taking tonight off from South by Southwest."

Kip's jaw drops. "Are you kidding? With that apartment of his, you're in prime position for star-spotting! I was even hoping you could check on the Sandra Bullock reports for me."

"Not tonight. One of my art projects has been on the back burner too long. Time I got back to work."

"Art projects?" This earns me a frown from Kip. "But Jonah's helping you? I thought he stuck to tremors, of either the seismic or erotic variety."

"Let's call him my muse." I head for the door with a smile. "But tomorrow? I'll be your eyes and ears downtown, all day."

"You'd better," Kip calls as I leave. "Because rumor has it Taylor Swift just flew in, and if I don't get her? My list's reputation will be ruined!"

"Is the studio always this quiet?" Jonah says as we walk inside. He slides shut the dead bolt as I flip on the lights. "Before it was only three people; now it's just you and me."

"Usually it's a lot busier. Sometimes there's a sculptor in one corner, a potter in another, and four different sketch artists working while I make my prints. But I figured South by Southwest would clear everyone out, as usual."

Jonah hangs his leather jacket up beside my coat as I head into the bathroom to change into my work clothes—leggings and a loose, stained smock in case I want to work with some inks later. Through the door he calls, "It must be easier to work when you're alone."

"Most of the time. But not tonight." I emerge from the bathroom and gesture toward a nearby chair. "Take a seat, sir."

He gives me a bemused look. "You said you needed my help. I thought I'd be—moving equipment around, carrying supplies, something like that."

I pretend to be intrigued. "I like how you think. But tonight? All I need you to do is pose."

"'Pose'?"

Once again, I point to the tall chair in front of the worktables. "A few months ago, after we got back together, I decided I wanted to make an etching that would symbolize you. Everything that you mean to me. Your strength, your courage, your scars, your grace—I wanted to capture all of that in one image."

Jonah climbs into the chair, expression dubious. "Okay, I'm not an artist. But that sounds like a difficult goal. I could never come up with one picture, or phrase, that sums up what you mean to me either."

As lovely as the compliment is, I don't let him distract me. "The goal wasn't just difficult. It was impossible. Symbols can carry so much meaning, but they can carry false meanings too. Or be misinterpreted. They're never portraits of the thing symbolized, really more a peek into the mind of the artist than anything else. So I don't want a symbol of you, Jonah. I only want to capture *you*. The real man that I love. Just as you are."

He shakes his head, but not in negation. In wonder. "You captured me already. Don't you know that?"

And now I want to lay aside my pencils, climb atop him, and take him right in that chair. Instead, I take a deep breath. "Shhh. Sit still. Eyes forward."

Jonah settles himself into the chair, and I begin.

Obviously I can't create an entire etching tonight—even if I tried, that would take well into the morning, and I learned the hard way that it never pays to rush it when transferring a draft onto the etching plate. My goal for tonight is only to create my first sketches for the drawing. To copy every one of Jonah's beautiful features precisely, and evocatively, in a way that will speak to anyone who looks at the page.

So far, yet no further: That's not unlike the way we've handled sex the past few weeks, since Mack's arrest. Jonah and I have slept together every single night, usually at his place, but now sometimes in my house too, now that the "crime scene cleanup" van has taken care of the mess. (That is an actual business. Can you believe it?) We've settled in, started creating the habits we'll keep as long as we live in Austin. And we've begun learning how to be together in bed without our games. Jonah has introduced me to a few new toys, and begun making a few experimental strokes with the vibrator while the two of us are naked together, kissing frantically.

Yet so far, I haven't climaxed. And that's okay.

Because—for the first time in my entire sex life—I am learning how to be myself while I make love. Before, I pretended to enjoy things that left me cold, or shut my eyes to enjoy a fantasy completely detached from whatever my lover was really doing to me. Then I found Jonah, and we began our games. Rich and passionate and exhilarating as our role-playing is, we are in fact playing roles. I hope we'll play those roles again someday, and maybe not even too long from now. Other games appeal to me too. For the time being, however, I'm focusing on learning how to reach orgasm in my own skin.

And Jonah Marks is the first man from whom I feel no need to hide.

Normally Jonah is good with silence, but silence plus observation appears to be the only combination of factors that can make him self-conscious. "I would've worn something better, if I'd known this was the outfit you were going to immortalize."

"You look great." Like he ever doesn't look great. But what he has on is perfect, really: tight-fitting jeans, a black sweater that fits snugly enough to outline his spectacular frame.

"Have you done etchings of the other people in your life? Has Carmen had to pose for you?"

"No. One time she held a tree branch over a still life for me, for a few hours, until she got muscle cramps. I still owe her one for that." My pencil has sketched out the rough parameters of his form. Time to begin filling in details. "Oh, hey, by the way, Carmen decided to go to Stanford for her Ph.D."

"Good for her," Jonah says. By now he knows my friends' hopes and problems nearly as well as I do. "She's not too worried about Shay and Arturo?"

"This is Carmen we're talking about. She's still incredibly worried. But I'll be here for at least the next two years. Geordie will be here too until September. So it's not like the new family has to go it alone for a while." I grab the sketchpad and step closer to Jonah. "Can you tilt your head to the right slightly? Like—there. That's it."

Jonah obediently remains in place. "Geordie must be doing well, then."

He never explicitly brings up Geordie's recovery, allowing Geordie or me to do that instead. "Four months sober now."

"That's impressive."

"Yeah, it is."

Geordie always reminds me that recovery is never final. It's a lifelong process, a state of being rather than a chore to be accomplished. But during the past couple months he's regained some muscle tone. His usual color. He laughs more often, and the laughter sounds genuine. It's impossible not to sense that the progress he's made is real.

"Hmm." I step back from Jonah, trying to decide on the exact right angle. "Maybe if you leaned in this direction?"

A slow, hot smile dawns on his face. "You know what's holding you back? Too many details. You need to simplify."

"What do you mean?"

Jonah doesn't explain. He simply kicks off his shoes, and begins to strip off his sweater.

My eyes widen. "Jonah—we're in a shared studio!"

"Where nobody's coming in, because they're all looking for celebrities on Sixth Street." He nods toward the door. "You saw me slide the dead bolt. Even if someone did show up, I'd have time to get dressed again before you let them in."

"I guess so . . ."

Really I should be protesting more than this. Which is to say, protesting at all. But now Jonah's slid out of the chair, and his hands are at the button of his jeans, and even if I could stop him, I don't want to.

With a grin, he adds, "Besides, isn't this the artistic ideal? Sketching a nude model?"

And with that, his jeans and boxers hit the floor.

No matter how many times I see Jonah naked, the sheer beauty of his body always blows me away. He would be an ideal nude model for a drawing class; his physique has the symmetry of a Praxiteles sculpture, and yet so many of his features are arrestingly unique—like his long, tapered torso, the unreal dimensions of his cock, and his unexpectedly narrow throat. His muscles still possess that rough-hewn quality that has always reminded me of stone. He is too rugged for beauty, too perfect for anything else.

The gleam in his eyes as he looks at me tells me he hopes I'll toss aside the pad and pencil and drop my clothes on the floor beside his own. Well, too bad. Because this is an opportunity I don't intend to waste.

"Standing, then." I flip to a brand-new page of the sketchbook and quickly fill out the most basic lines. Jonah raises an eyebrow, but obediently clasps his hands behind his back, willing to serve. "Hmm, let's see. How can I best—"

I set down the pad, step forward, and put my hands on his hips, my thumbs catching the notches of his hipbones. Jonah breathes in sharply as I turn him slightly to the side and run my fingers along his lower abdomen. I brush the edge of the dark thatch of hair leading down to his groin.

"That's it. Stand like that." As I slide my hands upward, I relish the warmth of his skin, the rippling of his abdominal muscles and pectorals. When I get to his neck, Jonah even lets me turn his head; I point his face toward the sky, exposing his profile and the long line of his throat.

Satisfied, I step back, to see that there's been one very dramatic change to my model's pose.

"Think you can hold *that* the entire time?" I whisper, brushing my fingers along his now fully erect cock.

Jonah smiles. "Motivate me."

I step back as I unbutton my smock. Didn't bother with a bra beneath it, because sometimes the ink sinks through. He wasn't expecting that, so when the fabric falls to the side, exposing the inner curves of my breasts, he sucks in a deep breath.

"How's that for motivation?" I say.

"Very, very good." He's harder than ever, so much so I ache to touch him.

But I want to touch myself even more.

I sketch a few more lines, taking care to re-create the lines of Jonah's lower abdomen and cock. Those muscles that create a V straight toward his erection—I shade those in fully, because it's impossible to look at them and not know the strength behind his every thrust. When I've filled in a few shadows along his muscular arms, I set down my pencil. Locking my eyes with Jonah's, I slide my leggings and panties down to puddle at my feet. He groans softly, but he doesn't move.

"You need even more motivation," I say as I stretch my hand between my legs and start to rub. A slow warmth begins to dawn inside me. "Because you'll need to stay hard for me a long time, Jonah. Even for a guy like you, that's going to be rough."

"Just keep doing that." His voice betrays the desire he feels. It's taking all his willpower not to tackle me here and now. "Let me watch you."

I hop up onto the sketching table, so I can spread my legs wider for him as I keep going. Jonah's cock twitches, but he remains perfectly posed for me.

Smoothly as possible, I switch hands—so while my left hand keeps playing with my clit, I can pick up my pencil with my right.

"You can't possibly draw like that," Jonah murmurs.

"Mmm. Watch me." Pun intended. Honestly, my focus and my grip aren't their strongest at the moment. I'm becoming a lot better at masturbating without getting out of my own head, and even if I can't get myself over the brink, I can dance right here on the edge. It feels so fucking good.

With my left hand I circle faster, then slower, then slide two fingers deep into my cunt to watch the desperation in Jonah's eyes. This is too much fun.

I really want to create this portrait of Jonah—but it can wait.

"You know," I whisper, "models sometimes find it difficult to hold their positions for a long time. You're doing a good job, though."

"You're doing it for me," He says hoarsely. His cock remains stiff and thick, yearning for me.

"Even professional models sometimes need to take a break, though. What about you, Jonah? Would you like to take a break?"

Instantly Jonah crosses the two long strides to reach me. I laugh in exhilaration as he pulls my hips up to meet him. The pencil drops to the floor.

My head lolls back as Jonah sinks in.

"Mmm." I don't stop using my hand; Jonah's got plenty of room to work anyway. He pumps into me faster, clearly already nearly at the brink. Watching me might have gotten him off on its own, without my even touching him—

That idea really turns me on. Or the sight of Jonah's muscles working as he pumps into me. Or maybe it's the tempo I've hit with my hand, because this is good. This is really good.

Really—really—

There's a moment when orgasm becomes inevitable. The split second between detonation and explosion. I feel the shift inside me, and I know that delicious sensation so well, and yet I can't believe it because it can't be happening but it is. *It is.* White-hot pleasure claims every inch of me from the inside out. A cry of ecstasy escapes from my throat, long and loud and good, rising in pitch with every one of Jonah's thrusts.

"Oh, God," he says, going faster. "Did you—"

"Yeah." I can't tell if I'm laughing or crying. My whole body is shaking with the release. Before I can even wrap my mind around what happened, Jonah's coming too, sinking deep inside me, then slumping over my trembling body.

For what seems like a long time after that, I can hardly think. We keep kissing, and he pulls me into his arms and down to the floor, where he can cradle me in his embrace. I stroke his body, burrow closer to him.

"That was good?" he whispers.

"Oh, yeah." It wasn't lesser than the orgasms I've had during my games. Not automatically better either. But it felt completely fucking amazing, and more than that—I know now that my body, my pleasure, is my own.

Someday Jonah and I will play another game, many more games, when we choose to. Because we want to.

Sexually, I will never be *forced* to do anything again.

THIRTY-THREE

We're not jerks. We clean up the studio afterward. I slide my unfinished nude sketch of Jonah into my portfolio case, to take it up another day.

After we're dressed again, Jonah and I head home for a celebratory glass of wine—and maybe, if we're up to it, round two.

As he starts his car, I say, "What am I going tell my advisor when he asks what I've been working on lately?"

It's just a joke, but Jonah answers. "Life drawing, right?"

"Mmm. That works."

South by Southwest blows out of town like a cyclone, leaving scattered debris in the form of screening tickets and promotional swag. The weather warms by fits and starts, days of tantalizing warmth broken up by the occasional chill that sends us all searching the back of our closets, where we stashed our coats away too soon. Students relax, shedding layers of clothes like molting birds, until the guys are running around in board shorts and girls have on dresses skimpy enough to be shirts. They're looking toward spring break, and then summer.

So am I.

"South America for summer vacation?" Doreen says as she sits with a mug of coffee cradled in both her hands.

"Southern Chile—Patagonia." I smile as I recall the spectacular images Jonah showed me on his laptop; the scenery down there takes my breath away, with its surreal landscapes of mountains, fjords and glaciers. "Jonah's going to be down there for about ten weeks. I'll join him for maybe five of those. That gives each of us some alone time to work, but makes sure we get to be together."

"You realize it's going to be winter down there."

"Suits me fine. I've lived through enough Southern summers. An extra winter sounds amazing." And where else will I ever get to wear the cold-weather gear I bought for Chicago?

Doreen nods with the weary look of a woman who has endured many Julys in Texas. "I can guess from your vacation news how things are going with Jonah, but I'd like to hear it in your words."

I lean back on her sofa as I search for the best way to put it. "The past few weeks have been an entirely new chapter in our relationship. Jonah and I are closer than we've ever been, both in bed and out of it."

"Tell me about the part in bed first."

"You're getting a dirty mind, Doreen."

"I'm no Freudian." She raises an eyebrow. "But with you two—and with you alone, Vivienne—the sex matters a lot."

"Yeah. It does. Fortunately, the sex is *incredible*. I'm reaching orgasm maybe sixty percent of the time? And it's still getting better."

I wish I could say that night at the studio changed everything. That a switch flipped or a dam broke and from that moment on, I could have an orgasm every single time we had sex. Unfortunately neither the human body nor the human psyche obeys such simple rules. Jonah and I have had some nights of pure frustration—but we've also had some of the hottest sex I can imagine. My body and my heart have connected. I am becoming whole.

Doreen holds up her hand for a high five; laughing, I lean forward and deliver. She says, "Is he as happy with this as you are?"

"Pretty much. Of course, he wishes I was at a hundred percent, but he's not putting pressure on me any longer. He understands that we can't fix this overnight."

But of course nobody is ever entirely fixed. I've learned that much. Once I would have found that depressing, but now I know it's liberating. Like the song says, Freedom is what you do with what's been done to you.

"And your fantasy?" Doreen asks. "You don't need it any longer. How does that make you feel?"

"More centered. More relaxed." A deep breath, and then I admit, "But just because I don't need that fantasy doesn't mean I don't still want it."

Jonah's body—his strength—the fires he keeps banked down inside—they still excite me to the core. I still crave his hands gripping my wrists, holding them over my head as I beg for mercy. I will never stop dreaming of that.

"Does Jonah know this?" This is a genuine question from Doreen. She is no longer seeing Jonah, who decided to finally go into counseling on his own. He's skeptical about the process, and to be honest, I share some of his doubts. Jonah has always understood what happened to him and a lot of how it's affected his life; on his own he's learned to cope better than most people do after decades in therapy. But he's finally ready to try doing the "hard work," as he called it, not only for me but also for himself.

"Yes," I tell her. "Jonah knows. He's willing to play the games with me again once we're both ready. I feel like I'm there, but Jonah still needs a while."

Doreen nods. "And that's okay with you?"

For a moment I remember last night, the way Jonah's mouth felt between my legs. Pleasure arcs through me at the mere memory, and it seems as if I can hear my own cries of ecstasy echoing in my ears. A smile spreads across my face. "So far I'm enjoying the wait."

I know Carmen's getting a head start on her moving preparations because she's one of the most organized people on earth. I know she's not actually going anywhere until August, and that between now and then I'll be able to see her pretty much every day I'm not in Chile. But as we sit together on her living room floor, going through the "give away or donate" items, I get all sentimental anyway.

"You can't give this away," I say as I hold up a T-shirt with the *Twilight* actors on it. "This was my present to you!"

"You bought me that tee at a gas station after you spilled strawberry milkshake on the blouse I was wearing."

"So?" But by now I'm laughing, and I toss the T-shirt into the donate pile.

"Are these really all your books?" Geordie says as he pores through the short stack of paperbacks. "Tell me you've got a fully loaded e-reader."

Carmen shrugs. "I'm not much into fiction."

"They write nonfiction books too, y'know." He picks up a copy of *The Hitchhiker's Guide to the Galaxy*, smiles, and tosses it by his backpack.

"How would I have time to read?" Carmen asks, genuinely confused.

Geordie gives me a look like, *Some people*. Did I really try to set these two up? That seems like a weird dream I had one time.

That said, my matchmaking had one wonderful, if unintended,

effect—as Geordie proves by leaning toward the baby seat on the floor near us. "Don't worry, Nicolas. I'll teach you to read. Your Tia Carmen can handle the math part of your education."

Nicolas wraps his chubby hand around Geordie's two fingers. At this point, Geordie might as well be an adoptive uncle; he genuinely loves taking care of the little guy. At the moment, Arturo and Shay are out enjoying an actual "date night"—which only involves an early dinner so they can be at home to put Nicolas to bed, but Shay says it counts. It gives them time to be together just as a couple, which is the main thing. And taking care of Nicolas seems to ground Geordie. To keep him stable. *Easier to hold it together for somebody else than for your own sake*, he said to me recently.

Geordie catches me smiling at him with the baby. "What?"

I shrug. "Just never saw you as the paternal type, I guess."

"Never saw myself that way either. But now? I think I want five or six of these."

"I can't wait to see this. One word to the wise, though—don't mention the five-or-six-kids thing on the first date."

He shakes his head ruefully. "It's going to be a while before I'm on one of those."

I knew it was a bad idea to start romantic relationships while in early recovery, but beyond that, I'm ignorant of the details. "How long? Just when you feel steady enough to date again, or when your sponsor gives you the go-ahead?"

"Kitty tells me the rule of thumb is plant, pet, love."

Carmen and I exchange confused glances, and she says, "Run that by us again?"

"Well, I'm supposed to get myself a houseplant," Geordie explains. "If I keep that alive and well for a year, then I can adopt a pet. And if both pet and plant survive the next year in good health, then I can give romance another try."

"Two years?" Maybe I shouldn't make my dismay so clear. "I mean—that's probably smart."

"Probably. It's *definitely* one hell of a dry spell, though." He sighs, resigned.

"I can help!" Carmen hops up and goes to the windowsill, then comes back bearing her gift. "I wasn't going to give this away until I moved, but hey, we might as well get your two years started now, right?"

Geordie looks down at the flowerpot and laughs. "I think a cactus *might* be cheating."

I lift the tiny cactus from Carmen's hands and set it before Geordie. "Take your breaks where you find them."

It's dusk when I walk out of Carmen's bungalow, a bag of books and T-shirts over one shoulder and her ceramic mixing bowl in my other hand. So when my phone starts ringing—Jonah's ringtone—it takes me a minute to set things atop my car hood and answer. "Hey there."

"Hey," he says, low and soft. "Where are you?"

"Just leaving Carmen's. What's up?" We'd talked about going out for dinner tonight but hadn't made any solid plans. The night's warm enough for food trucks—breezy and perfect.

I'm just about to suggest one when he says, "Could you wait until later for dinner tonight?"

"Sure. Did something come up with work?" Is it a volcano or an earthquake this time? Damned plate tectonics, screwing with my social life.

I'm about to make that joke to Jonah when he says, "Actually, I was wondering whether you'd like to . . . play."

My heartbeat quickens. "Really?"

"Yeah."

Cradling the phone to my ear with both hands, I lean against the side of my Civic. "Why tonight?"

"It's nice out. Seemed like a shame to spend the whole evening inside. So I was thinking we could go to the park, find an isolated spot, and—improvise."

He could take me on the ground, dirt under my back. Or make me brace my hands against a tree trunk while he hitches up my skirt from behind. I'm so glad I wore this dark sundress. Just have to make sure he doesn't tear it in his enthusiasm. As for my own anticipation, it's all I can do not to whimper at the thought of his rough hands on me like that again.

But still . . . "I like that idea, but it's not what I meant. Is there some reason tonight feels, I don't know, safer for you? Better?"

Jonah thinks it over for a moment before replying. "Nothing in particular. But the idea came to me, and I started fantasizing about all the things I could do to you—and it didn't make me wonder whether my stepfather got into my brain. It didn't make me hate myself. It only made me think about how much you'd love it."

"I would. Oh, God, so much. But—only if you're sure—"

"Positive." He sounds good. Strong. And nearly as excited as I am.

Before I had wondered whether returning to our games would feel like a step backward. It doesn't. It feels like an exhilarating leap forward. Jonah and I own our fantasy in all its dark glory. But it will never own us again.

"We'll have to be careful in the park," I say as I fish my keys from my purse and start getting my stuff in the car. "Make absolutely certain that nobody's around."

"And we'll need a cover story in case we're wrong."

Oh, man. I do not want to subject some innocent bystander to any sex acts, much less one that appears nonconsensual. "We won't be wrong. And I won't scream to attract attention."

"That means I'll need to hold my hand over your mouth." His voice lights up every nerve ending I have. "Take you fast and hard."

"Yes," I whisper. He's got me turned on already.

Then Jonah repeats, more firmly, "But we'll still need a cover story."

"We'll figure it out when we pick the place. Don't worry. I'm good at improvisation." I settle everything into the passenger's seat and start my car.

"We have a lot of cover stories, don't we?" Jonah says. "For Maddox, for your family, for your professor, for our friends—"

"Gosh, Jonah, what are we going to tell the kids when they ask how Mom and Dad met?"

That was a joke too—except kind of not. In my heart, I've believed for a while now that Jonah and I would go the distance. That this is forever. But we're not engaged; neither of us has ever spoken of this before, the idea of our marrying, having children, or making a life together. At first Jonah says nothing, and I wonder if I've gone too far. If I've rushed him. If this is when we have to have the talk about the immense amount of counseling we'd need before becoming parents.

Oh, no. I mean, I want to have this talk someday, but this is the last possible moment I'd have wanted to kill the mood—

"We tell the truth," Jonah says. "Just not all of it. Like, I'd say to the kids, your mother had a flat tire. I stopped to help change it for her. Soon afterward we ran into each other, and it turned out we had mutual friends."

Softly I chime in, "Your Aunt Shay and Uncle Arturo."

When Jonah speaks again, it's as though I can hear his smile. "At the party, I came up to you and said we ought to get together sometime. Then we met up for a glass of wine, and the rest is history. The children should believe that, right? What do you think?"

I lean back in my car seat and smile. "Works for me."

Warning (will include spoilers): This book contains multiple explicit scenes that graphically simulate sexual assault, although every encounter between the hero and heroine is fully consensual. There is also discussion of past nonconsensual sexual encounters. The hero is not the perpetrator of any nonconsensual sexual acts. Potential readers should be aware of the intensity of these scenes, and those who find such depictions triggering or traumatic are advised not to read.